6·07

YA 10/12

INN⊕CEN✝
DARKNESS

INNOCENT DARKNESS

DARKNESS

The Aether Chronicles • Book 1

SUZANNE LAZEAR

Woodbury, Minnesota

First Edition
First Printing, 2012

Book design by Bob Gaul
Cover design by Kevin R. Brown
Cover art: Background image © iStockphoto.com/Shutterworx
      Background image © iStockphoto.com/AlexMax
      Woman © iStockphoto.com/Studioxil
Cover illustration © John Kicksee/The July Group

Flux, an imprint of Llewellyn Worldwide Ltd.

This is a work of fiction. Names, characters, places, and incidents are either the product of the author's imagination or are used fictitiously, and any resemblance to actual persons living or dead, business establishments, events, or locales is entirely coincidental. Cover model used for illustrative purposes only and may not endorse or represent the book's subject.

Library of Congress Cataloging-in-Publication Data
Lazear, Suzanne.
    Innocent darkness / Suzanne Lazear.—1st ed.
        p. cm.—(The Aether chronicles ; bk. 1)
    Summary: In 1901, on an alternate Earth, sixteen-year-old Noli rejoices when a mysterious man transports her from reform school to the Realm of Faerie, until Noli learns his sinister reason.
    ISBN 978-0-7387-3248-0
    [1. Fantasy. 2. Fairies—Fiction. 3. Magic—Fiction.] I. Title.
    PZ7.L4494In 2012
    [Fic]—dc23
                                                    2012007196

Flux
Llewellyn Worldwide Ltd.
2143 Wooddale Drive
Woodbury, MN 55125-2989
www.fluxnow.com

Printed in the United States of America

In memory of Dr. Cheryl Mabey—mentor, teacher, friend.
Thank you for teaching me how to "work backwards."
Otherwise, I would have stopped trying to achieve
my dream before I'd ever begun.

Come away, O human child!
To the waters and the wild
With a faery, hand in hand,
For the world's more full of weeping
than you can understand.
—William Butler Yeats, "The Stolen Child"

PROLOGUE

The Runaway

Whatever happened, she could not allow them to catch her, nor could a single drop of her blood spill upon the ground. The only sounds were of her labored breath and the hum of night in the wildwood. Soon, the horns and hoofbeats of pursuit would follow.

Annabelle's lungs screamed, as did her body. She'd grown soft, enjoying the lavish lifestyle of the high court, only realizing too late what she'd unwittingly accepted. The sound of the hunting horn echoed in the distance, making her run faster. The lake lay to the right.

Somewhere.

She continued fleeing into the dark chill of the night, her wispy gown tearing on branches that reached out of the shadows of the wildwood like ghostly limbs. A root tripped her, sending her sprawling through the forest growth. Pain shot up her leg when she landed among the dirt and the leaves, scraping her elbow in the process. The ominous tattoo of hoofbeats filled the air and her heart raced. She stumbled to her feet in a mad panic, heart beating so fast she feared the wild hunt would hear it.

Ignoring the pain, she continued running, not bothering to stop when she lost a slipper. She kicked off the other. If they caught her, they'd kill her.

Not tonight, though. No, they'd continue to charm and cosset her as they'd done since the night Kevighn spirited her away in his airship, rescuing her from being forcibly married to an old drunk three times her age. Then, when the time of the sacrifice came, they would ritually slaughter her to enable the magic of their world to continue for seven more years.

Gasping for air, she summoned the last of her strength, going right and pressing on, praying she'd reach the lake before the hunt reached her.

The horn's call cut through the night air. Fear of being caught—especially being caught by Kevighn—nearly paralyzed her. His betrayal burned Annabelle's soul like a branding iron. She would willingly die this night to keep them from getting her blood; it would do them no good if she was already dead when they found her.

A body of water glimmered between the tree branches. Shouts pierced the air.

"Annabelle, Annabelle, where are you?" Kevighn's voice reverberated through the dark woods, sending a flock of leather-winged creatures into the air.

She pictured him in her mind's eye, dark, beautiful, strong, and deliciously rakish despite the gentleman aeronaut persona he'd worn when they first met. Sweet words rolled easily off his lips, enchanting her, making her feel special, beautiful. Now she understood why they called him Kevighn Silver-Tongue.

It was not for his kisses, but for his lies.

Her leg cramped and she fell again, terror gripping her. Warm, salty tears rolled down her face. No, this couldn't be. When she tried to push herself up, her arms crumbled beneath her weight. Her lungs, her limbs, had had enough. She crawled toward the lake, knees growing raw, fine gown torn and dirty. But that no longer mattered. Freedom—and revenge—lay within reach.

Kevighn had lied to her, stolen her from her world, betrayed her trust, her innocence. In return, she promised herself she would deny him and his queen what they wanted most.

"There she is," Kevighn shouted.

Her hands entered the water. The warm, blissful liquid welcomed her like loving arms. When her body gave up, she allowed it. *Yes. Release.*

"Annabelle, no! Come back—let me explain."

Too late. Water covered her face as she sank into the depths of the very lake where Kevighn had professed his love for her. How ironic that it should be the place of her death.

The moment her heart stopped, the magic broke, setting her free. The last sounds she heard were the screams of those on the shore.

The land began to shake as the magic mourned the loss of her gift.

We must not look at goblin men,
We must not buy their fruits:
Who knows upon what soil they fed
Their hungry thirsty roots?
—Christina Rossetti, "Goblin Market"

⊕NE

An Afternoon Drive

Six Years Later, Los Angeles, 1901

"Still working, Noli?" V's voice startled her, making her bang her head against the undercarriage of the automobile. Rubbing her forehead, she tightened the last bolt with her wrench. She wheeled herself out from underneath the old clunker.

"She's nearly finished." Noli sat up on the dolly and patted the auto. The old Hestin-Dervish Pixy belonged to her father. He'd always said he would restore it, fancying himself a gentleman tinker. After her father disappeared, her older brother had said the same. When Jeff left to become an aeronaut she'd decided to fix the Pixy herself—much to the chagrin of her ever-proper mother.

"Don't you have a book to read?" Noli smiled at her

best friend as she pushed up her old brass goggles. V possessed an insatiable thirst for knowledge.

"Don't you have homework to do?" Furrowing his brow in mock disapproval, V put his hands on his hips and raised his voice to mimic her mother's, making Noli laugh. Eyes green as oak leaves sparkled through wire-rim spectacles.

Steven Darrow, or V, as she called him, lived on the other side of the wooden fence. A year older than she, he was gangly, lanky, and deceptively strong. As always, his blond hair didn't quite lie flat. Every day after school, he climbed through the loose board in the fence to visit her— not entirely proper anymore, with her being sixteen and him seventeen, at least according to her mother.

Then again, her mother seemed stuck in the last century.

"I'll do my homework later." Still holding the wrench, Noli grinned. Her gaze fell to her long, navy skirt. Despite her heavy leather apron, oil stains spotted it. How would she explain the stains when she shouldn't be tinkering in the first place? The well-worn wrench went back into Papa's battered old toolbox.

She patted the side of the flying auto. The "bug eye" two-seater convertible possessed giant headlamps in the front, and the mesh grill underneath looked like a smiling mouth. The black retractable wings reminded her of bat wings.

"We should go for a test drive."

"Noli!" V shook his head. Unlike her, he'd changed out of his school uniform and wore beige trousers, a rumpled button-down white shirt, and brown bracers.

"A quick test drive, that's all." Standing, she rolled the dolly away. She'd made it herself from a broken hoverboard and cast-off wheels from a handtrolly. "Please? I've loaded her up with coal." Like all good autos, the Pixy was steam-powered.

Noli always worked behind the dilapidated shed in her backyard, away from prying eyes who might tell her mother. V wouldn't tell. In fact, he'd helped her reupholster the interior with scraps from her mother's dressmaking shop, and they'd painted the exterior purple. They'd also scrawled the flying auto's name on its side in silver paint: *The Big Bad Pixymobile.* The brass gleamed; the wood was refinished and waxed.

Fishing another pair of goggles from her toolbox, Noli threw them at him.

Catching them, V turned the goggles over in his hands. "I can't drive that."

He couldn't drive worth a lick, but was an ace hoverboarder.

"I can." She was an ace driver and an even better hoverboarder.

V's expression contorted to one of utter terror. "Remember what happened last time?"

An escaped strand of hair fell into Noli's eyes and she blew it out of her way. "That was a hoverboard. Stop being a fussy old bodger. You have an operator's license. All you have to do is sit in the passenger's seat. Please?" She cast a long glance at her beautiful, rebuilt automobile.

"And if someone tells your mother?" V pulled the goggles on.

"She'll restrict me to my room. Again. She'll hide my tools. Again." Noli loved her mother, even if she didn't always obey her. But after Jeff left, Mama had gotten difficult to live with.

"What if she sells the Pixy for scraps?"

"It belonged to Papa," Noli replied. "She might put it in the shed with a lock, perhaps, but to the scrap yard it will never go." Her mother treasured everything of her father's. Jeff's things—well, one day her mother threw her brother's things away without a word of explanation. Noli hid what she'd rescued in the back of the shed.

"Do you have a spare leather cap?" V eyed the one covering the mop of chestnut curls that threatened to escape from her braid. Her hair never cooperated in this sort of weather.

"V, you're such a girl." Rolling her eyes, Noli took off her cap and tossed it to him.

V pulled the leather aviator's cap over his wayward blond locks and repositioned his brass goggles, which looked peculiar over his spectacles.

"Don't I look handsome?" he teased.

"Wear that and your card will be full at the next ball," Noli joked back. His being odd, bookish, shy, and a repository for useless information put many girls off, despite his looks, skill at writing poetry, and good family.

Then again, she, as distressed gentry, would be lucky to find a suitor at all, even if she left Los Angeles. Not that she wanted one. Why did she need to marry well to save her family? Really, she was perfectly capable of saving them herself. It just might take a while. Besides, tinkering was always preferable to stuffy dances.

Climbing into the driver's seat, Noli adjusted her own goggles. V hesitated, one hand on the passenger door.

A huff of exasperation escaped from her lips. "If you don't get into this automobile right now, Steven Darrow, I'll take it for a drive all by myself."

He made an annoyed noise. "You know you can't."

Women weren't allowed to hold full operator's licenses. If they wanted to drive an auto or fly an airship, they needed to possess a provisional permit and be accompanied by a male over eighteen with a full license. Given that hoverboards were one-operator conveyances, women couldn't operate those at all. The women's rights movement had yet to reach Los Angeles. Not that she'd ever let that stop her.

She nodded to the passenger's seat. "Then get in." The fact V hadn't turned eighteen yet wouldn't stop her either—or that fact that when she'd gone to get her provisional permit, she'd been denied one.

With a sigh, he climbed into the passenger's seat.

Noli grinned. "Thanks."

V shook his head in mock despair. "I don't even indulge my sister the way I do you."

"Elise can grow up properly. I'm a lost cause." She adjusted the mirrors. Her chance to grow up properly had ended the day her gently born mother went to work, which had enabled them to keep their house; the upkeep of the house was proving another matter entirely. Noli had no problem with the idea of going to work ... or even going to the university like her father had.

Unfortunately, people like her mother *did*.

"Ready?" She pulled the lever that ignited the boiler. When puffs of steam rose from the smokestack on the hood, she tugged on the lever that started the engine. It only sputtered. She caught a jubilant smile on V's face. Gritting her teeth, she pumped another lever furiously. Resetting the first, she tried again.

"Come on, come on. Please?" she pleaded. This time the sweet purr of an engine greeted her. The rough grumble sounded more like a hungry beast than a kitten. But it ran. Such a blissful sound.

"That's a girl," she cooed at the Pixy as she pressed the button on the dash to start the wings. The gears creaked, making her wince. After a moment, a pleasant mechanized hum replaced the squeal of grinding metal and the wings flapped. Elation and excitement bubbled inside her. "Here we go."

"I'll drive." V's hand covered hers. A gentleman's hand, large, smooth, and pale contrasted with one small, rough, and an unladylike shade of tan.

"Too late. It'll be *fine*." She flipped switches on the dash, which was covered in an assortment of lights, buttons, and gauges. Finally, after nearly two years of work, her beloved automobile could set off on its maiden voyage.

Cranking another lever and pushing on the thrust, she took off. The auto zoomed forward with an awkward lurch. When it appeared as if they would hit the fence, they angled up, taking off into the air. Noli pulled up on the steering wheel and gave the engine more power.

The flapping of the wings and their ascent caused her hair to whip in her face. Maybe she shouldn't have given V her cap.

"Look." Leaning over the side of the auto, she gazed down. Her house was a stark contrast to V's house and the others in their wealthy Los Angeles neighborhood.

Despite V having no mother, his house always looked impeccable. In contrast, the shutters of her house sat askew, paint peeling, awning sagging. The neighbors complained, though it was hardly Miss Havisham's. Loose shingles dotted the roof; tomorrow after school she'd fix them. Perhaps V would help. They could only make repairs on the house while her mother worked at the shop—and only do things requiring no money, or that she could barter for. Maybe she could fix something for someone in exchange for paint.

"We'll just go once around the block." Noli switched gears and pushed on the thrust. The Pixy was flying! Even V had said she couldn't actually make it fly.

"Okay, now that we know we can get airborne, let's take her down." V's green eyes were darting around like a fly in the kitchen, but no one stood on the streets below. No hovercops loomed in the distance. "Give me a land lesson in how to fly, and I'll take you for a ride tomorrow."

"What did you say?" With a grin, Noli pressed the thrust, going even faster. "I can't hear you." Laughing, she zoomed through the air. A single auto puttered away on the street below and Noli waved. Flying autos didn't have quite the popularity regular autos did; well, not among old people like her mother. She couldn't imagine why. Flying was so much fun.

She pressed too hard on the thrust, making the auto jolt into a higher gear.

"Slow down. Please? We should return home before we get caught by the air patrol," V told her.

While she knew it was illegal, Noli hadn't actually thought about getting *caught*. Her driving became erratic as she turned toward home.

"It'll be fine—just ease up and steady your wheel. We're nearly there." V laid a cautionary hand on her arm, his voice even and soothing.

Yes, ease up on the thrust and steady the wheel. That was it. Her backyard came into view, the garden next to her favorite climbing tree the nicest part.

At that moment, a small, solar-powered hoverboard appeared in her rearview mirror. Noli's hands trembled as she noticed the red and blue lights flashing along the bottom. Dread made her palms sweat.

"This is the Los Angeles Air Patrol," a voice boomed through his megaphone. "I command you to pause your vehicle in the name of the law."

TWO ⊕

Consequences

Panic coursed through Noli as she slammed her foot on the thrust, her mind screaming at her to go faster and flee the officer. The engine squealed as she pushed the limits of the Pixy's speed. A bug flew straight into her goggles, leaving a brown smudge in the center of the left lens.

A siren pierced the air—the hovercop was pursuing them. The Pixy couldn't outrun a hoverboard, which was why hovercops were the ones to patrol both the skies and the streets below.

"Pause your vehicle," he ordered again, his voice booming through his megaphone.

"Pause, Noli, pause!" V gripped the side of the auto, knuckles white.

The engine thumped. She eased up on the thrust. Nothing happened.

Noli's heart skipped a beat. "V, the pedal's stuck."

The gears shrieked as metal ground together, and Noli lost control. The Pixy plummeted toward the ground. She pumped the lever and flipped switches. Nothing. Paralyzed with fear, she could only stare at the rapidly approaching ground.

"Cut the engine, cut the engine," V shouted.

V's instructions brought her back to her senses. Cutting the engine, she locked the wings and pulled up on the wheel to keep them from crashing headfirst. Her backyard loomed ahead.

"The fence, Noli. Watch the fence." He pointed at the wood fence separating their yards.

Gritting her teeth, she pulled harder, struggling to avoid it. It wasn't enough. She shut her eyes and braced herself as her beloved Pixy smashed through the barrier, crashing into her backyard. The sound of crunching metal roared in her ears and she jerked forward, her chest hitting the steering wheel with a thud. When her eyes opened, the sight of crumpled metal, a broken wing, and smoke greeted her. Her heart continued to race.

"Switch places, now." Pulling her into the passenger's side, V climbed over her, taking the driver's seat. The hovercop descended. Noli sank into the passenger's seat. "Go along with whatever I say." V squeezed her hand in reassurance. His cap sat askew.

She nodded, her heart in her throat. As usual, V remained the calm voice of reason while she became the impetuous wreck. Given her previous violations, she could be in all sorts of trouble. Hoverboarding in the hills was one thing; flying an unregistered automobile over a residential neighborhood without a permit was another.

The hovercop landed his shiny brass and wood hoverboard in her backyard. He wore the standard Los Angeles Air Patrol uniform—a black leather airsuit, a black aviator's cap, and matching goggles. A pistol hung from his utility belt, next to his megaphone and other interesting gadgets.

Perhaps Fortuna would smile upon her and they'd get off with a scolding and an order to rebuild the fence. They excelled at rebuilding fences.

V fiddled with the gold and green medallion he wore hidden under his shirt. He only took it out when nervous, so Noli had never gotten a good look at it, but she knew it was shaped like a gold sunburst with a green stone in the middle.

"Halt in the name of the law." The officer pulled up the mask of his helmet and Noli's heart sank. Officer Davies and she went way back.

Officer Davies approached the wreckage. "Names?" He pulled out a pen and pad of paper from a pocket on his airsuit.

"Steven Darrow and Magnolia Braddock, sir." Answering for them both, V gripped the wheel so tight she feared he might break it. Noli tugged on the navy ascot at the neck of her white blouse, trying to not look too guilty.

At the mention of their names, the officer sighed. "You're in the wrong seats."

"No, sir. I drove the entire time." Reaching into his back

pocket, V brought out his billfold and handed the officer his operator's license.

Officer Davies examined the paper, his eyes skeptical. "You don't have a flying auto addendum." He returned the permit to V. "Do you even have a permit, Noli?"

Squirming in her seat, Noli bit her lower lip. "No, sir."

"Registration."

Her heart thumped like the Pixy's engine. Opening the glove box, she withdrew the long-expired registration papers and handed them to the officer with bated breath.

"This expired years ago." Exasperation filled the officer's face. "Magnolia Braddock, what were you thinking? Flying in a residential neighborhood, without a permit, with an unregistered auto. After everything we've been through, everything we've talked about."

"What seems to be the problem, Officer?" Mr. Darrow, V's father, appeared, fresh from work in gentlemen's dress.

Noli groaned softly as terror swam in V's green eyes. She noticed how he smoothed his shirt over his medallion.

"They took the auto for a ride, sped, and crashed." Officer Davies shot them a look.

Noli made a face. Obviously, they'd crashed, considering the lack of fence and the various and sundry auto parts spread about her already cluttered backyard. It would take a long time to repair everything. Her mother's shrieks already echoed in her ears. *Magnolia Montgomery Braddock what were you thinking? Have you not humiliated this family enough? When will you grow up?*

"Magnolia possesses no permit, the auto is unregistered,

and Steven doesn't hold a flying auto addendum," the officer added. He shook his head, making a noise of dismay.

"I see." Mr. Darrow stood tall and imposing, regal even, with broad shoulders and a narrow waist. His angular jaw clenched as his muscular arms crossed over his chest. Maybe when V finished growing he'd look like that. Yet Noli liked V as he was—not that she'd ever tell him she found him attractive.

"Are you hurt?" Mr. Darrow looked them up and down, scanning both with unspectacled green eyes that always seemed to read their very souls.

She stretched a little, testing for injuries, then rubbed the center of her chest. That would bruise, but she'd live. "A few aches and scratches. V?"

"The same." Dirt streaked V's face and he didn't meet his father's gaze. He never quite lived up to his father's expectations, and it weighed on him.

"Since it is our property, Officer, perhaps you could remit them into my custody with a warning?" Mr. Darrow offered.

His proposal certainly outweighed going to the station. But Noli knew she would still get in trouble; Mr. Darrow would ensure that. He didn't like Noli much, and thought her a bad influence on V.

Perhaps she was.

Officer Davies pondered this and Noli held her breath. Then the officer nodded. "I can let Steven go with a warning. Truly, he should know better."

"Excellent." V's father crossed his arms. "He'll be punished, I assure you."

V's face fell. His father's punishments got creative.

"And Magnolia?" Mr. Darrow added belatedly.

Officer Davies frowned. "I'm sorry, Mr. Darrow. With her past history, I'll have to bring her into the station."

Noli exhaled sharply, the blood in her veins turning to ice. "The station?"

"Should I send for her mother, Officer?" Mr. Darrow shot Noli a disapproving look. She hung her head as her cheeks burned in shame.

Officer Davies shook his head. "No, I'll send someone to the shop to notify her."

"Come along, Steven." Mr. Darrow walked toward his house.

V turned to her with concern-filled eyes. He squeezed her hand in reassurance, his cheer forced. "We'll fix the fence and the Pixy, don't worry."

"Of course." Noli's voice went glum. Maybe Mama *would* sell the Pixy for scraps.

With one last squeeze of her hand, she watched as V gracefully eased his way out of the broken auto. Giving her half a wave, he made his way over the wreckage and across the broken fence into his own backyard, leaving her alone with Officer Davies.

•••••••••

Kevighn Silver walked the dark, foggy streets of San Francisco, his soul weighed down in defeat, his long coat brushing his legs. His walking stick tapped on the cobblestones, beating the tattoo of his failure. Another candidate lost. Again.

Desperation rode him, like a rider on the hunt rode a horse. The time of the sacrifice quickly approached.

If he didn't find a suitable girl…

Annabelle's suicide had weakened the magic more than he'd ever let on. The replacement girl they'd found hadn't been nearly powerful enough, leaving the magic hungry. Some of the lesser creatures were already weakening, and parts of the Otherworld grew unstable. This cycle, the chosen girl must be extraordinarily special—not only to satisfy the magic's hunger, but to atone for the shame he still suffered because of Annabelle.

It was all his fault.

As the high queen's huntsman, he was responsible for finding one special girl every seven years. She only needed to possess the Spark—that special something some mortals possessed. It was joy, creativity, *life*. It was that extra-rare something that propelled mortal brilliance to sheer genius.

Chosen girls lived a charmed life in the Otherworld, spoiled and cosseted by all. When the appointed time came, her blood was spilled, nourishing the very magic that composed their world. Without the magic, the Otherworld would fade away—along with the creatures who dwelled there.

The loss of the Otherworld would affect this strange

human world, too. Unbeknownst to mortals, it was magic escaping from the Otherworld that fueled their creativity. If the magic disappeared, human creativity would as well.

Kevighn entered an older part of San Francisco. He liked this area better than the rebuilt ones, with their technology, gadgets, and shiny bits of metal. At least the dismal weather was keeping everyone indoors, leaving him alone with his troubled thoughts. Holding his desperation at bay proved difficult but necessary; anxiety made him stupid. Finding a girl used to be simple. If he didn't succeed, they would all die. Him included.

Tomorrow, he'd figure out where to travel to next.

He should probably leave San Francisco, a city known for its high concentration of aether. Aether was actually magic, seeping into the mortal realm from the Otherworld through rifts between the realms. It enhanced creativity in mortals but too much of it could be dangerous, especially to those with the Spark; so finding a girl with the Spark here could prove difficult. He'd caused this problem, too. Six years ago, the magic had mourned the lost sacrifice of Annabelle so fiercely she'd caused a huge rip in the barrier between realms. This rip not only triggered the San Francisco earthquake, destroying most of the city, but enabled large amounts of aether—raw magic—to leak into the area.

Tonight he'd drown his sorrows in opium. His step, but not his heart, lightened at the thought. Mortals did have vices down to, as they would say, a *science*.

Ah, opium and soft women. The very thought made

him toss and catch his black and silver walking stick. Yes, just what he needed—and he knew the perfect place to go.

●●●●●●●●

"Noli, your mother's here." Officer Davies entered the empty room at the local Los Angeles Air Patrol station. She was sitting on the bench, knees drawn to her chest, arms wrapped around them, head resting on her arms.

"Noli." Officer Davies sat down next to her on the bench. "We're not singling you out. We're not out to spoil your fun."

"I know." Not raising her head, she sniffed.

"I understand how losing your father—"

"He's not dead." Passion colored Noli's voice. "He'll come home. It's only been six years." Six years. She'd begun to lose hope. Not that she'd ever admit it, even to V.

"No one wants you to follow the same path as Jeffrey, which is exactly where you seem headed no matter how many warnings I give you or how many chats we have."

She raised her head, her jaw clenched in defiance. "What do you mean, *follow the same path as Jeffrey?* What's wrong with being an aeronaut? Someone needs to fly cargo vessels. Jeff travels all around the United States and sees so many wondrous things."

"That's what your brother says he does? Fly cargo vessels?" Officer Davies was still wearing his airsuit, but not his helmet, revealing messy brown hair the same color as his eyes. He wasn't a bad sort—for a hovercop.

"Of course. My brother would never lie to me." She crossed her arms over her chest.

The officer sighed, his kind face weathered with age and elements. "Talk to your mother. You're a good girl—a smart girl. Not a girl who fails school and spends her time hoverboarding illegally or tinkering on that deathtrap."

She glared at him for calling the Pixy a *deathtrap*. "I'm not quite failing."

Not quite failing everything. She excelled in botany. Noli loved botany, and had secretly dreamed of becoming a botanist. Once. Before Papa disappeared. When her parents had told her she could do anything.

Lies. To do anything you needed money.

If she got a job after she graduated from school, she could not only help support her mother but save up for university and become a botanist anyway. Maybe.

Officer Davies' expression hardened. "This might appear silly; you were just two young people out for a joy-ride. But with your record, the judge will see a troubled girl with no guidance on the path to more trouble. Flying without a permit one day, stealing autos the next, perhaps even air piracy ... "

"Judge?" A lump formed in her throat as the word barely squeaked out.

"You were in a residential neighborhood. If we take this before the judge, you'll probably lose."

Noli's chest tightened. That would mean a detention center. Her mother's social status was balanced precariously on them being distressed gentry. Noli getting in trouble and playing the hoyden didn't help. Their biggest hope lay in her marrying well—not that anyone expected her to. She possessed no great beauty and too much intelligence; thus her idea that she should simply get a job and save her family. If she was sent to a detention center—basically a prison for children—her mother's reputation would plummet. It might even affect her mother's shop if people refused to buy her dresses. Also, who would take care of her mother? Right now, Noli didn't earn much in the way of money, aside from doing the occasional repair, but she did a lot to keep their little family together.

"There is a place … " he began.

Her eyebrows rose. Already, it sounded dreadful.

"A boarding school with an excellent reputation," he finished, as if sensing her hesitation. "I'll speak to your mother and the captain about it. Perhaps we can get you back on track before you become an air pirate."

"I'll *never* become an air pirate." Even if they went to the poorhouse. Air pirates were nothing but terrible, horrible criminals.

"Good." He offered her a hand up. "Your mother is waiting."

Noli brushed her skirt and apron with her hand, steeling herself. The true yelling would wait. Distressed gentry or not, the Braddocks still possessed their pride.

• • • • • • • •

Steven kept watch on Noli's empty house while he picked up the pieces of wood that were strewn across his yard, making it resemble a picture of a battle. He hoped the air patrol hadn't come down too hard on her. What he had to tell her would be difficult enough.

His father had lectured him severely: Irresponsible, reckless action such as this disrespected their family name and weren't expected behaviors from someone of his rank and station.

As punishment, he was to clean up the mess in both their yards. He would rebuild the fence, paying for it out of his pocket money. Every day after school he would work until dark, before starting his lessons and chores. This seemed reasonable, and he'd perform the tasks without complaint.

The final part of his punishment seemed most unfair. No longer could he associate with Noli—no fixing the Pixy or helping make repairs on her house. He'd even been forbidden to speak with her. The idea alone made his soul hurt. He'd do anything for Noli, as he would for his own brother and sister. More, even.

Picking up another splinter of wood, V threw it into the wheelbarrow, wiping the sweat off his brow with his handkerchief, his stomach grumbling with hunger.

His father reminded him constantly that he and Noli *weren't* brother and sister—or children, anymore. It pained him, but he would obey his father and tell Noli they could no longer be friends. She'd be destroyed, since nearly all her friends had abandoned her after her mother opened the dress shop. But he'd pretend his father was right and that he was better off ignoring her.

Still, he vowed to keep watch over her in secret. After all, he could hardly tell his father why Noli meant so much to him, why he'd continue to protect her as much as he could.

No, no, he couldn't tell his father that at all.

THREE

Conversations

"Noli?" Her mother stood in the doorway of Noli's room, holding a small oil lamp, the slightest of frowns on her face.

"Yes, Mama?" Noli sat at her desk, doing her homework by candlelight. Running the gas lamps got expensive.

"We need to chat, you and I. Could you please join me in the parlor?"

"Of course, Mama." Time for a scolding. Standing, Noli blew out the candle and followed her mother down the staircase, the tiny flame of her mother's lamp casting eerie shadows on the walls.

Mama had been pale and mostly silent when she'd claimed Noli from the station. Actually, tears had glinted in her eyes. Noli figured it was a valiant act by her mother to maintain her dignity. Everything they did now was a pretense to uphold their pride, even though *why* her mother clung to the idea of being high society, when high society shunned them, Noli didn't know. The middle class seemed to have much more fun and not be so stuffy and constricting.

Supper, a simple affair since they no longer could afford a cook, had also lacked the expected yelling. Silence unnerved Noli far more than shouts. After supper, she had done her chores and started her schoolwork without being asked.

A small fire crackled in the seldom-used parlor—the nicest room in the house. Noli tried to keep it dusted, fresh, and in good repair. Just in case. Not that suitors would come a-calling. No one would want her for a wife—not even V, who was the only interesting man she knew whom her mother would deem suitable.

The floral settee she sat upon only smelled mildly of disuse and dust. Her insides twisted into anxious knots. Mama sat across from her in a matching chair. The low table between them held her mother's silver tea service and fine china cups. She'd refused to sell them, saying Noli needed them for her dowry. Mama also refused to use the money Jeff sent, tucking it away in a place even Noli couldn't find, claiming she was saving it, too, for Noli's dowry.

Did anyone even *have* a dowry anymore?

Noli eyed the table setting, especially the plate of rare bakery cookies. Her mother poured the tea like they were at a tea party. Dress shop aside, Mama remained the same proud, wellborn woman Henry Winston Braddock had married twenty-two years earlier back east, then spirited away to the wild west so he could build cities, bridges, and other urban marvels.

Edwina Braddock's chestnut curls were like Noli's, only hers weren't unwieldy. Her eyes glowed a startling blue, while Noli's were an uninteresting gray. Still slender, Mama possessed curves in the right places—curves Noli lacked.

Her mother put the teapot down and held out the fancy plate of cookies, the kind she kept at the shop for her clients. Her hands remained pale and fine. "Would you like a cookie?"

"Thank you, Mama." Reaching out, conscious of her own rough hands with nails bitten to the quick, Noli took a cookie and bit into it, allowing the crisp shortbread and sweet chocolate to spread across her tongue. Delicious.

Looking around the room, she spied the photograph of her parents' wedding back in Boston. No photos of Jeff—not even family ones—hung on the striped, blue-papered walls. She missed Jeff and wrote to him often.

"These have been trying times for us, with your father disappearing and your brother leaving us." Her mother took a sip of steaming tea, looking tired and worn, shoulders hunched from fatigue. "You've always been clever and willful. Raising you alone is difficult."

The chocolate cookie soured in Noli's mouth. Certainly she hadn't made her mother's life easier, rebelling and getting into mischief. Tinkering instead of helping in the shop. Failing at school because she often fell asleep in class.

"I … I'm sorry, Mama." She took a sip of tea to wash the sour taste out of her mouth.

"I know. You don't mean to be naughty; you simply need more attention. Attention I can't give you because of all the time I spend at the shop." Her mother's beautiful face, with her high cheekbones and aristocratic nose, grew forlorn, her eyes downcast.

Noli knew guilt was consuming her mother, who believed that her place was at home raising children, not at work. If anything went wrong, ultimately she held full responsibility.

"I should have sent you away to school years ago as planned," Mama added.

Plans which had gone astray when Papa disappeared. Most young ladies of their social class went to fancy day or boarding schools; Mama had wanted to send Noli all the way to Boston to attend the same posh school she had.

"If I went away, who'd help you?" Fear seized Noli's heart. So her mother was sending her away now. Whether it was to a detention center or a school, she'd still be far from home. Remorse, for taking pleasure in vexing her mother, consumed her.

Mama turned the china teacup in her dainty hands, looking into its depths instead of at Noli. "They're going to drop the charges—"

"Truly?" Noli brightened, ready to bounce out of her seat in excitement. "Wonderful."

Mama held up a hand to silence her. "You see"—her lower lip quivered—"they don't consider me fit to care for you anymore."

Noli sucked in a sharp breath. "What?" Shock gave way

to outrage and her hands balled into fists. "It isn't anything you did. *I* rebuilt the Pixy, *I* made V go with me, *I* panicked…"

Again, her mother held up a hand. "They'll drop the charges if I send you to boarding school where you can get the attention you need. It's called Findlay House. Officer Davies spoke highly of it."

"You mean reform school," Noli pouted. Officer Davies had been threatening her with reform schools and detention centers for ages, but she always thought they were empty threats.

"Of course not. You're not a criminal, you just need guidance. Guidance I can't give you because I'm working." Mama smiled a sad smile.

Noli knew it must have been a blow to her mother's pride for them to blame everything on her lack of parenting. Some dutiful daughter she turned out to be. She'd promised Jeff she'd take care of her mother, and she'd done a dreadful job.

"We still have your dowry; perhaps you'll make a good match yet. Lots of girls go to boarding school, and you're only sixteen. When you're finished at Findlay House, I'll send you to Boston, to my parents, where you can come out to society and have a fresh start." Mama's smile brightened.

"But I don't want to leave, Mama. I'll try harder, I promise. We can use Jeff's money to fix up the house and pay some bills so you can take on less work. I'll spend afternoons with you at the dress shop instead of here… or I could get a proper job fixing things, even if it's just after school. We'll make this work together. I know we can." Tears pricked Noli's eyes. She turned away, catching sight of a photograph of her father. Her mother was all she had left.

"You are a lady and we don't get jobs." Mama's voice reverberated with sadness. "If you go to this school and do well, not only will they drop the charges, but they'll wipe your record clean. Think of what this means for our future."

"Who will take care of you?" Noli asked. Her mother couldn't do everything herself. Who'd do the washing and cleaning? The shopping and repairs? Tend the yard and garden?

"It's not open for negotiation. You've played the hoyden long enough. Do you wish to bring more disgrace upon this family than you have already?"

Noli drooped over her teacup. "No, Mama."

What would Papa say? But never would she have done such things with her father home. Her father also believed in upstart notions—like women getting jobs and attending the university.

"The school, Findlay, is quite successful in educating proper young ladies. Even with your, ah, adventures, they not only agreed to admit you, but we don't have to worry about the tuition." Her mother nodded, as if in agreement to an imaginary conversation. "We leave for San Francisco in the morning."

"San Francisco?" Noli's voice shook as her heart skipped a beat.

"It's far, but they say San Francisco is quite safe now." Mama sounded unconvinced.

Noli's belly flipped. Six years ago, a terrible earthquake had struck San Francisco. The quake and subsequent fires decimated most of the city. Urban engineers—including her father—had come from around the globe to help the city rebuild.

San Francisco was where he'd disappeared.

This wasn't the first earthquake in recent times to rack the United States. Several decades prior, a series of violent quakes struck dozens of cities across the county within hours of each other. That chain of quakes ended the Civil War and started the Great Reconstruction. That, in turn, led to the American Renaissance, which had given the world many incredible discoveries and technologies—including hoverboards, flying autos, and airships.

She still didn't like the idea of going to San Francisco. "But…"

Her mother frowned in that special way that meant Noli was being difficult. "No one has died or disappeared for quake-related reasons in five years."

Noli continued to fidget in her seat. Unlike the Great Quake Chain, the San Fran quake had no official cause. Many simply blamed it on the aether released by the Great Quake Chain. Some thought it was aether that had caused her father and the other men in his group to disappear. Apparently a little aether was good, but too much wasn't. Some people avoided San Francisco for that very reason.

Noli wanted to avoid San Francisco because it stole her

father from her ... although part of her wanted to see the rebuilt city, in all its gleaming brass and steam-powered splendor.

"Do we have to leave tomorrow?" she asked. Would she have a chance to say goodbye to V? He'd stood by her after her father's disappearance, through Jeff's departure and her mother going to work. How would she get through anything without him? Sure, she called him a fussy old bodger when he acted stuffy, but as her best friend, he'd always come with her on adventures, helped her fix things, told her bits of useless knowledge and stories, and often taken the fall when they got into too much trouble.

"We'll depart on the morning train." Her mother squared her shoulders, a look of finality etched on her tired face.

Noli's nose scrunched. "That's so last century. Can't we take an airship? It's so much faster."

"You know I don't like airships. Now go upstairs and pack your things." Mama's mouth set in a firm line. Not everyone embraced the rapid technological progress the American Renaissance had brought them.

Couldn't her mother have told her this *before* she started her schoolwork?

"I'm going outside for a little bit first, Mama."

Her mother sighed heavily, shoulders rising and falling like something heavy weighed them down. She considered tree climbing improper. "Only for a little while."

"Thank you." Putting her teacup on the table, Noli walked out of the sitting room. As soon as she left her mother's line of sight she took off running, slamming the kitchen door in the process. She didn't stop until she reached her tree. When confused, angry, or scared, she liked to scale it. Everything seemed better among its branches.

Up the trunk she went. The gnarled old oak had been knocked down in a storm, but it continued to grow, curving like a J. The rough bark under her fingers felt comforting and familiar. Overgrown branches reached nearly to the ground, like a weeping willow.

V called it a faery tree—"but not a real one," he'd always add.

As if faeries were real. Science had disproven them a thousand times over. That was V for you, believing in the fantastic even in the face of science. She'd miss him so much. Sometimes Noli liked to imagine what it may have been like, had her father not disappeared and she'd actually been considered a possible match for V.

Even though she teased V, she adored him, including his nonsense and scholarly rambles. They'd been best friends for so long, helped each other out, confided in each other. Also, he was the one person who would never laugh at her for wanting to go to the university. It would be so easy to become more than friends.

But that would never happen, and the closer V got to being of a marriageable age, the less she let herself entertain such a silly thoughts. Faeries would be proven real before they could be together. And V didn't even think of her in that way, anyway.

Higher and higher she climbed, the pleasant April air

kissing her face, until she reached her favorite place—the tree house she and V had built with her father's help. The little house was made of scrap wood, metal, and whatever they could forage. Once inside, she leaned against a wall that had once been part of an old wagon, drawing her knees to her chest, wrapping her arms around them. Resting her head on her knees, she began to sob.

• • • • • • • •

Steven looked out his bedroom window as he sat at his desk doing his schoolwork. The gas lamp on the wall flickered softly, scattering ghostly shadows across his books and papers. Out of the corner of his eye, he watched as Noli ran out the back door of her house, heading straight for her faery tree. Well, no faeries actually lived it in. Not anymore.

They needed to talk. This would be a good time— his father occupied by business, his nosey little sister asleep. He crept down the stairs, through the kitchen, and grabbed the knob of the back door.

"Where are you going? To talk to her in your tree house?" James rolled his green eyes. "I don't understand what you two talk about."

His younger brother looked like a man, while Steven was still all arms, legs, and feet. They stood nearly the same height; James wasn't much younger, and reminded Steven of it often. His curly blond hair drove the girls wild.

"Yes. I have to tell her about Father's edict."

"Oh. Good luck with that. Flying figs, I'm glad it's you and not me." James' eyes held sympathy. He, too, was fond of Noli.

Steven let himself out, walked across the backyard that still resembled a war zone, climbed through the broken fence, went past the crashed remains of the Pixy, and scaled the tree.

Her cries reached his ears, stabbing him in the heart like a knife. Safe within the canopy of oak leaves, he made his way to the tree house. He had many memories of this place and how they'd scoured the neighborhood for months to find the wood, sheets of brass, cogs, gears, and such they'd built it out of. Neither of them could stand up inside it now.

Letting himself in, Steven drew her into his arms, although he shouldn't do such things anymore. "Noli."

Pressing her face into his shirt, she sobbed so hard her whole body shook.

"Why the tears? They're not sending you to a detention center, are they?" he asked. She hadn't cried this hard since Jeff left.

"Worse." Lifting her head, she looked at him with those amazing, steel-colored eyes. Incredible eyes, currently watery and red-rimmed in her tear-streaked face. He took a handkerchief from his pocket and handed it to her.

"They're sending me to boarding school," she sniffed. "When I'm done, they'll wipe my record clean and drop the charges. It's called Findlay House. They're going to make me into a lady. They even waived my tuition because of the court order." Her tone became dry and her eyes dull and lifeless. For once, she looked utterly and totally defeated.

His blood ran cold. Boarding school? Not likely. After all, why would the Air Patrol send her to an ordinary school? No, the likely story was they were actually sending Noli to reform school—where they'd suck out everything that made her special and beautiful. While part of him felt relief that he no longer needed to tell her his own bad news, the other part didn't want to believe they'd send her to such a place.

Even if it was truly boarding school, a place for young ladies was not the right place for Noli. They'd still try to break her, crush her spirit and individuality. Couldn't they understand how incredible she was?

But they didn't. Not the police. Not her mother. Not his father. Her tinkering, her gardening, her curiosity were gifts, not hindrances. No one understood this but him.

"Everything will be fine." He rocked her gently in his arms as they sat on the floor of her tree house, both aware of the lie.

"I leave tomorrow. It's in San Francisco." Her voice was a whisper.

Steven paused, his face scrunching in confusion. "She's sending you to San Francisco?"

It made no sense to send your child to the place where your husband disappeared.

Noli's face contorted in pain. "She says it's safe. They gave her no choice, but still ... "

33

"You're afraid because your father disappeared there."

"They say the aether did it." Her words held the feeling of rhetoric.

"Too much aether can be unhealthy," he replied. The release of aether fostered either creation or destruction. Los Angeles had a higher concentration than many cities, a reason why the blossoming moving picture industry excelled. But ever since the earthquake, San Francisco had retained dangerous levels of aether—high enough to attract unsavory types.

"I'll write you often and send books," Steven added. Even if he must defy his father. "Maybe I could even concoct a reason to visit. If you do well there, perhaps you'll get into a university and study botany, just like you've always wanted." He forced a smile.

Sometimes he wished Noli's family had tried to meld into a lower class after her father's disappearance. It would have meant she wouldn't have continued to be his friend and neighbor, but at least she might have had a chance to achieve her dreams. In this new century, post Civil War and with all that the American Renaissance had brought them, classism and elitism still ran rampant, even out west.

"I'd like you to send me letters and books." She smiled shyly, her face lighting up. Noli hadn't inherited her mother's classic beauty, but she was pretty, especially when she smiled.

"Here." On an impulse, Steven pulled his medallion over his head and placed the golden necklace around her neck, its green stone gleaming. "For protection. Never remove it. No matter what."

"To protect me from aether?" Noli laughed. "You're such a fussy old bodger, V."

Her words made him smile sadly. He loved her laugh, which reminded him of bells. Would she laugh like this after her time at the school, or would she twitter mindlessly? Would she still call him V? It was a silly nickname, given to him when they were small and she couldn't quite say his name, but he loved it.

"Tell them that, if they try to take it from you," he replied. People did wear amulets to protect them from aether; not that they actually worked.

"I will." She tucked the medallion into her blouse. "You take such good care of me. Thank you. Did you get into a heap of trouble?"

Absently, he stroked her curls. Her thanking him always made him nervous. "Just the usual. Clean up the mess, fix the fence."

She sighed, leaning against him, the gesture relaxed and comfortable. "I made such a dreadful mess. It will take forever to repair the Pixymobile. Do you think we get vacations in boarding school?"

"I have no idea." If he were older, they could run off together and go to a university far away—despite the fact he had dreams of his own to attain.

Noli looked back toward her dark house. "Mama wants to send me to Boston afterwards, for a fresh start. Perhaps even find a husband."

He watched her toy with the medallion, fingering the intricately woven gold wire, stroking the crystal the color of oak leaves in its center. It wasn't supposed to leave his possession, and his father would be displeased. But she was worth it.

"I worry about Mama," she confided. "How will she get on without me? Or will she be better off?" Her eyes misted.

"Don't think such things." Gently, he tilted her face, wiping away her tears with his thumb. "James and I will check on her for you." He knew how much Noli loved her mother.

"Would you?" Her whole being brightened. "Thank you." Her forehead wrinkled. "Officer Davies said he didn't want me to travel down the same path as Jeff. Do you have any idea what he meant?"

For a long moment, Steven didn't speak. Everyone else knew. It was time Noli knew as well. "Have you ever wondered why your mother hides the money Jeff sends, even though you desperately need it?"

"She says it's for my dowry. But who'd marry me?" She snorted in an unladylike way.

"Noli, there's someone out there for you, and you'll need that dowry one day." It pained him to force out those words. Sure, she wouldn't be the perfect society wife. But she grew flowers like few he'd ever met and created life from hunks of junk. For the millionth time, he wished things had happened differently.

No matter what, he'd lose Noli in one way or another. But she was never his to have in the first place.

36

He pulled her close, savoring her scent—the soap she made from herbs in her garden coupled with auto grease and earth. "Jeff's money comes from the wrong side of the law. Your mother doesn't want to use ill-gotten gains. Instead, she saves it for you—her hope for a better life."

"He flies cargo vessels." The light in Noli's eyes went out completely, her shoulders rounding in defeat.

"That he does—vessels of stolen cargo."

"I can't believe he's an air pirate," she sobbed into his arms.

Noli was sheltered, naive. Steven often wished he still lived in an innocent world as well. But this way, he could protect Noli and his little sister. It was one of the few duties he didn't mind. Even here, in the wilds of Los Angeles, his father insisted they uphold their ways.

He, too, was his family's hope for a better life.

Finally, her sobs slowed. Putting his forehead to hers, he looked into her amazing steel-colored eyes for what would probably be the last time. "Go on inside, it's growing late."

"I still have to pack." She hiccupped.

"Be careful, please? Watch for aether and don't talk to strange faeries." He smiled.

She smiled back. "Faeries? You're such a fussy old bodger. I'm going to miss you."

"I'll miss you too. Good night, Noli."

Would she ever call him a fussy old bodger again? Would they ever sit in the tree house discussing philosophy, history, or her favorite—botany? Probably not. The idea both saddened and angered him.

"Good night, V." With a wave, she climbed down the tree.

"Goodbye, Noli," he whispered as she went inside. "May the Bright Lady keep you safe."

With all that lurked in San Francisco, she'd need it.

FOUR

Findlay House

Noli looked out the window of the hired motorcab onto cobblestone streets filled with cool gray mist. A flying car darted above them, and she wished it would take her far away from San Francisco. She, her mother, and Officer Davies had made the long and tiring journey from Los Angeles to San Francisco by steam train. Her mother, who didn't like autos any more than she liked airships, had been complaining about the motorcab since they'd left the train station. Just one more indication she was stuck in the past.

Officer Davies had come with them for two reasons: one, to make sure Noli didn't give her mother any trouble, and two, because respectable women never traveled alone. Even cities like Los Angeles and San Francisco had out-dated conventions of propriety.

"We're nearly there." Her mother's voice held forced

cheer. She believed she always needed to have a sunny disposition no matter what—except when she scolded Noli.

Noli didn't respond, continuing to stare out the window as a steam trolley puffed by. She couldn't believe they were sending her to school in San Francisco.

Did her mother secretly hope she'd disappear, too?

No. It was coincidence. That's all. Her father would return. He had to.

"This is a good opportunity for you, Noli," Officer Davies told her.

Ignoring him, she continued to brood in silence as the motorcab slowed to a stop. Their nice lunch at the train station sat in her belly like a lump of lead. She played with her gloves until her mother reached out and put a hand over hers. Scenarios about cruel headmistresses, dreadful conditions, and mean girls, pulled from every book she'd read about boarding schools, danced through her mind like a zoetrope.

The imposing gothic house sent shivers down her spine. The yellow paint did little to make it seem cheerful. The spires and large windows reminded her of spiteful eyes watching her every move. A tall, wrought-iron fence surrounded the house like a prison. Her stomach sank all the way to her toes. Next she'd spy a sign reading "Findlay School for Wayward Hoydens."

The entire street looked gray and worn. Its previous opulence remained evident in the fine homes and brass gas lamps and cobblestones. This neighborhood of mansions once probably held society's elite. According to her teacher, the city had changed when it was rebuilt after the earthquake. Slums gave way to vibrant arts districts, poverty gave way to wealth, and the old industrial ways, polluted and dirty, gave way to new innovation and ideas. San Francisco was now a true steam-powered city of progress—much more than any other city in the nation, even Los Angeles. Perhaps they'd take a school trip to visit the new steam-power plant here. Noli had read about them and wanted to see one in person.

The driver opened the door and helped her mother out. Mama looked like a fine lady in a rose-colored travel gown, complete with corset, bustle, hat, and gloves.

Next, the driver gave Noli a hand and she tried to remember her manners. Most of the train journey, when she hadn't been sleeping, had proved a refresher course on a lady's manners.

"Regardless of our current situation," her mother had lectured in her Boston clip, "the Braddocks and the Montgomerys are fine families. Your breeding shows in every word, every move. I hope you haven't forgotten everything."

"Yes, Mama," she'd muttered, shoulders rounded. What choice did she have? And truly, was being a lady so awful?

Yes. As a child, she'd been discouraged from thinking, reading, questioning. "Oh, Magnolia, a lady doesn't need to worry about such things," they'd told her over and over.

Her mother's beautiful face softened when she noticed Noli's expression as they stood outside the motorcab. "Noli, I understand that you don't want to go away to school. I don't want for you to go either. But the court..."

Tears pricked her eyes. "Afterward, I'll send you to Boston and no one will ever know about your many…adventures in Los Angeles."

Noli gave Mama a hug. She was the shameful one, sent elsewhere so no one would learn what she'd done. Noli didn't entirely regret her many "adventures," but she felt sorry for the pain they'd caused her mother.

She pulled her cape closer. Mama had quickly altered one of her own gowns for Noli since she didn't possess anything "suitable for traveling." Shiny brass buttons gleamed on the blue traveling suit and its matching short cape with crisp blue braid. The cream gloves on her hands were kidskin and butter soft. The uncomfortable corset and bustle made her fidget even more than usual.

"I'm so happy the bustle is still in fashion. It does wonders for a lady's figure." Mama adjusted Noli's hat. The little blue derby, with the feathers and a tiny bird, had always been Noli's favorite.

"You look every inch the lady. Now act like one."

"Yes, Mama." Dread pressed down on her chest until it became hard to breathe, but Noli resolved to grit her teeth and bear this dreadful place. As her mother often pointed out, she'd shamed her family enough. Hopefully, by the time she finished with Findlay, she could talk her mother out of sending her to Boston to find a husband into something more practical—like allowing her to build steam sewing machines for the shop, to increase productivity.

Officer Davies got out of the motorcab and handed them their valises. The driver carried Noli's steamer trunk.

Mama had insisted she pack her nicest things, which included the two new dresses she'd made for Noli's sixteenth birthday and a ball gown she thought would fit with a few tucks in the bust, waist, and hips.

A ball gown? Did her mother honestly expect her to attend balls? Not that she'd want to attend such dreadful things. Society boys were so boring.

A few other possessions, which she'd placed in the trunk when her mother wasn't looking, hid under the clothes ... books, letters from Jeff, and a few photographs, including one of her father.

Officer Davies took her mother's arm. The building looked lifeless, abandoned. It was in excellent repair, but lacked the warmth that inhabited homes possessed. The school seemed to have large grounds. Hopefully they were allowed in the gardens. If kept indoors, she'd go mad.

They passed through the gate and walked down the path, Noli's heart growing heavier with every footfall. When they walked up the front steps to the porch, she noticed the polished brass sign: *Findlay House. Educating young ladies since 1869.* That was all. Perhaps Findlay really was a boarding school.

But her stomach wouldn't loosen; her fists wouldn't uncurl. Something about this place made her want to hide in her tree house.

Officer Davies rang the bell. A young woman about Noli's age opened the door. She wore a green day dress, and her blond hair was hidden under a white lace cap. She carried a piece of fine embroidery in her lily-white hand.

She smiled listlessly. "May I help you?"

Officer Davies replied, "I'm Franklin Davies and this is Mrs. Braddock and her daughter Magnolia. I believe Miss Gregory is expecting us."

"Of course, please come in." She showed them to the sitting room and went to get Miss Gregory. Her blue eyes didn't sparkle; her step held no bounce.

"What a lovely young lady. This looks like such a nice place." Mama beamed as they sat down on the uncomfortable, overstuffed furniture. The stiff and formal sitting room reminded Noli of a museum they'd visited once in Boston. The stale air smelled of bleach, supper, and a scent she couldn't quite identify.

Noli stifled a snort at her mother's comment. Back when she'd associated with girls like that one, she'd hated them. She sat next to her mother; Officer Davies took a matching chair.

"They have an excellent reputation. I'm sure Noli will acclimate quickly." Officer Davies gave her a pointed glance.

A woman entered. "Good afternoon. I'm Miss Gregory."

Miss Gregory looked every inch the archetypal evil headmistress—from her tall, thin appearance and shapeless gray suit to her stiff walk, beady eyes, and prim, graying bun.

Officer Davies stood and led the introductions. Miss Gregory took a seat in another uncomfortable-looking chair and Officer Davies sat down.

"Do you require anything else, Miss Gregory?" the

girl in the green dress asked from the doorway of the stuffy sitting room.

"Thank you, Rosemarie. Please ask Claire to bring in a tea tray before you return to your sewing." Even Miss Gregory's smile looked pinched. Rosemarie curtsied and left.

"Rosemarie's one of our very successful girls." Miss Gregory folded her pale, bony hands into her nonexistent lap. "She'll return to her parents soon, and may even be ready for the season next year. She will make any gentleman a good wife."

"Ah, the season." Her mother sighed as if remembering the good old days. "Perhaps Noli will soon have a season of her own. I have family in Boston willing to sponsor her."

The headmistress's eyes focused on Noli. "How lucky you are, Magnolia."

Noli simply smiled, trying not to fidget or blurt anything out. Ladies were silent, quiet, demure. She didn't want to go to Boston, and was secretly glad they hadn't been able to afford school. Of course, Mama hadn't told Grandfather Montgomery that, afraid he'd make them return to Boston. Mama also refused his money, saying that Jeff supported them. Because if they moved to Boston, they wouldn't be at home when her father returned.

"Here at Findlay House, we take girls and teach them to be ladies, dutiful daughters, good wives, and productive members of society." Miss Gregory looked at Noli's mother. "We give girls what they need in order to live up to our and society's expectations. Many of our girls go on to make good matches, bringing their parents great pride."

Ugh, enough with the marriage already. Why couldn't being a scientist or inventor be considered a respectable profession for a woman?

A soft rap echoed on the open door and another girl entered. This one had neatly plaited, wheat-colored hair, topped by a white fabric cap. She wore a blue, high-necked dress with white lace and buttons, and a starched white apron. The dress hung to the floor in soft folds and had the appearance of a uniform. That wasn't what they wore ... was it?

"Your tea, Miss Gregory?" The girl carried a silver tray set with a tea service and was shorter, younger, and plumper than Rosemarie had been. Noli could tell that her strong and slightly calloused hands did more than embroider and wave a fan.

"Thank you, Claire," Miss Gregory replied.

Claire set the tray on the table and turned. "Anything else, Miss Gregory?"

Miss Gregory stiffly smiled and gestured at Claire. "We have little in the way of service staff here at Findlay House. Instead, the girls assist in upkeep. This provides discipline and teaches them how to run a household efficiently."

"Even manual chores?" Mama's lips pursed in disapproval. Although fine ladies did many things around the house, manual chores weren't among them. Noli privately wondered who would clean their own house and do laundry with her gone. Not only was her mother too tired at the end of the day, but such tasks were below women like her. She might be distressed gentry and forced to work in a shop, but she'd never stoop to scrubbing her own floors, or admit that Noli did.

Miss Gregory poured the tea. "Here at Findlay we find hard work good for the soul. It pushes out impurities. Girls do equal parts work around the house, schoolwork, and lessons on decorum. They spend their free time sewing, playing an instrument, sitting in the garden, and for some, learning skills that they can contribute directly to society."

Noli didn't mind hard work, but her stomach still wouldn't unclench. Something about this place just felt *wrong.* What, she didn't know.

"How long have you been here, Claire?" Officer Davies asked, glancing at the girl who was still standing uncertainly at Miss Gregory's side.

"Nearly a year, sir." She didn't meet his gaze.

"Do you like it here?" Concern lurked in Mama's eyes. Good.

"Findlay's a wonderful place." Her words felt rehearsed and insincere.

Miss Gregory gave a curt nod. "Thank you, Claire. You may return to the kitchen now."

Claire curtsied and left. She seemed nice enough, unlike that stiff, mindless Rosemarie.

"Claire is one of our girls who is making very good progress. Being unmarriageable, we're teaching her to cook and bake so she'll find a position at a fine house."

What made Claire unmarriageable? Plumpness might be unfashionable, but some men liked women with certain large parts. She didn't seem brain-addled.

During tea, Miss Gregory went over the curriculum and expectations. Noli sat up straight; not that her corset permitted her to slouch. Ankles crossed, she kept her gloved hands folded in her lap when not holding her teacup. Every time she squirmed, her mother glared.

"Would you prefer being assigned to mending and sewing, Magnolia? Being a dressmaker's daughter, I expect you're quite accomplished already. Do you wish her to be trained?" Miss Gregory asked.

Mama took a sip of tea. "I'm a dressmaker out of necessity, since my husband disappeared, as I explained in the aethergraph. I'd like to have Noli educated as a lady, in order for her to marry well and carry on our family's good name."

"I see." Miss Gregory looked down her nose at Noli, as if she found the notion preposterous but wasn't about to say it out loud.

"May I work in the gardens?" Noli asked softly. "I'm fond of bo—" Botany probably wasn't ladylike. "Flowers … and flower arranging."

"Noli grows lovely roses." Mama smiled, pride radiating in her voice. She always kept vases of them in the shop.

Miss Gregory sniffed again. "For now, you may."

Since she had to be there, she might as well do something she enjoyed. Noli could hardly picture Rosemarie working in the gardens. Hopefully not all the girls were like that.

After tea, Miss Gregory gave them a tour of Findlay. Rosemarie and friends sat sewing in a parlor. The half-

48

dozen thin, pale girls had vapid expressions and wore lovely dresses, although none of their gowns were half as nice as what Mama made. They were chattering inanely, the way polite ladies should, as they sewed or worked on complicated embroidery samplers.

A web of unease continued to wind around Noli as the tour continued. Everything at Findlay was immaculate, from the perfectly straight photographs on the walls to the polished hardwood floors. There wasn't a cobweb in sight.

Yet it lacked something. A soul. Yes, Findlay House lacked a soul.

"When do the girls take their summer vacation?" Mama kept looking around, as if trying to absorb the austere sobriety of Findlay House.

Didn't she see what a horrible place this was?

Miss Gregory looked down her pointed nose at them. "I'm afraid we don't do home visits, nor do we accommodate visits from our students' families. They interfere with the continuity of the curriculum."

"What about Christmas?" Mama's face creased with worry. "Don't most boarding schools observe the holidays?"

"We do things differently here at Findlay." Miss Gregory shook her head. "Here, students have control over their educations and how fast they work through the curriculum. Depending on how hard your daughter works, you'll have her back in a year or two. After all, if she's too old, she'll never find a husband. I assure you, she'll make you and your family proud."

Startled, Noli curled her fists and opened her mouth

to protest, closing it when her mother glared. She took a deep breath, trying to calm herself. Some girls stayed in boarding school until age eighteen. But she'd figured on a couple of months, not years.

"I understand. Continuity is central to your program?" Her mother's voice softened.

"Continuity, order, and discipline are the pillars holding up Findlay House, and have been since Mrs. Findlay started it back in 1869." Miss Gregory squared her shoulders proudly as she said that.

Discipline? Noli's stomach knotted.

"When Magnolia shows good progress, she may write letters," Miss Gregory added.

Noli's heart skipped a beat and it was hard not to make a sound. She'd been counting on letters from V, Jeff, and her mother to keep her sane in this dreadful place.

She didn't get even a glimpse of any other girls on the tour, nor did they view the sleeping rooms. Actually, they didn't venture upstairs at all. They returned to the sitting room.

Miss Gregory turned to her mother and Officer Davies. "I'd like to speak to the both of you privately." She turned to Noli. "Be a good girl and sit quietly. I'm sure you have some sewing to occupy yourself with."

"Yes, Miss Gregory." Her valise held a sampler—and a book. After they left, she withdrew the book and the sewing. The book belonged to V: *Nicomachean Ethics* by Aristotle, one of his favorites and quite fascinating. Miss Gregory probably wouldn't approve. Noli read until footsteps echoed down the hall. She tucked the book into her valise and began sewing as her mother, Officer Davies, and Miss Gregory entered.

"Magnolia needs to say her goodbyes now if she's to settle in before supper. I'll leave you alone for a few moments." The headmistress left and Noli put her sewing away, leaving her valise on the floor next to the settee.

Her knees shook under the heavy fabric of the blue traveling gown as she hugged her mother, wishing she didn't have to say goodbye yet. "Please don't make me stay," she whispered. "I'll be good, I promise."

"We don't have a choice, remember? Adjust quickly; learn well, so you may come home." Her mother's eyes glistened with tears and she drew her thumb down Noli's cheekbone.

Emotion choked Noli. "I won't ever become an air pirate, I promise."

Mama's eyes widened, but she didn't comment on Jeff. Instead, she gestured to the room. "It's school, Noli. Boarding school, like I went to, like I should have sent you to long ago. It looks like a lovely place. Such nice girls."

Such vapid, pretty dolls. That's all most society women were. While her mother proved a bit of an exception to this rule, she nevertheless always struggled to hide anything that could possibly be construed as "improper," or even worse, "madness."

"I want you to give Miss Gregory your full cooperation, Noli." Officer Davies' tone held a finality she felt down to her very core.

"Yes, Officer." Noli stared at the toes of her dainty black boots. Before she could add anything, the ominous clack of heels signalled Miss Gregory's return.

The headmistress gave them a pinched smile. "It's time for you to go, Officer Davies, Mrs. Braddock."

Noli gave her mother one last hug and she choked back a sob. "I love you."

Her mother stroked her hair. "I love you too, Noli. Be good and come home soon."

"Yes, Mama." That would be the only way she'd get out of here honorably. Even if her mother hated this place, bringing her back to Los Angeles meant Noli would go before the judge.

Miss Gregory showed Mama and Officer Davies to the door. "Thank you again for choosing Findlay, Mrs. Braddock. I'll send you regular progress reports." She smiled again. Noli noticed how her smiles never met her eyes.

"Goodbye, Noli." Her mother waved sadly, Officer Davies escorting her down the path and through the gate to the motorcab.

"Goodbye, Mama. Goodbye, Officer Davies." Noli waved from the doorway. Her heart swelled with sadness. How would she manage?

When the motorcab left, Miss Gregory ushered her inside and shut the door. "Come now, Magnolia. We'll go over the rules and you may meet the other girls."

"Yes, Miss Gregory."

Miss Gregory's hand made contact with Noli's cheek. Pain shot through her face as a loud crack resounded in her ears.

"That didn't require an answer," Miss Gregory scolded. "Your mother wants you educated like a lady, though from the looks of your record, I'm not sure how we'll manage to reform a hoyden with your temperament. Good daughters only speak when spoken to. Understood?"

Her heart racing, Noli cast her eyes down, rounding her shoulders in defeat and humiliation. That didn't make sense—she *was* spoken to.

Miss Gregory's bony hand made contact with her face again. "Are you brain-addled, besides being disobedient and willful? A question demands an answer."

"I … I understand, Miss Gregory," she whispered. Her cheeks burned where she'd been struck. Again the contradiction baffled her, but maybe rules here didn't have to make sense. They only had to be obeyed.

"Good." Miss Gregory stood in front of her, tall and imposing. "Understanding is another core foundation of Findlay, as is obedience. If you are obedient, your stay at Findlay will be as brief and pleasant as one can expect. Come now."

Turning, Miss Gregory quickly made her way through the foyer, heels clacking on the polished, dark wood of the floor. Noli followed.

Understanding and obedience? Discipline? Hard work?

Prickles of foreboding shot up Noli's spine, chilling her through and through until she wanted to wrap her arms around herself and shiver.

Where in the world had they sent her?

FIVE

Charlotte

Pulling the rough gray blanket over her head, Noli curled up on the rickety cot, burying her face in the lumpy pillow. There was no doubt about it—Findlay House was a reform school, pure and simple. They simply sugarcoated it, passing it off as a fancy boarding school so society families wouldn't feel shame for sending their daughters to such a place.

Had her mother known? No. Mama never saw the bad in things, even when it was obvious. Officer Davies had told her it was boarding school and she'd believed him, no matter how the place might seem. It was just the way her mother was.

If Mama had had any idea they'd take her things away, she never would have filled her trunk with finery. Miss Gregory had taken nearly *everything*. Her clothes—*New girls don't have the privilege of wearing their own clothes.* Her books—*Socrates, Plato, Shakespeare? Much too stimulating. No wonder you have Ideas. Certainly, you don't wish to become a bluestocking.*

Miss Gregory had allowed her to keep her botany book, a gift from her father that she'd hid her photographs in. But not the letters from Jeff or anything other than basics such as soap and undergarments. The headmistress gave her some ugly gray dresses and head covers, and scratchy gray nightdresses.

Findlay House had two rules: *Always do what you're told or you'll be punished,* and *If you're punished, perform your punishment quickly and silently.*

"Privileges are earned here at Findlay." Miss Gregory had looked sharply down her nose at Noli. "The further you progress, the more privileges you'll earn. You control how fast you progress by being obedient and polite; mastering your private, scholastic, and decorum lessons; doing your chores and duties correctly and quickly; and taking to your treatments."

Treatments? Her blood had turned to ice and her belly churned. No one had said anything about treatments.

Next, the school doctor, Dr. Martin, examined her—a violating, humiliating experience.

First, he did innocuous things. He took her heart rate. Tested her reflexes. Looked in her ears and eyes. Tested her hearing and vision.

When he started asking questions, she squirmed on the hard wooden stool in the sterile little doctor's office.

One set of glass cabinets held a variety of jars and boxes. Another held other strange things—geared metal boxes, odd contraptions, and large brass spoons.

"Do you have any urges, Magnolia?" He'd circled her, looking her up and down.

"What sort of urges, Doctor?" Something about him made her want to hide.

"What makes you do naughty things? Does something whisper in your ear? Do you have dark feelings deep inside?" He'd given her a look that tried, and failed, to be fatherly. "You may tell me anything."

"I don't mean to do bad things. I didn't mean for everything to happen this way." If only she could do it over …

"There, there." He'd patted her shoulder, his hand moist and sweaty. "It sounds as if you simply have too much unsupervised time. Easy to remedy. Any other urges? Yearnings to touch yourself—or perhaps be touched by a man?" His expression became a leer.

Noli had shaken her head, shocked that he'd say such a thing. "Good heavens, no."

Taking his clipboard, he'd asked more questions, asking about school, illnesses, even her monthlies, which made her blush. He'd even asked if she'd ever lain with a man, been touched intimately, or been kissed.

She'd answered with a resounding *no*. Why did he need to know? It smacked of impropriety and her cheeks burned with embarrassment.

Finally, Miss Gregory returned. "How did we fare, Dr. Martin?"

He glanced at his clipboard. "Splendid. I'll administer her first treatment tomorrow."

"Does she need to start in isolation?" Miss Gregory seemed to relish the thought.

The doctor shook his head. "No, a girl like her needs to be kept busy with meaningful work. I see no reason to keep her from the other girls."

The corners of Miss Gregory's lips twitched downward in a slight frown. "Any other restrictions? What about mental stimulation?"

"Yes. The things she reads are far too taxing. Your normal curriculum is fine, but anything other than ladies' magazines will be far too strenuous."

Since when were books overtaxing? She wasn't feeble-minded. Noli opened her mouth to protest. How dare they not permit her to read books!

One well-appointed glare from Miss Gregory caused her to remain silent.

At supper, Miss Gregory introduced her to the other girls, who, if they responded at all, replied only with a vapid *welcome* or *how do you do?* The girls in gray, who sat at the far end of the table, didn't speak much. Unlike the others, their eyes still held some sparkle—especially one with red hair, freckles, and green eyes.

Noli's "private lesson" after that soulless supper had terrified her. Miss Henderson's expression while she drilled the lesson over and over—with the aid of a long, black, leather whip—lingered in her mind's eye. Aching welts covered Noli's legs and bottom.

"A lady doesn't play with tools or fix autos." *Crack.*

"A dutiful daughter *always* obeys her mother." *Crack.*

When Noli cried out, the punishment intensified.

After her lesson, Miss Gregory had excused her from the evening activity, permitting her to retire early. Noli had washed, pulled on the itchy gray nightdress, and returned to the tiny, plain room she shared with five other girls. A pale, sickly green covered the walls—to promote calmness. Nothing decorated them, not even pictures. No rugs lay on the polished wooden floors. Crisp white curtains covered the barred windows.

Four narrow cots with tattered gray blankets were lined up against one wall. Over each bed hung a single shelf where a few personal possessions sat tidily. The other side held two proper single beds, made neatly with blue quilts and fluffy pillows. A trunk rested at the foot of each bed. Four "new girls" lived in the room. Two "girls making good progress," the blues, served as examples. The "very successful girls," the fancies, had their own rooms.

Noli curled in the narrow cot, afraid and unsure, bruised and humiliated, her legs still burning from the whipping. Clutching the necklace from V, she sobbed.

The door opened and she froze, not wanting to be punished for crying. Excessive weeping signified many womanly problems.

"Are you all right, new girl?" The sweet voice held a slight accent. "The first few days are the worst. They're still at the evening activity. Because I showed signs of overstimulation, they sent me to retire early." She sounded relieved.

Tucking the medallion under her dress, Noli turned to see who spoke. The girl with the red hair and mischievous green eyes sat on the next cot. She looked about Noli's age.

"I'm Charlotte Wilson. What are you in for?" Charlotte was dainty and pale, but something in her eyes made her look like trouble, as Mama would say. Girls like that always seemed more fun.

"In for?" Her legs screaming in pain, Noli eased into a sitting position, pulling her knees to her chest, wrapping her arms around them.

Charlotte spread her hands. "Everyone's in for something. Moodiness, willfulness, hysteria, and nervousness are the most common. We have one trouser wearer, and a few girls who are overly independent or frigid. I'm a nymphomaniac."

Noli blinked as Charlotte cheerfully labeled everyone as if going over the supper menu. "I'm Noli—Magnolia—Braddock," she said. "I'm a willful hoyden prone to youthful disobedience."

"Three labels?" Charlotte grinned. "I'm surprised they didn't start you out in isolation."

"What's a nymphomaniac?" The unfamiliar word rolled uneasily off her tongue.

Charlotte giggled. "They say I'm man-crazy and suffer from overstimulated genitals."

How exactly did one treat *that*? None of these "illnesses" sounded scientific at all.

"How long have you been here?" Noli asked. Could

she withstand a year or two of "private lessons" and not become a vapid pile of mush? Perhaps that was the point.

"A year." Charlotte seemed nonplussed.

"A year? And you're still a new girl?" Noli shivered, pulling the threadbare blanket around her.

"I'm not showing enough progress. But I don't understand why being a little flirtatious is a problem. It's not as if I'd actually do anything." Charlotte rolled her eyes.

"Don't you want to have more privileges?" Noli couldn't wait to write letters.

"And become one of *them*?" Charlotte shuddered. "Progressing means letting them suck out your soul and make you into a mindless doll. That's exactly what the successful girls are—nearly perfect girls who starve themselves and never have an original thought in their heads."

"If you don't improve, you don't get out, right?" Somehow she needed a way to get out without bringing more shame to her mother. How would her mother explain her going away to boarding school in the middle of April, anyway?

"If you get worse, they send you someplace else. Any place is better than here."

Noli didn't agree. A detention center might be better. But an asylum...

The very thought made bile rise in her throat.

"Watch out for the blues," Charlotte added. "Some of them are nasty, especially Margaret." She jerked her chin toward one of the blue beds. "Claire's nice enough."

Claire. The girl with the tea tray. The unmarriageable one.

"What makes a girl unmarriageable?" Noli asked.

Charlotte's face contorted in pain. "Never let them classify you as unmarriageable." With a sigh, she stood and got something off her shelf. "I should go before someone checks on me. We get in trouble for *everything*." She held a gray bundle, a washcloth, and a bar of soap in her hand. "You get used to it—the chores, punishments, treatments, even private lessons."

How did one grow used to being beaten?

"Welcome to Findlay House." With a smile, Charlotte left to wash.

Welcome indeed.

SIX

Enemies

Morning came too soon and Noli's legs ached. Charlotte assured her the whip wouldn't leave marks—on her body, at least.

Before breakfast they all did their chores. Noli had to scrub the kitchen and dining room floors. Bland mush eaten in virtual silence masqueraded as breakfast. Inspection came after. Lessons disappointed her. She'd covered these simple things years ago.

Her mind could easily rot from boredom here. That, too, could be the point. More bland gruel for lunch. Miss Henderson taught decorum, sans whip. Both she and the schoolmistress, Miss Nelson, used their canes liberally. Noli scrubbed more floors, then worked in the garden until supper.

After supper, the new girls did their schoolwork in the

library in silence, under Miss Gregory's watchful eyes. An eerie hush blanketed the room. Charlotte caught her eye and smiled. Earlier in the day, Margaret had tattled that Charlotte "smiled excessively" and Miss Gregory had sent Charlotte to lie down for "overstimulation."

"Magnolia." Miss Gregory's voice sent chills down her spine. "Dr. Martin wishes to see you in his office. Put your things away, then go directly there."

Noli gathered her books and put them away. Nervously, she made her way to his office.

Rosemarie stood in the doorway. "Thank you, Dr. Martin," she simpered, eyes wide, cheeks flushed. She left, completely ignoring Noli. Findlay had a pecking order.

"Hello, Magnolia," Dr. Martin greeted her. "Today we're going to go to Treatment Room A; that's where you'll meet me each day for your treatments unless I tell you otherwise."

Noli nodded, having been slapped several times and caned once for answering when she wasn't supposed to. Dr. Martin's smarmy smile and memories of yesterday's exam caused her to shudder involuntarily. She followed him, belly fluttering in anxiousness.

The little room known as Treatment Room A contained a box resembling a brass coffin with some sort of crank attached. Noli stared at it, trying to determine what exactly it was.

"This is a sensory deprivation box," Dr. Martin explained. "Your body needs to be kept busy with meaningful work, but your mind needs to be taught to relax. In this box you will see nothing, hear nothing. You'll be completely alone. All you have to do is relax and breathe deep. There is no need to think or do anything." He smiled in that creepy way which made her skin crawl. "Doesn't that sound nice?"

"Yes, sir." A blatant lie. It sounded positively dreadful.

He rotated the big brass crank and gears turned, retracting the lid with an ominous screech of metal on metal. It seemed like something needed to be oiled.

"Into the box you go." Dr. Martin gestured at it.

Noli did as she was told, although parts of her screamed at the mere thought of climbing into that small box. Lined with soft red fabric, the box was large enough to lie down in, but just so. When he closed the lid, there wouldn't be much more than a few inches between her nose and the lid. At least she didn't need to undress.

Panic rose within her. What would happen once he closed the box?

"Don't worry, you'll have enough air. Just relax and breathe deep. Clear your mind of all your thoughts and worries. I'll be back for you in a little while. He turned the crank, closing the lid over her.

Complete darkness blanketed her. She took a deep breath and tried to clear her mind of the many thoughts crowing her head. Closing her eyes, she took another deep breath as weariness consumed her.

....

"Well, well, fell asleep, did we?" Dr. Martin's disapproving tone made Noli's eyes fly open. He was staring at her with his unblinking eyes. He always seemed to look at her as if she weren't wearing any clothes.

"I ... I'm sorry. I didn't mean to." Her entire being braced for the worst.

"Don't worry, Magnolia. I won't tell ... this time." His voice held sinister notes that made her belly clench. "However, you're not supposed to be sleeping."

"Yes, Dr. Martin." She sat up and he helped her out of the brass box.

"Be a good girl and run along. Miss Henderson is waiting for you."

The crack of a whip echoed through her mind. "Thank you, Dr. Martin."

His hand caught her wrist. "What do we have here? An unauthorized piece of jewelry? Do I even want to know where you hid this to keep it from Miss Gregory?"

The doctor's eyes sparkled with delight as he fingered the medallion around her neck, which had worked its way out from under her dress. His hands brushed lightly and deliberately against her tightly corseted breasts.

"Please, Dr. Martin." Her knees shook under her thin gray dress. What could she tell him? "It's an amulet to protect me against the ill effects of aether."

"You fear aether, yet you aren't afraid to hoverboard?" A bushy white eyebrow rose.

"My father disappeared here in San Francisco right

after the earthquake. He's an engineer. His whole team disappeared." She hiccupped. "They say the aether caused it."

"You're trembling. You fear aether?" His expression softened. Once again, he tried, and failed, to appear fatherly.

"Of course." What she really feared was parting with the necklace.

Nodding, the doctor tucked it back into her dress in a way that sent shivers shooting up her spine. He smiled an unnerving smile. "I see. I'll permit it for now. Certainly we don't want this fear to overstimulate you."

Relief washed over her like spring rain. "Thank you, Dr. Martin."

"Take some deep breaths, and go on to Miss Henderson." He had her inhale and exhale deeply, then watched as she left, in a way that made her feel sullied.

....

Noli fell into a tiring routine of chores, lessons, and abuse, of rough sheets and shapeless clothes. Her muscles always ached from hard work and whippings, and she continued to fall asleep in the sensory deprivation box.

Findlay possessed two saving graces that kept her from curling into a ball and refusing to get up. Charlotte was the first. They could seldom talk, but all she needed was a smile, a stolen whisper. They did laundry together, laboring side by side, putting clothes through the hand-cranked washer and hanging sheets up on the line. It allowed them to talk on occasion.

Charlotte liked to make things—bracelets, blankets, necklaces. Technically an orphan, her aunt and uncle had raised her on the family tobacco farm in Georgia. She claimed she'd really been sent to Findlay because her aunt found her "inconvenient." Whenever she spoke of her uncle, the light went out of her eyes. Privately, Noli wondered if that was the reason Charlotte wasn't in a hurry to leave Findlay.

Gardening proved to be her second saving grace. Unlike many of the other girls, Noli didn't mind weeding or tending the garden for hours because she could be outside among the plants. The matron left her alone as long as she worked and didn't dally. It was quiet here, out of the path of airships. The rare hoverboard or flying car seemed to be visiting a neighboring estate.

The rose garden in the back corner of the grounds quickly became her favorite. The first few days, Noli had missed it, assuming that the stone wall around it belonged to the estate behind them rather than to a separate, walled-off garden. Then she discovered the door, an old brass key still in the lock.

Fragrant climbing rosebushes, not yet in bloom, grew wild on both sides of the garden's walls, mixing with ivy and honeysuckle and concealing it from the rest of the grounds. Faery lilies, rosebushes, sweet peas, foxglove, bluebells, lady slippers, milkweed, and fragrant herbs like thyme, lambs ear, and lavender filled the garden with fragrance and color. The whole place seemed wild and abandoned, adding to its magic feeling. She could practically see the faeries dancing among the blossoms.

Magic? Faeries? Bah. Noli rebuked herself for sounding like V, all fancy, no practicality. They were far too old to believe in such nonsense. Still, he'd like this place, and she could see him coming here to read one of his dusty old tomes.

A giant oak tree stood guard in the center of the garden, reminding her of her own faery tree back in Los Angeles. A sharp pang of homesickness pierced her. No tree house hid among the foliage of this old tree, but a worn rope swing dangled from a branch. Someone had once loved this place. The tree's huge branches made for perfect climbing. Ivy and honeysuckle festooned the trunk, adding to its magical appearance. A ring of toadstools circled it.

Noli's hands itched to climb the tree, but memories of Miss Henderson's whip made her legs burn at the thought. Hoyden-like behavior would earn her extra private lessons.

Instead, she cut bouquets of sweet-smelling blooms and brought them into the house to arrange in vases in the front hall, in the fancies' sewing room, and in Miss Gregory's office. She'd been praised for her thoughtfulness and skill at arranging. Good—a reason to go back often. She had no desire to tame the wild garden, but the roses certainly could use some attention.

....

"Miss Gregory?" Margaret's whiney voice cut through the soft din of lunch, her thin face flushed, her brown eyes gleaming with spitefulness.

Inwardly, Noli sighed as she focused on yet another bowl of bland food. Ever since Margaret had realized that Noli and Charlotte were friends, she'd tortured Noli, too. She made stains on her clothes and fussed when Noli couldn't get them out. Tracked dirt onto clean floors. Claimed to be allergic to the flowers. Found fault with the way Noli made her rickety cot.

"Yes, Margaret?" Miss Gregory looked up from her conversation. She, Miss Henderson, and Miss Nelson sat at the head of the long table. Next came the fancies, then the blues in the middle, and the new girls at the end.

"I believe Magnolia has an illegal piece of jewelry. A necklace." Margaret smirked. "New girls aren't permitted jewelry."

Noli writhed in embarrassment on her hard wooden chair. How did Margaret know? She'd been so careful to keep it hidden.

Miss Gregory's eyes narrowed as she looked down her pointed nose. "Does she? Thank you, Margaret. Magnolia Braddock, come here."

Margaret beamed, probably imagining her reward, and swished her brown braid in delight.

The fancies continued their inane conversations, completely ignoring everything else around them. The blues whispered clandestinely as Noli left her seat, making the walk of shame to the head of the table. None of the grays spoke, since they weren't permitted to speak unless spoken to at meals, but Charlotte's forehead furrowed in worry.

"What is this?" Miss Gregory grabbed her medallion

and yanked it clear off her neck, breaking the chain in the process.

Noli tried to maintain a facade of calm. Anything else would earn her extra lessons and punishments.

Miss Gregory clucked her tongue, beady eyes narrowing in dismay. "I'm disappointed in you. What do you have to say for yourself?"

"Miss Gregory, this isn't a piece of jewelry but an amulet to protect me against aether. I'm afraid of it, you see." She told the headmistress about her father. "They say the aether did it. Dr. Martin said I could keep the amulet for now."

"Did he now?" Miss Gregory blinked in surprise. Her chin jutted out. "If you're lying, it's the water room for you."

"Rosemarie, please fetch Dr. Martin," Miss Gregory ordered.

"Yes, Miss Gregory." In a flurry of pale green skirts, she got up from the table and left.

While they waited, Noli stood while everyone else ate, enduring hard looks and smirks, especially from Margaret. She got a compassionate look from Claire. Claire never made any outright overtures of friendship, but she'd never been mean, and she occasionally passed on small bits of advice or warning.

Dr. Martin finally arrived. He inclined his balding head. "You called, Miss Gregory."

"Indeed." Standing, she handed him the broken medallion. "Magnolia Braddock had this. She claims it's a medal to protect her against aether and *you* permitted her to keep it."

Noli prayed that he would tell the truth.

"Why, yes, Miss Gregory. I did permit Magnolia to keep her amulet." He looked Noli up and down in a way that seemed highly inappropriate. He turned the gold sunburst over in his meaty hands.

"You did?" Miss Gregory's thin lips pursed.

"Indeed. She has a deep fear of aether—and this city. I didn't wish her fear to impede her initial treatment. I decided it would be better for her overall adjustment for her to keep it until we are ready to deal with her deep-set fear." He smiled at Miss Gregory. "But even in today's society of progress, what god-fearing woman isn't a little afraid of aether? Plenty of ladies wear protective amulets."

By the look on Miss Gregory's face, she wasn't one of them. Her lips formed a hard line. "I see. I know you wouldn't allow a breach of rules unless you found it absolutely necessary to aid her course of treatment. Next time, please inform me."

"Why yes, Miss Gregory. It must have slipped my mind." He handed Noli the broken necklace. "There you are. Will that be all?"

"Yes, that will be all." Miss Gregory's mouth puckered as if the words tasted bad.

He left the room. Charlotte shot Margaret a triumphant look. Noli tried to keep her expression bland as she made her way back to the table, her belly unknotting.

She'd won, but she knew there'd be a price to pay for her small triumph.

As soon as Noli sat, Miss Gregory clapped. "Lunch is over, ladies."

Noli's belly rumbled in protest as she looked forlornly at her half-filled bowl. With a sigh, she followed the girls out of the room, hunger gnawing at her. She'd be punished if caught eating anything out of the vegetable garden.

"Good job," Charlotte mouthed.

Carefully, Noli knotted the broken ends of the chain together; it now barely fit over her head. She tucked it back under her dress.

Claire stopped her on the way to the garden shed. She probably wanted her to tend to the vegetable garden or pick something for the cook.

"Watch out for Margaret." Claire's blue eyes darted around nervously. "She didn't get in trouble, but she didn't get a reward either. She might try something."

As much as Noli wished that weren't true, she had a sneaking suspicion it was.

• • • • • • • •

"Quinn, I need a new sigil." Steven sat hunched over the desk in the library, working on his lessons. Quinn was many things to his family. Right now, he was playing tutor, and hopefully he wouldn't ask many questions.

Tall and pale with naturally silver hair, Quinn had an air of dignity about him, even if he didn't look older than twenty. His eyebrows arched at Steven's question. "How exactly did you manage to lose your old sigil?"

It wasn't that Steven regretted giving it to Noli, but he didn't look forward to explaining its absence, either. Sigils weren't easy to procure. It would be simpler to say that he lost it, but if his father discovered he'd lied and given it to Noli... well, only the Bright Lady could help him then.

"If I don't tell you, you can't tell my father," Steven finally replied.

Quinn gazed at him with sharp eyes the color of flint. "I'll get you another, but you have to pay attention in our lessons. What has gotten into you?"

Never had Steven anticipated that Noli's absence would affect him so much. But it had. According to her mother, he couldn't even write to her. "I promise to try."

"Good." Quinn nodded in agreement. "Now let's get back to our lessons."

Once again, Steven's mind wandered back to Noli. Should he hope she did well at school, or poorly? Not that it would change anything, either way. He just hoped she was safe.

SEVEN

The Spark

"Should we go for a walk?" She shot Kevighn a winsome smile. Her name was Annette, or was it Maryanne? He couldn't remember. Whatever the mortal called herself, she was charming, curvaceous, and flexible. Very flexible.

Truly, he should be out hunting instead of haunting the Red Pearl. But after the last missive from the queen, he needed to indulge briefly. Essentially, the message read: *If you don't find a girl soon, I'll find someone else who can.*

While few possessed the ability to see the Spark in mortals, he wasn't the *only* one. He just happened to also be good at tracking and seducing young women and stealing them away.

Well, he used to be.

There weren't fewer girls with the Spark in the mortal realm. They were just more wary of running away with him, especially with all this emphasis on virtue and chastity. What nonsense. He liked mortals better before the recent spurt of technology and science. Back then, they were more likely to believe what they were told than seek out answers.

Also, after Annabelle, he lacked motivation.

"We can walk briefly, if you wish." He'd rather take the harlot back upstairs. After, perhaps.

They walked outside; the afternoon was overcast. She carried a lace parasol like a fine lady. To give the strumpet credit, she didn't prattle on as they strolled the gardens of his favorite opium den.

"Poor girls." She jerked her chin toward the other side of the tall fence.

Two girls in gray were silently hanging laundry on a line. The tiny one had freckles and red hair. The other possessed a mop of chestnut curls and eyes like steel. They were about the age he usually stole—the magic preferred girls who hovered on the brink between child and woman.

Personally, he couldn't fault the magic for her good taste.

"What precisely is this place?" He gazed at the girls as they worked. A hoverboard flew overhead, probably to visit the Red Pearl.

"They take willful society girls and beat them until they become submissive, fine ladies." Taking her fan, she fluttered it. "Horrible, terrible, place. I know the cook. The doctor there is creepy. He seems to enjoy his job of treating the girls a little too much." She shuddered slightly, making her large bosom shake in her tight pink dress.

A place where they actually sucked the life out of young girls in their prime? Terrible. He'd never claim to understand mortals.

The girls on the other side of the fence continued to hang laundry. The eyes of the redhead went alight with mischief. She whispered something to the other girl and grinned. They both laughed.

Kevighn winced, as if the sun had come out from behind the clouds. The Bright Lady smiled upon him. Both girls possessed quite a bit of the Spark. One of them shone with it, but with them so close together, he couldn't tell which. Either girl would do. Maybe he'd bring both.

After all, how hard could it be to lure girls with the Spark out of a place designed to drain them of just that?

....

The next day, Kevighn strolled the grounds of the Red Pearl alone hoping to catch a glimpse of the two girls. No laundry hung on the line. He continued walking along the fence. Near the back of the garden he felt something hum under his skin, something surprising, pleasing, and startling all at the same time.

Things just got better and better. As he crept to the back corner of the property, the magic grew so thick he could taste it.

Ivy, roses, and honeysuckle covered the bars of the fence. Quickly, he pushed some to one side and peeked in. Ah, a fine faery garden if ever he saw one. Someone had planted all the right things. In the center stood a *bona fide* faery tree ringed with toadstools, gleaming with so much power he could see it. Tiny wood faeries flitted around.

Oh, it wasn't *just* a faery tree, but an old portal to the Otherworld, one that had gone wild, probably with disuse. Wild portals were unstable, capable of accidently transporting people to who-knows-where.

Hearing movement in the garden, Kevighn peered through the foliage. A flash of gray caught his eye. The girl, in her gray dress and little gray headscarf, positively shone as she pruned the roses, unaware he watched.

Faery trees drew those with the Spark. Wary mothers cautioned their girls about such dangers. Even children's poems held warnings. Once he'd seen girls with a skipping rope, chanting *Mama said I never should, play with faeries in the wood.*

With bated breath he continued to watch her, as he read her Spark. Piling her arms with flowers, she seemed oblivious to the wood faeries flying around her. One spied him and Kevighn placed a finger on his lips. The mortal turned. Ah, it was the girl with the mop of chestnut curls and the steel eyes. Putting her nose into the flowers, she breathed deeply and glowed.

He drank in her power, her potential. Oh yes. She'd do nicely.

Now to plan his next move.

EIGHT

Stronger Measures

Something was wrong with Charlotte. She was quiet and avoided all attempts at conversation. As they hung the wash in the summer sun, Noli wondered if Charlotte's unusual silence had to do with being told that if she didn't make better progress, she'd be sent elsewhere—since stronger measures hadn't worked.

Charlotte had confided that "stronger measures" included a hand-cranked box with brass, spoonlike paddles that produced something called an electroshock.

"Why do you continue to fight them?" Noli had asked.

"If I don't, they win. Besides..." Charlotte's green eyes lost their glimmer. "I don't want to go home. Beatings, treatments, even electroshock are *nothing* compared to my uncle."

Charlotte had been right; Noli had adjusted to the hard work and beatings. She missed her mother terribly, but the quicker she progressed, the quicker she could see her—and V. She missed that fussy old bodger, too.

Still, Noli yearned for her books. She'd managed to recover *Nicomachean Ethics*, which had been in her valise when it was left in the sitting room that first day, and read it in secret. In public, she devoured the inane prattle of *Harper's Bazaar* and other ladies' magazines simply to have something to read.

When they finished hanging the laundry, the matron who supervised them appeared. "Cook would like me to gather some thyme," Noli lied. "May I bring Charlotte with me?"

The portly matron scowled. "Make it brief."

Noli inwardly sighed with relief. If she could get Charlotte to the faery garden, they could speak freely. They went off. Charlotte shot her a look when she walked right past the kitchen garden.

"Cook likes the thyme from the other garden better." Noli led Charlotte to the back corner of the grounds, pushed the roses aside, turned the key, and pushed open the old wooden door, revealing the hidden garden.

Awestruck, Charlotte stood in the doorway and drank in her surroundings. "I had no idea this was here," she whispered.

"I don't think Miss Gregory does, either. There's another rose garden." Noli had found that out the hard way. "Will you tell me what's bothering you? Please?" She picked thyme, relishing the scents of the herbs and flowers in bloom, the sensation of leaves under her fingers.

Squirming, Charlotte bent forward, hiding her face in the flowers. "They want to send me elsewhere. My uncle asked them to give me one more chance. If not, I'm to return home."

"Return home? You don't want to return home, do you?" Noli's voice gentled

"No, I don't." Charlotte's voice broke. "Uncle Nash... hurts me. Down there. He never actually compromised me, so I'm still *marriageable*. But the things he did are far worse than being strung up on a bar and beaten with a whip, shocked, and everything else they do here." Tears pricked her eyes and she shuddered.

He did *what*? The horrific thought made Noli cringe. Putting down her bundle of thyme, she wrapped her arms around Charlotte.

"I can't win," Charlotte bawled, tears streaming down her freckled face. "I don't want to go back—either as myself or as some perfect, marriageable drone. Even an asylum would be better than this. But no. He won't let me go." Her voice rose. "Why won't he let me go?"

Noli stroked Charlotte's hair, holding her tight. "Why did he send you here?"

"My aunt did," Charlotte hiccupped. "She discovered what he was doing and blamed it on me—hence the flirtatious label." For a moment she went quiet. "We... we could run away."

"Escape?" Noli's voice hushed.

"Why not?" Charlotte cocked her head. "I don't know

about you, but I want my life to mean something, and it won't here."

"Where would we go?" Noli's heart skipped a few beats.

"Anyplace but here," Charlotte replied.

"I suppose we could go to my house. Maybe even dress as boys and work for our passage to Los Angeles on an airship. Still, escape?" The word barely passed Noli's lips. "If they caught us … or even suspected we'd entertained the thought … "

"The water room and isolation, at the least. But think about it. Do you really want to be a mindless lady? To never fly a hoverboard or read a book again?" Charlotte looked at her through tear-filled eyes.

Actually, flying a hoverboard illegally was wrong. But to never read another book? Never learn more about plants? Never make her mother that steam-powered sewing machine?

Still, running away could have serious consequences even if they weren't caught. Noli took a deep breath. "Let me think about it. I'm not sure I want to end up in a detention center."

Disappointment crossed Charlotte's face. "Think fast. My chance won't last long."

A rustling sound made them look up. Noli's mouth grew dry with fear, and she hoped no one had overheard them.

The movement came not from the garden's entrance, but from the other side, beyond the fence. Someone had cleared the vegetation away. A face peered through, belonging to a handsome man with long black hair tied back in a tail and piercing dark eyes flecked with gold. For some reason, he reminded Noli of V. Though poised and polished, he still looked a bit like a ruffian—or at the very least, a rake.

"I'm sorry; I didn't mean to frighten you." His voice sounded silky and accented. "This is a lovely garden—a faery garden, I should think."

Noli and Charlotte moved closer together, seeking each other's safety. "It is, isn't it?" Noli said, unsure if she wanted him to go away or not.

"Do you believe in the fae, the fair folk?" He arched a dark eyebrow.

"No, I don't. They're just pretty stories for children." She picked flowers to go with the thyme, to cover her nervousness at a stranger talking to them so freely.

An odd smile played on his lips. "You think so?"

Charlotte went pale. "You won't tell, will you?"

"Tell what to whom?" His smile stretched. "Besides, who'd believe anyone from over here?"

After being at Findlay House for two months, Noli had seen the stream of men and occasionally women entering, seen the painted fancy-women strolling the gardens with men on their arms. She'd heard groups of people laughing eerily late at night, and the hoverboards flying in and out at all hours.

"It's a house of ill-repute, isn't it?" She knew she shouldn't speak to him; as soon as he'd appeared, she should have grabbed Charlotte by the arm and dragged her out of the garden. Just the fact that he approached them meant either he or his intentions were improper. If someone found out, they'd be punished. They were supposed to ignore the neighbors on all sides of them. To talk to a patron would be worse than speaking to one of the painted ladies.

Still, there was something about him.

"It's more than just that. I'm Kevighn, Kevighn Silver." Taking off his hat, the man bowed. His hypnotic eyes made Noli want to trust him, despite common sense saying she shouldn't.

"I'm sorry, sir, but we should go." She pulled Charlotte toward the gate. They took their flowers and herbs and fled the garden, hearts racing.

"I can't believe we spoke to him," Charlotte whispered, once they were outside of the walled garden. "But he was handsome."

"That he was." Something in him had also seemed dangerous.

As long as he didn't tell.

....

"Magnolia Braddock, come here," Miss Gregory demanded at supper.

Noli approached the head of the table, her heart growing heavier with each step. Had the man from next door told? Had someone overhead her and Charlotte's conversation about escape?

"What is this?" Miss Gregory's face became even more pinched as her thin lips pursed together in disapproval. Today she was wearing all black, which made her look spindly. She displayed the old copy of *Nicomachean Ethics* for the whole table to see.

"It's a book, Miss Gregory." Noli tried not to fidget or sound disrespectful. Margaret. It couldn't have been anyone but. She must have gone through her things and found it.

Miss Gregory's eyes narrowed. "Who is Steven Darrow?"

V's name was written inside the cover in his neat hand. "My neighbor. It's his book."

"Ah, the neighbor boy. Why on earth would he give you such a thing to read?" Miss Gregory's voice dripped with disbelief.

Noli tried to compose an acceptable answer. "He's from a scholarly family. He has no mother. Even his younger sister reads such things."

Miss Gregory squinted, as if that might help her process Noli's answer. "He encourages you to have Ideas and do naughty things?"

"Actually, he thought taking the auto out was a bad idea." Noli's voice softened as she braced for a blow for contradicting the headmistress.

Her eyebrows rose but her bony hand didn't fly out. "Yet he didn't stop you."

In Miss Gregory's opinion, as a man V should have stopped Noli from doing such things. Ugh. She couldn't escape this horrid, outdated way of thinking.

"I'm glad you're away from such influences. It must be because he has no mother, so he doesn't understand how women should be. But the real problem isn't him giving you the book, it's the book still being in your possession.

Not only did I take all your books, save one, but you heard the doctor say reading such things aren't good for your current state. How did you get this?"

Noli tried not to flinch at Miss Gregory's tone. "I'd never steal my books back, Miss Gregory." That would be suicide. Things taken from the girls were kept under lock and key. "It was in my valise. The one I left in the sitting room by accident when I arrived. When I remembered I'd left it, I took the book out and hid it before I brought you the contents."

"What? You insolent girl." She smacked Noli across the face with the book.

Tears of pain pricked Noli's eyes as her face stung. Parts of the table filled with whispers. Others simply looked on, appalled or smirking. Even the fancies paused their conversations.

"Since it wasn't my book, I wanted to make sure it didn't leave my possession," Noli whispered, fear balling in her belly.

"That's deceitful, Magnolia. Hiding a book and disobeying me like that." Miss Gregory's tongue clucked in disapproval. "You were starting to adjust. You'll be punished for this. Severely. Deceit and disobedience are not tolerated. Do you hear me?"

"Yes, Miss Gregory." Her heart skipped a beat at the idea of severe punishment.

She shoved the book in Noli's hands. "Tear out a page."

Noli blinked. Tear a page out of a book?

Miss Gregory slapped Noli's face so hard her teeth rattled. "Did you not hear me?"

"Yes, Miss Gregory." Biting her lip, Noli tore the first page out of the book, hand trembling. Hopefully V would understand.

"Throw it into the fire." Her beady eyes gleamed with pleasure.

"I will not." Noli bit her tongue as soon as the words left her lips, but it was too late.

Miss Gregory boxed her ears. "Insolent, disobedient girl. Do as you're told. Now."

Ears ringing, Noli threw the page into the fire, trying to ignore the titters and stares.

"The next one." Miss Gregory's voice cut through the tense silence of the dining room.

Her hesitation earned her another hard smack. One at a time, she tore the pages from V's book and watched them burn to ashes. Tears of defeat streamed down her face.

Then Miss Gregory dragged her off to the water room by her elbow. Charlotte shot her a sympathetic look. *It will be okay*, she mouthed. Margaret smirked.

In the water room, Miss Gregory used big leather straps to buckle Noli to a table. She elevated her feet, also strapped down, on a box, putting Noli at a slant, and tied her hands at her sides with brass manacles. She shoved Noli's head into a leather cradle so she couldn't turn it, then blindfolded her. Noli felt a cloth being placed over her mouth. Every time she fought or screamed, Miss Gregory smacked her. Fear lay like lead in her belly, making her bland supper threaten to come back up.

It sounded as if someone pulled a chain, and ice-cold water sluiced over her head. The shock of the water's frigid temperature made Noli scream, enabling water to enter her mouth and nose. It burned. As she sputtered and gasped for breath, more water came down continuously. She thrashed at her manacles and the wide leather straps, trying to free herself. Miss Gregory smacked her again.

The cloth became suffocatingly heavy with water. Terror seized her. Just as she thought she'd die, the cloth lifted, allowing her to breath. But only for three or four breaths.

Water choked her, drowned her. Each time she got to the point where she could take no more, Miss Gregory allowed her to breathe for a brief moment, then continued.

Noli's life flashed before her eyes as she gagged and choked on the water pouring through the cloth. Images of her father, her mother, Jeff, V …

Yes, she was going to die. All because she hid a book. Her mother would never know how much she loved her, how sorry she was. Tears rolled down her face as she waited for death.

The cloth rose again. Air. Sweet air. Noli gasped for breath. Heart speeding, she waited for Miss Gregory to put back the cloth. But she didn't.

"Never be disobedient again, Magnolia," Miss Gregory warned, every word making Noli tremble in terror. "I guarantee that you won't like the consequences."

Noli dragged herself to the washroom. She couldn't get

over the feeling of suffocating. Of drowning. Of imminent death. Even washing her face triggered memories. What kind of place made girls think they would die as *punishment?* It made the beatings seem civil.

If Mama knew, surely she wouldn't make her stay. They'd find some way to make everything right with the air patrol.

Someone entered the washroom and Noli froze. Charlotte didn't say anything. She wrapped her arms around Noli and held her tight.

Sobbing softly, Noli whispered one word in Charlotte's ear. "Yes."

NINE

The Wish

Escape plans moved slowly. The best way to flee would be from the faery garden; they could climb over the fence and into the yard of the joy-house, then make their way to the street from there. Noli didn't know how they'd get to Los Angeles without any money. Nevertheless, Charlotte's time was running out.

As she replaced flowers in the entryway, she heard shrieks from the visitor's parlor. Charlotte's shrieks.

"Please let me stay," Charlotte cried. "I'll cooperate, please, let me stay."

Noli's heart raced so fast she feared it might beat right out of her chest. She crept toward the parlor. From the doorway, she saw Charlotte throw herself at her uncle's feet and beg him not to take her away.

"I'm sorry, but obviously this place isn't suited to you."

The smarmy look on the gentleman's face reminded Noli of Dr. Martin.

"Please, Uncle Nash? Please let me stay. I beg you." Charlotte's plea, more sob than words, made Noli's heart wrench.

"No." He stood. "Now come along."

When he reached for Charlotte, she swatted at his hands and shrieked that she didn't want to leave. Noli watched in horror as Uncle Nash picked Charlotte up, threw her over his shoulder, and carried her toward the door as if she were a sack of flour, his top hat not even going askew in the process.

Bile rose in Noli's throat. He was taking Charlotte away for good, without even letting her say goodbye.

Pressing herself against the wall, Noli put a knuckle to her mouth as the screaming Charlotte was carried into the entryway. Neither Nash nor Miss Gregory noticed her. The usually unflappable Miss Gregory seemed distraught, wringing her hands and asking if he'd come into her office and talk.

"May I please say goodbye to Magnolia?" Charlotte cried, her arms flailing.

"I'll tell her for you." Miss Gregory frowned in a way that made deep creases on her forehead as Uncle Nash carried Charlotte out the front door.

Noli took off running, right past Miss Gregory, not caring about the ramifications. She wasn't going to let Charlotte leave without saying goodbye.

"Charlotte! Charlotte!" she cried as she sped down the front walk.

Uncle Nash didn't stop, but Charlotte raised her tear-stained face. Her eyes glimmered with life, with hope. "Magnolia!"

Miss Gregory rushed out onto the front porch in a flurry of long black skirts, the matron and Dr. Martin at her side.

As Noli reached for Charlotte's small, pale hand, a sense of failure consumed her. They'd waited too long to escape. Her friend, her lifeline to sanity in this dreadful school, was leaving for a place even worse than this. She'd never see her again. Their fingertips brushed.

"Don't leave, Charlotte, please." Tears streamed down Noli's face. Dr. Martin, who had run after them, restrained her, preventing her from grasping Charlotte's outstretched hand. "No, let me go." She thrashed at the doctor's grasp. His arms tightened around her, keeping her immobile.

"Is there a problem, Miss Gregory?" Uncle Nash finally stopped. He looked down his nose at the headmistress, his drawl more pronounced than Charlotte's.

"Magnolia and Charlotte are friends." Miss Gregory's lips pursed as she joined them on the front walk. "I thought it would be too much for Magnolia's delicate condition for her to see Charlotte leave. I didn't realize she'd already come inside."

Noli flinched as if a bony hand had smacked her across the face. Miss Gregory had planned on letting Charlotte leave without saying goodbye.

"I see. Well, good day to you." Uncle Nash continued toward the motorcab waiting outside the tall gates, nonplussed.

"Don't leave, Charlotte, please don't leave." Noli struggled against Dr. Martin, trying to break free before Charlotte became lost to her forever.

Still over her uncle's shoulder, Charlotte kicked and twisted. "Let me say goodbye to Magnolia. Please?"

"Please, let me say goodbye," Noli shrieked in return.

"Come now, Magnolia," Dr. Martin soothed. "Let's go to my office."

"No." She continued to scream for Charlotte as she watched Uncle Nash wrestle her only friend at Findlay into the waiting motorcab.

Even after the motorcab drove away in a cloud of steam and dust, Noli refused to move. Finally, the matron helped Dr. Martin drag her to his office. The matron held her down on the exam table.

"I'm going to give you something to calm you down so you may rest. Won't that be nice?" Dr. Martin swabbed down her arm and stabbed her with a long, sharp needle.

She didn't get to answer, because it took effect immediately. Sleep consumed her.

• • • • • • • •

Kevighn hadn't seen either girl in a few days. He'd watched them quietly, looking for an opening in which to act. It also gave him a legitimate reason to frequent the Red Pearl.

Still, time was of the essence. Never before had his people gotten this close to the time of the sacrifice without a girl. This uncertainty was what was causing the magic to weaken. Usually, he found a girl far in advance. It also gave the chosen girl time to enjoy her reward.

As he walked through the gates of the Red Pearl, a commotion from the school drew his attention. The girl with the red hair was screaming like a harpy as some man in an expensive suit carried her to a motorcab. Kevighn's heart sank; he'd wanted to take both girls. At least it was the other who contained more power.

The girl with the steel-colored eyes barreled down the path, calling for her friend. He watched in morbid fascination as the redhead was forced into the motorcab while they restrained the girl with the chestnut curls and carried her back into the house.

Could this work to his advantage? She'd just been stripped of her dear friend. Hmmm…

He needed to catch her alone in the garden. Maybe it was time to go over the fence.

●●●●●●●●

When she awoke, Noli found herself alone in a tiny room with rose-colored wallpaper, on a little bed with a pink quilt. Beside the bed, a small table proved the only other object in the room. No mirror, no magazines, no sewing. The barred window was too high to see out.

Isolation.

Brass manacles built into the bed secured her arms and legs. The reason why crashed down on her like frigid water. Charlotte. One of the two things holding her together at this place had been taken from her. She'd probably never see her again. Tears rolled down Noli's cheeks. With her arms tied, she couldn't even wipe them away.

After a while, Dr. Martin came in, untied her, and gave her supper and another injection. This one didn't work as fast, but she barely finished eating before falling asleep.

When she awoke, Dr. Martin came in and sat down on the little bed. "This place isn't suited to everyone, Magnolia. We couldn't give Charlotte what she needed, so her uncle brought her home. I don't agree, but it's his choice." For once his unblinking eyes didn't leer. He touched her, but only on the shoulder.

"But..." It came out like a sob.

His eyes met hers as if willing her to understand. "She kept you back from your own progress. If you work really hard, you might be able to progress by Christmas. Don't you think a Christmas letter would make your mother happy?"

As much as she ached to write Mama, to read her letters, Noli refused to believe that Charlotte had anything to do with her lack of progress. Rather, it had everything to do with Findlay House being the wrong place for her.

Actually, this was probably the wrong place for everyone.

Dr. Martin looked at her expectantly, so she nodded.

"You may rest here for as long as you need." His creepy

smile sent prickles down her spine. "I'll be back to check on you." He left, locking the door behind him.

....

Noli didn't know how long she spent in isolation. When she cried, she got more drugs. Finally, Dr. Martin released her. She bathed while everyone else went to evening activity. When she returned to her room, she found her botany book gone, along with her photographs.

Shaking, she sank down on her rickety cot. Gone. The botany book from her father. Her parents' wedding portrait. A photograph of her brother. She needed the memories to keep her sane, to remind her of happier times until she could get out of this dreadful place.

"Dr. Martin wants you to rest." Miss Gregory's voice startled her from the doorway. "No books or magazines of any kind—you are to lie down instead of doing schoolwork. You will help with the mending and in the kitchen instead of with gardening and washing. He feels being outside is much too stimulating in your delicate state."

Or did they fear she'd run away?

"Please, can't I garden?" Realizing she'd spoken, Noli slammed her mouth shut.

For once, Miss Gregory didn't hit her for speaking out of turn. "Not at this time. You should go to bed."

Noli put on her scratchy nightgown and crawled into her rickety cot. But sleep wouldn't come. They'd taken away everything that meant something to her, everything that made her herself. Without those things, her sanity would crumble in this place.

Perhaps that was the point.

She needed to go to the garden one last time, to say good-bye to it. They'd be watching her closely now, to make sure she didn't escape, which was probably why she wasn't allowed to garden. By the time they let her go outside again, she'd probably no longer have the will to escape. She'd be just another one of their mindless ladies.

The other girls hadn't returned from their evening activities. Noli crept down the back stairs on full alert. If caught, she'd say she sleepwalked. After all, she was barefoot and in her nightdress. Almost nothing remained for them to take from her.

For once, Fortuna actually smiled upon her; Noli managed to make it outside without being caught. Closing her eyes, she breathed in the warm summer air as twilight began to fall. She took off running, not stopping until she reached the sanctuary of the faery garden.

In the distance, the full moon was rising in the not-quite-dark sky. The air prickled with . . . something. Perhaps it would rain. But the sky remained clear, the breeze warm. She pushed open the door, palming the key instead of leaving it in the lock. She'd take the key back with her, something to trigger her memories when her brain turned to mush.

Inhaling the near-intoxicating scent of flowers, Noli spun round and round until she was dizzy, like she was once again a little girl. What would she do without this place?

The toadstools around the tree glistened and sparkled in the twilight; the sky was streaked with brilliant pinks and purples. The big tree itself seemed to glow. It was time she did something she'd wanted to try for months. Crossing over the ring of mushrooms, she walked to the tree. For a moment she simply savored the sensation of the bark under her fingertips. Then, hiking up her scratchy gray nightdress, she scaled the giant old oak, dropping the key in the process. Whoops. She'd pick it up on her way out.

Noli climbed until she found a sturdy branch to perch on. Gazing at the moon, she held her medallion. It was only a matter of time before they took it, too. They wouldn't stop until they had her soul—or her sanity. If she could do it all over, she would listen to V and never be sent here in the first place.

Gathering her knees to her chest, mindful of her balance, Noli wrapped her arms around them and laid her head on her arms.

"I . . ." Tears rolled down her face. "I wish I were any place but here."

TEN

Midsummer's Eve

Kevighn's ears perked as he lay on the brocade settee in a hazy room in the Red Pearl, with yet another nameless woman and some rather good opium. Something was calling to him; something so powerful it cut thought his marvelous—and costly—drug-induced haze.

Today was Midsummer—hence, he was trying to drug himself into oblivion. He didn't wish to join his people this night. It would cause his queen to summon him, and he had no progress to report. Since the redhead had been dragged away, he hadn't seen the chestnut-haired girl at all. When he'd tried to visit, posing as a "relative," he'd been rebuffed.

"What's wrong?" the soft woman beside him asked lazily. Oil lamps flickered through the miasma of opium smoke.

"Nothing." If he failed at his task; the high queen

would punish him. And if someone else was not able to rectify his failure, an entire world—one much older than the mortal realm—would perish.

Yet part of him no longer cared what happened to his people. He'd taken the position of huntsman ages ago, when he'd lost his reason to love, to fight, to protect. But now the position no longer offered the diversion it once promised. If he were to fade away, he'd much rather do so in the company of good drugs and pretty women. He held the pipe over the oil lamp to vaporize more of the drug, releasing it into the air, and deeply inhaling the intoxicating vapors.

The call persisted, buzzing annoyingly in the back of his mind until it cleared him of his drug-induced stupor. He sat up, anger fueling him. What treachery was this? His stomach tightened. It didn't feel like his queen, but a call from her could not be ignored.

He'd just check, from a distance. Lost in her euphoric state, his female companion wouldn't miss him. She would undoubtedly still be there upon his return. If not, he'd find another.

The influx of fresh air startled his senses as he emerged from the opium den, bringing him out of the remainder of his stupor. After he investigated this persistent call, he'd make it up to himself.

A summer breeze kissed his face as he headed straight toward the back corner of the garden where the wild portal lay. The call couldn't be coming from anywhere but the faery garden. The closer he drew, the stronger the call became. Yet he didn't sense any fae other than the usual tiny inhabitants. He felt tempted to turn around and head back.

Sobs reached his ears. Sobs of a mortal girl. A girl with quite a bit of the Spark.

He peered through the hole he'd made in the brush covering the fence, but he couldn't see anyone, only hear her cries. Without a thought, he scaled the fence and landed in the enchanting little garden that radiated wild power.

For a moment he didn't see her. He scanned the garden. Ah, she sat *in* the tree.

Tiny faeries surrounded him, pleased by his presence. They asked him to join in their Midsummer celebration. Placing a finger to his lips, he pointed to the tree. He crept around the perimeter of the garden until he could get a better glimpse of her.

Magnolia, the dark-haired one, fair as the blossom she was named for, sobbed into her knees as she perched high in the tree. Wood faeries sought to comfort her, but either she couldn't see them or ignored them.

The air sizzled with magic, amplified by the full moon and Midsummer energy. Yes, this neglected old portal was quite wild. Really, he should send someone to look at it. The earthquake must have made it unstable. Not that wild portals—ones not regularly maintained or anchored to a specific spot in the Otherworld—were ever truly safe and stable.

Kevighn felt elation course through him. The moment was perfect—if not to act, at least to extend the hand of friendship. Perhaps he could offer her the escape she'd never achieved.

Closing his eyes, he inhaled the raw power of the garden. Why it existed here, or what it had been once tied to, had been long lost. He crept closer to the tree, crossing the ring of mushrooms that served as a warning. Did she not know what it meant, or had she ignored it? The magic hadn't pushed her away. It must feel her Spark and want her close.

Her whisper pierced the silence of the garden. "I . . . I wish I were anyplace but here."

The air shimmered and spun like a vortex of light and life. Kevighn held on to the tree and prayed that she would as well.

Too perfect. Magnolia was about to get her wish.

Now, to manipulate the situation to his favor.

• • • • • • • •

Steven stood in his backyard, gazing longingly at the moon as twilight fell around him. The fence had long been fixed, both his yard and Noli's had been cleaned, and the battered remains of the Big Bad Pixymobile had been put back behind the shed and covered.

He missed her. Mrs. Braddock shared Noli's progress whenever he and James went over to make small repairs. She truly seemed to think Findlay was just another boarding school. But he couldn't shake the thought that Findlay *must* be more—after all, why *that* school? He easily read between the lines, the lies, of the school's letters, which only cemented his fears.

Lifting his face to the sky, he breathed deeply of the summer air, of the full moon and the radiating power of the summer solstice. If only he could join the melee happening tonight, even here in Los Angeles.

His father forbade it, so he could only look on with longing. All of his people here in the mortal realm felt something on nights like this. His particular magical gifts made it worse. Perhaps he should convince James to go hoverboarding in the hills with him, just to get away from the house. But it wasn't the same without Noli.

A hand clasped his shoulder. Not his father, who hid shamefully from the night's call, but someone who was many things to him—father, brother, uncle, tutor, advisor, friend.

"The full moon makes it stronger. I didn't realize you were so sensitive." Quinn gazed up at the moon as well.

"Why do we have to hide?" Bitterness dripped from Steven's voice. It was an old argument; they were lucky to have been allowed to take refuge among the mortals.

Still, he remembered. He longed.

Quinn shook his head. "One day you'll be a man. Then you may do as you like."

"I know." Steven planned on reclaiming his family's kingdom and honor. If only Noli could be part of it. But his love for her could never be. Bringing her into his world would be dangerous because of the sheer amount of Spark that she possessed. Many dark things liked such girls. Of course, there were also the obvious reasons, such as her being mortal.

"How's my sister?" Steven added. Elise had suffered

from a bought of hysterics because a clan of wood faeries she liked to visit had disappeared. He'd told her they'd migrated, though he knew they hadn't.

So did she.

"Asleep. Things are amiss with the magic. Can you feel the instability?" The moonlight made Quinn's silver hair gleam white, and his flint eyes look like steel, reminding Steven of Noli.

He nodded slowly. One good thing about his father's distance was that he hadn't noticed Steven coming into abilities beyond his family's usual magical gifts. His gaze focused on Noli's tree. Because he possessed an affinity for the earth, especially plants and trees—a family trait—he loved that tree as much as she did.

Perhaps that was another reason for his fondness for Noli. He was earth court—how could he not enjoy spending time with someone who liked plants and trees as much as he did?

The plants and trees liked her as well. So did the wood faeries. It had been difficult to keep her faery tree faery-free. But wood faeries drew other things, and he wanted to keep Noli and her beautiful Spark a secret.

Not that it mattered anymore. It was only a matter of time before they beat it out of her. If they hadn't already.

He toyed with his sigil, a twin of Noli's, thinking of her. To the untrained eye his family's crest might look like a sunburst of golden wire. The sunburst held the image of a tree, the roots and branches intertwined to form a never-ending circle. The green stone set in its trunk symbolized the tree's heart. Had they taken it from her?

Steven could imagine her looking longingly out the window, not understanding why the night called to her. On nights like this he'd find her in the tree house and they'd sit there, looking up at the sky, talking, or else sneak out on the hoverboards for a moonlit ride.

"You miss her." Quinn's voice remained neutral.

"I know, she's a bad influence and I shouldn't form attachments to mortals." Steven blew a lock of hair out of his face. If they knew about her Spark they'd use her, especially with the magic in flux. Something needed to be done soon or the effects might become irreversible.

Also, he didn't want anyone to know that he could sense the Spark in mortals. If the high queen's huntsman failed, she'd annex every one of their people who could see the Spark and send them to hunt. Personally, he'd rather die than trick a mortal girl into being the sacrifice.

"Truly, what you and Noli did is hardly comparable to the scrapes you and James used to get into." Quinn grinned at the memories.

The hairs on the back of Steven's neck stood up as the magic shifted. Fear knotted in his belly—*a potential sacrifice had been found.*

He could tell that the girl had not yet been bound, which would settle the magic. Of course, the Otherworld would not be truly saved until the sacrifice was actually completed; only when the girl's blood was shed would the magic's hunger be sated.

But a sacrifice had been fully identified, perhaps even taken to the Otherworld. He prayed to the Bright Lady that the huntsman hadn't found Noli.

Was using a girl's Spark to save an entire world better than letting the mortals beat it out of her? That was a question of ethics to ponder. It depended, he surmised, on whether or not the girl was *willing*. The biggest problem he had with the way the queen handled the sacrifice was that Kevighn Silver-Tongue *tricked* the girls.

If they were informed and willing, well, that posed another question altogether. Some argued that a mortal would never willingly give her life, not anymore. He'd beg to differ. Not that anyone cared to ask him.

But not Noli. Never Noli. For the millionth time, Steven wished things had played out differently.

"You felt that, too." Quinn's flint eyes grew searching, as if trying to see inside his head.

"I think I'll stay outside for a while," Steven replied. That wasn't an unusual statement. Because of his affinity for the earth, he always wanted to be outside.

Quinn nodded. "I'll check on James and your father."

As soon as Quinn returned to the house, Steven slipped through the board he'd kept loose in the new fence and scaled Noli's tree. He climbed as high as he could, avoiding the tree house. Getting comfortable, he sat with his back against a branch, feeling the tree's life, its energy.

The stone in his sigil reflected moonlight as he played with it. Maybe Kevighn wouldn't take her because she wore the mark of an earth court house. Even if it was a house in exile.

No. It wasn't her. Besides, plenty of other girls possessed the Spark.

The golden moon sat full and high. Raising his face to the sky, Steven drank in the night, listening to the hum of the city, the creatures of the night, and wishing that he weren't alone.

"Happy solstice, Noli."

• • • • • • • •

A strange sensation, one both hot and minty, filled Noli as she sat in the faery tree. Just as she thought she caught movement out of the corner of her eye, everything began to spin round and round like she was on the carousel at the pier back in Los Angeles. It made her feel odd, even odder than the time she'd gotten drunk on wine leftover from a party at V's house.

The air shimmered with colors—pinks, blues, and golds. Little lights danced around her and she gripped onto the branch with all her might, afraid she'd fall off.

Perhaps she was reacting to the drugs. Or going mad. Yes, that was it. The isolation and everything she'd endured had made her mad.

Holding tight, she sat back, enjoying the colors and sparkles.

Suddenly they stopped, jolting her back to reality. She

looked around—she was still perched in the tree, the same tree. Yet no longer was she in the faery garden at Findlay.

Yes, she'd most definitely gone mad. How could she not be in the garden?

This was *a* garden but not *the* garden; the plants were more wild, the colors more brilliant. Everything shimmered and sparkled as if dipped in diamond dust.

Tiny balls of light flew around her. One landed on her hand, tickling her palm. It seemed to be a glowing butterfly.

A glowing butterfly with the body of a person?

Noli shook her head, startling the little ball. They'd put poppy syrup in her food to keep her passive, and she must have fallen asleep in the tree. She needed to wake up and return to the house or she'd be in trouble.

"Wake up, Noli, wake up." She squeezed her eyes together. When she opened them, she still sat in the strange garden. The sky above held stars unlike the ones she'd gazed at so many times with V. This dusky-rose sky held no moon. No flying cars or hoverboards darkened it.

Noli pinched herself, hard. That didn't work. Neither did slapping herself. She jumped out of the tree. Pain shot through her foot. *Ow*. Dreams didn't hurt. Did they?

Little balls of light surrounded her as she sat on the ground, cupping her bare foot. They reminded her of illustrations of faeries from one of V's books.

That was silly. It was all a hallucination. Faeries weren't real. Science said so.

V said they were. But that was V. He always spouted nonsense about faery trees, faery flowers, faery rings …

She drew in a sharp breath as realization cascaded over her with the force of a punch in the stomach. All those things V had told her to watch for, things she'd discounted as poppycock, were present in the garden—a giant oak, the wildness, flowers that faeries liked, a ring of mushrooms. She sucked in a short breath.

A little ball of pink light landed on her hand. She studied it like she might a plant or an engine. Little eyes blinked at her, as if examining her right back. Blue eyes, attached to an all-too-humanlike face. Pointed ears peaked out of blond hair flowing down to her shoulders. Truly, the creature in her hand looked like a miniature person with translucent wings. Her pink dress resembled flower petals.

"Faeries are real?" Noli scrubbed her eyes with her free hand, then looked again. No, it was still there. Gently, she touched the hair of the creature with her finger. It flew off her hand as if startled. Then it flew closer, tugged on an escaped strand of Noli's hair, and flew a few feet away in a fit of giggles. A few other balls of light joined the pink one. A purple one flew up and perched on Noli's nose, making her go cross-eyed.

No this wasn't a hallucination. Everything she knew about science and the world was collapsing on her, making her gasp for breath. They were little people, real things with curiosity.

If faeries were real, what else existed?

The silence was eerie. Her heart thumped at the thought of things like ogres and trolls.

Right now, the bigger problem was how she'd get back

to Los Angeles. "Where am I?" she asked, hoping they were intelligent.

The little purple faery joined the others and they flew around her as if trying to say something, but she couldn't quite understand. Wherever she was, it was wild and beautiful. There was no Miss Gregory, no Dr. Martin.

But no Charlotte. Or V. Or Mama.

A crack of a branch made Noli's head whip around. Her body tensed as she tucked her medallion under her nightdress. "Who's there?"

"Hello, Magnolia." A figure emerged from the shadows. While there seemed to be no moon in this place, she could see him perfectly. There stood the man from next door. The one who'd spoken with her and Charlotte. The one who called himself Kevighn Silver.

ELEVEN

The Otherworld

Noli's heart raced as the strange, ethereal man approached her. The faeries swirled around her like a miniature battalion of protectors.

"Who are you? Where am I?" she demanded, still huddled on the ground.

"I won't harm you, Magnolia." The words dripped from his lips like liquid silver. His black hair hung loose, and his piercing eyes sparkled wildly in the moonless night. He was a beautiful man, like a Greek statue from a picture in one of V's books. Kevighn might be dressed as a gentleman, but tonight it seemed out of place, as if he wore a costume.

Yes, Kevighn Silver seemed far too untamed—ferocious even—to be a true gentleman. Yet he didn't seem to be a truly dangerous hooligan, like an air pirate.

"How...how do you know my name?" Something about the way he spoke her name made her uncomfortable, but not in the way Dr. Martin did.

"How did you come to be here?" Smiling in a way that made the hairs on the back of her neck stand on end, he gestured to the shimmery, magical garden they stood in.

"Where are we? Who *are* you?" she retorted.

"I'm Kevighn, as I told you before." He looked around. "I'm not precisely sure where you've brought us."

It took a moment for his words to register, and when they did, fear, confusion, and anger rumbled in the pit her belly.

"Me? *I* brought us here? How could I bring us here? And why would I bring *you*, Mr. Silver?" If she could bring someone, it would be Charlotte or V, not some man she didn't know.

"Your *wish*, Magnolia. You brought yourself here with your beautiful wish. I was simply caught in its magic. Didn't anyone ever tell you to not make a wish in a faery tree under a full moon on the night of the solstice?" He arched an eyebrow as if she'd ignored a basic rule.

"What are you talking about?" Perhaps she really was in some poppy syrup-induced dream. That was easier to believe than that her wish had brought her someplace...else.

"Words have power, especially on nights such as this. The magic heard your wish and brought you here." He flashed her a smile that did nothing to reassure her.

Noli crossed her arms over her chest. "There's no such thing as magic."

A dark eyebrow rose. "No?"

"No." Her voice soured to hide her fear. Standing, she brushed off her gray nightdress. "If you'll excuse me, I need to return before I'm missed." Turning on her bare feet, she walked toward the exit of the strange garden.

"Magnolia, wait," he called.

Ignoring him, Noli continued toward the familiar walls. When she reached the gate, she threw it open. Instead of being greeted by the familiar, orderly grounds of Findlay House, she saw only chaos.

Chaos. That best described the disordered wilds stretching as far as she could see. For a moment Noli simply stood there, one hand on the gate.

"This area isn't safe for you, Magnolia." Kevighn stood behind her.

This wasn't San Francisco. The thought chilled her to the bone. "Where am I?"

"You're in the Otherworld, Magnolia. A place very different from your own realm."

"Another world? Are you serious?" she scoffed. "That's even sillier than magic and wishes. Everyone knows there's no such thing." As she looked around, Noli knew in the pit of her belly that she could be nowhere *but* in some other realm. "Where exactly is this Otherworld? I have to get back to Los Angeles."

"What is in Los Angeles?"

Turning to face him, she blinked in surprise. "My home. I'm certainly not returning to that dreadful school."

Not even if they made her.

"Of course not." He smiled in a soothing way.

"But I don't know how to get to Los Angeles from here." She blinked, hoping she'd reappear someplace she knew, like her backyard. Little fairies settled on her shoulders in reassurance. She looked at Kevighn, who seemed to not be bothered by this situation. "Can I get to Los Angeles from here?"

"The Otherworld isn't on any of your maps, and you can't get home by steamer, train, or even airship. You can only get there by portals, like the one you brought us through," Kevighn said smoothly. "These portals connect our two worlds at many, many points. You can't get home from this place specifically, but, yes, you can get to many places from the Otherworld. Los Angeles included."

Noli felt relief flow through her and her tense muscles began to relax. "Will you please take me there now?"

Trusting this stranger was better than getting lost in *that*. She didn't want to think too hard about his rather convenient appearance. Instead, she'd concentrate on getting back to Los Angeles. To her mother. To V. Hopefully, they'd both be happy to see her.

He frowned and shook his head. "I'm very sorry, but I don't know how. But don't fret. You can come with me to my home and we'll figure it out from there."

He offered her his pale hand.

Noli eyed it. It was one thing for him to take her home;

it was another for him to take her to *his* home. She could take her chances and just try to find Los Angeles herself, but another glance at the chaos beyond the gate told her that the notion was utterly ridiculous.

Could she get back through the tree? Yet if she could do that, which also sounded ridiculous, it would most likely take her back to Findlay. Kevighn, at least, had the ability not only to take her away from this garden in the middle of nowhere, but to take her *home*.

She glanced at the tree, then back into the chaos. No, she wouldn't take her chances in the chaos. But to go to the house of a strange man?

"And then we'll go to Los Angeles?" Noli gave him a measured look.

"Come with me, and I promise that everything will be fine."

Noli cocked her head. Really, she didn't have much choice. "Promise?"

"Promise." He smiled and his face lit up like sunlight streaming in through stained glass in church. How could one not trust such a smile?

Noli took his outstretched hand.

....

"This is where you live?" Noli asked as they approached a log cabin set deep in a wood filled with the biggest oak trees she'd ever seen. They towered over her like giants.

"Whenever I can." Notes of wistfulness tinged his voice. "Often, I'm at the palace."

"Palace?" They walked down the dirt path. They'd used the faery tree, a "wild portal" as Kevighn called it, to connect to other portals, other places, in this strange world. The Otherworld. The sky held the same twilight as it did in the wild garden, but here it appeared duskier, more purple than pink. Unfamiliar stars winked at her, and two strange moons rose in the distance.

"Yes. I'm in the service of Tiana, High Queen of the Otherworld. If I'm not elsewhere, doing her work, I'm generally at the palace. And yes," he added, "we have a queen."

Noli squinted, as if doing so would bring this whole odd situation into focus. "I … I'm having trouble believing I brought you to another land, one you happen to be from … "

A land with tiny faeries. But this place had a queen, not a king. That could be progress.

Stopping in her tracks, she turned and studied him. It seemed to be quite the coincidence, him being nearby when she'd made her wish. "Why *were* you in San Francisco?"

"Business for the queen." He met her gaze and shrugged.

Noli's eyebrows rose. "In a joy-house?"

Kevighn continued down the path. Noli trotted to keep up, not wanting to be left behind. The cabin turned out to be larger than she'd expected, but not nearly as large as her home in Los Angeles. It was made of roughly hewn logs with windows and a chimney. It looked so … normal.

Putting his hand on the door, Kevighn whispered something that wasn't English. The door opened. By itself.

Noli drew in a sharp breath. "Magic."

"There's much magic here." He smiled. "What you call aether, we call magic."

"What?" She stopped in her tracks. Yet it made sense. The qualities aether supposedly possessed did sound, for lack of a better word, magical. Also, what had made her father disappear if not magic?

"We have many wondrous things," Kevighn continued. "Perhaps you'd allow me to show you a bit of my world before you depart?"

She shook her head. "I need to get home. Immediately."

Before Miss Gregory told her mother she'd run away.

"Very well." He ushered her inside. The door closed magically behind him.

The multiroom structure looked a bit like a woodsman's cabin from a story. A workbench occupied one corner. Another held a case of unusual weaponry that she itched to examine more closely. A large, comfortable armchair sat in front of the cold stone hearth, reminding her a bit of her father's chair—the one she wasn't supposed to sit it, but did. The rug in front of it certainly hadn't graced the back of any animal she'd ever seen. Hunting trophies of unfamiliar animal heads gazed at her with glass eyes.

It didn't look as if Kevighn entertained much. No flowers, pictures on the wall, or anything to indicate a feminine presence. "It is apparent you're unmarried, Mr. Silver."

"True." He nodded toward the far side of the room. "Let's go into the kitchen. I have two chairs at the table." He smiled; it didn't reach his eyes.

Beyond the masculine front room was an airy little kitchen with a wooden table and two wooden chairs. He gestured to one, and Noli sat. The tidy room was simple and utilitarian, made of wood and stone. The window over the sink looked into an unkempt garden.

"Tea?" He gestured to the shiny copper stove. A pile of wood sat next to it.

As anxious as Noli was to get home, tea did sound nice, wherever she was. What harm could come from a cup of tea? "Please."

She watched as Kevighn lit a fire in the potbellied stove, put the kettle on, and busied himself with setting the table. He went outside and returned with a basket of dark pink fruit the size of golf balls.

"I'm afraid I have no milk, but I do have honey." Kevighn smiled as he placed a honey pot on the table along with a bowl of fruit. Such a handsome smile.

As handsome as V's? Maybe. Goodness, she missed V. What would he say about this grand adventure? *Don't talk to strange faeries.*

Yet those tiny balls of light didn't seem like they'd cause any harm.

"Here you go." Kevighn placed a cup of golden, steaming

liquid in front of her. The delicate blue cups and saucers looked handmade.

Noli started to thank him when another one of V's old stories surfaced: *Never thank a faery.* Of course, the man in front of her was hardly a faery—he stood taller than V. Still, something within her warned her to be cautious. As Noli sipped her tea, she tried to recall everything else V had told her. All she could remember was not to dance in faery circles and something about salt.

"I do appreciate it." Taking the cup in her hands, she blew across the surface. It smelled minty and sweet. Tentatively, she sipped it. The intense, near-burning mint balanced perfectly with the sweetness, which reminded her of sucking the nectar out of fresh-picked flowers with V on lazy summer days.

Adding honey to his own cup, Kevighn took a drink. "You look tired. I know you're in a rush to return home, but it might take time to figure out the safest way to get there. There are few direct paths to anyplace here."

Noli set her teacup down in dismay. "How much time?"

"I don't know. After all, I must be discreet in my inquiries."

"Oh." Staring into her teacup, she mulled this over. "Am I not supposed to be here?"

His eyes met hers. Where before they'd been flecked with gold, now they looked completely yellow. "Not precisely."

"Oh." Another land. A magical land. Some in her

world might seek to exploit it. It was difficult not to readily accept the fact she was elsewhere, given what she'd seen so far. Still, it was odd being in some strange man's home in an unfamiliar land. "You'll hurry, Mr. Silver?"

"I'll try." He took a fruit from the bowl and bit into it. "Have one. I just picked them." He pushed the bowl toward her.

Her belly rumbled. "Maybe just one."

When she bit into the firm, fuzzy fruit, the light pink flesh dissolved in her mouth like spun sugar. Juice squirted down her face, making her laugh.

Kevighn tossed her a napkin. "They're perfectly ripe, aren't they?"

"They are." After finishing it, Noli put the pit in her saucer and took another. After she polished off her tea, she felt drowsy.

"Why don't you take a nap?" Kevighn took another piece of fruit from the bowl. "I'll see what I can discover, and you may sleep in my room."

As tired as she was, warning bells were going off in Noli's head. "Perhaps I could doze in your chair?"

"Your honor's safe with me, Magnolia. I would never try anything with an unwilling woman." Kevighn flashed her a genuine smile that made her want to trust him.

She yawned, eyes heavy. "Just a short nap."

He stood. "As you wish."

TWELVE

Kevighn's Cabin

Light streamed through the window as birdsong greeted her ears. Sheets caressed her skin. This wasn't her narrow cot at Findlay. Nor was she in her bed in Los Angeles. She hadn't even fallen asleep in the tree house.

The previous night's events crashed down on her. She was at Kevighn Silver's. The house of a stranger. It definitely hadn't been a dream. The good thing was, she no longer was at Findlay. The bad thing was, she wasn't home.

Feeling refreshed, Noli stretched and looked around. The room was simple and neat like the rest of the house— a bed, a chest, a chair, a wardrobe. A single decoration adorned the wall, a painting of a field of flowers.

The door opened and she pulled her covers up. Kevighn walked in, holding something. He'd changed into tan trousers, a deep yellow shirt that complemented his eyes, and a brown vest. It made him look ... normal, unthreatening.

"Did you figure out how to get to Los Angeles?" she demanded, feeling her cheeks warm at the blunt question. She could at least say something pleasant first.

Instead of being angry, he chuckled. "Not yet."

"Hurry, please?" Noli's cheeks burned again. "I could get in a lot of trouble for leaving, and I want to go home and explain before they tell my mother I ran away." Memories of Dr. Martin, Miss Gregory, and Margaret made her flinch.

He stood in front of the bed. "Are you *positive* you wish to return home?"

She crossed her arms over her chest. "Of course I am. Why wouldn't I be?"

"As you said yourself, leaving the school could get you in trouble. What if your mother doesn't understand?"

Noli erased that terrifying thought from her mind. After all, it was *Mama*. No mother would want her daughter to be abused and beaten—even in the name of propriety.

"She'll understand." If not, she'd go find Jeff. The address she sent letters to was only a postal box, but they might know where to find him.

"Do you have hoverboards?" Noli asked. Perhaps the laws were different here, and she liked hoverboarding an awful lot.

Kevighn shook his head. "No, but we have magic. I took the liberty of running you a bath and finding you something else to wear." He handed her the bundle. Noli dropped her blanket and he eyed her gown critically.

Again, she bit her tongue to keep from saying *thank you*. "I'd like that."

"Excellent." He smiled. This one reached all the way to his eyes. "It's the room across the hall with the open door. When you're finished, come to the kitchen. I have a surprise."

· · · · · · · ·

Kevighn sat at the kitchen table nursing a cup of something much stronger than tea. What had possessed him to bring Magnolia *here*, to his private home, his refuge?

Never had he brought any of the girls here—not even Annabelle. Certainly, the queen would be unhappy he hadn't brought Magnolia straight to the palace.

Magnolia reminded him of Creideamh. Silly, really, because the mortal girl didn't physically resemble his baby sister at all. And his thoughts toward Magnolia were hardly brotherly. They never were, toward the chosen girls. He usually took it upon himself to … personally ensure the girls had a satisfying stay in the Otherworld.

He'd also given Magnolia one of Creideamh's dresses. That, too, smacked of poor judgment, something he could ill afford right now. What would he do next? Unlock Creideamh's room and allow the mortal girl to stay there?

Of course not. Once he put the girl at ease, they'd go to the palace in the guise of seeking information. When she saw the palace, she'd be so amazed by its wonders she'd never want to leave. Just like the others.

Yet this girl was different—smarter, sharper, quicker than his usual quarry. On past hunts he'd occasionally run across girls like her, but passed them over for more malleable prey. He'd have to be careful. Right now the magic hadn't even begun to bind her—yet even that hadn't helped with Annabelle, in the end.

Annabelle. Sighing, Kevighn drained his cup and refilled it from the bottle on the table. Never before had any of the girls committed suicide to escape being the sacrifice. Annabelle hadn't even been the sharpest of his victims. Her actions had devastated his ego, his reputation.

Yes, he hardly needed something to go wrong again, especially with the magic already so unstable. It would destroy them all. For good.

So much rode on this girl. On him. Still, he wasn't ready to care about anyone again.

Why *had* he brought her here?

Footsteps drew him from his ruminations. He exhaled sharply, feeling as if he'd been punched in the gut. The dark blue of Creideamh's dress made Magnolia's steel eyes and creamy complexion glow. The gown hung a little long, but otherwise fit perfectly.

It also complemented her dark hair. Those headscarves she always wore hid its splendid curliness. He could easily imagine tangling his fingers in those glorious tresses.

The mere thought made his trousers tight. Actually, for a mortal, Magnolia was quite pretty. He was glad he was sitting. It wouldn't do to frighten her. Like with the others, he'd win her trust first, *then* seduce her.

"I'm glad the dress fit." He took another drink, suddenly unsure why he'd given her Creideamh's dress. But it wasn't as if he possessed a supply of gowns and feminine fripperies like they did at the palace. If he planned on keeping her here, he'd have to make due.

What would his little sister think of a mortal wearing her clothing?

Actually, Creideamh would have dressed Magnolia in her best dress, then fixed her hair. She had a soft spot for mortals.

The look Magnolia gave him wasn't grateful, but skeptical. "Who did it belong to?"

The question took him aback. Clever girl.

"My sister. Don't fret, she won't mind." He'd need to tread lightly.

Her inquisitive steel eyes flashed. "She painted the picture in your room."

Again, her words surprised him. "Indeed. Please, sit." He stood and gestured to the other chair. "Let me make tea." He busied himself with making tea, hoping she asked no more questions about his sister. "Everything was to your satisfaction?"

"It was quite nice." She smiled.

Interesting. By now most mortal girls would have thanked him many times. Magnolia had readily accepted the existence of the wood faeries and the Otherworld, but not blindly. Her eyes read like a book as she weighed and analyzed everything with her sharp mind.

As the water boiled, he set a bowl of fresh, ripe berries on the table. "I found these in the garden this morning and thought you'd like them for breakfast."

Her eyes sparkled. "Really? How … thoughtful."

"No berries at school?" He took a teacup down from the cupboard, not missing how her face darkened like a storm cloud. "It was a horrid place, wasn't it?" He spooned the herbs into a tiny metal net and put it in the cup, then poured in the boiling water. When he set it in front of her, he spied quiet tears running down her face.

Pulling the chair next to her, he placed a tentative hand on her shoulder. She seemed uncomfortable at first. "You're safe now. They can't hurt you here."

After a while she calmed down, growing used to his touch. She sat up and took a sip of her tea, her expression determined. "I'm never going back there."

Kevighn had heard that before. "Would you like to talk about it?"

"Not right now." She gazed out the kitchen window as she absently sipped her tea.

"Of course." He needed to lighten the mood, quickly. "See anything you like?"

"I like gardening nearly as much as tinkering." Magnolia smiled shyly, probably spying Creideamh's garden behind the cabin, which had long since gone to seed. The palace had splendid gardens beyond a mortal's imagination, but personally, he'd always preferred Creideamh's.

"After breakfast why don't you explore while I do some research?" he offered.

She beamed. "I'd like that."

Excellent. By supper she'd have forgotten all about going home.

THIRTEEN

Seeds and Seedlings

"Still working, Magnolia?" Kevighn walked into the garden holding a basket in his hand. A few days ago the garden had been naught but tangled wilds.

"Of course." Her voice came from someplace near the roses.

He'd noticed she had an extreme fondness for roses. She possessed a true knack for plants—and fixing things. Also, she unconsciously did little things to make the cabin feel like a real home again.

It would be too easy to get used to this.

He made his way toward her voice, taking in the progress she'd made. She'd weeded, replanted, pruned, and sheared. Once again, the window boxes held flowers; the kitchen garden was orderly, filled with fragrant herbs and vegetable seedlings. The roses and hedges sat in neat rows. In another week, you'd never know it had been abandoned.

No. Another week was out of the question.

Kevighn hadn't expected it to take this long. The magic should have chosen her by now, marking her, binding her irreversibly as the sacrifice. But the binding hadn't even started—perhaps because, unlike the other girls, she hadn't yet decided she belonged here. Once she acknowledged that, the magic would accept her.

Instead, Magnolia pestered him about returning to Los Angeles. If she didn't stop soon, he'd run out of diversions, not to mention that it grew irritating.

Schooling his face into a smile, he clutched the basket containing today's distraction. He'd found out how to take her home, but he wasn't going to. However, he couldn't tell her the truth, either. So every day he pretended to do research, then found something to distract her when he didn't return with the information she wanted.

Hopefully it wouldn't take much longer for her to decide she belonged here. When the magic bound her, her annoying questions would cease.

In the rose garden, he found her up to her elbows in dirt. She wore a brown skirt and blouse of Creideamh's, her hair tied back with a scarf. Dirt streaked her pretty face. Looking up from her task, she grinned, the smile lighting up her face like the moons lit up the night.

Kevighn grinned back, this smile genuine. He liked seeing her happy.

"Any luck?" Sheers in her hand, she looked at him with expectant eyes.

He suppressed a sigh, careful to not let his voice, expression, or posture show how tiring he found her questions. Distraction time. "Not yet. But I found this while researching."

Her beautiful, steel-colored eyes glimmered with excitement as he held out the basket. She folded back the cloth and drew in a sharp breath. "They're beautiful, Kevighn."

His name played hesitantly on her lips. He'd had difficulty getting her to use it.

"They're called star blooms. They bloom at night. I have pink, purple, and blue. They're rare." And taken from the palace greenhouse. Every visit to the palace, or to some place even remotely public to find things to delight Magnolia, held the risk of someone seeing him and reporting his whereabouts to the queen.

If he took much longer, the queen would look for him. She'd want an update, to meet the girl. Sweet Magnolia wasn't quite ready to meet the ruler of the Otherworld.

Certainly, he wasn't ready for them to meet.

He liked having the mortal girl about—a dangerous notion. This situation necessitated caution. It would be too easy to become attached her.

Already Kevighn found himself going beyond mere diversion, seeking out things that would truly amaze and delight her. She possessed an extra bit of charisma that made her difficult to resist—hence, his taking of rare seedlings from the royal greenhouse without permission.

For some reason, it was blooms, not dresses, and herbs, not jewels, that pleased this girl. Nevertheless, herbs and flowers were easier to obtain without drawing attention. He also knew a little bit about plants because of his sister.

"Where do you wish to plant these?" he asked.

"Oh, I know." Putting the basket in the crook of her arm, she stood, absently wiping the dirt from her hands onto her apron. "I found an amazing place today." Her eyes glimmered with excitement.

Magnolia took off, going deeper into the garden. He followed, curious to see what she'd found. When they crossed the barrier from Creideamh's garden into the surrounding woods, he knew exactly where they were headed.

Uneasiness crept through him. He hadn't told Magnolia *not* to go into the woods. With the enchantments on this place, she couldn't leave the grounds unless he wished it, anyway.

Despite this, anger consumed him as they entered the little grove. Creideamh's dominion, where her secret sanctuary, her tree house, lay.

"I don't want you to come here. You have no right to be here," he snapped, reaching out to yank her away from this sacred place.

"Ow." Magnolia stumbled as he dragged her away. She fell to the ground, coming free of his firm grip.

Kevighn was so focused on getting this mere mortal away from his sister's refuge that it took him a moment to realize the girl no longer remained in his clutches. His focus shattered the moment he turned around. Magnolia sat crumpled in the dirt, cradling her arm. Tears streamed down her dirty face. Curls escaped from the brown scarf.

Regret stabbed him. What had he done?

Little balls of colored light surrounded the girl like a rainbow guard, comforting her. The tiny beings loved her so much.

When he approached her, several swarmed him, trying to fend him off. "Please, let me pass," he told them. "I ... I didn't mean to."

He put out a hand, but either Magnolia didn't see it through her tears or she ignored it.

Not that he blamed her.

One little faery zoomed at him with a tiny stick. He caught the bugger with one hand. "None of that," he chided. "It was an accident." It had been a long time since he'd let anger get the best of him. It had been even longer since someone affected him so. He crouched in front of her. "Shhh. It's all right." Taking a handkerchief from his pocket, he wiped away her tears. She flinched, sending arrows of pain through his heart.

For a moment, he flashed back to another time he'd crouched in the woods, comforting a sobbing girl as balls of light kept guard.

"Shhh ... It's all right, Creideamh. I won't let them hurt you." He wiped the tears off his younger sister's face as she sat in the dirt, sobbing, clutching her leg, broken and lifeless, shaking in pain. "I will protect you always."

In the end, he couldn't. For that he'd never forgive himself.

"This place was hers."

Magnolia's voice brought him back. He wasn't comforting Creideamh, but a slip of a mortal.

"Yes, it belonged to my sister. Even I thought twice about coming here uninvited." His voice went soft as he tried to push away the painful memories.

"You made her the tree house? It's such a wondrous tree house." Magnolia cocked her head, holding out her uninjured hand for a little purple wood faery to perch on.

"I did, when she was small." Kevighn would do anything to make Creideamh smile. The day he'd led her from the big house, blindfolded, to this grove of oaks still burned bright in his memory. He'd made the little house in the faery tree just for her. How proud of himself he'd been. How happy she was.

"I have a tree house in Los Angeles. My father helped V and me build it." She brightened.

"You have a father?" A mother she'd mentioned, but no father. She hadn't mentioned V either. A brother? She'd been cautious, revealing little personal information.

Her face screwed up and she looked as if she'd cry— but to give her credit, she didn't.

Had. Magnolia *had* a father. Ah, it made sense now.

"He disappeared right after the San Fran quake." Her voice quiet, she focused on the little faery in her hand.

"How?" Los Angeles and San Francisco weren't close, in mortal terms.

"They needed engineers to rebuild the city after the earthquake. His whole team disappeared. They say the aether did it."

Uh oh. Kevighn tried not to make a startled noise. Indirectly, he was responsible for her father's disappearance since the quake itself was, in a way, his fault. Her father and his team weren't the only mortals to disappear, either.

"He'll come back." Magnolia squared her shoulders, so sure. "It's only been six years."

How hopeful she seemed. Her father had probably fallen into one of the many small rifts between here and the mortal realm that were caused by the earthquake. It took his people a while to fix them all.

She looked around. "Do you think he ended up here?"

Her cleverness never ceased to amaze him.

"Perhaps. Some may have fallen through into this world after the earthquake."

"Could we look for him while we try to find Los Angeles?" Her eyes lit up.

"You can't get your hopes up. The Otherworld is vast," Kevighn said. There was a good chance her father would never be found. Most likely, he and his team had perished ages ago. Many, many creatures dwelled here—not all as nice as he was. Some thought mortals who fell through the rifts between realms made tasty snacks.

"Let's get up," he added. Standing, he offered Magnolia his hand. The faery fluttered away, eyeing him warily, as he took Magnolia's hand. Her small cry of pain reminded him that she'd hurt herself in the fall. The basket of star blooms lay on the ground.

"You're injured. Should we go back to the cabin?" He picked up the basket of seedlings.

"I didn't know I couldn't visit the grove. I'm sorry," she sniffed. "I like trees."

Of course she did, considering how much Spark she possessed. She'd be just as attracted to Creideamh's grove as she was to the faery tree behind the school.

"It's not your fault. I never told you. Actually, I didn't think it would affect me so." How badly would this mistake set back his plan? "You … you may still show me, if you like, and if that's where you wish to plant the blooms, you may. Or we could just return to the cabin."

"I may plant the flowers there?" It was as if the sun had emerged from the clouds. "I don't want to intrude on your sister's special place."

"Creideamh wouldn't mind as long as you treat it well. Besides, trees like that need love and attention." He smiled at her, leading her back toward the grove. Often, he'd joked that Creideamh spent as much time there as in the cabin. The familiar hideaway came into view.

"Magnolia, does your tree house look like this?" He'd formed this one with magic, making the house out of the very branches of the old faery tree itself.

"Not at all. Mine is made of boards and sheets of metal, of cogs and gears and bits of things." She smiled at the memory. "Your sister died, didn't she?"

"What?" He heard anger and hurt flow through his voice, and she flinched. "I'm sorry." He softened his tone, putting a hand on her narrow shoulder. "Thinking of her still hurts." Magnolia's very presence dredged up painful memories. "Yes, she died. But I don't wish to speak of it."

That, too, was his fault. His sister had relied on him to protect her. He'd failed.

"I understand." Magnolia took his hand and squeezed it.

Her simple gesture of comfort caused numerous thoughts to invade Kevighn's mind, none of them innocent or brotherly. But her face held no coy look, no brazen glimmer lurked in her eyes—only innocence and joy.

For some reason, injuring her—even by accident or carelessness—seemed like a far greater sin than what would happen at the time of the sacrifice. It was a privilege to be the sacrifice. She needed to be cosseted and honored, not yelled at and hurt.

"Let's go back to the cabin and I'll tend to your arm." He touched her face in a bold and intimate gesture, getting a little closer to her. "I'm sorry. Will you ever forgive me?"

She gave him a look of mock consideration. "I suppose." A smile played at the corners of her lips. "But only if you bring me more seedlings tomorrow."

"Anything for you." His voice might drip with mock-gallantry, but those words rang much truer than was comfortable.

After all, she was only a mortal. The mortal whose death would save them all.

• • • • • • • •

"Here, let me take a look." Kevighn sat down at the kitchen table and reached for her arm. On the walk back to the cabin, all traces of that fearsome man in the grove, who'd hurt her and yelled at her, had disappeared.

Noli suspected he still lurked within.

"Do we have to go to the hospital?" she asked. Did they have hospitals here? So far she hadn't seen anything but Kevighn's cabin and the grounds surrounding it. Her left arm hurt; it felt bruised and twisted, but not broken. Once, she *had* broken her arm, when she'd fallen off the roof of the shed. Still, this hurt.

"You'll be fine." With feather-light fingertips, Kevighn took her arm in one hand, the other hand running down the length of her arm but not quite touching it.

Her arm grew warm. Such a comforting feeling, like hot apple cider with cinnamon sticks on a chilly evening.

"What are you doing?" Noli eyed him, unsure if she wanted to hear the answer.

"Magic." He looked at her arm, not her. "I'm not jesting. You know magic exists here. It makes sense that we have it, too."

True. After all, in V's stories, fairyland *was* magic. Not that Kevighn actually ever called this place fairyland.

"You formed the tree house by magic?" It would be difficult to build a house that looked as if it were made of the tree itself. Perhaps you could grow one.

"I did." He continued to move one hand up and down her arm. "With extreme difficulty, since I'm not of an earth affinity like my sister."

"Earth affinity?"

"Her magic lay in gifts from the earth; she had a gift

for gardening and would rather be outside than anywhere else—or else painting what lay outside." He smiled sadly.

"What's your talent?" The pain in her arm was fading.

He flashed her an impish grin, eyes dancing. "I have many, many talents."

She laughed, and her belly tightened. "If you have magic, what does that make you?"

Kevighn's eyes met hers. "What do you think?"

She sucked in a breath. "Fae, right?"

"Yes, we are called fae by some." He continued to work in silence.

Kevighn was a faery. With magic.

No wonder his world didn't need hoverboards. As V might say, one's man technology was another man's magic.

"I know you don't wish to speak of it, but could you at least tell me your sister's name?" Noli asked.

"What?" He looked startled and nearly dropped her arm. "Ow."

"I'm sorry." He held it gently, but that tender gesture seemed like much, much more—though Noli was certain it wasn't. Him being this close, touching her this way felt … well, *nice* only began to describe the feelings this beautiful man occasionally caused within her. Obviously, from his clothes, stories, and even his speech, he could be a bit of a rake. No good ever came from falling for someone like that.

For a faery like that.

Still, he tempted her. She felt a bit like she'd been left alone in a room with a tray of sweets.

"Her name was Creideamh." Kevighn pronounced it *Kray-jif.* "My younger sister. I raised her mostly on my own. Her magic could do marvelous things."

"Oh, what happened to your parents?" Immediately, Noli felt a kinship with him.

His expression grew stormy. "I don't wish to speak of it."

"It's all right." She patted him on the shoulder, hoping he didn't think she was being too familiar.

"I appreciate your understanding." He touched her injured arm with both hands and it grew hot, like a steam boiler. Then he let go. "It might be stiff for a few days, but it's better. Just sprained, not broken." A look of regret crossed his face. "I'm sorry."

"I know." She could see it in his eyes. Given the circumstances, she would forgive him this time.

"I have a surprise for you." He stood up.

"Another? Are you trying to spoil me?" Every day there was some new treat or surprise.

"More like a bribe, so you won't be angry with me. I haven't lost control of my temper in a long time." For a moment he looked as if he were elsewhere.

She followed him down the hall of his little cabin to a locked room. Taking a key from his pocket, he unlocked it and opened the door. "It would probably be more proper for you to stay in a room of your own."

"Creideamh's room?" Noli looked around the small, comfortable bedroom. It wasn't dusty or stale. The wood furniture was covered with intricate carvings of flowers, and pink curtains resembling flower petals topped the four-poster bed. The rugs on the wood floor resembled grass and the window looked out into the garden. A small painting of the tree house hung on one wall.

Shoving his hands into his trouser pockets, Kevighn gave the room a wistful look. "After my parents died, we moved from the big house into my cabin. We liked it better here."

Noli wondered what it would have been like if Jeff had raised her. "Was it difficult?"

"Very. Make yourself at home. You may use anything here." He gestured to the room.

Overwhelmed, she bit her lip to cut off a reflexive *thank you*. They'd never discussed it, but she'd noticed that he never said it either.

"I appreciate your kindness. But truly, I'll only be here another day or two. Right?" She fidgeted. She'd been here longer than anticipated. Soon, if not already, the school would tell Mama she was gone. Had they looked for her? Would her mother? V would help search. Oh, how she missed V. She also missed her mother and Jeff.

And Charlotte? How was she faring with her uncle? The thought made her shiver.

"I'm doing the best I can." Kevighn's voice pulled her out of her thoughts.

"What exactly do you do when you go out researching?" After all, he'd never said.

"Find people who can answer my questions truthfully, without alerting everyone. It's tedious work, so you might as well be comfortable. Are you hungry?"

Her belly rumbled and she grinned. "I am."

He jerked his head toward the door. "Let's go have something to eat."

After supper they sat in the front room, which now had two chairs. Usually he'd work on things and she'd read one of the books he found for her. She and Kevighn never really conversed like she and V did. They didn't have much in common, it seemed.

That didn't stop her from stealing glances at him as he worked in the firelight. Tonight, he was sitting at his workbench, making arrows for one of the many giant bows hanging on the wall. He called it fletching, and it involved lots of colorful feathers.

"Will you tell me how you ended up at that school?" he asked, breaking the easy silence.

Noli didn't feel like talking about Findlay, but Kevighn *had* told her about his sister. She marked the page of her book with her finger. "I wasn't exactly a model daughter." Guilt shot through her at the admission. "V and I took the flying auto out for a drive. It was unregistered, I didn't have a permit, and V didn't have a flying auto addendum, and, well ... " She looked away. "We crashed."

His dark eyebrows rose. "Whose flying auto?"

"Mine. Well, it belonged to my father. He won it in a card game and always said he'd fix it up. He never got the chance, so I did."

Kevighn stopped fletching, mid-gear. "You *fixed up* a flying auto? What kind?"

"A Hestin-Dervish Pixy. I called her the Big Bad Pixymobile." Noli's face crumpled at the memories. Two years she'd spent fixing her. "I think she's destined for the scrap heap now." She wished she could repair the auto so she could go get Charlotte.

Kevighn laughed a deep belly laugh that shook his entire body. "You fixed up a Pixy? There's a good reason why they discontinued the Pixy model. Those are death-traps. You must be an ace mechanic to be able to fix one by yourself."

"They're not deathtraps," she retorted. "Wait, you know about flying autos?"

"A little. Personally, I like airships better. I'm a better pilot than hoverboarder."

"Really? My brother is an aeronaut." Who would have thought someone like Kevighn would know about flying autos and airships?

"What kind of airship does he fly? I once had a spar-row-class schooner."

Noli put a hand to her mouth to stifle a laugh. "Spar-row-class? That's a girl's airship."

Kevighn's yellow eyes flashed. "No it's not."

She rolled her eyes. "The only good thing about the sparrow is that you can jerry-rig the engines to make them out-fly everything else in the sky."

"How?" Kevighn put down his arrow and gave her his full attention.

"Well, there's this gas called nitrous..."

....

Yawning, Noli pulled on a soft, ruffled nightdress and crawled under the quilt. The bed certainly was pretty with its petal-like curtains. It seemed a bit like sleeping in a flower, which may have been the point. Like she did every night, Noli held her medallion, closed her eyes, and thought of home, of V, as she drifted off to sleep.

She sat in her tree house, looking up at the full moon, unable to sleep. Often, she'd have trouble sleeping when the moon sat high and heavy. V would find her and they'd sit and gaze at the stars and talk—usually about books.

"Are you up there, Noli?" A soft and familiar voice cut through the night, clear, crisp, and breezy, just as she preferred.

"No, I'm in my room fast asleep like a proper young lady instead of up in a tree like a hoyden." She grinned. Seconds later, a familiar face greeted her. As always, his hair was a mess. He wasn't in his nightclothes.

"Noli. Oh, Noli, I missed you so much." He flew at her, wrapping her in an embrace far more comfortable than was proper.

"Why?" She laughed. "We saw each other after school, like always. Oh, did your father punish you again?" V often needed to talk to her after he'd been punished.

His forehead furrowed in confusion. "Where have you been?"

She pressed a hand to his cheek. "Are you feeling well? After school, you helped me re-hang the shutters, then drilled me on my Latin while I did the wash."

"Please, where have you been? Are you still at the school...or are you...elsewhere?" His voice held so much yearning she wanted to cry.

"Why would I be at school, silly? It's evening. I don't understand." A strange feeling formed deep in her belly.

"Don't fret." He reached out and tucked a wayward curl behind her ear. "You still have the necklace I gave you?"

"You gave me a necklace?" Her hand went to her chest. A lump lay under her nightdress. "You did. How could I have forgotten?" Pulling it out, she examined it. "It's so pretty. Why did you give me a necklace?"

He sat close to her, and for some reason it no longer seemed brotherly. Suddenly, neither did her feelings for him. It seemed...

Oh. Was this what Mama meant when she said they were too old to be best friends?

"Please wear it always, Noli. Promise me you'll never take it off." His fingertips traced the necklace chain and when they made contact with her bare skin, little shocks of...something...reverberated through her.

"I will. What is it? Is it a love token?" Noli writhed. "I'm sorry, that's such a silly—"

V's lips pressed to hers, sweet and light, like feathers dipped in honey. When she tried to pull back, his arms wrapped around her, bringing them so close together she could feel his beating heart. Could he feel hers as it raced?

When he pulled back, his spectacled eyes looked at her, concerned. His finger traced her cheekbone. "Are you all right?"

"I'm fine." Not really. Her belly was aflutter and deep

places, secret places, seemed to have awoken. "Why did you kiss me?"

"To see what it was like." A boyish grin played on V's lips. For some reason he looked even more handsome than usual. It must be the moonlight.

"Why?" Her heart raced and her skin blazed. If he touched her again something would happen—but she wasn't sure what.

"Because." V tapped her on the nose, making her laugh.

"Did you like what you found?" Oh, that sounded so idiotic.

His green eyes danced with excitement and desire. "I did. Did you?"

Before she could answer, his lips pressed to hers again. This time, she kissed him back.

FOURTEEN

Progress and Lack Thereof

"Why are we doing this again?" James complained, as they painted the front of the Braddock residence. The July weather stifled the city like a sticky blanket. He wiped the sweat off his brow with his sleeve. "I can't believe Noli never made some gadget to make this faster."

Painting a house was proving harder than the brothers had expected.

"Because we promised Noli we'd look after her mother. Remember?" Steven shot his younger brother a look. Actually, *he'd* promised Noli. "She really wanted to paint the house." Slowly, they'd been working their way through her list.

"You miss her." James dipped his brush into the blue paint.

"And?" Steven missed her more than he'd admit—especially to his father. Oddly enough, their father approved of them doing chores for Mrs. Braddock. Since school was out for summer, it kept them occupied.

"I miss her too, and I'm not even sweet on her like you," James teased. "After all, I'm here helping you and not off hoverboarding."

Steven dropped his brush, sending splatters of blue paint all over the front porch. "I'm not sweet on her. After all, she's..."

Picking up the brush, he sighed. She was a mortal with the Spark. Being with her would mean endangering her; bringing her to his world could make people aware of her gifts. Of course, she might be in danger right now. He wasn't sure.

Weeks ago, on Midsummer, he'd sensed the magic shift. But the magic hadn't shifted again, which always happened at the binding—the acceptance—of the sacrifice. Not only was that odd, since according to Quinn it usually happened quickly, but it meant that the magic continued to deteriorate.

He should be relieved that Mrs. Braddock kept receiving progress reports. Yet the arrival of each one convinced him more and more that Kevighn Silver in fact had Noli. There were also his dreams—which served him right for trying to dream-search for her without actually knowing how to do it correctly. One night, he swore she was in pain.

"I won't tell," James prompted, stretching on his tiptoes.

"I ... " If he said it out loud, it would make it real. Their father didn't think mortal girls suitable for serious relationships—especially for royals. Even exiled ones forced to live in the mortal realm.

"When you take back our kingdom, will you marry her?" James' seriousness held a wide-eyed innocence.

With a sigh, Steven cleaned up the spilled paint. "It'll be a long time before I'm ready, and it's not that easy— don't you ever listen to Quinn?"

Mortals were playthings. Usually. Even ones with the Spark. Their gifts added entertainment and beauty to the Otherworld, but they were still just diversions. It was complicated. Then again, everything in the Otherworld was complicated. Their exile included.

"But you want to, right?" James made a face. "You're such a romantic. You won't catch me being all mushy, wooing some girl and the like."

Steven tried to hide his smile at his brother's distaste. "It's better for Noli if she finds someone ... else."

Someone mortal. If she had a chance to grow up at all. Still, he worried.

"My, what a lovely color." Mrs. Braddock came up the stairs of the porch looking tired and worn, a basket of sewing on her arm.

"Good afternoon, Mrs. Braddock. Quitting time already?" he asked. These past months had taken their toll on Noli's mother, not that she'd ever admit it. He could see it in the way her shoulders hunched and in the dark circles under her eyes.

"It's Saturday." She held up a letter. "I got another report on Noli. Would you like to take a break and hear it? I'll make tea."

"I'd like that." It was too hot for tea, but Steven felt he needed to stay connected to Noli, even if only through the inane letters the school called "progress reports." Part of him felt relieved that Mrs. Braddock took everything at face value. Part of him wondered how anyone could be so stupid. But Mrs. Braddock was a fine lady, reared to only see the pleasant.

"Sure." Putting the brush down, James shoved his hands into the pockets of his brown trousers and shuffled inside. Being a younger son, James didn't bear the brunt of their family's exile, and their father's wrath and melancholies, like Steven did. James wasn't as innocent or sheltered as Elise, but she was a girl. It was their job to shelter her, protect her, take care of her when their father got too wrapped up in business or depression to give her attention.

Also, Elise didn't remember much of their former life. Memories of their home, the palace, even their mother were only kept alive by the stories James, Steven, and occasionally Quinn told her when their father wasn't around.

And their father had no wish to return to their old life. No… "wish" wasn't the right word. It was more like "will." As much as he wanted his kingdom back, he no longer possessed the heart to do what needed to be done.

But Steven would. He'd decided that as soon as he became of age, he'd first go to the high queen and see if he could negotiate for the return of his family's kingdom and honor. If he couldn't accomplish his task with reason, he'd do it the easy way—kill his uncle and take it back by force, though he'd much rather fight with logic than with swords.

He and James sat in the dusty parlor and allowed Mrs. Braddock to feed them weak tea and stale cookies. While they did what they could to make repairs on the house and keep the outside tidy, the inside was another matter. Despite the dust, the parlor wasn't too bad, but Steven had peeked and seen the disarray that had befallen the rest of the house. Noli may have been a bit rebellious at times, but she did most of the household chores—usually at the expense of her schoolwork.

"Is Noli permitted to write letters yet, Mrs. Braddock?" He was growing desperate for actual news from her to put his mind at ease.

James caught his eye and mouthed the word *mushy*. Steven narrowed his eyes at him.

Mrs. Braddock shook her head sadly. "Not yet. By Christmas, perhaps."

"Christmas?" Five months. "What does this letter say?"

She read the innocuous letter out loud. Noli excelled in her lessons, she loved the gardens, she needed extra work in deportment.

"It sounds so much like the last one," he replied. Identical, actually.

"Does it?" Mrs. Braddock sighed tiredly, rubbing her eyes.

"Are you sure Noli is well?" The feeling that she wasn't rode him like a savage beast, making him restless, cranky.

Even his father had noticed. Unfortunately, he hadn't managed to confirm Noli's whereabouts through dream searching.

Mrs. Braddock held up the letter. "She seems fine. She has friends. The letters mention Charlotte and Claire often. Certainly Miss Gregory would alert me if something were amiss."

Would she? How would such an establishment react to a girl *disappearing*? Surely, that would reflect poorly on their reputation.

But would they *lie*? Search for her on their own, hoping to return her to the school before anyone became the wiser? Perhaps they'd bide their time until they found a suitable excuse like an accident or winter sickness.

"I miss her so much." Mrs. Braddock sniffed.

"Why don't you bring her home?" Steven asked.

She looked at one of the many photographs of young Noli on the parlor wall. "It'll be best for her future to stay there, then go to Boston. I know you miss her, but ... "

It might be best for her future—their future, since unless Mr. Braddock miraculously returned, their best chance for survival was for Noli to either marry well or get a job. He knew her mother would rather remain at her shop twenty-four hours a day than allow Noli to work.

What of Noli and her dreams? He knew she still clung to her dream of going to university and becoming a botanist.

But even if she came home tomorrow, how badly had that place damaged her?

"We're going to work more on the house, Mrs. Braddock. The tea was lovely." He smiled at her.

"It looks beautiful. Thank you for doing this." She smiled, which lit up her weary face. Her smile reminded him again of Noli.

They returned outside to paint, James grumbling about the heat. Again, Steven fervently hoped Noli wasn't captive in the Otherworld with Kevighn. If she was, he had to save her before the magic bound her. Yet what of his people? Certainly, he couldn't condemn them—his family—to death to save one mortal life. He pondered this ethical dilemma, trying to shake the feeling that Miss Gregory's letters lied.

· · · · · · · ·

Once again, Noli was working in Creideamh's garden behind Kevighn's cabin. Right now, digging in the dirt kept her sane. She'd lost track of how long she'd been here. Miss Gregory had probably notified Mama of her disappearance by now.

Oh, how Mama must worry. Noli hated to think how her disappearance must be hurting her mother.

So far, she hadn't seen anything of this strange world other than the cabin, the garden, and Creideamh's grove. Kevighn always went out to research alone. Whenever she asked about Los Angeles, he distracted her. She knew it was a ruse, yet it was difficult not to be distracted by the likes of him. They often spoke of airships, flying autos, and even zeppelins. His knowledge of mortal mechanics astounded her. He even knew a little about plants.

Noli felt a pang of homesickness shoot through her, slicing all the way to her soul. She needed go home so her mother wouldn't think both her children had abandoned her.

What if, like in one of V's tales, years passed in the mortal realm while only days passed in Faerie?

The trowel fell from her hand at the thought. No matter what, she *had* to get back to Los Angeles. As much as she enjoyed this place, and Kevighn's company, she'd insist that if he couldn't help her get home, he take her to someone who could.

"How was your day?" Kevighn walked toward her. He was wearing his green Inverness coat, one of his bows strapped to his back; it was quite a different look than the black coat she always saw him in back in San Francisco. He reminded her of a huntsman from a fairy tale. All he needed was a hat with a feather in it.

"Good, and yours?" Noli's original wariness of Kevighn had faded. It was as if she'd known him for years; she even called him by his first name. She hadn't seen his temper since that time in the grove. Not that Kevighn was a pushover, or softhearted like V.

V. She'd always been secretly attracted to him, and lately she'd had dreams about him that made her blush in the morning. She found herself looking forward to sleep, hoping these dreams would come.

Her and V? She chuckled to herself. That was as ludicrous as her and Kevighn. It would only happen in her dreams.

"What is so funny?" Kevighn shot her an amused look.

"I was thinking of my friend V." What was he doing in her absence? When she returned to Los Angeles, perhaps he could help check up on Charlotte. If they couldn't fix the Pixymobile, maybe she and V could earn airship fare to Georgia.

"Oh, he's your friend? For some reason I thought he was your brother." Kevighn's brow furrowed, and Noli detected the slightest hint of disapproval in his voice.

Jealousy? Her belly jumped a little.

"My brother is Jeff. He's the aeronaut. V—Steven—is my best friend. He lives next door." She finished planting her seedlings and stood, brushing the dirt off her hands with the apron she wore over her dress.

"Come inside. I brought you a surprise." Kevighn smiled. His smile wasn't boyish like V's. It was alluring, tricky.

He always brought such lovely surprises. But she needed to stand firm. "What did you discover today? I'd like to go home soon."

"Come inside and I'll tell you." He held out a hand.

"No. Are you distracting me on purpose?" If she went inside she'd forget, or allow him to distract her as usual. If it wasn't a trinket, it was a story. Not only had he owned an airship, but he'd once stolen a zeppelin.

"What?" Hurt flashed in Kevighn's eyes. "I simply find things I think you'd enjoy—especially when I don't have any information for you."

His shoulders hunched and he looked so ... wounded. Noli berated herself; she shouldn't say such things after he'd been so kind to her.

"Oh ... I'm sorry. I'm just frustrated. I really need to return home. I've been here for ages." Of course he wouldn't *keep* her here. He had no reason to.

"I know how much you want to go home." His voice softened. "But you haven't been gone that long. I did make a little progress today."

"Good. I'd like to return home tomorrow." She added a little nod for emphasis. She wasn't even sure why she'd stayed so long and not stormed off to look for home on her own. Normally she wasn't this patient.

Kevighn's face fell. "I haven't made *that* much progress."

"Oh." All the hope that had built up inside her deflated.

"Soon." Smiling, he tried to take her hand. "Wouldn't you like to see your surprise?"

Noli felt all the frustration, fear, and turmoil inside her—regarding this place, her mother, V, and even Kevighn himself—explode like a steam engine with no release valve.

"'No, I wouldn't!" she yelped. She crossed her arms over her chest. "I'm not going anywhere until you tell me when I'm going home. Now."

His eyes flashed. "Be reasonable. I must make discreet inquiries. It takes time, and I do have to say your impatience is tiresome. Now, be a good girl and come inside so I may give you your surprise."

Something about his tone, the words he chose, grated like sandpaper. "No."

"What do you mean, *no*?" Puzzlement, not anger, lurked in Kevighn's voice, as if he was unused to being told no. Actually, someone like him probably was.

"I don't want a surprise. I don't want to hear about more leads that don't work out. Most of all, I don't want to be a *good girl*. All I want is to go home. *Now*." All her pent-up frustration flowed through her voice.

"Stop this," he snapped. "You don't understand. Everything is complicated."

"Why can't we just go?" she retorted. "I'm so sick and tired of being told that it's complicated, dangerous, that you must be discreet. I haven't seen any danger. For all I know, you're keeping me here on purpose." Her pitch rose as anger stoked the flames of fury. "Did you even *have* a sister, or is it all a pretty lie? How many lies have you told me, Kevighn Silver?" Turning on her heels, she ran, and didn't stop until safe inside Creideamh's tree house.

FIF+EEN

Truth and Lies

Curled in the corner of the tree house, Noli clutched the medallion from V, feeling the coolness of the stone in the center of the wire design against her palm. The little faeries danced around her, trying to soothe her. They brought her small things: feathers, acorns, leaves.

The tree house was cozy, with a chair and small table. It seemed perfect for someone with an earth affinity. According to Kevighn, the four main kingdoms in the Otherworld each aligned with an element, the fae in each court possessing gifts in that sphere. He still hadn't told her what kingdom his cabin sat in, or the element in which his own talents lay.

Several faeries approached her, carrying a large pink star bloom that they offered to her. Taking it, Noli inhaled its sweet fragrance. She'd planted these flowers all around the base of the faery tree, filling the grove with heavenly perfume.

"I appreciate the kind thought." She couldn't understand the tiny beings, but they seemed to understand her.

Darkness fell, the mauve sky darkening and the two moons rising in the distance. Noli wasn't sure if she should stay until Kevighn came for her or just return to the cabin. Somehow, she needed to make him understand that she must return to Los Angeles immediately.

She decided to make him come to her. Yes. Returning would be acquiescing. Her stomach rumbled and she foraged for the berries she'd picked earlier and left in a bowl. Sighing heavily, she ate them, absently sharing bites with the little faeries.

Full dark fell upon the grove. Since she had no candle, the only illumination came from the faeries, who cast soft-colored shadows on the wood walls, and from the light of the moons through the window. The rustling of branches in the breeze startled her, as did the call of some unfamiliar animal. Perhaps she should go back.

Crossing to the widow, she peered into the stark purple darkness, where the thick branches now hid the moons. Out here in the wilds, no gas lamps illuminated the night. She'd become lost the moment she left the grove.

The air chilled and her stomach rumbled again. She hadn't thought to bring a blanket here.

"Noli, Noli!" Kevighn's voice rang through the night.

Much to her chagrin, his voice caused a little tingling

feeling deep inside her and her anger faded. But she couldn't allow him to charm her.

"Noli, please tell me you're up here?" He stood at the bottom of the tree, a lantern with blue fire in one hand, a worried expression on his face.

He'd come to her. That meant she'd won, right? Hopefully he'd take her home tomorrow. She'd tolerate no more tales.

Several little faeries swarmed Kevighn. One pulled on his dark hair.

"Let me pass, please? I only wish to speak with her. Please, Noli, call them off!" he shouted.

"Let him up," she told the faeries.

A moment later, Kevighn appeared, setting the lantern and a basket she hadn't noticed on the table.

"What do you want?" Noli made her voice tart, but she hoped the basket held something to eat. No—she needed to keep her mind on the task at hand.

Brazenly, the tiny faeries poked at the basket, one going so far as to lift the cover, grinning at Kevighn daringly. Leaning over too far in curiosity, the faery disappeared under the cloth. When he surfaced, he triumphantly held a berry and presented it to Noli with a mock bow.

"You may keep it if you'd like." She laughed. With another bow, he went to devour his prize, but other faeries tried to take it away from him. "None of that, I'm sure there's more," Noli admonished. Without looking at Kevighn, she took the basket and set it in her lap, warding off swarming faeries as she made sure everyone got a berry.

"They like you." Taking the basket from her, Kevighn set things out on the table. "They liked my sister as well."

"Why would they like me? I'm not one of you." She watched the good-natured warfare among the faeries, as some finished their berries faster than others.

Kevighn set some fancy sweets on the table. "They're wood faeries, and this is their faery tree. Creideamh took care of their tree and of them. They loved her for it. Being wood faeries, they're naturally drawn to those with an affinity for the earth. They now see you as tree-keeper. Even if they didn't, they'd still love you. Your kind draws them, just as faery trees draw you."

"Mortals draw them?" Noli tried not to eye the feast on the table—stew, rolls, fruit, sweets...

"Special mortals." Kevighn spooned some stew into a bowl and set it on the table before her. "You're special. *That* is why I keep you here, to protect you. They may not have understood you in your world, but here, those such as yourself are valued by most. Some, however, might seek to use you for their own devices. I wish to keep you safe."

"You value hoydens?" Noli asked skeptically. She wasn't special. Special girls were pretty.

"We call it the Spark. It's that extra something some mortals have. Often it manifests in the arts. Many of the great artists in your world—painters, dancers, musicians, poets, writers, and sculptors—possess it." He made himself a bowl.

The delicious aroma of stew made Noli's mouth water,

but she didn't reach for it. "I'm not gifted in any of those things. Passable in some, but not gifted."

Kevighn took a bite. "It manifests in other ways— philosophers, scientists, bakers, your great designers and builders. You may think of it as genius or being talented, but we named it the Spark because it's as if you have an extra-bright light inside you. I see it in your ability to fix things and your affinity for plants."

"My talent is gardening?" She laughed. "Painting might make me more marriageable."

"My sister's element was earth," he teased, his eyes sparkling. "Don't mock it. Yes, I really did have a sister named Creideamh who loved to garden and paint and hid in this very tree house when scared or angry, though she came here often at other times, too."

Noli looked away. "I shouldn't have said that. But I don't regret the other things."

"I know you're frustrated … "

Scrunching her nose, she thought about what he'd just told her. "Does sewing count?"

"What?" He handed her the bowl in front of her. "Eat."

She took the bowl but didn't take a bite. Yet. "Sewing. Does it count as a gift?"

Kevighn pondered that for a moment. "I should think the Spark could manifest in sewing."

"My mother sews amazing dresses. Could she have the Spark? Maybe I inherited it from her." Noli took a bite of stew, savoring the complexity of the textures and flavors.

The whole idea of the Spark, of certain mortals possessing special talents, sounded plausible.

"I suppose. Her dresses are lovely?" Scraping the last of the stew out of the bowl, Kevighn mopped up the remainder with a roll.

"Better than anyone else." Even better than the dresses Kevighn had brought her, both his sister's and from wherever else he got things. Where *did* he get things? They may not have the same advanced technology she was used to, but they probably had shops in the Otherworld…

"I'm frustrated." She brought the conversation back on track between hungry bites. "Los Angeles is my home. I miss my mother. Most importantly, after Papa disappeared, my brother left to make his way in the world. I can't disappear too. It would devastate my mother."

Kevighn nodded thoughtfully, finishing his roll. "Then why did she send you to that dreadful place? Crashing a flying auto isn't that bad."

Noli looked away. "Because I'm a disobedient, willful hoyden."

"Who told you that? Your mother?"

"Of course not." Putting the empty bowl on the table, she reached for one of the green fruits whose sweet pink flesh reminded her of a cross between figs and plums.

"But she sent you there."

She bristled. "Mama had no choice. I told you that. Unfortunately, women still don't have the choices men do."

"Well, you are none of those things. I told you, they

don't understand you." Kevighn touched her face, forcing her to look at him.

"And you do?" Noli felt her belly flutter at his touch.

"Yes."

Their faces hovered so close she could imagine him kissing her. But the face she pictured in her mind's eye wasn't Kevighn's. It was V's.

She shook her head, trying to shake the strange feelings away.

Kevighn misunderstood her gesture, pulling her close. "You're safe here."

The crack of Miss Henderson's whip reverberated through Noli's memory, making her flinch.

"What did they do to you?" He toyed with her hair like V often did.

"They … they beat us. Starved us. Gave us terrible punishments and treatments." For a moment she struggled to breathe, recalling the water room.

"They did what?" He pulled her closer to him.

She closed her eyes to ward off the memories. "That's how they fixed us, trying to turn us into the vapid, insipid piles of mush that pass for society ladies."

Kevighn shook his head. "I never did like society ladies."

Noli's eyes flew open. "Instead, you consort with fancy women and steal zeppelins?"

"Perhaps." Kevighn chuckled, twirling a lock of her hair around his finger. "I can't believe they hurt you. It seems like they sought to beat the Spark right out of you."

"Did we all have the Spark?" So the girls at Findlay

weren't hysterical, willful, or moody? Just Sparky? Geniuses in ways others might not understand or appreciate?

"I didn't see many of you, but your redheaded friend had it."

Charlotte. The forgotten piece of fruit in Noli's hand fell to the floor with a soft thud. How badly had her uncle hurt her? "I miss Charlotte."

"I know you desire to return home. Who could blame a girl for wanting to be with her mother—especially if she didn't willingly send you to such a place?" Kevighn's voice soothed her. "We may not have the technological delights you are used to, but there's so much in my world that I want to show you. I promise no one will ever beat you here. You'll be treasured beyond your wildest dreams."

"I just want to go home. Since it seems that you cannot, or will not, help me, you must take me to someone who can."

There. She'd said it.

Kevighn sighed. Something about his expression, his posture, seemed apprehensive. "Selfishly, I wish to keep you to myself. But there is indeed someone who has the knowledge you seek. I'm unsure if she'll help; she can be … difficult. I'd rather not have to ask for her help, but I could take you to her if you desire."

"I'd like that very much."

Finally, progress. By supper tomorrow, she'd be home.

SIXTEEN

Wanting

Steven hovered in the doorway of the library, too afraid to go inside but unwilling to leave. Quinn might have the answers he needed. He only *looked* young; once, he had been a noted scholar.

Quinn sat curled in a leather armchair by the unlit hearth. Finally, he looked up from his tome. "Are you going to stand there all evening?"

"Perhaps."

"Sit." Leaning forward, Quinn put down the old book. "What's been bothering you?"

Entering the library, Steven slumped into a chair facing his tutor. He loved this place, so cozy and full of books. "What makes you think something's bothering me?"

Quinn raised a pale eyebrow. "Because I know you."

"Good help is so hard to find." Steven rolled his eyes in an exaggerated gesture.

The silver-haired man chuckled; Quinn knew he was hardly "the help." "Hmm, let me see. You spend all your time either brooding in your room, brooding outside, or at Mrs. Braddock's working while you brood. I've also caught you reading some very odd spell books."

"There are no off-limits books in this house," Steven snapped. He'd been looking for things beyond the usual, things that might raise eyebrows if he asked. Like how to dream-search.

"True." Quinn rubbed his chin. "Does it have to do with Noli?"

"How did you…" Steven shook his head. "I know, you know me."

"Yes. And I've observed that you're coming into some rather remarkable abilities. You're also extraordinarily worried about the state of the magic. I'm aware that you fear the queen's huntsman has Noli." Quinn met his gaze. "I also know how you feel about her. Don't worry; your father hasn't noticed any of these things."

Steven sucked in a breath. "You know what she is? I didn't realize you could do that."

"Not the way you do. I don't have that gift, Bright Lady bless." Quinn frowned, tapping his lip with his finger. "If Queen Tiana discovers what you can do, she'll call for your help. She's already sending out others, since Kevighn's gone missing with whomever he found on Midsummer."

Missing?

"She'd like it if I became one of her men," Steven muttered, not hiding his bitterness.

"You know she would."

A request from the high queen was a command. She'd find great pleasure in forcing him to do her bidding—mostly because it would infuriate his father.

Steven crossed his arms over his chest. The queen was the reason they were in exile. She was the reason his father became a mess, a king without a kingdom. Most of all, she'd taken away their mother.

"I won't do it," he announced.

"She could make you; after all, she *is* the high queen. Our queen." Quinn's tone remained emotionless.

"She won't." Steven knew she'd try, though if it came down to it, she wouldn't. But the price would be painful; she'd ensure it.

"Why *are* you lurking in doorways instead of moping in a tree or something?" Quinn shot him a pointed look.

Steven fiddled with his sigil. "Noli has my sigil. Could I use this one to find her?"

"Yes. In theory, she could also find you—or anyone in your family wearing a corresponding one." Quinn held his gaze. "That is why they are rare and protected."

And enchanted. Steven had a feeling that Quinn had given him his own sigil, so his father wouldn't ask why he needed a replacement.

"Um." He fidgeted in his seat. "Could you show me how? Please?"

"Of course. It's relatively easy. You hold it, speak the

word of power associated with it, and think of her. It'll act as a compass of sorts. But it doesn't work well in this realm," Quinn warned. "Too much interference."

Steven wasn't going to track her in the mortal realm anyway. "Can I ..." He bit his lip, looking away. "Can I *feel* her through this sigil, since I gave her mine? I think I have. Last night she seemed so sad ... and once, not long after Midsummer, I felt pain in my arm, and a deep sense of shock and hurt that wasn't mine."

That night, he'd attempted to dream-search for the first time. He'd felt other things, too, especially after his various failed attempts. They might be tied together. And last night the magic had seemed to shift ever so slightly, but to what end he didn't know.

"Bright Lady bless." Quinn sat ramrod straight. "You *felt* her?"

Steven tried not to squirm in his chair. "So I am feeling her through the sigil? Am I not supposed to?"

"*You're* not supposed to." Quinn's eyes narrowed.

Oops. It wasn't impossible, then. Good. "Oh. Why?"

Quinn rubbed his temples, for a moment looking *tired*. "What possessed you to give her your sigil in the first place?"

"She's afraid of San Francisco; I told her it was an amulet to protect her from aether." He cast a glance toward the window; her house was dark. "She shines so brightly with the Spark. I know what lurks in San Francisco, post-earthquake. I wanted to protect her. Stupid, I know. After all, if Kevighn does have her, it didn't protect her from the likes of him."

"You've marked her as yours." Quinn swore softly.

"I put her under my protection. Is that wrong?" Steven wished he could become invisible. He couldn't do anything right.

"Not wrong. But your father won't like it one bit. Truly, you should ask before doing something of that sort." Quinn's voice grew stern.

"Everything angers Father now. I hadn't meant to, it was … impulsive." Steven braced for a lecture on impulsiveness. A good leader wasn't impulsive.

"I know." Quinn's ageless face held no disapproval. "Just like I know that making her your own was an accident. It's different from bringing someone under your protection."

Steven cocked his head. "How?"

"Bringing someone under your protection can simply be undone, revoked with a few words, unless there's a sworn oath involved." A grave look filled Quinn's eyes. "To undo what you did, you must take the sigil back from her and smash the stone."

Steven winced, not only at the thought of oath-breaking, which was punishable by duel, but at the idea of smashing the stone in Noli's sigil. "Really? I suppose Father will make me. Will it hurt her the way it would hurt us?"

"I don't know. As for your father … " Quinn's shoulders rose and fell as he sighed. "It depends on a great many things, including Noli's own intentions and desires."

"And whether or not Kevighn has her," Steven muttered.

"Steven, your father won't permit you to burst into the Otherworld without proof." Quinn's expression hardened. "Neither will I. I suppose that is why you seek to track her? At least go to the school first and see if she's there."

"Of course." That was one reason why he was sitting in this chair.

"I presume you want my help in you getting to San Francisco?" Amusement tinged Quinn's voice.

"I'll owe you. I promise on my honor." Steven held up a hand. He needed Quinn to help him—not only get there, but to deal with his father.

"Your father is leaving for business in three days. If you're going to catch an airship to San Francisco, you should wait until then. But," Quinn cautioned, "you need *proof* that Kevighn has Noli before you charge into the Otherworld. We're a house in exile, remember. We're not supposed to be in the Otherworld to begin with."

Unless it was to beg for mercy from the high queen.

"Also, remember what's truly at stake," Quinn warned. "If she is the chosen girl, you'll need to replace her with another. No one—not me, not your father, and certainly not the queen—would allow a whole people to die for one mortal."

"Of course, Quinn." Steven's mind sped. Three days. In three days he'd know for certain. This feeling plaguing him would cease. "So, can I feel things because I'm tied to her through the sigil?" He didn't wish to break the bond. If those dreams held true, she felt the same way about him. If the

Otherworld knew of her, he no longer needed to deny his feelings, as long as he protected her fiercely so that no one could abuse her Spark.

"Yes. It's complex; something we'll speak of soon."

"Of course." Three days. "Oh, I need help in dream-searching."

Quinn put his head in his hands as if he had a headache. "You've tried searching for her? What happens? Anything?"

"Um…" Steven could feel his cheeks warm. "If I'm actually successful, and not just falling asleep and merely dreaming of her, I think she's taking control of my searches, manipulating them to her whims."

"Prince Stiofán, please don't tell me you're having dream… relations with a mortal." Quinn looked as if he wanted to poke himself in the eye with the fireplace poker. His use of Steven's real name and title was never a good thing. Steven's cheeks burned.

"We only kiss," he stammered. "I always wake up before we do anything improper." Sometimes he wished he wouldn't.

"That's it." Quinn stood, clearly flustered. "You, me, my office, now. Your father thinks you're too young to learn certain things. Clearly, you're not."

That wasn't what Steven had expected. His heart quickened. "You'll tell Father?"

"Not tonight." Quinn's eyebrow rose. "Unless there are other things you've left out?"

Squinting, Steven thought for a moment. "I think I got them all."

Quinn shook his head. "Come along."

"Of course." Standing, he followed Quinn out of the library.

••••••••

Noli curled up in the bed in Creideamh's room. She was quite comfortable in this little room, more so than when she'd slept in Kevighn's bedroom—not that he'd ever tried anything, sleeping out on his chair instead.

How would she react if he *had* tried something? Hoyden or not, Noli understood the dangers of engaging in any sort of … relations … while unmarried.

Something about Kevighn utterly terrified her, and also drew her. He'd had such amazing adventures. Yet as soon as she thought of V, she forgot all about Kevighn. Every cell in her body recognized V as the better choice.

She'd never told V about her attraction to him; she didn't want to ruin their friendship. And since his father didn't like her, he'd probably never allow them to be together.

Would she dream of V again? Sometimes it seemed as if V was reaching out to her, seeking her. No, it was just her imagination. V might be a fussy old bodger who believed in faeries, but he was hardly some knight errant who'd barge in on a white horse with a sword to save the day.

Her fingers reached under her white nightdress, looking

171

for the comfortable shape of the medallion. Holding it, she thought of V and drifted off to sleep.

"Oh good, you're here. I was hoping you'd be here." She sat in her tree house next to V.

I'm glad you're here, too. But we need to talk." V caressed her cheek.

She didn't want to talk. "Why?"

"Where are you?"

"Here with you, of course." She grinned. *"Mama's asleep. No one will know."* Already parts of her grew warm with the anticipation of his touch.

"Noli, what are you speaking off?" V's expression grew shocked.

She turned away, her cheeks burning with embarrassment. "You didn't meet me here to kiss me again?" Taking a deep breath, she met his gaze straight on. *"I hope I don't sound like a dollymop, but I enjoy kissing you."*

He put a hand on hers. "You do?"

"I do." She couldn't help but smile.

"Why?" He pulled her into his lap, holding her tightly, stroking her hair. She luxuriated in the warmth of his body, the rhythm of his hands playing with her curls.

"Because..." She couldn't form the words. *V kissing her didn't mean he loved her—or that he would pursue her against his father's wishes.*

His hands moved down her neck and over her shoulders, sending shivers down her spine. Warm breath tickled her ear as his lips brushed it.

"Because you care for me as I do for you," he whispered.

Without waiting for her answer, his lips captured hers. Like always, his soft kiss tasted sweet, like the nectar sucked from a flower mixed with morning dew. One hand delivered just enough pressure to the back of her head, making her feel safe and secure. The other slowly ran up and down her back, the thin fabric of her nightgown the only barrier between him and her bare skin. Her arms wrapped around him, one hand tangling in his unkempt blond hair.

Oh, she was such a dollymop. But here she could, and would, do things she'd never do otherwise. She deepened their kiss.

His leg brushed her in a place that made her insides tighten with pleasure. She tried to shift positions to capture the sensation…

He wouldn't let her. She tried again. Frustration took over. She broke off the kiss so she could speak. "Please, V?"

"Not tonight, Noli. Not here." Green eyes brimmed with regret. "I'll stay with you if you wish, but only kisses." His hands continued touching her neck, her shoulders, her arms. They lingered in her hair, on the small of her back. "I want to, truly. And I will. Simply tell me where you are and I'll come for you. No one's angry with you, I promise."

She tried to press herself into him, to satisfy that feeling inside. Then Noli found herself flipped over so that her back was pressed to his chest—not nearly as satisfying.

"Please answer me." His lips trailed kisses down her neck.

"I'm here with you, in our tree house." She twisted to capture his lips with hers, wanting more. "And I'm kissing you like a dollymop."

"You're no dollymop. But you are missing. Are you in the Otherworld? Are you with Kevighn? Has he hurt you?" V's tone grew urgent. Something in his words rang familiar.

"I don't want to talk. Just hold me, kiss me." Love me, she thought.

Sitting up, he pulled her into his lap again, but this time he didn't cuddle her; his arms held her like iron bars. "After we talk, please?"

"I... " Fright consumed Noli as she tried to sort everything out. If she weren't here, where was she? What did he want to speak to her about? Surely it wasn't as important as kissing.

Her belly turned to lead. It could only be one thing. There was another girl, a proper one, with manners, breeding, and money. One who didn't dream of unladylike things such as going to the university or saving her family through hard work instead of marriage.

"What's her name?" Noli's voice broke.

He frowned. "What are you talking about?"

She fought against his grasp, her surety of another, a proper lady from a good family with money, growing with each second. "Let go of me, Steven Darrow." She smacked him across his face, not allowing him to answer. "How dare you toy with me? I thought you cared for me."

Jerking herself away, she threw herself down the ladder, running for the safety of her home, not bothering to hold back the tears.

"Noli, wait. I don't understand... I do care for you, much more than you know, come back, please. Where are you?"

She continued to run.

Noli woke with a start, tears streaming down her face and a fire deep within her she didn't know how to quench. Hugging her pillow, pressing her body into it as if it were a lover, she cried until she fell into a deep and dreamless sleep.

SEVEN+EEN

Preparations and Realizations

Steven turned his sword over in his hands. If he went into the Otherworld, he'd need it, but he could hardly board an airship or walk the streets of San Francisco with the weapon strapped to his back. Uttering a word of power, he watched as the sword shrank, becoming a pen. He tucked it into his shirt pocket, grinning at his own clever joke.

"Nice trick." James leaned against the doorway, a satchel dangling from his hand. "Ready?"

"For what?" Steven slung his own satchel over his shoulder.

James rolled his eyes. "To go to San Francisco to save your sweetheart. I've got the airship fare right here."

"You're not going." Steven eyed his younger brother.

"At least you didn't deny it. I'm surprised Father hasn't caught on."

"I've tried to be discreet." It had been three days of pure agony, both because he needed to wait for his father to leave town, and because he hadn't been dreaming of Noli. In the last dream, she'd fled in tears and he still wasn't sure why. Girls were so confusing.

"Oh, come on. You're so sweet on her it's not even funny." James made another face. "I'm not watching your reunion." He flopped onto Steven's bed. "Quinn's been covering for you, too."

"True." Steven grinned. "You're still not going."

"You're not actually leaving me here with Quinn and Elise while you go adventuring, are you?" James expression became a cross between hurt and disbelief. "I could help."

"I'm only going to the school to see if Noli is there." In theory.

"And that's why you're bringing your sword?" James arched an eyebrow. "Let me go. Look, Quinn's the one who gave me the fare, which means he wants me to go."

Steven looked out the window at Quinn playing a game with Elise in the backyard. "What if I have to go into the Otherworld?"

James huffed. "Oh, come on, V. I remember home. I remember the palace. I'm not Elise. I know the dangers and I know enough to be a help. I'm not that much younger."

Every word rang true. "Since when do you call me V?"

"Someone has to keep you from being a fussy old bodger." James grinned. "Besides, I need to go."

"Why? Aside from being a royal pain."

James' foot shot out as he tried to kick Steven. "No. Um, because..." James' cheeks flushed. "I've been having dreams about the Otherworld. But I can't remember anything other than they're in the Otherworld and involve a girl."

"Don't tell Quinn." Steven had gotten quite the education from Quinn, and now he could actually dream-search correctly. But he still couldn't figure out where Noli *was*.

James snickered. "I overheard most of it. Are you really having clandestine trysts with Noli on the dream plane?"

"I am *not*." Their meetings were a bit naughty by mortal standards, but hardly trysts.

"Girl or no, you won't catch me being mushy like you." James made a face of disgust.

Shaking his head and suppressing a grin, Steven made to leave.

"Good. I've been ready for ages." James hopped up off the bed.

Steven turned around. "You're not going. Someone has to protect Elise."

"Nice try, but we both know Quinn has it under control."

Steven knew there really was no good reason to leave James behind. Honest and loyal, his brother was better than he was with a sword, and decent enough in magic. Also, James understood the intricacies of the Otherworld. He'd be an asset—especially if they needed to split up.

"I know you care about Noli." James put a hand on his shoulder. "I know you and Quinn are worried about what's going on with the magic. Let me help. Please? I *am* the better swordsman, you know," he teased.

Steven thought for a moment, carefully considering the risks. "You understand I might have to break some of our laws?" How far would he go for a mortal, desperation aside?

"Since when have we been afraid of breaking rules?" James shrugged.

"These aren't child's pranks. This could lead to our deaths. You know how the high queen is. The sacrifice is under her dominion. If Noli is—"

"I don't understand why you're so sure it's Noli; why you're so afraid, so desperate. But you're my brother, so I'll go and help the best I can. Besides..." James grinned devilishly. "If you leave me behind, I'll tell Father."

James would do nothing of the sort, but it made Steven laugh. He turned and left the bedroom. "Well, if you put it that way..."

• • • • • • • •

Kevighn paced the kitchen, trying to work out his frustration. The magic still hadn't bound Noli, who hounded him constantly for information. The queen knew he'd gone missing with the chosen girl. It was only a matter of time before she came here. She'd sent hunters out for more girls, but so far they were unsuccessful. He'd also continued to search for another girl, partly out of duty, partly out of selfishness.

Never had they gotten this close to it being time without

179

a sacrifice. This morning, he'd gone to light the hearth, and needed to try over and over like a small child. Soon the wood faeries would sicken and die. Ones in the mortal realm already were. Portals had closed themselves off. One of the smaller realms had disappeared completely, along with everyone in it.

Once again, it was his fault. Yet he didn't care.

The problem didn't lie in Noli's stubbornness to give in to the magical binding. No, the real problem lay in the fact that he'd fallen in love with the very girl he had to kill. He wasn't in lust, as with the other girls, or merely attracted, like with Annabelle. No. If he professed his love to her, as he had to so many others, he'd be speaking the truth.

At first, Kevighn had thought Noli drew him because she reminded him of his sister. But then he'd been ensnared by her spunk, her spirit, her gifts, and the fact that she'd made his cabin a home again. He could easily imagine a quiet life here with her ...

That couldn't be. Unless he managed to find another girl before the magic bound her, Noli must die. But Kevighn knew he played a dangerous game; he wasn't going to find another girl. It had been hard enough to find her. With every moment that passed, he became resigned to the idea that he must take Noli to the palace to see the one person who could "help" her, as he'd promised, and entrust her to the queen. He had to finish with it all before he got himself, and his heart, in trouble.

No rule said he must be the one to amuse and seduce

the sacrifice, and he'd let others do the job before. Yet the thought of anyone else touching Noli made his blood boil.

He wanted to kiss her, to love her. That could make the magic set—it had worked in the past. It would be easy. She often woke up … frustrated, as girls that age often did. He'd walked by her open bedroom door more than once to see her cradling her pillow while she slept as if it were a man.

Yet as good as it would be for his people—for the magic to set, irreversibly binding her as the sacrifice—it would be bad for him.

Out of all the girls, and all the times, why this girl, why now?

A familiar sensation rippled up his spine. Someone had arrived at his private portal—the secret doorway into his domain. This wasn't the one he'd brought Noli through, a seldom-used public one. Rather, someone had come through the proverbial back door, using his personal portal. Only three people besides himself possessed access.

Creideamh was dead. The other would never use it unless necessary.

The high queen herself had decided to visit.

Surely, nothing good would come of this.

Where's Noli?

"This place looks dreadful," James whispered as the two of them approached the imposing yellow house. They'd taken the steam trolley from the air terminal.

"It's a reform school, not a resort." But Steven concurred. The soulless house seemed to watch them sinisterly, like dark-court spies.

"What's your plan? Walk through the gate, knock on the door, and ask to see Noli?"

Steven's eyebrows rose as he pushed open the tall, ominous gate. "Do you have a better one?" Hopefully they looked respectable enough.

James shrugged, top hat askew. "No."

As they walked down the cobblestone path to the front door, Steven looked around. This entire place made an uneasy feeling settle over him.

After ringing the bell, he straightened his coat. *Please let Noli be here.*

A rather bland blonde in a fancy green dress answered the door. "May I help you?"

"Good afternoon." He tipped his hat. "We're here to see Magnolia Braddock." All he needed to see was the girl's expression to get his answer.

"Let me summon Miss Gregory." In a flustered flurry of skirts and petticoats, she left, leaving them standing on the front porch.

A few moments later, a spindly woman in all black came to the door and looked down her nose at them as if they were beggars looking for scraps. "I'm Miss Gregory. I run this establishment. You are?"

Steven bowed, trying to be every inch the gentleman. "I'm Steven Darrow, and this is my brother James. We've traveled from Los Angeles to see Magnolia Braddock."

Unlike the blond girl, the headmistress's face remained stone-cold and blank. "I'm sorry, but our girls aren't permitted visitors."

"Please," James wheedled, turning on the charm. "We've traveled a long way. All we are asking is for a few moments, chaperoned of course. We'll even stand on the porch." He flashed her an ice-melting smile.

For a moment Steven caught a glimmer of something in her eyes. Fear.

"She's not permitted visitors. Her mother is aware of this and should have told you. If I allow you, I'd have to allow everyone. Good day." She slammed the door in their faces.

"What a dragon-lady," James whispered.

"I think real dragons would be offended by that," Steven replied.

James grinned. "I think you're right."

Steven peered through the windows to see if someone was watching—he didn't see anyone. He made his way down the porch steps, but instead of heading straight out the gate, he walked along the side of the house.

"What are you doing?" James jogged to keep up.

"I need to check something." He could feel the buzz of magic under his skin, pulling him like a lodestone. He needed to see what it was, where it came from.

A side door opened, startling them. A plump blond girl in a blue dress and white apron stepped outside, a basket on one arm. She seemed more … alive than the girl who'd answered the front door.

When she saw him, her eyes widened. "Oh!"

Steven's finger went to his lips. Quinn would *not* appreciate it if Miss Gregory called the authorities. Neither would his father.

"We aren't here to harm you or cause mischief. Do you know Noli Braddock?" he whispered.

Blue eyes wide, she nodded and lowered her voice. "She isn't here anymore. It's a dreadful scandal. But we're not supposed to speak of it."

"Is it now?" His heart sank.

"Who are you? Her brother Jeff or her best friend V?" The girl smiled shyly. "Magnolia was my friend. Well, I considered her my friend."

Noli spoke of him? Steven's heart jumped. "I'm V, and this is my brother, James."

She bobbed a curtsey. "I'm Claire. Charlotte and Magnolia were close. When Charlotte's uncle took her back to Georgia, Magnolia became upset and they locked her away in isolation. When they took her out, she simply … vanished." Claire looked around again, trembling. "I think she and Charlotte had planned on running away. She might have carried out the plan, perhaps gone to Charlotte's."

Charlotte. Claire. The letters mentioned the both of them. Run away? Steven wouldn't blame her. This place made his skin crawl.

"Do you have Charlotte's address?" He doubted that Noli ran away—or if she did, that she'd gotten all the way to Charlotte's. Certainly she hadn't run back to Los Angeles. Maybe she'd gone to Jeff. Still, he just couldn't imagine her abandoning her mother with no word.

Claire looked startled. She seemed to startle easily. She also shone, ever so slightly, with the Spark. "Oh, silly me, I forgot my shears. It's hard to cut herbs without shears. It should take me time to find them, at least ten minutes. Excuse me." She went back inside and shut the door.

"Odd." James blinked in puzzlement.

"Come on, we have ten minutes." Steven dragged his brother toward the back gardens, the magic he'd felt earlier still tugging at him. Had they ever let Noli out, or did they keep her inside? The thought of being kept inside made him shudder.

"What do you mean, ten minutes?" James scratched his chin, frowning.

"Are you daft? She's going to try to get the address and come back in ten minutes." They crept past a kitchen garden filled with vegetables and fragrant herbs.

James blinked, once, twice. "Oh, that's what the babble meant?"

Shaking his head, Steven continued following the magic, like a bloodhound on a trail, until they came to a stone wall overgrown with ivy.

"There's something on the other side of the wall," James whispered.

Steven walked along the length of it, looking for the door. Perhaps Noli had simply scaled the wall? "Ah, there we are." At his push, the unlocked, vine-covered door opened.

"Flying figs, what is this place?" James stood at his shoulder.

"Language, James," Steven teased, taking it in. "It's a garden, of course." A secret faery garden. This place—a tangle of roses, vines, and other blooms—would draw Noli like the proverbial moth to a flame. Little wood faeries flitted about, playing tag. In the center of it all stood a faery tree, inhabited and radiating power.

He laid a hand on its gnarled trunk. "Flying figs."

"Language, Steven." James grinned. The faeries flew around them, one landed on James' shoulder. "Is that … is that a wild portal?" His voice hushed.

"It is." What luck that Noli would end up in a school with a faery tree that not only was inhabited, but was a portal to the Otherworld as well. He'd love to learn one day why this place existed.

Using his gift, Steven tried to "speak" to the tree—to see when the portal was last used. He got the sense of a sad girl with the Spark and a male fae. Finally, he got the impression of a burst of power and the faint tang of Midsummer.

"James, this was last used at Midsummer. Two people went through—a male of our kind, and a sad mortal girl with the Spark."

"We should still get proof," James replied, as a faery landed on his hand.

"Proof?" Steven didn't hide his surprise.

James glanced up. "Okay, the faery tells me that a girl who sounds like Noli came here a lot and then disappeared from the tree at Midsummer. She often brought a redheaded friend, who shone nearly as brightly."

Steven nodded. "That sounds like proof to me."

"I'll go try to find Charlotte and Jeff, to see if Noli went to either of them," James offered. "Remember that Father and Quinn won't let us charge into the Otherworld without *solid* proof."

"You as the voice of reason is humorous. Next, you'll be the mushy one," Steven observed with a snort. "If you're checking on them, what will I do?"

The wood faery flew off. A grin spread across James' face so broadly it went all the way to his ears. "Why, charge into the Otherworld without proof and find Noli, of course."

For a moment, Steven paused. Would James be safe? Yes, he could take care of himself. After all, it was only the mortal realm. He returned his brother's grin. "Now that's more like it."

James took off his hat and mock-bowed. "I'm here to serve."

A glimmer caught Steven's eye, near the oak, and he bent down. An old brass key lay discarded by the roots. Probably the key to the garden door. Unsure exactly why, he pocketed the key.

"Let's see if the kitchen girl has the address yet," he said. "Are you sure you want to find Charlotte and Jeff on your own?" Steven didn't really want to go to the Otherworld without James, but the sense of urgency to find Noli, to protect her, continued to build inside him like a maelstrom. They both knew Noli didn't dwell anyplace here. Yet James was right; they needed proof she *wasn't* in the mortal realm.

"Yes, I'm sure. But don't think I won't join you in the Otherworld as soon as I'm done," James replied as they left the faery garden.

"Hurry up, or you'll miss all the fun."

James' eyes flashed in the afternoon sunlight. "Never."

• • • • • • • •

Kevighn didn't go looking for Queen Tiana. *She'd* invaded *his* home. Noli was working in the grove, making window boxes for the tree house. As long as she stayed there, she'd be safe. Now wasn't the time for them to meet.

As soon as he'd sensed the queen nearby, Kevighn began to make tea. When she appeared in the kitchen doorway, he turned and bowed low. "Would you like some tea, Your Majesty?"

"And here many think you have no manners." The queen's cool voice cut through the cozy kitchen like a winter wind. "Please. After having to look for you, I deserve to take advantage of your hospitality."

He busied himself to hide his nervousness. No fear, no weakness, could be shown in front of her or she'd exploit it. "What brings you here, Your Majesty?" He took down two cups. "My apologies for making you look for me; I've been here the whole time."

"With false trails and safeguards," she said, her pretty face screwed up in disbelief. "Whatever are you doing with the girl? I've actually had to send out other hunters—not that anyone has found anything." Her lower lip jutted out in a slight pout.

In some ways he felt relief—it was a testament to his skill. The thought also saddened him. "With all due respect, I need more time, Your Majesty."

"For what? Where is she? Why hasn't the magic bound her? Why ever did you bring her *here* and not to the palace … as charming as this place is?" Looking around the simple kitchen, she raised a pale blond eyebrow in distaste.

This high queen talked far more than the previous one. And although no one would ever say it aloud, everyone knew that this queen had killed the previous one. Perhaps Tiana had talked her sister to death.

"I don't know why the magic has yet to bind her," Kevighn said. "She shines like no other in my memory. She's smart, curious, and not like the usual girls. That's why I brought her here. She's a wary one, not entranced by gems and gowns." He set two steaming cups of tea on the table, trying to keep his face and voice neutral. The queen would blame him no matter what he said, but he didn't need to give her ammunition.

"You should still have brought her to me, like you did the others." The queen frowned. Her beautiful regal features looked carved out of alabaster. Blond hair was gathered at the top of her head, parts cascading down in ringlets. Jeweled mechanical flowers, which opened and closed before his eyes, decorated her coif. She also wore a tiara made of tiny spires.

"I always spend some time with them before bringing them to the palace. I simply happened to bring her here to do so." Kevighn toyed with his cup. The last thing he'd counted on was feeling the way he did. Bright Lady bless, Noli was only a mortal.

"I still don't understand *why* it is taking so long." The queen took a sip, the sleeves of her heavily embroidered, plum-colored dress rustling with her every movement. "The magic always binds the girls quickly."

"Yes, I know." It galled him, too. After all, he was the best.

"Meanwhile, my kingdom is falling apart. My subjects

are frightened. And you—" Her blue eyes flashed with rage as she pounded her fist on the table, nearly upsetting her teacup.

Uh oh. He steeled himself against her wrath.

"You have taken your sweet time. Then, when you found her, you hid her away and haven't made any progress. Time has run out. Either make the magic bind her immediately, or I'll do it for you." The queen's cheeks flushed.

A frightening prospect. "What if I find another girl?"

"There is no time for another," she snapped, her voice rising in pitch. For a moment he thought she might pop the laces on the black leather corset she wore over her dress. "I hope you pray to the Bright Lady this mortal has enough power to repair the damage you've personally caused."

Kevighn flinched at the accusation, but didn't say a word. He *had* caused it.

"I'm going to hold you accountable for everything that doesn't return to normal—and you'll pay dearly for it with your hide." She gave an eerie laugh, and her eyes had a look of macabre delight as she sipped her tea, pinky up.

"Of course, Your Majesty. I've brought her here, plied her with gifts, and shown her wondrous things. I rescued her from peril. What else do you wish for me to do?" He allowed a little frustration to leak into his voice. But only a little. This queen didn't make idle threats. She might seem silly or shallow, but she had forfeited her own family to be queen.

"I don't care how you do it." She set her cup down with such force it spilled onto the table. "Lie to her. Trick her. Seduce her. Whatever it takes. If you can't do it, I will."

Her chilly voice held veiled threats. It was within her right to end his life if she pleased. After all, she was the law of the land—outside of the magic itself.

"You think you can succeed where I cannot, Your Majesty?" It was a dangerous question.

"Yes, I do. You used to be such a good huntsman, too," she sneered. Standing up, she brushed at her purple skirts with a pale hand. "You have two days to bind her, or I will employ drastic measures. Remember what's at stake." Her voice became a hiss and her eyes narrowed.

"Yes, Your Majesty." The intensity of her words nearly bowed Kevighn over. He needed to work quickly, even though he didn't want to. If he didn't succeed in two days, the queen would make her move, and Kevighn would have failed.

He'd never failed.

"Good." Turning on her heels, Queen Tiana marched out of the room.

He'd done everything he could—except seduce Noli. Perhaps that would work. Could he mix lies with truth, telling Noli how much he wanted her, wanted to care for her, while also feeding her falsehoods? There didn't seem to be a choice. He must please his queen even if he had no taste for it.

Even if it cost him what he wanted.

As soon as he felt the queen leave, the back door opened. Noli walked in, anger clouding her face.

NINETEEN

Confrontations

"You liar." Anger at both Kevighn and herself welled up inside her like unreleased steam. How could she have been so stupid?

"I can explain." Those words dripped so easily off his lips. Clearly he'd said it before. To how many girls?

She'd been in the grove, planting, and came in for something to drink when she noticed someone in the kitchen with Kevighn.

Her hands went to her hips. "Explain fast."

"Remember when I told you someone could help, but might be unwilling? That was her." Kevighn looked displeased. He *should* be ashamed, Noli thought.

"The one you promised to take me to, but haven't yet? Like you promised to help me find the way home, but haven't done that either?" She didn't try to hide her hurt; it flowed into her voice with the force of a waterfall.

"Noli." Kevighn's expression softened. "I told you, things are complicated. What did you hear? You probably just took it out of context."

"More lies." But guilt overcame Noli as his face crumpled, since she hadn't really heard anything other than that they were speaking about her.

"Have a seat." Kevighn gestured to the table. "Perhaps I should have told you the truth from the beginning…"

"You should have," she snapped. She sat down in the wooden chair that she thought of as *hers* and arranged her skirt, smoothing a bit of dust off the russet fabric.

"If I had, would you have come here with me?" He went over to the cabinets and rummaged through them.

"No." She never should have gone with him to begin with. No, she should have marched up to the faery tree and demanded it take her back to Findlay.

Wait. That sounded so silly. Noli stifled a laugh.

"What are you laughing about?" Kevighn took down two glasses and a bottle.

"If I'd walked up to the faery tree that brought me here and demanded to be taken home, would it have listened?" She continued to laugh at the notion.

"You aren't a tree-speaker, so it probably wouldn't have listened unless you knew how to use a wild portal." He smiled, carrying the earthenware goblets and glass bottle over to the table. "I like it when you laugh. You're so beautiful when you laugh or smile."

She stopped laughing and narrowed her eyes. "I will have none of your honeyed nonsense, Kevighn Silver—is that even your real name?"

Shrugging, he opened the bottle and filled both goblets with a dark liquid that seemed to shimmer in the light. "One of them. Usually they call me Kevighn Silver-Tongue."

"For your lies?"

"Or my kisses, depending on whom you ask." He said this lightly, easily.

She stared at him in partial disbelief. "You really are a rake, aren't you?"

For a moment he looked sad—but only in his eyes. "Only when I need to be. My job is complex, and I often must do a variety of things you'd deem distasteful. Things are different here." He pushed a goblet toward her. "Here, try this. My friend made it. It's nice—strong, but nice."

Taking the brass goblet in her hands, she eyed the burgundy fluid. "This isn't tea."

"Not at all." He took a sip. "It's made of those berries you like so much, and honey."

Fermented until they became alcoholic, most likely. Noli took a sip. It exploded over her tongue in an overpowering sensation, bringing forth memories of summer days, berry-picking, and lounging in meadows blooming with flowers. "It's like summer in a bottle."

"That it is."

She took another sip, drinking in the heady experience. The act of drinking it was even better than the drink itself.

He chuckled. "Careful. It's strong."

"Who is she and what does she want?" Noli realized how jealous she sounded and her cheeks blazed. Hopefully he had missed that. When she peered at him, she realized he hadn't.

He arched a dark eyebrow. "Jealousy becomes you, sweet Magnolia. But you need not worry about her. She's not the kind of woman I prefer to relate to."

"You prefer painted ladies." Noli took another sip. It didn't taste strong to her, but she was hardly an expert on spirits.

"Not always. I told you that you weren't supposed to be here. I should have brought you directly to her, but I didn't wish to … for a number of reasons." He toyed with his goblet.

"Why?" She took another swallow. It was so good. Better than anything she'd ever had.

"To protect you, as I've said before. She has uses for those such as yourself, and is extremely powerful. Yes, she has the power to send you home. However, you'll only be permitted to leave if she wishes. As you probably heard, she doesn't wish it."

Noli's forehead wrinkled as she tried to understand. "But why?"

"Here, we understand people like you. We treasure those with the Spark and adore your gifts. I knew from the moment I met you that she'd be enchanted and delighted by you, that she'd want to keep you."

Her heart froze at his words and her voice dropped to a bare whisper. "She will?"

"Yes. That's why I've been discreet in my questioning, so I wouldn't draw her attention." Kevighn looked right at her, with such intensity that it felt like he was looking clear through her.

"Oh. So how did she come here?" Travel in this world seemed so strange.

"Like we did, through a portal. But not the one I brought you through." Noli noted that he didn't look pleased at the idea of that woman's visit. Good.

He eyed her glass. "You might want to go easy."

Defiantly, she took another swallow. "I'm fine."

He took a sip of his own drink. "It looks like I have two days to convince you to stay here with us. After that, she'll take you from me."

"She won't let me go?" Noli felt her fear growing, and she took another drink to fortify herself.

"Unless … " Kevighn looked away. "Unless we can convince her to send you back. Your argument would have to be clever. I had planned on doing that, if needed— bringing you to her in hopes you could enchant her so much she'd allow you to go home."

"Oh. I don't think I'm that clever. Who is she, again?" Noli felt hopelessness pressing down on her. Looking into her glass, she found it empty. Without asking, she filled it.

"She's my queen—high queen over all the kingdoms. We all must do as she commands." Kevighn sighed unhappily, taking another swig.

"Oh."

"Usually, when mortals find themselves here, they want to stay, having fled terrible situations in their own realm. Not all are lucky enough to have people who love them." For a moment he looked far away.

Noli pondered all this, her thoughts heavy. It was like trying to wade through molasses. "I don't want to stay. I want to go home. Are you close to finding a way home for me?"

He put a hand on her shoulder. "It no longer matters. I can't defy an order from her even if I wished, and she wishes for you to stay with us, either here or at the palace."

"Do you want to?" Swirling the liquid in the goblet, she drank more.

"Want to bring you to her? No." He looked into his cup, shoulders rounded in defeat. "Do I want you to go home...no. But if she permits it, I won't stop you."

"You don't want me to go home? Why?" Noli's stomach fluttered with several different emotions. She finished the rest of the drink to hide her face.

"Why do you think?" His voice grew ragged.

Startled, she nearly dropped her empty cup. Kevighn took it from her and placed it on the table in front of him.

"It's true," he added.

"Lies," she spat. It must be.

"Look into my eyes. I'm not leading you false." Taking her hand, he pulled her up out of her chair and toward him.

She looked into his eyes, biting her lip. "Why?"

"I don't know." For a moment his eyes flashed and his

voice was unsteady. "I've seen many, many girls in my day, Noli. I'm far older than you could understand, though I'm relatively young for my people. No one, not *one* of my people, nor one of yours, rich or poor, beautiful or plain, debutante or strumpet, has ever drawn me the way you do."

A sharp breath escaped her lips and her heart pounded like a million drums. "Stop lying, please." Noli's voice broke, but she refused to look away.

"Tomorrow, I'll take you to the queen so you may plead with her to send you home." Kevighn took her hand. Noli felt her insides go wobbly at his touch, and everything seemed as if she were viewing it through a dense fog.

"Tomorrow?" she murmured. "You said she's giving us two days."

"Why wait?" He shrugged.

True; this would enable her to get home one day sooner. *If* she could get home. Why wouldn't the queen send her home? Surely there was no good reason to keep her here. If she were an opera singer, a harpist, or a ballet dancer, perhaps. But Kevighn himself said her talents lay in gardening and fixing things. What use would that be to the high queen?

They walked down the hall and Kevighn pulled her into his room. When Noli started to speak, his mouth met hers.

He kissed her hard, lips crushing hers, tongue darting into her mouth like a snake. His arms tangled around her like vines, pressing her body against the length of his.

Noli had never been kissed before—outside of her dreams about V. Kevighn's kisses were most unlike those.

No, these fiery kisses consumed, tasting of spice and passion. The arms around her weren't feather-light and comforting, but possessive and stalwart.

She felt fear building, but also a sudden—and strong— yearning. Putting a hand in the center of Kevighn's chest, Noli pushed him away hard enough to break off the kiss. Even though the thought of curling her hands in his long dark hair was tempting, she needed to pull herself together and take control of the situation before it got out of hand.

"What are you doing, Kevighn? I'm not one of your fancy women." Her heart raced.

"No, you're not, and I'm glad." His hands stroked her hair as she gasped for breath. "This is your last night here, and tomorrow..."

"Tomorrow I'll be home." The fear faded, replaced by excitement and anticipation.

"We hope."

She nodded blithely. "Of course."

"But tonight..." He kissed her again, moving her backwards toward his bed.

Kisses could easily lead to other things, especially when in someone's bedchambers. She should break this off right this second. Her head seemed so fuzzy, so heavy. It seemed so much easier to simply go along with things, rather than muster up the strength to stand up to him—or think.

Also, part of her liked this. His fiery kisses seared her, making her toes curl. A fire blazed deep in her belly—one of those unquenchable infernos that came to her at night.

His hands roamed her body, sending shivers of pleasure through her, causing little gasps to escape her lips. She allowed her hands to tangle themselves in his unbound black hair.

"That's my little blossom." His whisper caressed her ear as his hands roamed her still-clothed body. "I can give you a memorable night—one that, if it doesn't convince you to stay, will at least keep you company in your dreams all your days. And if you wish, I could visit you as well."

One hand cupped her bottom; she could feel the warmth of his fingers through the fabric of her skirt, blouse, and petticoats. The other hand moved from her lips to behind her head. His heat scorched her very soul as he pressed against her. She could nearly imagine them fitting together.

Warning bells sounded in her head. She should stop this. Poverty aside, she was a lady.

"But . . ." It took all her willpower to break off his searing kiss and force out that single word.

He laid a finger upon her lips. "I'll not harm you. It will be sweet, gentle, and beautiful—just like you."

She opened her mouth, but once again, instead of words, his mouth pressed to hers, hands picking up the pace, sending thrills shooting through her body.

Her dreams of V were nothing like this. But this wasn't a dream.

"Kevighn." That single word was a warning, a plea for help, and a cry for more all at the same time.

"I'm right here." His kisses trailed down her neck, each one sending tingles to her very core as his fingers undid the buttons on her blouse. Next, he pulled the strings of her skirt-waist. Free, the skirt slipped to the ground, leaving her in her chemise, corset, and petticoats.

More than cold chilled her. It hurt to think, to stay in the present; it would be so much easier to float away on clouds of sensation and delight. Clearly, he had ideas—ideas that, at the moment, sounded good to her. They also frightened her.

But she wasn't sure she wanted to stop.

"Noli, little blossom, what's this? I haven't seen it before." His hand hovered close to the medallion resting on top her corset, but didn't quite touch it.

"Oh, my best friend V gave it to me, to protect me from aether and other such things." Noli laughed. "He told me to wear it always. Some help it's been."

"Did he now? This is your friend who lives next door?" Kevighn continued to examine it with his eyes, his expression unreadable.

"He did. He's such a fussy old bodger sometimes, going on about such nonsense as faery trees and aether—" She paused as her words made sense, a little. "Oh. I suppose he was correct."

Would she tell V about her adventures? Probably. He'd believe her, not simply pat her on the head and dose her with poppy syrup and a cold compress like her mother would.

"Could you take it off for me? Please?" Kevighn was eyeing the medallion as if it were a bug.

"Why? I said I'd always wear it." Why she clung to this, Noli didn't know.

"I can't take it off you, and I fear we can't go forward until you do." Kevighn kissed her again. Pulling away, he cupped her face with his hands so he could look straight into her eyes. "Don't you wish to continue?"

Things became as clear as freshly washed windows.

"I ... I'm sorry, Kevighn, but I don't think I want to go any further." Taking a deep breath, Noli tried to sort out her thoughts and feelings. After all, as nice as this was, she didn't want to become some sordid cautionary tale.

If only the fire within her would cease.

"I'm sorry as well, little blossom." Close to her, he continued to trace little kisses down the back of her neck like they were little breadcrumbs left as a trail. "Could you take it off for me anyway? I'll give you something far nicer. Green does nothing for you." He kissed that place between her neck and ear, and she gasped. "Please, take it off for me. It's just a silly necklace."

Something about his voice compelled her, and she raised her hand to take it off.

"Yes, that's it," he murmured, his voice smooth as imported silk.

Noli stopped, letting the medallion drop back around her neck. "If it's a silly necklace, why do I need to take it off?"

She stepped away, breaking contact with him.

He closed the space between them but didn't touch her. "Perhaps the idea of you wearing a gift from another man makes me jealous."

"He's just my best friend." A lie. V was far more than her best friend. She felt confused and weary. Couldn't she just go to sleep and deal with everything later? A thought pierced the cobwebs of her brain. "It's protection against faeries, isn't it?"

"Of sorts. I'd like to know why he possessed such a powerful token."

She shrugged, not actually surprised that the medallion had such properties. "V has all sorts of odd things and bits of odd knowledge. It's part of what makes him so interesting."

"I see. You seem tired. Why don't you lie down with me?" He offered her his hand.

Tempting. But...

"I want to go home." She turned away from him, as if doing so would make dealing with this—with him—easier. So many emotions churned within her. "I appreciate all you've done for me, but truly, all I want is to go home."

"Please, sweet blossom, is there not anything I could say or do to make you stay?" Kevighn's voice sounded so wistful, so full of want, that it was difficult to not say yes.

Noli steeled herself against those traitorous feelings inside her, the ones that urged her to embrace the moment. "I only want to go home. Perhaps it would be best if you took me to the queen right now."

"I could, if that's what you desire. When I told you I care about you, I spoke the truth. I do care about you, and can love and cherish you as no mortal can. But"—his expression turned hard and her stomach clenched—"I guess your friend never told you that if you should happen to find yourself in the realm of Faerie, don't eat any food that's offered."

She thought for a moment. "I don't remember that one. Certain words, dancing circles ... "

Then his words hit her like a sack of flour, and her hand went to her mouth.

"I'm very sorry, my little blossom, but you've eaten faery food. That means you are no longer able to return to the mortal realm." Kevighn didn't sound rough or mean, but the words were poison nevertheless.

Noli looked up at him, betrayal coursing through her as if she'd been shot with one of his feathered arrows. It made her knees shake, and for a second her heart ceased beating.

"You are nothing but a rake and a liar, Kevighn Silver." Anger flowed into her voice as a lump formed in her throat. "I never should have trusted you."

Breaking out of his arms, she shoved him away with all her might and tore out of the room.

TWENTY

Noli's Flight

Noli ran straight out of the cabin, trying not to cry. A fiend like him wasn't worth tears.

"Wait! Please, Noli. Wait!" he called from the back door.

Fueled by betrayal, she continued to run, not even turning to see if he followed. When she reached the grove, her chest heaving with exertion, she gazed up at the tree house. No. He'd expect that. Like last time, when he'd lure her back with pretty words and surprises.

Ignoring the little faeries who vied for her attention, Noli continued through the grove, even though she'd never been beyond it before. The trees grew into a dark tangle of branches. Everything seemed darker and scarier here, causing her skin top break out into gooseflesh. Still, she pressed on as her legs burned and sweat tricked down her back, making her chemise stick to her skin.

Kevighn Silver-Tongue, indeed. Fortunately, she hadn't done anything other than kiss him. Such pretty lies he'd woven, and she'd walked right into his glimmering web.

What an idiot she'd been. She'd looked forward to the treats and his company.

And her heart still jumped a bit from those kisses.

A look down revealed that she was wearing only her undergarments. Not only was she an idiot, but a dollymop as well. She tried to shake off the feeling of his hands, his lips. She needed to focus in order to find her way out of here—and home.

The large, ramshackle house that appeared ahead of her looked to be straight out of a gothic novel, and cast an air of abandon and neglect. Truly Miss Havisham's place if there ever was one. Noli ran toward it anyway. Perhaps someone still lived there.

Once inside, she found it empty. Exhaustion pressed down on her and she wished she could crawl into one of the beds and sleep. Instead, she returned outside. The garden behind the house had taken over and seemed to be attempting to keep her there as she twisted, tore, and thrashed her way through.

Where was she?

She was lost, plain and simple.

Hopelessness nipped at her as she stumbled into what may have once been a clearing. A faery tree grew out of the center of the lifeless wilds. As she gazed at it, the air around her seemed to change, humming with something she couldn't quite identify and making prickles shoot up her spine. This tree didn't hold the joy and life of the others she'd seen. Nothing grew on it; no wood faeries played within it. It seemed as lifeless and soulless as Findlay House.

Her fingers brushed the bark, and she yanked them back as a shock shot through her. The outward appearance of the tree remained the same, but it now seemed to thrum with power like a steam generator.

Was it a portal?

"Take me away from this place," she whispered to the tree, wiping her nose with her bare forearm. Nothing happened. Perhaps she wasn't a tree-speaker, but one of these blasted trees had brought her here. If they could do that, they could take her away.

For some reason, she couldn't remember what Kevighn had done each time they'd passed through a portal on the way to his cabin.

Perhaps if she made a wish, as she had before, it would work. "I wish you would take me away from here." She waited. Nothing.

"Flying figs." The unladylike epithet was a favorite of V's younger brother. Noli pounded on the trunk of the tree with her fists, anguish welling up inside her and threatening to spill over. "I know you have the power. As ludicrous as it sounds, I can feel it. Now take me away from this place! Please?"

Still nothing.

She should start running again, before Kevighn caught up with her. But tiredness consumed her, filling her head with cotton, making her limbs heavy and reluctant. Sinking to the ground, her back against the trunk, Noli laid her head on her knees.

"I only wish to go home," she whispered. "Please. Take me away from this place and bring me anywhere that could lead me to home, I beg of you." Holding her medallion, she wished with all her might to go home to her mother—and V.

A flash of heat surrounded her. It was so cozy and soothing that she ignored the strange tingling in her body and let the warmth lull her to sleep.

•••••••••

With a heavy heart, Kevighn approached Creideamh's grove. He clutched Noli's clothing in one hand and a necklace in his other. A basket hung on his arm. The things he did for his queen and country. Trying to seduce Noli had been painful, in some ways. After all, unlike with the other girls, where he mostly play-acted, some of the things he'd said to her held true.

Hopefully she'd had enough time to calm down—his reason for not following her immediately.

The little faeries looked on but didn't stop him. His shoulder unrounded and his confidence increased with every footfall. Noli had certainly been responsive to his touch, his kisses. His little blossom had probably fled in confusion and fright. The Bright Lady knew what strange things they told mortal girls these days, especially those in the highest social classes.

Her medallion disturbed him. Yet it might answer

the question of why the magic hadn't bound her—it was the crest of an old faery house, a royal house of the earth court…although which house, exactly, he wasn't sure, having been born into the fire court. There was no love lost between the two courts. Earth quelled fire, fire destroyed earth. Keeping Creideamh's throwback earth talents a secret had proven an impossible task.

He couldn't believe that Noli was the mortal lover of some earth court fop. She'd know far more about the Otherworld than she did, if she meant enough to one of them for him to give her a sigil.

There *was* an earth court house that had been exiled to the mortal realm. Once, it had been *the* earth court royal house, as in the royal family. It had been quite the scandal when the high queen took away their kingdom, forcing them out of the Otherworld. Perhaps this friend of hers, the one she called V, was one of the young exiled princes.

Or the sigil may have also been lost or pawned over time by the former royal owner, and somehow wound up in the hands of a clever mortal.

Somehow, wearing the mark of a royal house, even an exiled one, had kept the magic from binding her. He couldn't think of another explanation. The idea of some earth court prince paying her attention disturbed him even more than her being the good wife of some ponderous mortal.

He couldn't touch the medallion, and he was less than royal in all respects. If somehow he could convince her to remove it, perhaps the magic could do its work, marking her as the chosen sacrifice and allowing the Otherworld to stabilize.

The necklace he carried in his hand sparkled, its little gem fiery red at first glance, then deep orange, then golden. A pretty bauble. His father had given it to his mother as a betrothal gift. The basket held a picnic—and more honey wine. He'd give her back her clothing, present her with the necklace and his apologies, and go from there.

Hopefully this would work. If not…

"Noli?" He scaled the tree, which was only slightly difficult with his parcels. The tree house was empty. "Where are you?" A faery nudged him, indicating the basket. "Have you seen Noli?"

The faery told him she'd run by, but hadn't stopped.

His stomach sank and an uneasy feeling settled over him. He could stop her from leaving his own personal land; however, a tiny rift existed between Creideamh's grove and their parent's land. This had allowed his sister to come and go when he'd first made the tree house. When he'd assumed full responsibility for Creideamh and they moved to his little cabin, he never sealed it, since she went back there occasionally.

Noli may have made it through the rift and found herself in his parent's land. The old portal there probably had gone wild. If Noli discovered it, only the Bright Lady knew where it could take her. When he'd told her that terrible things lived in the Otherworld, things which would want to hurt and use her, he'd told the truth.

Pocketing the firestone necklace, Kevighn dropped the basket and clothing and left the tree house, running at full speed for his parent's land as the inquisitive little faeries looked on.

TWENTY-ONE

The Wild Hunt

Steven looked around as he walked across the once-cared-for grounds of his home, blanketed in moonless twilight. Not the palace—his uncle lived there now—but their real home. The rambling estate put even the largest Los Angeles manor to shame; it resembled a cross between a European farmhouse and an antebellum mansion.

This place used to teem with servants, members of the royal court, and their extended family. That included his uncle, who then happily took the earth court throne when the high queen banished his father.

Once, this place had also included his mother. If he listened hard, he could almost hear her shriek at him and James as they did yet another naughty thing. The grounds held such wondrous places for hiding, pranks, and other acts of youthful mischievousness.

Quinn was right; he and Noli's joyride in the Pixy paled in comparison to some of his and James' antics. Swords were only meant to be found in rocks in stories told to mortal children.

The queen had tried to take this place away from them when his father was exiled. But the magic wouldn't permit her to do so. This place belonged not to his father, but to his family and the House of Oak; it couldn't be taken away if suitable family members remained alive. After all, while he and James had chosen to leave with their father, they weren't actually *exiled*. There was a difference.

Steven still clung to his dream of reclaiming his family's honor so that they could all come home. If his father regained his kingdom, perhaps he'd stop being crotchety and become the man they remembered.

While Elise barely remembered their mother, she did remember when their father had played with them, loved them. Before Queen Tiana's selfishness and true nature reared its ugly head and stripped them of their life.

Being back here brought on an onslaught of memories. But it made a good home base, and the high queen wouldn't notice him here. As Quinn had said, she'd take great pleasure in forcing him to use his gifts on her behalf—which would be her punishment for his choosing to stay with his father.

Steven made his way through the overgrown hedges toward his favorite faery tree. No tree house lurked in its branches, but he'd spent plenty of time in it—as had his father. It hid at the center of a hedge maze, which wasn't as overrun as he'd expected. No wood faeries flew about. He couldn't blame the little beings for abandoning his family. Most everyone had. The only member of their court who'd accompanied them into exile was Quinn. The others had all pledged allegiance to his uncle.

He laid a hand on the tree, and surprise shot through him. Some wood faeries still occupied it. But a look into a knothole made his stomach churn. The tiny inhabitants weren't dead—yet. They would be soon if the magic didn't stabilize. Somehow he needed to fix this, and without Kevighn's trickery.

First and foremost, he needed to find Noli. Taking his sigil in his hands, Steven recalled what Quinn had taught him about using it as a compass to find someone. The sigil tugged, indicating Noli's direction.

Then the air changed, charging, making his skin prickle. Eerie horns that had no mortal counterpart pierced the air, followed by the clop of hooves and the bark of dogs.

"The host is riding from Knocknarea, and over the grave of Clooth-na-Bare," he whispered, quoting William Butler Yeats. Mortal writers produced so many works based on the fae. Most were incorrect; Yeats got a few details wrong, but did manage to capture the essence of the wild hunt.

The essence, but not the fearsomeness.

A terrifying host of riders and hounds, the wild hunt was known to chase its quarry across the Otherworld. Once the hunt started, they wouldn't stop until they got their prey. The only way to escape being the chosen prey was death.

According to Quinn's stories, the hunt was said to possess horns that compelled the guilty to run, but Steven had never actually seen this. He *had* seen men ripped to shreds by the giant, sentient hounds that accompanied the riders.

For a moment, his insides clenched—did the hunt come for *him*? They were known to hunt the high queen's quarry, unless granted special permission to hunt for pleasure. He grew still as they rode through the sky, and didn't relax until they'd passed. "The host is rushing 'twixt night and day; and where is there hope or deed as fair?" he murmured.

But now wasn't the time to quote Yeats, Chaucer, or even Aristotle. Putting a hand on the tree, Steven fed it a little of his own power, trying to keep the faeries alive. "I'll be back. I promise."

• • • • • • • •

A blast of horns in the distance startled Noli awake. Their clamor made her want to run, but something deep within her told her she shouldn't. Something about those who start running can't stop—or perhaps they don't escape? She couldn't remember. Her head ached and her mouth felt stuffed with cotton wool.

Where was she? Still lost, no doubt. A forest of spindly branches surrounded her. Shadows played on the dense growth, making it seem as if the branches were reaching for her. Shivers crept up her spine; this wood was even spookier than the one between Creideamh's grove and the abandoned house. The sky hung heavy with a starless, moonless, dusky purple dawn. The faery tree must have sent her here. Now, to figure out how to get home…

The horns echoed through the woods again, upsetting something winged in a nearby tree. This time, supernatural barking and the pounding of many hooves accompanied the horns, making her heart quicken. Were they after her?

The third time the horns called, they drove her to her feet, but she caught herself before starting to run. This *was* in V's stories—if she remembered correctly, if they wanted her, they would get her no matter what. In any case, she should give them no reason to make chase. She walked slowly away from the sounds, trying to focus on how to get home.

Charged and tingly air wrapped around her, like just before a lightning storm. A chill took her, and she wished she'd remembered to grab her clothing before she fled.

With every step, the horns and hoofbeats grew louder like approaching thunder. Suddenly, they filled the sky—a fearsome melee of giant horses and hounds, of formidable riders armed with swords and axes. That, too, made her feet yearn to flee.

How could horses flying through the air without wings make hoofbeats? But this world didn't have the same constraints as her own. The hunt swooped closer and closer, led by a warrior with snow-white hair whose very presence made her want to hide.

Noli continued to walk, though her instincts squealed at her to run. Her stomach tightened and her skin broke out in gooseflesh—not from the air, but from the sinking sensation that they *had*, in fact, come for her.

They hit the ground, heading toward her in a terrible, beautiful sight—horses neighing and tossing their heads in anticipation, hounds the size of ponies barking and gnashing their teeth, warriors with weapons poised and ready. The hooves of the giant horses never seemed to actually touch the forest floor.

What had V called them? Ah, the wild hunt. Yes, running away was out of the question.

The hunt surrounded her, horses pawing at the ground, hounds wagging their tails impatiently. Even the warriors looked irritated, as if stopping posed a major inconvenience. The one with the white hair rode toward her on his imposing horse, a canny look in his eyes, two daunting black hounds on either side.

"You are the mortal they call Magnolia?" He stopped in front of her.

Would he know if she lied? Would it help? "Yes, I am."

"I am Fionn, the leader of this hunt. The high queen sent me to retrieve you."

Noli suppressed a shiver. She'd caught a glimpse of the cold, regal queen and didn't relish the thought of meeting her, even if she did possess the power to send her home. Of course, Kevighn could have been lying—about the Spark, about eating faery food, about getting home. Then again, if anyone could undo the trap of eating faery food, if anyone could send her home, it seemed logical that it would be the high queen.

"Do I have a choice?" she asked. Under her petticoats,

Noli's knees shook at the leers and looks of the men accompanying Fionn.

His eyes gleamed. "Not a pleasant one." He offered her a large, rough hand. "You may ride with me; no harm will befall you."

She eyed the hand skeptically. "If I get on your horse, will I never be able to get off again, and be forced to ride with you for all my days?"

Fionn laughed a true belly laugh, making the woods seem less ominous. "No, you'll be able to get off. But that was shrewd. Here, it is prudent to be careful with one's words and actions. If you do not wish to ride with me, I'll simply throw you over my shoulder."

That didn't seem pleasant, and he probably wasn't joking.

She hesitated for another moment. "Where are we going?"

"To Queen Tiana, of course." He cocked his head, his horse snorting with impatience.

"And we'll go straight there, the fastest way, and I won't be harmed or hurt or frightened or ... " She couldn't remember what else to ask for.

He chuckled. "Little mortal, you'll be fine. Come, my hunt grows impatient, and no good comes from an impatient hunt."

"If you insist." As if she had a choice.

Giving Fionn her hand, she allowed him to pull her up in front of him on the giant horse. The horns sounded. "Hold on, small one."

The hounds howled, the horses neighed, and the war-riors cried out as they flew into the twilight in a flurry of hooves, paws, and weaponry, quarry in hand.

TWENTY-TWO

The High Queen's Palace

Kevighn stared out the window of his room in the palace as he watched the wild hunt depart through the darkness. Perhaps he hadn't done the right thing, going to the queen and asking her to retrieve Noli before his two days were up. After all, the last mortal girl the wild hunt chased drowned herself.

Noli didn't know about the sacrifice. She needed to be watched carefully to ensure she didn't find out. In some ways, it saddened him that she'd only get to enjoy the luxury of their hospitality for such a short period. In other ways, it could prove a blessing. If Annabelle had figured out how to thwart the sacrifice, someone as clever as Noli could wreak havoc.

He sighed, turning around to look at the sumptuous

quarters where he spent most of his time when in the Otherworld. He missed his cabin, especially now that it seemed like a home again—because of Noli.

"I don't think you should be here when she returns. You'll serve as an unwelcome distraction." Calm and cool, Queen Tiana stood in the doorway in one of her ridiculous outfits. Her bustle, which seemed to be made of spider webs, jutted out several feet behind her. A small mechanical dog sat in her arms. She was known for her fondness for intricate toys and silly gadgets, and always demanded that her subjects give her their best inventions.

"I don't know if that's wise, Your Majesty," he replied. If anyone was to lie to Noli, it would be him and him only. Noli would forgive him eventually—it was her nature.

"Are you questioning me, huntsman?" The queen stroked her toy dog as if it were real, and its tail wagged in reply.

"Of course not, Your Majesty." Kevighn turned toward the window. The wild hunt had disappeared from view. How long before they found Noli? Would she run?

"Good." The queen flounced out the door.

Perhaps he should have told her about Noli's medallion and his theories.

No. The queen could discover it for herself.

Right now he needed a diversion, and he knew the perfect place.

• • • • • • • •

"Is that the palace, Fionn?" Noli asked as the hunt flew over the Otherworld, the pink of dawn coloring the sky.

"Yes, that's our destination."

The structure looming before them reminded her of a photograph she'd seen once of a castle in Europe, only a hundred times more beautiful. Even in the early light it gleamed. The whole thing looked as if it had been dipped in brass. Tall spires, which reminded her of clock hands, rose into the skies. A moat surrounded it. It seemed like something out of a fairy tale. Yes, Noli realized, she was trapped in a gruesome, twisted fairy tale like those told by the Brothers Grimm or Hans Christian Andersen. She hoped she would fare better than the heroines in some of those stories.

The wild hunt landed in a large, grassy courtyard. Fionn disembarked from the horse, helping her down. "Come along."

He started off in one direction, the two giant dogs following. Noli followed as well, wishing she wore a gown. Even in the Otherworld it was probably considered improper to meet a queen while dressed in only your undergarments.

Fionn entered the palace and led her down a long hall, finally stepping into a large and airy room. Its high, gilded ceilings were decorated with murals grander than pictures of the ceiling of the Sistine Chapel, and its giant marble columns rivaled those Noli had seen in V's books. Different colors of marble formed intricate patterns on the floor. Some walls held giant mosaics; velvet curtains and ornate tapestries covered others. Strange sculptures sat on marble pedestals. A dais held a plush purple and gold throne with spires radiating out of it like the sun, or a clock gone mad. Behind it stood a mosaic with five circles, each a different color, in a pattern reminding her of a flower. The whole room was breathtaking and gaudy all at the same time.

Footsteps echoed in the chamber and she looked toward the far end of the room. She recognized the tall, blond, regal woman who entered. The queen's top was as tight-fitting—and as revealing—as a corset, glittering as if made of pink diamonds. The back of the skirt became a swirl of ruffles, sewn vertically and ending in a swath that reminded Noli of a mermaid's tail. It was beautiful, even if scandalous to reveal that much skin this time of day.

Fionn bowed as the queen approached them, and stayed hunched over. Noli stood there, eyeing the woman curiously. Only when the queen stood in front of them did she curtsey. Not knowing exactly how to do it, she simply curtseyed as deeply as she could, then stood.

"I didn't tell you to rise." The queen's voice sharpened. "But I suppose you come from that barbaric new country that doesn't need monarchs?"

"Yes, Your Majesty."

America wasn't new. It was well over a century old.

"You are the mortal Kevighn found—Magnolia?" She looked Noli up and down, her eyebrows rising.

Noli's cheeks blazed. "Yes, Your Majesty. I'm Magnolia Braddock of Los Angeles."

"I am Tiana, High Queen of the Otherworld. Welcome

to my palace." The ethereally statuesque woman drew herself up, speaking with the utmost authority. "Fionn, you may rise. I appreciate you bringing Magnolia to me. You are dismissed."

"As you wish, Your Majesty." Fionn bowed, winked at Noli, and disappeared out the door they'd come through. But they weren't alone. Noli spied stalwart guards in purple and gold livery. Nasty curved swords hung from their belts.

The queen might be beautiful, but she didn't seem warm in the slightest. No, this woman could rival the Snow Queen. She held some sort of mechanical puppy in her arms. Noli itched to see how it worked.

Her eyes, like sapphires, bore into Noli. As the queen looked her up and down, Noli noticed that it wasn't unlike the appraisal Mr. Darrow often gave her and V when they got into mischief.

"Is this the latest fashion in the mortal realm?" Her lips contorted into a cross between a smirk and a sneer.

"Um, no, Your Majesty." Cheeks burning, Noli bobbed again, remembering Alice's encounters with the Queen of Hearts when in Wonderland. *Curtsey while you're thinking…*

The queen's elaborate coiffure sparkled with what looked like tiny diamonds, and she wore an elaborate gold crown with clockhand-like spires tooled with the same five-ring symbol hanging on the tapestry behind the throne. Her necklace resembled a golden snowflake, the stone in the center a translucent gold, like a clear, polished piece of amber.

"I see. Do you normally run about in your undergarments?" She frowned.

"Um, no, Your Majesty." Noli traced her toe along the inlaid marble floor, trying to avoid eye contact, humiliation saturating her entire being. "I ... I didn't have time to grab my dress before I fled." What must the queen think of her?

"I see." Her expression became something nearly kind, but it didn't reach those hard eyes. "Why don't you come with me? I'll find something for you to wear, we'll have some tea and breakfast, and you can tell me all about it. Don't fret; you're safe now." She smiled again, but it seemed rehearsed.

The queen walked toward the far side of the hall, where she'd entered. When she noticed that Noli still stood there, she stopped. "Come along."

Not knowing what else to do, Noli followed.

....

"Much better, don't you think? Turn." Queen Tiana eyed her, nodding in what Noli hoped was satisfaction. She was tired of trying on ensembles. Currently, she was modeling the fourth.

Dutifully, she turned, having mastered this long ago. Her mother often had her try on half-made dresses so she'd have an idea of how things might look. The pale pink silk dress rustled softly. Its construction reminded her a bit of a nightdress, as did the dark pink ruffles at the cuffs and hem. The one-piece garment got its shape from the dark pink underbust corset with light pink piping worn atop the dress, like a bodice.

"Much better." The queen clasped her hands together in delight, still clutching the small mechanical dog, whose tail wagged.

But it was so *pink*. Personally, Noli liked the green dress she'd tried on previously. Apparently the queen wasn't fond of green.

She stifled a yawn, longing for a brief nap to clear her head. "I'm glad you approve, Your Majesty."

"That necklace doesn't go with the neckline, as striking as it is. Why don't we find you another?" The queen's voice seemed insincere. She stroked her toy dog's head.

Warning bells clanged in Noli's head. "Why *do* both you and Kevighn want me to remove it? I'd like to know exactly how it protects me from faeries." She put a protective hand over it.

The queen's laughter reminded her of champagne bubbles popping in a glass. "Perhaps it's an amulet against the likes of Kevighn, but *I'm* the high queen." She shrugged as if she found the notion utterly and totally ludicrous. "If you wish to look like some country bumpkin, I suppose it's your prerogative."

"How does the dog work? Is he mechanical or steam powered?" She drew close but didn't touch it. It was small, like a puppy, and made entirely of metal. The dog's tongue lolled as its eyes focused on Noli. Eerie.

"Isn't she charming? I call her LuLu." The dog's ears moved. "She's made entirely of clockwork. She winds up through her tail." Her voice rose in pitch and grew excited like a little girl, cheeks flushing.

Noli smiled back, taking in the marvelous toy. Did it walk? "It's wondrous."

"Now, come along." The queen and her dog left the room.

It was a command, not a request, and Noli scurried after her to keep up. "Come along" seemed to be the queen's favorite phrase, and it always sounded a bit condescending. Kevighn had never made her feel like a mere mortal.

Unfortunately, Kevighn had proved to be a liar extraordinaire. If she saw him again, she'd smack the lying cad.

The queen led her to a sumptuous parlor. The splendor of the ornate furniture, the art on the walls, and the chandelier of colored glass made the parlor of her mother's house seem like a hovel. It also made her miss home even more. This was her one chance to convince the queen to send her back to Los Angeles. She'd need to be articulate, concise, and most of all, polite.

Taking a deep breath, she composed her argument in her mind.

"You look deep in thought." The queen's voice roused her from her musing. "Please have a seat; you must be hungry and tired." She gestured to a little table set for two, complete with a shiny brass teapot. Next to the table was a roaring fire that just happened to be purple.

LuLu trotted to a little purple cushion next to the fire, lay down, and went to sleep.

Fatigue was now creeping through Noli's bones. The

back of her head thudded. Reaching up, she massaged it. That would teach her to not accept strong drink from fast-talking rogues.

"Tea." The queen clapped her hands.

Little legs, reminiscent of a spider, popped out of the teapot. The teapot crawled over to the queen's cup and tilted, pouring golden liquid into the teacup without spilling a drop.

Noli watched in fascination. Magic? Mechanics? Both?

"Noli's as well," the queen told it. She added honey from a gold and jeweled pot to her tea.

The teapot scurried across the table to Noli and filled her cup with tea. It returned to its place on the table and the legs disappeared into the pot.

Now that was something she wanted to take apart.

Parched, Noli took a sip from the elaborately painted cup, which was so delicate she could see light through it. Remembering Kevighn's words, she eyed the little pink and green cakes on the shiny brass tiered tray. Her stomach rumbled. Did it matter, at this point? She clung to the hope that he'd lied about faery food, or if it *was* truth, that the queen had the ability to fix it.

"Try one. They are quite splendid." The queen took one for herself. Everything about her was elegant and noble in a way that even the Bostonian blue bloods failed to match. She also seemed so young in many ways, yet old in others. Kevighn had implied that his people aged differently than mortals.

"I … I'm not hungry, Your Majesty." Noli's stomach gurgled, betraying her. Cake for breakfast? Why not?

The queen's lips pursed. "Do you think I would allow anything to happen to you?"

"Kevighn explained that you consider those like me … special." Noli busied herself by adding honey to her teacup.

"Indeed." The queen took a sip of tea, pinky up. "You practically glow."

"Do I?"

"Not everyone can sense the Spark, you know."

"So the Spark is real? How does it work?"

"I do not know the whys and wherefores. It simply is. Some mortals have it, most don't." The queen's expression became sisterly. "Your own people may not understand you. Traditionally, they don't—especially with the women. Men with the Spark don't fare much better; most mortals only realize their genius *after* their deaths. Sad, really."

Noli's brow furrowed as she thought of several artists, writers, and musicians that described. She took a slow sip of her tea and then blurted out a thought that had been nagging at her all morning.

"Your Majesty, Kevighn Silver told me he finds things for you. But as you have the wild hunt, why do you need him?"

Something flickered in the queen's eyes. "My, you are a clever one, aren't you? Kevighn handles the more delicate affairs; after all, I could hardly send the wild hunt into the mortal realm, now could I?"

Something about her tone, her face, made something

click in Noli's mind. Her heart sank and her hands shook, making the tea in the cup slosh over the sides onto the white brocade tablecloth. "Kevighn was *looking* for me ... why?"

"Not for you, specifically. But a girl with the Spark, yes. As I told you, we value your kind here. We find those who are unloved and unappreciated and bring them here—not unlike the stories you mortals tell about our people."

"You really steal children and leave changelings who waste away and die in their place?" Noli looked at the queen in horror. Did some simulacrum lie in her cot at Findlay, doing her chores and lessons, pretending to *be* her?

The queen laughed in a way that made Noli feel utterly stupid and waved her hands in amusement. "No, no. I said *not unlike*, not that they were completely accurate."

"I'm not unhappy or unloved, Your Majesty," Noli said quickly. "I never wished to leave the mortal realm, only that dreadful school. What I'd like most is to go home to my mother in Los Angeles. Please, Your Majesty, I beg of you, send me home. I simply wish to go home." She tried to keep her words from sounding like a wail—or a whine.

"There, there, dear." The queen patted her arm. "But didn't your parents scold you, not understand, try to make you into something you're not?"

Right now, Noli would give anything to hear her mother yell *Magnolia Montgomery Braddock, get down here right now.* "My mother did, sometimes. But only because she loved me, because she wanted to do right by our family."

"No one will scold you here. We'll encourage you, help your talents grow."

The queen didn't seem to understand. Noli tried again, the urgency of the matter building inside her. "She's all the family I have left. I miss her."

"Now, now, you should be happy here. What can I do to make you happy?" Sitting back, she looked at Noli expectantly. "Would you like to see our gardens? Kevighn said you adore gardens."

"Is Kevighn here?" Noli's voice rose in alarm.

"Not right now. You're safe. If you don't wish to see him, I simply won't allow it." Queen Tiana held out her dainty, pale hands in an empty gesture. "After all, I *am* queen. But a young woman like yourself needs friends. Perhaps you'd like to meet some of our young people? Since you seem intrigued by my LuLu, would you like to see my mechanical menagerie?"

A mechanical menagerie sounded tempting, but she must remain focused. "While I do appreciate your hospitality, the only thing I need to be happy is a one-way passage to Los Angeles. Anyplace in Los Angeles will do."

"You should word your requests carefully here," the queen warned. "At this moment, it does not please me to send you back."

Noli nearly dropped her teacup in her lap. "But you must."

Queen Tiana bristled, her eyes narrowing. "I'm queen; I don't have to do anything anyone asks—especially a slip of a mortal girl."

"But you're the only one who can send me home," Noli pleaded.

A pained sigh escaped the queen's lips. She folded her hand on the table. "I had hoped to acquaint you with this place better before I broached the subject, but you give me no choice."

Heart pounding, fear crept through Noli, freezing her to the chair. "Am I really stuck here because I ate faery food, like Kevighn said?"

"Kevighn is untrustworthy and a liar." The queen waved her hands as if dismissing the idea he might be anything but. "I tolerate him because he's good at finding things. You see, I need your assistance on an imminent matter."

Cocking her head, Noli blinked at the preposterous notion. "Me? What could I possibly do to help you?" She felt her panic subsiding. There was something about the queen that kept making Noli want to trust her—maybe it was because Kevighn *didn't* seem to trust her, or want Noli to have contact with her.

"Oh, you have no idea what you are capable of. Really, the fate of the Otherworld lies in your hands." Queen Tiana's grin was reminiscent of a tiger at the zoo.

A plan was forming in Noli's mind, and she tried to phrase her statement carefully. "That sounds very important. If I happen to agree to help you, will you send me back to Los Angeles in a timely manner when I'm finished? I don't wish to be gone long—a few weeks at most."

She didn't want to return to find everyone she knew and loved to be long dead.

A satisfied look crossed the queen's face as she steepled her hands. "Magnolia, darling, you are correct; it's an imperative matter. If you agree to help me, every whim and desire shall be yours."

TWENTY-THREE

A Rescue, of Sorts

In the pink, early morning light, Steven trudged through the Otherworld. He was using his sigil as a compass, trying to find Noli. In that it was made of magic, the Otherworld wasn't precisely linear. Portals generally provided the quickest way to get from one place to another, but even then it became a complex dance. More than once he backtracked, going to a different destination than the one he'd originally thought he needed.

As he made his way through the wildwood, he became surer of where Noli dwelled. The presence of the wild hunt made sense. *She'd* sent it after Noli. He really had hoped to avoid the high queen. In the eyes of his people, he was still a child, so she couldn't do anything that would prevent him from reclaiming his kingdom. Yet.

It still dredged up memories best forgotten.

She might even be expecting him. Kevighn Silver might not recognize which house Noli's sigil represented, but Queen Tiana would.

The magic shifted around him, tightening and loosening. Like the previous times, he couldn't tell what the shift meant—only that she still hadn't been bound.

What *would* he do once he found her? If he took the intended sacrifice, even if Noli hadn't been bound yet, he'd be responsible for finding a replacement. He resolved to first rescue Noli, then figure out everything else. Noli might have an idea what to do.

A shudder ran through him as he passed the Lake of Sorrows, setting every fiber of his being on edge. Something seemed amiss with the magic there, seemed broken. Soon after, he spied the bridge marking the division between the outermost regions of the high palace and the wildwood. The sigil pointed him directly toward the palace. Steven sighed in resignation. He hadn't imagined his return to the Otherworld would be like this.

This wasn't for his family honor. This was for Noli.

Taking a deep breath, he staved off memories of this place, of his mother. Then he crossed the bridge into the territory of the high queen.

• • • • • • • •

Kevighn was halfway to San Francisco when he decided that a visit to the Red Pearl could wait. The high queen wanted him out of the way, but he cared too much about Noli to throw her to the hounds.

Maybe he'd been huntsman too long. He liked to think all his experience made him immune to emotion. But perhaps the opposite held true.

He stood at the edge of the Lake of Sorrows. Despite its name, it was a pretty place, with its expansive depths, weeping trees, and the many creatures that called it home. More than one woman—mortal and otherwise—had been wooed by him on its shores, or out on its depths in a rowboat.

Where had he gone wrong with Annabelle? She hadn't been the first to discover where her fate truly lay. But no one had done anything of that sort before.

He picked up a rock and skipped it, watching it jump eleven times across the water before it sank below the silvery surface.

What *would* he do about Noli—tell her the truth and reason with her, as some suggested he do with the girls? The very thought made him laugh.

As if any mortal would give their life to save his people.

Shoving his hands into his pockets, Kevighn walked back toward the palace. He'd start with an apology; maybe bring her flowers. The palace greenhouse probably contained some rare bloom he hadn't shown her yet.

When he emerged from the trees, he spied someone crossing the bridge. The man wore mortal clothing and had a shock of blond hair that would make Creideamh itch for a hairbrush. Intently marching ahead, he held something in his outstretched palm. Interesting.

Stealthily, Kevighn trailed the intruder. It quickly became clear that the interloper was no mortal—or man. Not quite. What was this boy doing?

Wait. Perhaps this was Noli's V.

Rubbing his hands together in glee, Kevighn continued to shadow the boy. The whelp was too immersed in his task to notice that he was being followed.

••••••••

"Oh, my." Noli stood in the center of the garden. No words could describe its beauty. Hedges made of unfamiliar plants formed elaborate shapes. Blooms she'd never be able to describe in mere words filled the air with intoxicating perfume. Yet for some reason it made her miss Creideamh's simple garden—and her own little plot in her backyard in Los Angeles. Hopefully V had remembered to water it.

"They are lovely, aren't they?" The queen clasped her hands under her chin in posed delight, LuLu tucked under her arm. She rode on a golden jewel-encrusted, horseless chariot that floated above the ground but didn't have wings like the Pixy, or solar panels like a hoverboard. It didn't even puff steam like an auto. "You are free to use the gardens during your stay here. I've even arranged for you to have a room with a private garden."

A room? She didn't want to be here that long. But a nap did sound tempting.

"What exactly do you need me to do, Your Majesty?

If I am to agree to help you, I need to know about the task at hand." Every time she'd asked this, the queen had sidestepped the question, employing distraction much like Kevighn. Perhaps it was an Otherworld technique. Being mortal didn't make her stupid—or lesser.

"For the moment, I simply want you to enjoy yourself and be happy. We'll talk more about it later." Queen Tiana stretched out her hand as she floated along the path. "Some of my courtiers are playing a game in the center garden. Why don't we join them? We have many gardens here, including ones representing each of the courts."

Without waiting for Noli, the queen glided away on her chariot. Two guards in gold and purple livery trailed them, swords at their sides.

"What do the five circles mean, Your Majesty? I keep seeing them everywhere," she asked as she tried to keep pace.

"Oh, those represent the five courts. The outer circles represent fire, water, air, and earth, with the high court uniting them in the center. But that's so boring." She waved Noli off with an ungloved hand. "Let's go see what the ladies are playing today. I want you to meet them."

"Splendid," Noli lied. Courtiers? Would she ever escape mindless ladies? "Could we see the different gardens first?"

"We'll pass fire and water on the way."

The water garden was just as she imagined—a series of streams and ponds filled with water lilies and other aquatic flowers. A few children played a game with a ball under the watchful eye of what looked like a governess with a sword.

"There are children at court?" Realizing how idiotic

she sounded, Noli fidgeted. Of course there'd be children. She could hardly expect them to emerge fully-grown from flowers.

Queen Tiana waved at the children, who waved back. "We adore children."

"Do you have any, Your Majesty?" Noli clamped her mouth shut as the queen's expression tightened. Her mother would be ashamed of her uncouth manners. "I ... I beg your pardon. That was a very personal question."

"I do have children, but they're not here at court."

"Oh, do you miss them? I miss my mother so much." Perhaps Noli could use this as a bargaining tool. Surely, as a mother, the queen could understand.

"I do." For a moment the queen looked far away, then her expression hardened, her eyes flashing. The look disappeared as quickly as it had appeared, and she stroked LuLu's furless head. "Let's think of more pleasant things. Come along; the fire garden is quite the sight."

A sea of red, orange, and yellow flowers, looking like a cross between orchids and roses but smelling of lilies, greeted them in the fire garden. A river of molten sand cut through it, its heat searing her as they walked past.

The center garden burst with purple and gold blossoms, clearly the queen's colors. A group of strangely dressed, giggling women were playing a game, with what looked like umbrellas and translucent golden globes that seemed to have a life of their own.

It reminded Noli of croquet, both as they played it in Boston and as described in the book *Alice in Wonderland*.

The point of the game seemed to be to hit the ball, with the curved part of the umbrella-looking mallet, through one of the many hoops decorating the lawn. Only the hoops weren't made of metal or sentient playing cards. Looking like a cross between a wood faery and a walking stick insect, they stood about two feet high when not hunched over in an arch, and *moved* when the women hit the balls, which caused fits of giggling. The ball seemed to move this way and that with no correlation to where it had been hit, as if it was driven by a tiny, demented creature.

"Doesn't that look like such fun, Magnolia?" the queen cooed from her perch.

Not really. The women didn't hit many through the arches, and they giggled a lot. It made her want to retch. Hadn't she left all this twittering nonsense behind? For the first time since arriving in the Otherworld, she felt as if she'd fallen through the looking glass.

And their clothes! One woman wore skintight black trousers. Despite their practical implications, trousers on a woman were even more outrageous than wearing a corset on the outside of one's clothing. While she'd heard that some women did such things in the mortal realm, Noli certainly had never met one. After all, she could do everything she wanted to in a dress.

Another courtier wore an asymmetrical dress festooned with large buckles. It seemed to be missing chunks of fabric, revealing vast portions of skin. A third wore a bustled skirt made of completely sheer fabric, a bodice with nothing underneath, and long, fingerless gloves.

The two in skirts both possessed big blue eyes, heart-shaped faces, and straight brown hair worn loose and strewn with flowers. Their large breasts were disproportionate to their slender frames. The one in trousers had amber eyes and wore her black hair in a pompadour, covered by a tiny hat.

"Hello, ladies." The queen floated across the immaculate lawn toward them. "How's the game?"

"Splendid, Your Majesty," the woman in the bustled skirt replied as she hit the ball toward one of the arches, which promptly moved so that the ball missed. She erupted into giggles.

"Ladies, I'd like you to meet Magnolia," the queen announced. "Magnolia, please meet Breena." The giggling courtier waved. Noli couldn't help but wave back. "Nissa." The queen gestured to the one in the dress, who bobbed a greeting. "And we can't forget Donella." Noli smiled, and the woman in the trousers looked down her nose at her.

"Would you like to join us?" Breena asked, offering Noli her umbrella-stick.

"Oh yes." Nissa clapped her hands under her chin in delight. "You simply must try."

"Perhaps I could see the rest of the gardens?" Noli wanted to get away from these women and their inane game. She could feel herself getting stupider by the moment just from being around them.

"Oh, no, I must insist." Taking the mallet from Breena, the queen floated over and handed it to her.

"You hit the ball with it." Nissa mimed the movement.

"Do you ever actually get the ball through the hoop?" Noli hefted the umbrella-stick in her hand.

Donella scoffed. "You *lose* points if you get it through the hoop."

"Well, that's one way to play," Noli muttered.

Nissa placed the ball on the ground. Taking the stick, Noli hit the ball, which headed straight for one of the hoops—which promptly moved.

"Yay, you did it," Breena clapped.

Nissa hopped up and down. "I knew you could."

"It's not that difficult of a game," Donella sneered. "My turn."

She, too, missed the hoop. But it wasn't hard to miss the hoops when they could walk and the ball had a life of its own. Noli still wasn't sure how they kept score, if they did. Could Nissa and Breena even count, or would their heads explode?

They continued to play the insipid game, Noli sharing Breena's mallet, the queen not actually participating but staying perched on her chariot, holding LuLu, while a man in purple held a silken canopy over her head and another fanned her with a giant purple feathered fan.

"I'm sorry, you're not permitted here," she heard one of the guards yell from the side entrance.

Noli turned to see what the commotion was.

"Yes I am," a familiar but out-of-place voice retorted. "Let me pass."

Noli watched as someone tried to muscle his way through the guards blocking the gate to the garden. The queen stopped talking to Nissa and eyed the scene with interest, but didn't say anything.

Odd. The voice really sounded familiar. But it wasn't Kevighn, and she didn't know anyone else in the Other-world.

Another voice joined the melee. "Who are you and what are you doing here?"

That was Kevighn.

"Where is she, Kevighn Silver?" The familiar voice held authority, command even.

"Who?" Kevighn scoffed.

What was Kevighn doing here? The queen said she'd keep him away. Noli's hands curled into fists. Yes, just like she'd promised herself, she'd give Kevighn a good smack right in front of the queen and her simpering ladies, pro-priety be hanged.

Breena and Nissa craned their necks, straining to see who was arguing with Kevighn on the other side of the guards. Donella perked up at the mention of Kevighn's name.

"Noli, where's Noli?" the other person demanded.

Noli stood on her tiptoes to see if she could spy the interloper. All she caught was a shock of pale hair.

Wait, could it be? Her heart pounded.

The guards unsheathed their swords. Taking a pen from his pocket, the man waved it, and before her eyes it became a full-sized sword.

"Oh, what a splendid trick." Breena clapped.

"Do it again," Nissa called as the man began to sword-fight with the guards.

The queen simply watched, nonplussed.

Noli's heart skipped again as she realized who the swordsman was. How *had* V gotten here? But he was here.

As V and the guard fought in the garden gate, Kevighn hurried toward them. He didn't have a sword—or even his bow—and was dressed in the same gentlemanly gear she'd seen him in back in San Francisco.

He bowed in front of the queen's chariot. "Are you all right, Your Majesty? Did that rogue threaten you?"

Swords clanged in the background. V seemed to be winning.

Queen Tiana brushed Kevighn off with the wave of her fine-boned hand. "You may rise. I'm fine."

For some reason, the fight going on before her didn't seem to bother the queen in the slightest. Perhaps men with swords often burst in and started fighting with her guards.

"Noli, are you all right?" With a concerned expression on his face, Kevighn laid a hand on her shoulder. Breena and Nissa tittered in delight, and Donella threw her nose in her air, obviously jealous.

How dare he? He'd tried to seduce her. He'd lied to her. Noli felt anger whirl up inside her.

Her hand flew out, smacking Kevighn across the face. Hard.

His hands went to his face. The three courtiers looked on with horror, especially Donella. The queen smirked in amusement and muttered something to LuLu.

"What was that for?" Kevighn's voice dripped with hurt, eyes wide.

"Noli took a step backward, giving him a daring look. "Stay away from me. You're nothing but a rogue and a liar."

"Yes, stay away from her, huntsman." V ran toward them, sword extended.

"Oooh, he's cute," Breena whispered.

"Who is he? I've never seen him before," Nissa added.

Donella crossed her arms. "He's a little young, if you ask me."

"Who *are* you?" Kevighn strode up to V, eyeing the sword in his hands. It was a grand sword; a big green jewel bedecked the hilt.

"V!" Noli's heart burst with excitement. "I didn't recognize you at first, without your glasses." She fastened her arms around him, even with the sword still in his hand. "I'm so glad you're here. I missed you so much."

"I missed you too, Noli. Did they hurt you?" He held her tightly to him, which reminded her a bit of her dreams. He and Kevighn contrasted like the sun and moon.

"What are you doing here? How did you find me? Where are your glasses?" The words tumbled out. If he'd gotten here, surely they could get home.

"We'll talk in a bit; I wanted to make sure you were safe." He repositioned her, so that her back pressed against his chest and his sword stood between her and Kevighn.

"I didn't know you fenced," Noli added. Or that he owned a sword … but his pen had *become* a sword. That was so very V. Which was mightier? The thought made her chuckle.

"If I'd told you that, you would have asked me to teach you." His voice grew fond.

"Who are you and why are you here?" Kevighn's eyes narrowed.

The queen looked like the cat in the cream pitcher. "Yes, Prince Stiofán. What are you doing here?"

TWEN+Y-F⊕UR

Prince Stiofán

The courtiers perked at the word "prince." Noli stiffened. Who was Stiofán?

Still on her horseless chariot, looking self-satisfied, the queen approached. Her voice was cool enough to freeze a pond. "Not that I mind. But, if I remember accurately, weren't our parting words something along the lines of 'I'm not returning until I can reclaim what's ours'?"

"I believe you are correct, Your Majesty." V's arms tightened around Noli. "But I didn't expect your huntsman to take what belongs to me."

"You are from a house in exile, and still a child. You have no rights. Unless, of course, you're tired of playing mortal with your father." Queen Tiana sneered, clutching LuLu so tightly that if she were a real dog, she'd yelp.

"Playing mortal? What is she talking about, V?" Noli's mind spun.

The queen laughed eerily, putting a hand to her lips. "How quaint. You and a mortal. I never should have allowed you to join your father in exile. You probably picked up all sorts of bad habits."

A lump formed in Noli's throat as the meaning of the situation hit her. Her voice shook. "Is what she says true, V?"

Was her life nothing but a web of lies?

"Yes, Noli. I'm not a mortal like you. I'll explain everything in a moment, I promise." His green eyes shone in the sunlight with fondness and perhaps just a hint of regret.

"What?" Pushing herself out of his arms, she put her hands on her hips. "Steven Darrow, what the world is going on here?"

"Yes," Kevighn added, his eyes narrowing in anger. He took a menacing step toward them. "What is going on here? I still don't know who this is."

"He's a prince," Breena told him sagely, still holding the mallet.

"A young one," Nissa added.

"Indeed." The queen gave a regal nod. "Ladies, Kevighn, I'd like you to meet Prince Stiofán. Or perhaps I should say, the prince formerly known as Stiofán, since he chose to go into exile with his father, the former king of the earth court." Her lips puckered in distaste. "'Steven'? What a horrible bastardization of your name."

V's face tightened and he suddenly looked fatigued. "Please, Your Majesty, I've come for Noli. I'd like her back."

"I'm not going anywhere until someone explains." A firestorm of anger burned inside Noli. First Kevighn's lies; now V's.

"You're not taking her anyplace, *prince*." Kevighn's eyes flashed with anger.

"Yes, I am." V took Noli's hand. "This isn't the place to explain. Come with me?"

"Why? So you can lie to me, too?" Noli didn't bother to hide her hurt as she yanked her hand away.

"Do you really think I'd let you take her anywhere?" The queen shot V a haughty look as she resumed petting LuLu.

"With all due respect, yes, I do." V's eyes narrowed at the queen. It really was odd seeing him without glasses.

"Why do you all do nothing but lie? I don't want to be part of your games. I only want to go home." Tired of being here, tired of being lied to, and just plain tired, Noli wrested herself out of V's grasp and marched past Kevighn, the bewildered Breena and Nissa, and the disgusted Donella. She ignored V, the queen, and the guards, disregarding their shouts as she fled from the garden.

When she stopped running, Noli found herself in what could only be the air garden, filled with will-o'-the-wisps and pussy willows. A breeze blew through, soft like whispers—or kisses.

"Noli, wait." V ran into the garden after her, sword still in hand.

She turned her back to him, a lump forming in her throat. "Stay away from me."

"No." He came up behind her, pressing her back against his chest. "Never."

"You lied. Everyone lies here. I want to go home." Turning around to face him, Noli poked him in the chest with her index finger. "You know how I don't like to be toyed with, Steven Darrow."

"I'm sorry, I'm so sorry." His eyes gleamed with regret as he entwined his fingers with hers. "I know you want to go home. If we're to figure everything out, I need you to come with me. I didn't lie to you. I never said I was mortal."

"You hid large chunks of truth." She wanted to lay her head on his shoulder, like always, despite her anger and confusion. V had always been the one constant thing in her life.

"I hid them from everyone—on my father's orders. He doesn't know I'm here." V pulled her to him, and she let him.

"No?" Laying her head on his shoulder, she stifled a yawn. V's fingers traced her neck, sending little shivers down her spine.

"No?"

"No. Besides, would you have believed me if I'd told you?" His fingers found the medallion chain around her neck and traced it. It felt like her last dream.

The stories, all the odd things he'd said … it all made sense now. "Does the faery tree in my backyard have little wood faeries in it? Will I be able to see them when I come home?"

"Yes, it's a real faery tree," he told her gently, as if the very words might break. "But no wood faeries live in it.

I've had a devil of a time trying to keep clans of them from settling in it, too."

She looked up at him, blinking. "Really? Why?"

"Because it's a nice tree—and who wouldn't want to live in a tree cared for by someone like you? I kept them away because I feared they would draw attention to you."

Noli stepped back from his embrace as if burned. "What? You know that I'm all Sparky and whatnot?"

V looked around and held a finger to his lips. He lowered his voice. "I do, but it's important that you don't let the queen know I can sense it."

"Why?" Her hand went to the necklace and her eyes narrowed at him. "Did you know this would happen?"

"No." He took a step, closing the gap between them. "I didn't think Kevighn would find you. Strange things lurk in San Francisco, things even more dangerous than Kevighn. I gave you my medallion to protect you from them. I see you didn't take it off."

She fingered it, looking at the green stone and gold design, not him. "I do listen to you sometimes. Kevighn and the queen keep trying to get me to take it off."

V cocked his head, a lock of blond hair falling over his unspectacled eyes. "Do they?"

"Is it really-bad-faery repellent?" She felt a bit ridiculous saying it out loud.

He laughed and it reached all the way to his eyes. "No. It's the mark of my house—my family crest. That's also why it looks like a tree." Taking his own medallion out, he traced it with his finger. "These are the branches, these are the roots, all intertwined, and the stone is its heart."

V tucked his medallion back under his shirt. He waved his sword in the air and, before her eyes, it shrunk and became a pen again, which he slipped into his shirt pocket.

Noli grinned. "Is your pen collection really a sword collection?"

"Yes. Nice trick, isn't it?" He grinned boyishly and she felt the rest of her anger at him disappear. It was always difficult to be mad at V for long, especially when he smiled.

"You still owe me an explanation." Noli put her hands on her hips.

"I never meant to deceive you, only to keep you safe." Reaching up, he tucked a piece of hair behind her ear. His fingers trailed down her cheek, making her skin blaze.

"Because they like girls with the Spark here." Noli sighed. "I still don't know what exactly the queen needs my help with."

V's eyes widened. "She asked for your help? Did you agree?"

"Not precisely."

"Good. We really need to talk. I'll answer all your questions if you answer all of mine. Please, come with me?" He took her hand, like so many times before. Only this time it made her toes tingle.

"Then I may go home?" She sighed, suppressing a yawn. "I just want to go home."

"We'll figure it out together. I promise." He put her hand to his lips and kissed it as if she were a fine lady.

"I…"

His lips silenced her. It reminded her of the kisses in her dreams—gentle, sweet, and tasting of nectar. Their lips and tongues danced as his body pressed to hers as if he sought to unite them. Her hands ran over his back, feeling his muscles, him.

V broke it off. "I missed you so much."

"I…" Noli felt breathless. Her heart raced. It was one thing to kiss him in her dreams…

"This place isn't private, and we really need to talk." V led her toward a different garden gate than the one they'd come through.

Noli's lips burned with desire, as did other places. "Won't they stop us?"

"She'll let us leave, for now."

"Why?" She half-expected guards to come charging into the garden any moment.

V's cheeks colored and he looked at his feet, bashful. "I told her I just wanted to speak with you, and, well…" He kicked the ground. "She *let* me. It surprises me. But, then, there's no hiding from her in the Otherworld. She'll grace us with her presence soon enough." A worried look flashed in his eyes. "Please let me explain?"

"Don't think you can simply come in brandishing a sword, rescue me, kiss me, and everything will be fine. I'm not some ninny from a story." Noli tried to make her voice tough, but she could only think of that kiss.

"If only it were that easy. But we'll figure it all out."

Worry colored his voice, but that was V for you—always fussing about something.

"Promise?" Her heart fluttered like the wings of a wood faery.

V smiled. "Promise."

• • • • • • • •

Steven relished the sensation of holding Noli's rough, tanned hand as he led her through the wildwood and several portals. He knew the queen wouldn't pursue him . . . yet. It still surprised him that no one did—or that she'd allowed him to take Noli in the first place.

"Where are we going?" Her quiet voice didn't tremble.

"We're going to my home. I can't wait to show it to you." He had to give her credit for taking all this so well, but who knew what things she'd endured before his arrival.

"Another palace?"

"Our real home, where I grew up. We spent most of our time there, not at the earth court palace." His face contorted as pain pierced his heart. Coming here, facing *her*, was much more difficult than he'd expected.

She squeezed his hand, the corners of her lips twitching downwards into a slight frown. "I don't understand."

"I don't either, quite honestly." As high queen, Tiana's word was law, unless the magic—or the Bright Lady herself—objected.

"What happened?" Noli swung his hand back and

forth while they walked, reminding him of better, more innocent times.

"The short version is that my father was king of the earth court. He made a decision the high queen objected to, but he wouldn't reverse it. As punishment, she took away his throne, gave it to my uncle, and exiled my father to the mortal realm. As children, James, Elise, and I could have stayed here—with our uncle or with her—but James and I chose to stand by our father, since we understood why he made the decision in the first place." He would have made the same one. "Elise was too little to understand, but my father didn't want to separate us."

Noli took this all in, drinking the information like a plant did water. "Is that why he's so sour? Because once he was king and now he's simply a man?"

"Yes. We all lost a lot that day."

Noli squeezed his hand again. "Your home, your life."

His mother.

"Coming to the mortal realm, no longer being a prince and just being a boy, was difficult. To have to conceal our nature, use our magic in secret…" Steven looked away. "To be forced to hide in shame, even from those of our world who walk the mortal realm freely. Unlike them, we can't return at a whim."

"But you came for me?" Noli's face scrunched in confusion. "Will you get in trouble?"

Steven laughed. It was such a dire situation, and she was worried about punishment? That was his Noli. Too soon, she'd understand. "My father will be angry, but I needed to protect you."

"Why?" She looked at him with questioning eyes.

Stopping, he pulled her to him, planting a kiss on top her head. He'd missed her so much. "You know the answer."

She cocked her head, a lock of hair falling in her face. "Truly?"

The way she said it sounded so fragile, like she didn't dare believe it.

Stopping, he cupped her face with his hand and gazed deep into her beautiful, steel-colored eyes. "Truly."

"Why?" She blinked.

"Because you're my best friend. My creative, rose-growing, mechanic of a best friend. The one with whom I share my secrets and discuss books. Is it really such a stretch for me to think of you as even more?"

Noli's rough hand squeezed his in return. "No, because I feel the same."

They walked hand in hand. When they reached the edge of the property, Steven inhaled the rich woody scent. Home.

"You wanted to return and take your kingdom back? Like in a story?" Noli studied him with her big eyes.

"One day, yes. That was the plan—it still is, really."

"Will your uncle give it back?"

"Not willingly. My uncle had wanted the earth court throne for a long time. It's ... it's complicated." It was difficult to speak of it, even to Noli.

"I'm confused." Her nose wrinkled and he found the gesture adorable.

"I know, and I'm sorry. Desperately, I feared someone would discover how you shine with the Spark and seek to use you." His face crumpled as he kicked the ground. "Some protector I turned out to be."

Noli stopped. Gently, like feathers, her fingers brushed his face in a tentative, exploratory motion. He closed his eyes, drinking in her touch. When he opened them, she held his gaze.

"You came. I wished and wished, and you charged in with your sword like a knight from a story." She grinned.

"As everyone tells me, I'm no knight—or adult—yet. You... you aren't too angry with me, are you?" His belly tightened. "As I said, no one knew about us. Who'd believe it?"

"I... I'm not sure I would have... before all this." Noli held her hands out in an empty gesture, an odd look in her eyes.

He led her toward the grove. Maybe he'd take her to visit his tree and they could check on the wood faeries. Yes, she'd like that.

"I never meant for you to experience this. It uncomplicates and complicates things all at the same time." How would he solve this mess? But he would. He had to.

"How? Kevighn said my talents lay in gardening and fixing things. How could that help the queen? She said the fate of your whole world lay on me." Noli rolled her eyes in disbelief. "I can't save my family, how can I save a kingdom?"

"Unlike them, I'll be completely honest with you—

even if it's unpleasant or hurtful." They entered the grove and she grew in a sharp breath. "It's nice here. Isn't it?"

"It is." She looked around, her eyes widening in wonder. Giant rowan trees, as old as the land itself, towered above them. Soft moss covered the ground. Birds chirped in the distance.

"I ... I like trees and plants, too, Noli. I'd rather be outside than anyplace else. That's just another reason why I enjoy spending time with you. Because we both love the same things."

"You're earth court, right?" She made another darling confused face, scrunching it in an unladylike way. "Does the water court have tails and the air court fly?"

"Some do. My talents lie in trees and plants." Steven touched her face again. He couldn't stop touching her. No longer did he have to. Noli now knew the truth about him, and they knew of her and her beautiful Spark. He no longer had to hide his feelings to protect his secret, or to conceal her Spark.

"And your whole family has these gifts?"

"Pretty much, though everyone's a little different." Elise showed a dangerous propensity toward their mother's gifts. Frightening. Another reason for them to shelter her the way they did.

"Can you speak to trees?" Noli looked up at a tree that seemed to have no end.

"That's how I figured out you were in the Otherworld. The tree at Findlay told me."

Noli's face crumpled and her shoulders drooped. "I

didn't mean to come here. Findlay was so dreadful, and I wished I were anyplace but there, and suddenly I was sitting in some strange garden with faeries. Kevighn promised to help me find my way back to Los Angeles…"

Her words came out rapidly. Pulling her to him, Steven hugged her. "It's not your fault, Noli. It's not your fault."

They sat on the velvety moss under one of the giant trees, his back against the smooth trunk, her in his lap, his arms tight around her. The very weight of her against him made him certain they were no longer children.

He fingered her wayward curls. The sunlight streamed through the trees, making it shine. The pink gown she wore did nothing for her complexion, he observed. She would be radiant in his family's colors.

"Noli, will you tell me everything, from the moment you made your wish to when I found you? Please? If I'm to help you, I need to know every detail—even the ones you may not want to share." He laid a finger on her protesting lips. "I promise I won't get angry."

"Promise?" She looked at him with worried eyes.

His heart sunk and his insides knotted. But he needed to know in order to help her, to keep her, to prevent her from dying yet still save his people. "I promise."

"Very well." Noli said this with resignation, as if it were punishment—or schoolwork. Getting comfortable, she repositioned herself in his lap. "It's a long and strange tale, one I hardly believe myself…"

TWENTY-FIVE

Sometimes the Truth Hurts

Noli told him her tale as they sat under the giant tree. Parts of it sounded ludicrous even to her, and she'd lived through it. Would V believe her? He had to. After all, he was her best friend—who always believed her, stuck by her, and helped her out of sticky situations.

Despite his warning not to, she left parts out. Like the dreams where they kissed. Like Kevighn getting her drunk and taking off her gown. Kevighn and V were so different, yet both drew her. That realization made her stomach churn with guilt.

"When Kevighn told me that eating faery food had trapped me here forever, did he speak the truth?" Closing her eyes, she prayed it was just another one of the huntsman's clever lies.

He put his hand on hers. "I'm afraid so. We might be able to figure that one out, though. Right now it's the least of our problems."

"What? I only want to go home." She sniffed.

V cupped her face with his hand. "What things did you eat? Again, nothing you tell me will make me angry, but you can't leave anything out if we're to solve all this."

As always, he was the voice of reason. She had full confidence in his abilities to figure this out—whatever it was.

"Um," she thought for a moment. "Tea, berries, little fancy desserts, soups, stews, porridge—all manners of things."

"Anything...harder?" Trailing down her face, her neck, his fingers toyed with the chain of her medallion.

Her cheeks warmed and her shoulders hunched. "I got angry with Kevighn when I overheard him speaking with the queen in his cabin. He brought out some sort of honey wine while he explained and I got a little..."

Noli averted her eyes in embarrassment. Ladies didn't do such things—and to think that V, her best friend, was an actual prince.

"You got a little tipsy, did you? Like we did the time my father had the dinner party?" His voice held no blame, and his fingers ran up and down her arm in a feathery motion. "Ask James about the time we snuck into the great hall at the earth palace after a feast and decided to have a taste from every glass left on the banquet table." V grinned. "I've never had such a headache in my life. Mum was so angry."

Noli laughed, picturing the event as clearly in her mind as if it were a moving picture. "Where *is* James? I'm surprised he didn't join you."

"He'll turn up eventually; after all, he's the better swordsman." V chuckled. "We couldn't simply barge into the Otherworld without proof. James went to see if you'd run to your brother, or to your friend Charlotte's."

"He went to see Jeff and Charlotte? I hope they're both well. I miss them so much, and I'm especially worried about Charlotte. Her uncle is more dreadful than even Findlay House. He hurts her." Noli shuddered. How could anyone do such things to his own niece?

"I'm sure she's fine." V rubbed his hands up and down her arms. "After you got tipsy, what happened?"

Would he be so calm and gentle when she told him? "Kevighn … he … " She closed her eyes, as if that would change things. "He said things to me." Things she found scary and exciting at the same time. "Then he kissed me … "

Memories of his kisses, his touch, choked her, cutting off her voice.

His arms tightened around her, bringing her close enough to lay her head on his shoulder. "Did … did you lie with Kevighn?"

"No. Of course not." Noli's head popped up as she bit back disbelief and outrage and her arms crossed over her chest. "What sort of girl do you think I am? I might be mortal, I might be a hoyden, but I'm no dollymop."

V held his hands up in surrender. "I know, I know. You're none of those things. I know of his reputation—though I've never heard of him having to get someone drunk. If anything, you should be proud you've resisted his charms."

"He got my dress off, so I'm not that good." She averted her eyes. "After I ran from him, I got lost and the wild hunt found me. I met the queen while in my petticoats. Oh, the scandal!" Noli gave a little laugh. "Do you think I could start a new trend in Los Angeles?"

He grinned. "Meeting Queen Tiana while in your undergarments must have been quite the sight. So, the wild hunt brought you to the palace, and you met the queen, then I found you?"

"Thank you for rescuing me when you did; that game was dreadful." Realizing what she'd said, Noli put her hand to her mouth. "I'm not supposed to say that to you, am I?" She couldn't recall what happened if you thanked the fae, but odds were it wasn't nice.

"I won't take advantage of you, but others might—you didn't thank Kevighn or the queen, did you?" V's brow furrowed.

She smoothed his forehead with her fingertips. "No, I didn't thank them, but I forgot with you. I still see you as V, as my best friend, not some prince, even an exiled one. *Prince.* It still sounds so strange."

"I only want to be V when I'm with you. I do have to say…" His eyes met hers as a smile played on his soft, kissable lips. "I would like to be a little more than your best friend." Taking her hand, he kissed her palm, a slow, lingering kiss that left her gasping for breath even with his lips nowhere near hers.

"What?" The word caught in her throat.

"Did you dream of me, Noli?" His lips brushed her ear and warm breath grazed her neck, setting her skin ablaze. "I dreamt of you."

"I did. They were … " Her toes curled at the memory of her dreams, those kisses. "Pleasant."

"Pleasant? I seem to remember them being far more than merely *pleasant*." His green eyes danced in amusement as his hands caressed her body. Up and down, up and down. Rhythmic and hypnotic, they didn't touch any special parts of her, but warmed her all the same.

"You … you dreamt of me?" It seemed wrong, wicked even, that two different men could cause her body to react so.

"I did. I think we actually dreamed the same dream. We'd sit in your tree house and you wore only your nightdress, and we'd … " His lips met hers, demonstrating the kisses they'd shared in her dreams. First his lips toyed with hers, as if greeting them, then it deepened, their tongues dancing.

Noli's eyes widened and she broke off the kiss, her mind reeling. "We shared the dreams?"

V's cheeks pinked. "Um, yes. I'm afraid I'm to blame. I tried to dream-search for you, but you kept ignoring my questions and taking control. You liked kissing better than talking."

The last dream came back to her and she jumped up, clenching her fists. "You fiend. I cannot believe you."

"I'm sorry. I don't understand why you got so angry, but I didn't mean to betray your trust in any way. I needed to find you, but you kept getting me … distracted. " His face crumpled and Noli felt a tinge of regret.

"You know, I like kissing you as well," he added as he stood up.

He did? Her heart did a little dance of joy.

"So there's no other girl?" Her belly flipped a little at the thought.

"Is that what you thought?" He blinked in surprise. "Um, no, there's no other girl." He closed the space between them. "There's no girl but you, Noli. Promise."

All the sudden it became hard to breathe, and it felt as if the ground had evaporated, leaving her floating in midair. Only her. V liked her. *Her*. Hoyden, auto-fixing, troublemaking her.

"You are forgiven." The dreams were real? That, too, terrified and excited her. Several different emotions swirled inside her, like a tempest in a teapot.

V came up behind her and pressed his chest to her back, his arms draping around her like a necklace.

"Why do they want me? What can I help them with? Would you tell me?" she asked.

"It might be easier to show you." Taking her hand, V led her in a different direction. They walked and walked until he stopped short, pulling her toward him. "Careful."

She looked down. They stood at a precipice. Instead of there being a river below them, or a crevice, there was … nothing. It reminded her a little of the chaos that lay outside the gates of the garden she'd first arrived in. "What *is* that?"

"Wild magic. It's what makes everything here—and what keeps us alive." He gestured to the trees behind them.

"Wait." Noli's mind spun round and round like a runaway carousel. "Everything here is made of magic?"

"Just about. The magic makes it. This is magic in its natural, wild state."

"What?" She blinked again

V laughed. "I'll spare you from all that. Basically, the magic is sentient."

"It's *alive?* How can magic be alive?" Noli cocked her head, trying to understand the science behind it.

"It just is. Actually, it's a *her*. The magic is the land. Also, what you call aether is actually bits of magic leaking into the mortal realm."

"Oh." Her nose scrunched. So that was literally where the aether in her world came from.

Taking her hand, he led her away from the chasm of nothingness. "Like you and me, the magic has to eat."

Noli laughed. "What does wild magic like for breakfast?"

V's arm snaked around her waist as he led her back the way they came. "Blood."

"What?" Noli gasped.

"Every seven years, a girl is chosen by the high queen's huntsman. She's always a mortal girl on the brink between child and woman, bursting with the Spark, that extra bit of something some mortals have. Usually, she's plucked from some terrible situation and brought here to the Otherworld, to the high palace, where she's plied with gifts and amusements. She's treated like a princess. Everyone comes to see her; everyone wants to be her friend..." His voice trailed off as they left the giant trees and made their way through a hedge maze.

"In exchange for her life, they give her the time of her life?" Dread chilled Noli's soul.

"Yes. The problem I have is that Kevighn tricks these girls, deceiving them until the magic binds them. Once that happens, little can be done to reverse it." The maze ended in a little grove, with a grand tree in the center.

Noli stopped dead in her tracks. "Has the magic bound me? Is that what you mean by figuring it all out?" Her words barely eked out as her throat swelled shut with fear.

"No." He came up beside her and put an arm around her waist. "The magic hasn't bound you yet. I'm not sure why—not that I want it to. But the time grows near, and there's still no other girl. That makes things difficult for all of us. I don't want you to be the sacrifice, but someone has to be, soon."

Relief washed over her, but V sounded so concerned, looked so grave. He let go of her and approached the faery tree. No little wood faeries darted about.

"I don't understand." She felt overwhelmed by everything he'd told her.

"Let me show you." V crouched down and his fingers caressed the bark of the giant old tree. It was like the tree at Findlay, only much bigger, and even more gnarled and twisted than her tree in Los Angeles. A few pink star blossoms grew around the base, but not quite like the garden at Findlay. Yet at the same time it seemed just as enchanting—perhaps even more so.

"This is my faery tree, and my father's before that," V told her softly. "Without nourishment, the magic weakens. Eventually, like you and me, if starved, she will die. Magic makes this world, so if she dies, the world goes away. It will return to chaos, then fade into nothing."

He reached into a knothole. When his hand withdrew, it held something. The corners of his lips turned down in a frown. Noli crouched next to him.

"Hold out your hands," he told her.

She extended her hands and V placed something into them, still and cool.

"Right now the magic is weak," he explained. "She hungers, and some of the weaker parts of the land are fading away as the power does. We, too, will fade when she fades completely, even those of us who live in your world. As she weakens, our own magic becomes erratic. Some creatures are sickening and dying." His eyes fell to what lay in her hands, and a somber feeling cloaked her.

In her cupped hands was a tiny, pale wood faery. But she didn't dance around like a drunken firefly; she didn't even glow. Her green wings were lifeless. She simply lay there, unmoving, in her green dress that resembled leaves, her bare feet peeking out. Her brown eyes pleaded with Noli to help, but she seemed too ill to do anything more.

Everything fell into place. Noli felt bile rise in her throat. "If I don't die, everyone else will?"

V put an arm around her and one of his fingers stroked

the golden-brown hair of the faery in her hands. "If *some-one* meeting the requirements doesn't become the sacrifice soon, the entire Otherworld, and all the creatures calling it home, will cease to exist. Not only will we all die, but the mortal realm will be affected too. It relies on the magic that leaks into it from the Otherworld. That's what gives you mortals your creativity. If our magic ceases to exist..."

"Flying figs." The epithet wasn't strong enough, given everything that was at stake. "That's what you mean by figuring it all out together?"

V nodded. "You meet all the qualifications, but the magic hasn't bound you—"

"If we find someone else, quickly, could we fix this?" But it would be too late for this little wood faery. Noli watched the life fade from the little creature in her hands.

"Yes, but..." V sighed heavily. "Kevighn had a lot of trouble finding someone this cycle. Usually the magic doesn't fade, creatures don't die, it's a seamless transition."

"Oh. Who would willingly die to save an entire world?" Her mouth clamped shut. How selfish she sounded.

He shook his head. "Don't even think about it. I don't want you to be the sacrifice any more than I want us all to perish."

She nearly dropped the faery in her hands as a revelation smacked her. "You would die, too."

"I would, along with Elise, James, my father. I... I don't think we need to trick the girls. But no one else agrees with me." Defeat crossed his face as his shoulders rounded.

"What do we do?" Noli whispered, hopelessness pressing

down on her chest like bricks. "I don't want you to die, either. I don't want anyone to die. I ... I just want to go home."

V stroked her cheek with this thumb. "We'll find a way to get you home; we'll find a way to fix the magic. We have to."

But it was too late. The tiny faery in her hands was dead.

TWENTY-SIX

Plans

Kevighn watched the queen pace back and forth in her sitting room, that silly mechanical dog lounging in front of a purple fire. The arrival of the young prince had dealt a blow to his ego—especially when Noli lit up when he appeared, sword brandished, like a knight in shining armor from one of those idiotic mortal stories.

This Prince Stiofán had lied to Noli as well, hiding his true nature. But had she smacked him? Hardly. She *ran* to him. Why did they always fall for princes?

He didn't understand why the queen had allowed Noli to leave with Stiofán, either.

Oh. Interesting.

Kevighn glanced over at the queen. "If I might be so bold as to inquire, what is your plan, Your Majesty?"

"My plan?" She arched an eyebrow, her voice rising in

pitch. "Not only are you the huntsman, but we're in this predicament *because* of you. How are *you* going to fix this?"

Well, his plan involved going back to San Francisco and drowning his sorrows in opium. No matter what happened, Noli was lost to him. Like Creideamh.

Like Creideamh, in the end, Noli would die.

"Well…" She tapped her slippered foot impatiently. "Have you nothing to say for yourself?"

"Me? You're the one who let them go." No sooner had Kevighn spoke than he felt the energy bolt graze his arm, singeing the cloth and burning his flesh, although not actually cutting off his arm. A warning shot. The queen had peculiar abilities—all women who held the high queen's throne did.

"I don't have to explain myself to you, *huntsman*." Her face hovered inches from his. "It's not as if I let them go to the mortal realm. For all we know, he might hold the power to bind her."

Pain sliced through him, but all Kevighn could do in the queen's presence was put one hand over the wound to stifle the bleeding. "With all due respect, Your Majesty, none of us saw the Annabelle escapade coming."

"You didn't answer my question," she snapped. "What is your plan?" Another bolt left her fingertips, grazing his leg, causing him to nearly tip over in pain.

"I know you don't think we have time to find a new girl, but the place where I found Magnolia seems to be a holding pen for girls with the Spark." The pain in his leg grew so great it became difficult to speak. "I'll return there, Your Majesty." And conveniently located next to the Red Pearl.

"You do that." Her cool tone told Kevighn that if he didn't, his torture and death would be the entertainment at the next feast—if they weren't all dead by then.

"We can, I mean, *I* can fix this." He forced himself to sound as confident and sure as he could while bleeding all over her carpet.

"Yes, you will." She smiled at his discomfort.

"Of course, Your Majesty."

"I do have a plan of my own," she added slyly.

His stomach sank; if she succeeded and he didn't, there would be a price to pay. He wanted to leave before he grew weak from blood loss, but clearly, the queen wasn't finished.

"Excellent, Your Majesty. May I ask what?" Kevighn gritted his teeth at the pain.

She smiled in a way that would frighten the most seasoned warrior. "Magnolia still remains our best prospect. I'll go to Stiofán."

"Stiofán?" His face contorted in confusion at the unexpected plan. "Stiofán? Why do you think he'll succeed? He's not even a man."

The gleam in her eyes grew vicious. "I have something he wants more than anything."

"Very good, Your Majesty." He shifted his weight to keep the pain from overwhelming him. The poor prince would pay dearly for it, too; it was scarcely worth what he'd get in return. One must be exceedingly careful when making deals in the Otherworld—especially with the likes of Tiana, who'd betray her own family.

She looked him up and down and waved her hand toward the door. "You're bleeding on my carpet. Be off with you."

"Yes, Your Majesty." Kevighn bowed the best he could. Halfway to the door, he turned. "Your Majesty, what does Stiofán have that I don't?"

The queen laughed, a high-pitched, menacing laugh that sent chills ricocheting off his spine. "My dear Kevighn…" Her words held no sincerity. "You might be handsome and quick-tongued; you might even be an expert lover. But you're just my huntsman. Stiofán, as young and inexperienced as he may be, is a prince."

Why did women always think that? Being a prince didn't make you a better man.

"Of course, Your Majesty." He may have bedded many women, but he never claimed to be able to understand them—especially while sober.

• • • • • • • •

Steven stood in the doorway to the room he'd given Noli. It having been Elise's room, the decorations befit a young girl: pale colors, ruffles, and ribbons. They'd made camp in the nursery wing, the area of the house he and his siblings had lived in before they'd been exiled. Though it was dusty, spells had kept vermin and other riffraff out of their ancestral estate. Even after lying quiet and empty, it still felt like home.

He watched Noli sleep, her chest gently rising and falling with her breath. Every day she grew lovelier—to him, at least. She'd become distraught when the wood faery died in her hands. Noli possessed a connection to them, which he hadn't known, but it didn't surprise him either. They liked those with the Spark and those who held a connection to the earth.

Her anguish had led to him comforting her, and then to a disconcerting realization as he'd sensed the magic shift around them. Kevighn might not be able to get the magic to bind Noli—but *h*e might. Noli had become his when he'd given her the sigil, and that could be why the queen and Kevighn kept trying to get her to take it off.

Which again meant that he might be the only one who could get the magic to bind Noli.

Kevighn usually bound girls through seduction. By sleeping with him, they made an unconscious decision that they belonged to him, or at least belonged in the Otherworld. Steven was relieved she hadn't fallen for Kevighn's charms. He'd been even more relieved—and delighted—to discover she liked kissing him in person as much as she did in her dreams.

They'd have to be careful. It would be so easy for the magic to bind her. With each kiss, each stroke, he'd sensed the magic build. He couldn't allow the magic to bind her, even if it meant pushing her away until they figured everything out.

Really, he should explain it to her first, even if it sounded rather silly. But Steven didn't want her to bear that burden.

He'd just gotten her back, and he wanted to protect her with all his might.

Getting her home would prove a different matter entirely...

First things first. Perhaps James would have an idea. Where was he?

Shutting the door to Noli's room, Steven walked into the small library that always had been his favorite room in the house. He scanned the shelves, but nothing that could help him would be here. Perhaps there'd be something helpful in his father's library.

"How like your father you are, so ponderous with your books and studies."

He didn't need to turn around to identify the speaker, but he did, anyway, inclining his head as was proper from a prince to a queen, and not one iota more.

"Your Majesty, I wasn't expecting you so soon." He tried to keep any and all emotion out of his voice as he gazed at the high queen invading his library.

"Why, Stiofán, you'd think I wasn't allowed to visit my own son." The look she shot him was hardly motherly. She hadn't always been that way—not with them at least.

"You stopped being our mother the day you chose being high queen over us," he retorted.

"Really, Stiofán, you, of all of them, should understand." She didn't hug him or even approach; she simply stood there, cool and collected in a ridiculous lavender dress; it looked as if ruffles had been wrapped around her like thread on a spool. Little mechanical butterfly clips flapped in her upswept blond hair, and more of them decorated the dress.

"Ah, but I do, Your Majesty," he replied. "Séamus understands. Ailís doesn't. She believes she had a mother who loved her—and we try to keep it that way."

Her eyes narrowed at him. "You are your father's son, aren't you?"

"Why are you here, Your Majesty? I know this isn't a social call." He suspected what she wanted lay sleeping in Elise's room. Certainly, she'd only let him and Noli leave the high palace because she figured she could easily get Noli back—through him.

"Why *did* you choose him over me?" No hurt flashed in her eyes, no condemnation rang in her voice as she looked around the library.

While their father wasn't fun anymore, and tried to be away from home as much as possible, Steven knew he would never abandon his family. Deep down, their father still loved them, and he always sought to do the right things for them. Their mother had stopped loving them the day she decided that being queen of the earth court just wasn't enough.

"James and I support our father's choice," he replied quietly. "Why would he wish to go from being king of the earth court to a mere consort? He made you his queen. He loved you. You *promised*."

Her shoulders squared. "You don't understand how complicated this all is. You could return—you, your brother and sister. I exiled your father, not you three."

That's not what it had felt like.

"I came to get Noli, Your Majesty. That's all. What brings you here?" He could guess.

"I have a proposition." Her voice held a calculated chill. He found himself trying not to shiver even though the library wasn't cold, the door to the adjoining gardens tightly closed.

"I don't want to bargain. You have nothing I want," he spat. Lies. She had exactly what he wanted—and she knew it.

Tossing her head back, Tiana laughed and laughed until her chest heaved and her eyes glistened. "Silly, silly Stiofán. I hold the key to what you desire most. Do you want me to restore your father to his throne? Or should I make you king of the earth court and allow *you* to bring him back?"

Oh, she'd like to see that. His father would never return except as king.

"I won't give you Noli." When the time came, he'd get back his kingdom himself.

"I'm not asking for you to *give* me your little mortal." She smirked in the way that always made him feel like an idiot. "All I ask is for you to ensure that the magic binds her. Then the earth court, and all your family's honor, will once again be yours."

He crossed his arms over his chest. "I'm sorry, Your Majesty, but I won't."

Her jaw clenched. For a moment he was grateful that his status as a child prevented her from killing or exiling him. But she was queen, and he was close to being an adult. Suddenly this didn't seem like such a good idea. Still, he couldn't allow her to keep Noli.

"Do you not understand what's at stake? Have you forgotten everything?" she hissed. For a moment her hand raised as if preparing to strike him.

He tried to school his expression and show no fear. "I know precisely what's at stake, Your Majesty. Noli and I will try to find another."

"You do that. If you find another sacrifice, you may keep your silly little mortal. Truly, I don't understand why your father would allow you to become attached to her to begin with." She gave him a pointed look. "I'm *very* disappointed in you, Stiofán."

Steven watched his mother walk out of the library, just like she'd walked out of their lives. "I'm disappointed in you as well, Mum."

TWENTY-SEVEN

Mood Swings

"Good morning, V." Noli walked into the library where V sat on one of the settees, hunched over a large, dusty book. A good night's sleep had left her feeling refreshed, and ready to find a way home.

"Good morning, Noli." His voice echoed with fatigue. Dark circles ringed his eyes.

"I still can't get used to you not wearing spectacles." She laughed. Shelves and shelves of books, tall enough to need ladders, lined the walls. The room possessed a lovely view of a private garden. What would it be like to grow up in such a place?

"I'd never been to the mortal realm before our exile," V said. "When I saw spectacles for the first time, I was so fascinated I insisted I wear them." He shrugged. "I'm not sure I'll ever live that one down."

"Find anything helpful?" Reaching out, she ran her fingers through his unkempt hair. It was clear that the cozy library held well-loved furnishings. She could imagine V doing his lessons here as a child, or reading.

He shook his head, as if trying to shake her away, frowning. "She came here last night."

"Who?" Noli sat down next to him on the velvet settee.

"Queen Tiana. She offered me our kingdom back if I forced the magic to bind you." His fingers danced along the text, searching for information. "I didn't take her offer."

"I appreciate that." Reaching out, she took his free hand and squeezed it. Had it been difficult for him? She wouldn't blame him either way.

Taking his hand away, he continued to browse the tome, paying her little mind.

"Do you want to go for a walk with me?" She looked out the window, anxious and edgy, needing to work off her energy.

"Not right now." V didn't look up from the book. "There's some food for you on the table. Go amuse yourself. You may go anywhere in this wing or the private gardens. There's a door to the gardens right here."

"I can help you with your research." Standing, Noli put a hand on his shoulder. That, at least, would be something to do.

"Just go, Noli." He shrugged her hand off.

For some reason, that gesture, that brush-off, *hurt*. Never had he treated her like that, even when angry.

"Fine." Spinning on the balls of her feet, she turned and marched out of the room, leaving him alone with his tome.

•••••••

A door crashed open, rousing Kevighn from his slumber.

"Why are you still here?" The shrill voice made him cringe and want to pull the blanket over his head. The last queen had found had that amusing, but it made this one throw things.

He cracked one eye open. Really, he should jump out of bed and bow, but his head throbbed as if a goblin were taking a hammer to it.

"I planned on departing this morning, Your Majesty." After his hangover wore off. Last night, after he'd gotten his injuries looked at, he'd been about to head for San Francisco when he'd run into some friends and gotten ... distracted.

"Do you need another warning?" the queen snapped, eyeing the pink panties hanging from the bedpost. She aimed an energy bolt at his headboard, causing him to jump.

"Stiofán didn't wish to bargain?" That must have stung, being rejected by her own son.

"That's between Stiofán and myself." She looked down her nose at him, a vision in nothing but strings of deep purple beads made into something resembling a gown and another of those elaborate corsets, this one of purple velvet. Meanwhile, he was lying half on top his covers, reeking of alcohol and still dressed in yesterday's clothes, with one shoe on. The other one might still be at the pub.

"I expect you to be gone when I return. If not..." Queen Tiana sent another energy bolt at the bed. This one disintegrated the panties. Turning on her heel, she slammed the door.

Magnolia still remains our best prospect. The queen's words echoed through his liquor-induced fog like a hunting horn. As much as he didn't want Noli to die, she was still his best prospect. Also, the queen had failed to bring her back, despite being Stiofán's mother.

Why hadn't she simply demanded that her son turn Noli over? Perhaps she wasn't confidant she could make the magic bind her. Could that whelp of a prince do it?

He knew that *he* certainly could, if he could get that sigil off and get Noli alone. Oh, what sweet victory it would be to accomplish what the queen had failed to. That surely would redeem his honor. Also, it would be satisfying to wrest Noli away from Stiofán.

Kevighn vowed to personally make sure Noli got everything he could give her. He'd love her and cherish her the way that earth court brat couldn't.

When it came time...

Killing her would be difficult, but some time with her— even such a short time—would be better than not being with her at all, especially if she was associating with a prince.

He'd be doing her a favor. Being mortal, she didn't understand what dangers Otherworld princes posed. Earth court princes were far worse than any others—even those of the dark court.

Stretching, he hauled himself out of bed, trying to ignore his pounding head. He needed to get dressed and find Noli. Pity that she wouldn't have much time before she was sacrificed. He'd simply have to ensure their time together was so good it seemed like years.

· · · · · · · ·

Noli wandered through the halls of the big house, looking for V. His mood this morning puzzled her, especially after he'd been so … affectionate last night. Perhaps he was angry because *she* was the one to reach out. Her cheeks burned. The different rules regarding the sexes frustrated her. What was perfectly acceptable, or even encouraged for men, would cause a lady to be "ruined." Even the Otherworld probably held such conventions, as silly as they might be.

He wasn't in the library anymore, or the sitting room, or his room, or the garden. Sighing, she tried the library once again. No. Absently, her fingers rolled over the spines of a row of books. Maybe she should read until he found her. The library held a number of interesting books; she could take one into the garden.

Yet that didn't seem right after what she'd learned yesterday. The magic was growing weak from starvation. Little wood faeries—and other creatures—were dying. The land itself was fading away. A whole world would perish unless they did something soon.

Was it selfish she didn't want to be that something?

Surely, she and V could find a solution, and that meant doing something more than reading in the garden. Perhaps he'd been cranky because of his visit from the queen. It must have taken a lot to stand up to her. Maybe now he'd be willing to let her help.

She might not want to die, but she didn't want them to, either.

"That book, right there, is one of my favorites."

The voice startled her, and she yanked her fingers away.

"I'm sorry." V entered with a bundle in his arms. "I didn't mean to surprise you."

"It's all right. Which book?" She stared at the spines. He always recommended good books.

"Here." Getting behind her, he took her wrist and guided her hand to a red book with gold writing. "That one. My mum used to read it to me. Actually, she taught me to read using those stories." His smile became bittersweet, his eyes sparkling with sadness and memories.

Pulling it off the shelf, she thumbed through it. "*Strange Mortal Tales?*" She laughed. "What sort of book is that?"

It was hardly *Nicomachean Ethics*.

She nearly dropped the book as she remembered what had happened to the other one.

"It's a silly one. My father considered it dreadful nonsense, so she read it to me every single night." He cocked his head, a lock of blond hair falling into his eyes. "Is everything all right?"

Exhaling heavily, she looked at the burgundy rug, tracing

the black designs with her stocking foot. "They took away my books at Findlay House. I ... I hid *Nicomachean Ethics.* When Miss Gregory found it, she made me throw it into the fire, page by page, as punishment." Noli's cheeks burned at the memories. "I'm sorry. I'll replace it. I promise."

"It's only a book. Books are just things—unlike people, they usually can be replaced. I'm sure we can get another." He wrapped an arm around her waist making her heart flutter a little. That was more like her V.

"You think so?"

"Oh, I brought you something," he added.

Her body stiffened at his words as another man's voice echoed through her mind.

"What's wrong?" Reaching up, he tucked one of her unbound curls behind her ear. "You're still wearing yesterday's gown. Look, I found something else for you to wear."

Sure enough, he was holding a bundle of brown fabric on top of a giant old book. Yet it didn't help her relax. How different was her best friend from Prince Stiofán? Everyone else she'd met in the Otherworld seemed to be a liar. Who was the real Steven—V or Stiofán? And what was he like? Would he betray her, too? The thought made her knees tremble. Not only was he her best friend, but he might be more ...

"Noli, Noli, look at me." Strong fingers with a light touch canted her head, forcing her to meet his gaze. "What's wrong? What are you thinking?"

"Can the fae lie? In stories, they can't lie." It seemed liked everything she'd been told since coming here was a lie.

"Yes, they can lie. A lot of things in the stories aren't true."

"Oh. It's hard to sort through what's what." She shot him a measured look as she said what was actually on her mind. "Are you trying to distract me? Avoid my questions by bringing me presents?"

V's green eyes blinked back at her. "What are you talking about?"

She twisted out of his arms. "Every time I asked about going home, Kevighn distracted me with something—a new seedling for the garden, exotic blooms, sweets." Her face contorted at her own stupidity. "And I fell for it, like a silly child."

V's hand tangled in her unbound hair. "That doesn't make you a lesser person, and no, I'm not trying to distract you, I..." His cheeks colored. "I wanted to see you in green. I was in a hurry and couldn't find a green dress, so I brought a brown one. But I'll find you one."

"Green? You've seen me wear green before." Her eyebrows rose. Boys could be so strange sometimes.

He gave her a shy, bashful smile. "This is different. Besides, you look dreadful in that shade of pink."

"Some chivalrous prince you are." She gave a weak laugh, bumping him with her hip.

He laid the brown gown in her arms. "Do you want me to help you?" His grin went from shy to boyish. "I'm afraid there are no ladies' maids here."

"That is most improper, sir prince." She faked outrage, lips pursing as she tried not to laugh.

"That's 'Your Highness,'" he teased back, putting down the big book. "Here, let me help." Reaching around her back, he undid the laces of her dark pink bodice, his eyes on her the entire time as his nimble fingers made quick work of it. The bodice fell to the floor, leaving her in only the pale pink gown.

"I ... I'm going to change in my room." Her breath caught in her throat. She found herself wanting him to pull the dress over her head, to run his hands over her thin chemise, feeling her body underneath ...

No.

"I'll be right back." Before he could answer, she left the library. Once safe in Elise's room, she closed the door and leaned against it, her heart pounding. Why did he do this to her?

She washed her face with water from the pitcher on the nightstand. Elise's bedroom was pale pink with fluffy white curtains, colorful ribbons, and furniture painted with butterflies. Had James done that? He was an ace artist.

Noli pulled off the pink dress and laid it on the dresser. The soft fabric of the brown dress caressed her fingers as she shook it out, its rich chestnut color reminding her of cinnamon. The gauzy, nutmeg-colored underskirt had layers and layers, like a crinoline but softer, and the asymmetrical skirt of the cinnamon overdress looked like flower petals. When she pulled it on, she realized that it revealed her bare arms, and the neckline dipped in the shape of a V.

Part of the dress, above her waist but under her breasts, was a darker brown, and striped, similar to the underbust corset fashion that seemed all the rage here. But it was part of the dress, like a built-in waist cincher. She'd have to tell her mother about that clever idea.

Noli couldn't quite reach the back of the dress, which laced up with dark brown ribbons.

Someone knocked on the door and it cracked open. "Noli?"

"Come in." Butterflies fluttered in her stomach.

V walked in and drew in a sharp breath. "You look so lovely in that color."

Something about the way he was looking at her made her insides tighten. "You're so silly. But I think the dress is missing the sleeves. Did I drop them?"

Walking behind her, he tied the laces, his breath warm on her neck. The whole gesture seemed so ... intimate, but in a sensuous way that made her feel ...

It made her feel like a woman.

"Beautiful. Oh, I can't wait to see you in green." He gave a satisfied nod. "The dress is supposed to be this way."

"A sleeveless dress in the daytime?" Scandalous—like the things those courtiers wore. Yet she actually liked it. No sleeves meant nothing to get grease on or get in her way while fixing things. The dress was comfortable as well, especially with no corset—it would be perfect for fixing autos and repairing the roof. "And what exactly is your obsession with the color green?" she asked.

"We're earth court. Our colors are green and brown."

"Oh."

They stood dangerously close to each other, and she felt

the energy crackling between them like a Tesla coil. This mood of V's was strange, but better than him pushing her away.

"I didn't mean to offend you." His hand cupped her cheek, causing the sensation to spread across her body like gooseflesh.

"I...don't understand." Noli's voice came out breathy as her chest tightened.

"Don't be afraid." He pulled her tightly to him, his hands gently caressing her back.

Kevighn's words about giving yourself to a man you cared for came back to her. Noli buried her face in the crook of V's neck. He kissed the top of her head. Feather-light kisses trailed down her bare neck, her shoulder, her naked arms, her collarbone.

His lips met hers in a kiss so deep it seemed as if he was trying to reach into her, become part of her. Leaning into him, she kissed back, trying not to make a fool of herself as she explored his mouth with hers.

Part of her ached and she pressed her body against his, trying to relieve that longing. He groaned and she felt him press back. Ah, yes. A happy sigh escaped her lips.

One of his hands brushed across her uncorseted breast, making her body explode with inner fire and her lungs gasp for breath. Despite her fear, she wanted more.

In a bold and daring gesture, her hand found the waistband of his trousers and slipped beneath. She felt the small of his naked back with the flat of her palm. She wanted to float away on a cloud of pleasure between the texture of his form, the pace of his hands, and his kisses.

"Please." She didn't know what she asked for, but she wanted it now. His kisses deepened to the point where she felt as if she'd she could drown in them. Yes.

"NO!" V's pained shout broke her out of her pleasure-induced haze. His palm shot out, striking her in the solar plexus, forcibly pushing her body from his.

Her eyes widened and her stomach lurched, the breath going out of her from the force of his blow. She couldn't even speak.

"I . . . I'm sorry, Noli, but we can't do this." A look of terror crossed his eyes. "I told myself I can't do this. I didn't mean to do this. I'm so sorry."

"We won't, then." It was tough to force the words out. Her body burned with passion, with longing, with need, with shame. Her hand rubbed where he'd hit her in the chest. She reached her other hand to touch his face, to comfort him.

"Don't touch me. Don't you understand?" His voice sharpened.

"I . . . I only wanted to comfort you." She flinched, confused by his reactions. "And no, I don't understand. I'm frightened and excited, terrified and wanting all at the same time . . ."

V's face contorted. "Just go."

"What?" Her jaw dropped. Where would she go?

"Please, just go."

What had she done? She'd merely followed his lead.

"Fine." Shoving him as roughly as she could, she stormed toward the garden.

●●●●●●●●

Kevighn stopped at the magical barrier erected to keep out those who didn't belong on the lands of the House of Oak. Usually such barriers would stop him in his tracks. But here the magic had weakened. It was child's play to force his way through and enter one of the oldest ancestral lands in the Otherworld.

Where would Magnolia be? He made his way past the rowan forest that surrounded the grounds for protection. Their magic, too, had thinned enough for him to power his way through it. This time of day, she'd probably be in a garden or a tree. A place like the House of Oak probably housed more trees and gardens than the high palace. He was no tree-speaker who could ask the trees about her location, and no wood faeries danced about.

Kevighn became frustrated as he searched the vast gardens, groves, and mazes—she wasn't even at the magnificent faery tree. He saw that most of the wood faeries who dwelled there were dead, victims of the fading magic. A tiny tumulus lay at the foot of the tree, covered in smooth white pebbles. A wilted pink star bloomed on top of it.

He could imagine Magnolia crying over the faery's tiny, lifeless body. Had that whelp comforted her? Kissed her? Done other things with her?

Kevighn's hands fisted and he punched the faery

tree—an uncouth gesture, but it was nearly dead anyway. So many things were weak and dying.

Why *had* he waited so long to find a girl this time, other than apathy?

His knuckles smarted from the punch and he shook his hand, trying to shake away the pain. Then another sort of pain caused him to freeze. He could sense the rapidly building magic in his very core. Last night at the pub he'd sensed the magic building as well, which spurred the drinking contest, which lead to drunken revelry. The Otherworld might lack opium, but comely women abounded.

And also like last night, the magic suddenly ceased. Actually, this time it seemed more like a dull guillotine wielded by an inexpert executioner.

Ow. What exactly had transpired?

Why now? Unless it was the brat. How that puppy of an earth court prince could make the magic start to bind her, while he couldn't, made him furious.

It must truly be the medallion. He couldn't come up with anything else.

Sobs reached his ears as he drew closer to the residence—delicate, feminine, familiar sobs. Magnolia. Breaking into a run, he made his way toward the heart-wrenching cries. Dressed in a brown gown that made her look like a dryad, she sat crumpled in an oak, head on her knees, in a sheltered little garden dangerously near a large window of what was probably the main house.

"Please don't cry, Noli." He tried to keep his voice low and soothing as he approached the tree. His fists clenched, ready to hurt whomever hurt her—preferably Stiofán. Actually, even if it wasn't Stiofán, punching the whelp would make him feel better.

Startled, she nearly lost her balance. Clutching a branch, she steadied herself and assumed a defense stance. Well, as defensive as an unarmed mortal girl could get while in a tree.

"What are you doing here?" she hissed.

"I want to speak to you." Kevighn took a calculated step toward the tree—and her. The sigil hung between her breasts. She wasn't wearing a corset.

"You want to lie to me." Her red-rimmed eyes narrowed in suspicion and she sniffed. "V told me why you found me—he told me about the other girls and how you trick them, lie to them, seduce them, then kill them."

It sounded like such a terrible thing when she said it. "It's complicated," he murmured.

The look she shot him spoke volumes.

"I'm sorry, Magnolia. Truly, I never meant to hurt you." That was the truth.

"Just kill me?" Her tone was akin to a slap in the face.

"Noli, if you don't die, an entire civilization will." He hadn't meant for their conversation to happen this way.

"I'm selfish?" She sniffed again, but her look dared him to continue.

"Why are you crying?" He took another calculated step toward her.

"It's nothing." She clenched her jaw but didn't look away. Nevertheless, her eyes, her body, betrayed her, as did the red mark on her chest. He hadn't seen that at first. Anger built inside him, making his fists clench and unclench.

"Who hurt you?" It was hard to not yell out the question.

"It was an accident. I ... I went too far." A blush rose on her cheeks as she clutched the tree branch so hard her knuckles whitened.

He shook his head, gut wrenching. "Whatever you did didn't warrant that."

Her steel eyes flashed as she looked right at him, her gaze challenging. "I didn't warrant *you* hurting me either, but you did. Is it an Otherworld convention?"

"We shouldn't hurt you." Kevighn raked a hand through his loose hair in both anxiety and frustration. "Come with me?"

"What?" She tried to play it off with laughter and mock outrage, but that didn't hide the way her eyes brightened and her shoulders straightened.

Good. He still had a chance.

"I know he's your friend, but he hurt you. He made you cry." How could he make her understand she should spend her remaining time with him?

"It was an accident." Magnolia leaned against a branch and crossed her arms over her chest.

Shoving his hands in his pockets, Kevighn tried to block out another voice saying those same words. "Creideamh, too, thought it was an accident ... " He shook his head, shaking away the painful memories. "She loved an earth court prince, too. Once. She's dead now because of him. They're not outstanding citizens simply because they're princes; rather, they're the worst of the lot. He's not good for you."

She squinted. "I don't understand."

"I know." He closed the distance between them and laid a hand on her arm. "Please, give me one more chance."

"So you can kill me?" she spat, but she didn't jerk her arm away.

"You don't think your prince will do the same?" Kevighn put an edge to his voice. He had to make her understand.

Her eyes flashed defiantly and she did jerk her arm away. "Never."

"What are you doing here, Kevighn?" a voice interrupted.

Kevighn turned to see Stiofán holding that sword. His voice sharpened at his appearance. "She's too good for the likes of you, prince."

"Leave." Stiofán drew himself up to his full height in an attempt to be imposing. "Are you all right, Noli?" He walked over to the tree and put his arms out, bundling her into them.

The tender gesture made Kevighn's heart hurt. He longed for her.

"Don't let him hurt you, Magnolia. In any way." Kevighn met her eyes, willing her to understand that she could come back to him and be safe, happy. Despite what he told the other mortal girls, there was more to life here than the parties and fine gowns found at the palace.

"She's fine, we're fine," Stiofán snapped, walking toward the house, Magnolia in his arms.

"Sure." Kevighn watched them go inside, jealousy raging within. "We're all just fine."

TWENTY-EIGHT

James Returns

"He didn't hurt you, did he?" Carrying Noli in his arms, Steven brought her back inside the library. This way he could safely hold her close, show her he cared.

"No, only you did." She looked away from him, a wounded look in her eyes.

A handprint-shaped red mark colored her fragile chest, making him suck in a sharp breath. He needed to keep his strength in check; he wasn't some fire court rogue prone to displays of temper.

"I'm sorry." His lips brushed over the top of her wayward curls, but he didn't dared do more. Sensing the magic tighten around her when they'd kissed earlier had frightened him. Steven wanted to kick himself for that whole incident. He'd sworn last night to not do anything to make the magic even consider binding her. In the heat of the moment, he'd lost control.

Never had he wanted to harm her.

"What did Kevighn want?" Steven didn't keep the distaste out of his voice as he set Noli on the settee in the library, in front of the table set with lunch. How had the huntsman gotten into the estate? Tricky, conniving, bastard.

"He wanted me to come with him. He said you're not good for me because you're a prince." She looked up at him, questions dancing in her eyes.

"That's just silly." Busying himself so he wouldn't be tempted to touch her, Steven poured her some tea.

"An earth court prince hurt his sister once," she told him, her voice soft.

"Oh. I didn't know he had a sister." Steven wasn't sure what court Kevighn hailed from originally, but he knew it wasn't earth court. He handed the cup to Noli.

"Steven, where are you?" a familiar male voice called from the hall.

"About time," he muttered. "We're in the library!"

"James?" Noli grinned over her teacup. "I hope he has news of Charlotte and Jeff."

A moment later James barreled through the door, carrying something in his arms.

"Finally," Steven joked. He took a better look at the bundle. Tiny little shoes peaked out of the bottom of the ratty brown blanket.

"Sorry." A sheepish look crossed his younger brother's

face. "I got … distracted. Oh, you found Noli, great." He turned to her. "I brought you a present."

Noli brightened. As always, it radiated through her, like the sun coming out on a cloudy day. "You did? What did you bring me?"

Gently, James placed the bundle down on the settee next to her. "Charlotte, we're here."

"James!" Steven didn't keep the disapproval out of his voice.

"Really?" A sleepy voice with a southern twang came out of the blanket while James fussed over the tiny, freckled-faced redhead, making her comfortable on the settee. Seeing James fret over someone was both amusing and strange.

But it didn't diminish the severity of the matter.

Noli looked like she'd found the plum in a Christmas pudding. She hugged her friend. "Charlotte, you're here."

"Careful," James warned.

"I'm crippled; I can't get more broken," Charlotte teased back. Steven saw that she was pretty, with gleaming red hair and a pleasing, petite body. Her big green eyes danced with mischief. She glowed with the Spark—not as brightly as Noli, but brilliant nevertheless.

"Crippled?" Noli's forehead furrowed in concern. "He hurt you, didn't he?"

The light went out of Charlotte's eyes. "Uncle Nash is a dreadful man."

"You're safe here." Noli put her arm around her and looked at Steven. "She *is* safe, right?"

James helped himself to some fruit off the table. "That's why I brought her here."

Steven suppressed a sigh. As long as they were in need of a sacrifice, Charlotte too would be at risk. If he were less scrupulous, he'd convince Charlotte to be the sacrifice in order to save Noli.

"Um, James, will you come talk with me ... outside?" He nodded toward the door leading to the garden.

The girls put their heads together and whispered. He hadn't seen Noli this happy since she first saw him charge into the queen's garden to rescue her.

"Okay." Stuffing another piece of fruit in his mouth, James followed him outside.

Steven made sure they had a clear view of the girls through the window but couldn't be overheard. "James, what were you thinking?" He suppressed the urge to smack his brother. "Charlotte is mortal. She also has the Spark. Do you realize how dangerous it is for her to be here right now? The huntsman actually had the nerve to come here earlier, to convince Noli to return with him."

A frown tugged at James' lips. "She has the Spark? I didn't know, honest."

"I know. Still, what were you thinking?" His hands waved in the air for emphasis.

James leaned lazily against a tree, a wistful look on his face. "Charlotte is *amazing*."

Steven wanted to bang his head against the trunk. "Oh, no. You can't fall in love with a mortal."

"Do you know how much you sound like Father right

now?" James' eyebrow rose. "Besides, you're in love with Noli."

"That's different," Steven retorted.

"Is it?"

"And I don't sound like Father." As soon as Steven's mouth snapped shut, he realized he did. "Flying figs. Still...why did you bring her here?"

James shrugged, toying with a low-hanging tree branch. "I first went and found Jeff, who was deeply disturbed that Noli had been sent to that place, let alone was missing. He's got quite the airship, by the way. Then, I went to find Charlotte."

"And brought her back with you." Steven hoped to the Bright Lady that Noli didn't let Charlotte eat anything off the table.

"She wasn't at her home." James looked at his shoes. "She'd gotten some kind of tumor and the doctor had told her uncle it was fatal. He'd been counting on her making a good marriage to 'pay him back' for raising her after her parents died. Her uncle became angry and beat her so severely he crippled her, then threw her out on the streets. I found her crumpled in the corner of an alley, starving to death and in dreadful pain from both the tumor and her injuries."

That wasn't what he'd expected.

James' face contorted with pain, his eyes glowing with compassion. "I want—no—I *need* to help her. Do you think I could heal her? I'm making her pain go away, but I only took a quick peek at her injuries. I didn't want to risk anything else until I got here."

"How bad are they?" Steven asked. Neither of them were experienced healers.

"I can't believe anyone could beat someone so badly—and he did it with the intention to maim. Then there's the tumor..."

Steven shook his head. It was so sad. "I don't know if we can heal that. Her bones, maybe."

Defeat colored James' face, but Steven knew there wasn't anyone they could ask for help without endangering the girls and racking up a debt to someone. The best healers hailed from the water court, and, as allies of his uncle, they wouldn't deal with a couple of underaged, exiled princes.

"Anyway, I couldn't leave her to die alone and in pain. There has to be something." James raked his hand through his curly mop. "Charlotte is extraordinary. I like Noli well enough, but I never really understood how you two could spend hours in the tree house simply *talking*. Now I do." His face lit up with the light of a thousand lanterns.

Uh oh. "You're smitten."

"I'm in love." His head bowed, forlorn. "I'm in love with a dying mortal and I don't know if I can fix her."

"You were right to not leave her. No one should die alone and hurting." Steven understood that. After all, this was Noli's friend, not a stranger. Still, it made their situation all the more dangerous.

"By the way, Charlotte knows where we are and *who* we are. I needed to explain how I could make her pain go away."

Well, that solved one problem. He put a hand on James' shoulder. "We'll figure this out."

James grinned. "You're the best."

"I need your help, too." Steven glanced toward the window. Charlotte and Noli were chatting away, huddled together on the settee. Quickly, he filled his brother in on what had transpired—his rescuing Noli from the queen, the wood faeries dying, and the queen's visit.

"She did *what*? I can't believe it." James' voice was filled with outrage.

"I believe it. We have to find another girl. I won't let Noli die."

A look of horror crossed James' face. "I won't allow you to trade Charlotte for Noli."

"I don't believe in tricking them, remember?" The fact that James even thought that's what he'd meant hurt.

James' arms crossed over his chest. "Don't even talk to her about it."

Steven nodded, understanding completely. "Of course not."

"What do you suppose they're talking about?" James jerked his chin toward the window.

"Us, probably. After all, they're girls. What do you plan on doing with Charlotte?"

"Um." James' cheeks flushed. "Why don't we keep them here?"

"And do what, stay here with them? Father will be livid. What about school?" Privately, Steven had hoped to go to university, even if it was unrelated to his other goal. An institution of higher learning did exist in the Other-world, but it wasn't quite the same.

"We could stay here with the girls and you're worried about *school*?" James snorted.

"Father won't allow us to—and neither will *she*." Unless they agreed to certain things, which probably included moving into the high palace and playing good sons.

James slouched against the tree trunk. "I didn't really think about anything past keeping her from hurting and reuniting her with Noli. I'm not sending her back. I don't know how long she'll last. Bright Lady bless, I wish I could save her."

"Maybe we can."

"You think?" His face lit up. "Considering her situation, I think it would be best for her to stay here. I'll do whatever I need to, to be with her—including defy father."

Steven whistled. "You have it bad." Even he wouldn't defy their father that much. Truly, James' predicament wasn't that different from his own situation. "The queen might be able to help her. But bargaining with her is dangerous and desperate."

"It's an option." James lowered his voice. "She *is* our mother."

"Not anymore." Steven looked over; Charlotte seemed to be crying into Noli's arms. "There's still the problem that the queen needs a sacrifice and we have two girls glowing with the Spark."

James rolled his blue eyes. "That's not our problem."

True. It was his.

"Come on." James grabbed his arm. "Let's go back inside." Their eyes met; James' were pleading. "Will you help me, please? Help me see if we can fix Charlotte? Help me figure out what to do with her?"

It was rash and stupid. But Steven could hardly judge, having run off to save the mortal he loved. "Of course. After all, that's what brothers are for."

TWENTY-NINE

Choices

"Easy, Lottie." James helped the little redhead lie down on the bed in the room that used to belong to Elise's nurse-maid.

Steven still thought it odd for James to be so tender, so concerned, so smitten. After all, he eschewed all things *mushy*.

"Will it hurt?" Fear darkened Charlotte's freckled face.

"I won't let you hurt, I promise." James caressed her cheek.

Smiling, she closed her eyes. "I trust you."

Steven didn't miss Noli's look of longing, of jealousy. He'd been finding ways to avoid her all afternoon. Since she'd been closeted with Charlotte, he hadn't thought she'd noticed.

"I'll be gentle, I promise." James tucked a blanket around Charlotte.

"Don't make it tickle." She giggled.

Steven watched as James tried to magically take stock of Charlotte's injuries. Her legs were bent and broken, having healed improperly, and one arm hung oddly, limply. She looked pale and wan, her cheeks hollow. Her eyes still sparkled—she still shone with life, with the Spark.

"Are you all right, Charlotte?" Noli held her friend's hand.

"It tickles a little. You may call me Lottie too, if you'd like. You know how Miss Gregory was about nicknames," Charlotte replied.

Noli rolled her eyes. "I know. I prefer Noli. Only my mother calls me Magnolia, and that's with my other two names attached, delivered in a shout from the bottom of the stairs."

Charlotte giggled. "I can hear it now."

So could Steven. He saw Noli's eyes get misty; she was probably thinking of her mother, of home. He should go put an arm around her.

"I miss my mother, Lottie." Noli's voice cracked. "I want to go home."

"You don't want to stay here with me?" Hurt leaked into Charlotte's voice.

"I'll come and visit." Noli smiled. "Right, V?"

Tentatively, he put a hand on her shoulder. "We'll visit Charlotte and James together."

That statement assumed so much—Noli not being the

sacrifice, him finding a way for her to leave, his father not grounding him until he came of age.

Noli's brilliant smile made it worthwhile.

"Steven, can you help me?" James asked.

"Of course." He wasn't very good at this either.

Carefully, he repeated James' scan. He could sense every break in Charlotte's bones, every crack in her ribs. They could repair some of them, though it would be a long—and painful—process. But the tumor…

The large tumor in her brain wasn't something he'd even know how to *start* fixing. Magic could do wondrous things, but it didn't solve everything.

They finished and James looked as if he wanted to speak to him away from the girls.

"We're going to let you two talk some more." Steven tentatively touched Noli's hair. She'd been wearing it unbound and he really liked it.

"We'll be just fine." Noli flashed him a large smile.

"Bye." Charlotte waved.

"I'll come back soon." James squeezed Charlotte's hand.

"Me too. Come on, James." The two of them left to discuss what they'd found, leaving the girls to do whatever girls did when guys weren't around.

●●●●●●●●

"Let me help you sit up." Noli propped Charlotte up with pillows and sat on the bed with her. Charlotte had deteriorated from her vibrant, bouncy friend into someone who couldn't walk, who needed help to do the simplest things, who was dying. She hoped with all her might that James and V could save her. At least Charlotte was still herself on the inside.

Noli took a seat on the bed and sighed.

"Are you all right?" Charlotte leaned into her.

"I … I'm fine," Noli lied.

Earlier, Charlotte had shared the amazingly dreadful story about what happened after her uncle dragged her away from Findlay House, up until when James found her. And she'd confessed that she loved James. From the way James acted, he clearly loved her, too.

"Did James tell you why I'm here, Lottie?" Noli finally asked.

"He said his brother thought you'd been kidnapped by bad faeries and needed rescuing." She cocked her head. "Were there really bad faeries?"

Was Kevighn *bad*? He was many things—a rake and a liar being the first that sprung to mind. Exceedingly handsome and compelling were two more.

But bad?

Noli could appreciate the nature of his job. The high queen had charged him with an important task vital to his people's survival. She didn't like that he'd *lied*. Yet did that make him bad?

"Do you remember that man who spoke to us from the other side of the fence?" she finally asked.

Charlotte's nose wrinkled as she thought. "Long black hair, looked like a rake?"

"That's him," Noli replied. "He's the faery queen's huntsman."

"What does he hunt?" Her nose scrunched.

Noli remembered what Kevighn had told her about Charlotte. Did James and V know that Charlotte had the Spark? Her friend could be in danger too, and Noli needed to tell them that.

"Well, he hunts those like us." She told Charlotte about her wish and being drawn into the Otherworld, then explained about Kevighn, V's rescue, the sacrifice, what aether really was, the Spark, the fact that Charlotte, too, had it, and everything that was at stake.

"It didn't become real to me until the wood faery died in my hands." Noli sniffed. She'd buried her at the bottom of the tree. "I don't want to cause the death of an entire civilization. I don't want V to die—even if he's behaving most erratically—but … " She pulled her knees to her chest. "I don't want to die either." Her head rested on her knees. "I wish I'd never made that wish."

"If you hadn't, you'd still be at Findlay." Charlotte put a hand on her shoulder.

"Such a dreadful place," Noli agreed. "I would've run away."

"And done what? Gone home to your mother and hoped she didn't drag you back?"

Noli had forgotten about that little detail, but everything

looked better in hindsight. "Yes, I suppose, and gone to Jeff if I had to."

James had given her a letter from Jeff, who missed her and invited her to come and visit him on his airship—not that Mama would ever allow it. But it warmed her heart. Occupation aside, she missed him.

Charlotte smiled. "I can't believe your brother is an air pirate. I think I'd like to be one. Could you imagine? Some of the female air pirates even wear *trousers*."

Noli covered her mouth in mock dismay and they laughed. "Oh, a courtier in the high queen's court wore trousers. It also seems that the thing to do here is to wear corsets on the *outside* of your dress." She looked at her bare arms. "I still can't believe I've been running around all day with bare arms and no corset."

"Oh, you're such a scarlet woman," Charlotte teased.

"Actually, I keep thinking how this would be a great dress to fix things in. Perhaps I could even alter one of those corsets to hang tools from and such."

Charlotte's eyes danced. "I can help you with that. That's a terrific idea."

"Still, I feel like I've been nothing but a dollymop since coming here." For a moment she went quiet, then she looked at Charlotte, lowering her voice. "May I tell you a secret?"

"Of course." Scooting closer, Charlotte put an arm around her.

"Since coming here, I've been having…" She twisted a little in place. Saying such things aloud seemed so naughty.

"Feelings, urges, like the kind Dr. Martin always talked about. I didn't really know what he meant, until recently." Arms around her legs, Noli rested her cheek on her knees, the cinnamon fabric soft on her cheek. "V tried to find me in his dreams, and we did things."

"Really?" Charlotte's green eyes sparkled. "Like what?"

"We…" She closed her eyes. Was she truly ready to admit this? She needed to tell someone. Charlotte wouldn't judge her. "We kissed, and I let him touch me through my night dress, and…" Her voice hushed. "I liked it. Mama always said marital relations were a duty, but I think they could actually be pleasant under the right circumstances."

"They can be unpleasant." Charlotte's voice colored with pain. "But I'd think if it was out of love and not anger or perversion, it could be nice."

The two of them curled against each other, Charlotte's head on Noli's shoulder, Noli's head on top of Charlotte's.

"The heat in my dreams is still there—in person, I mean." Noli's voice broke as she remembered V pushing her away, yelling at her.

"What's wrong?"

"I'm so confused. One moment he tells me I mean something to him, but the next he won't even touch me. Is he toying with me? Kevighn said V's not good for me. I know Kevighn is a lying cad and a rake, but I never thought V would hurt me." Her hand went to her chest.

"Slow down. Isn't Kevighn the one who kidnapped you?"

Noli looked around, praying the boys were out of earshot.

"He is. Lying and roguish ways aside, he's not that bad." Her cheeks warmed—she sounded like a twittering idiot. "He... he's said several times that I should be with him. I don't know if they were pretty words meant to entrap me or not, but... he... he kissed me."

"Did he, now?" Charlotte's eyes danced. "Is he a good kisser?"

"I'm not sure if he kisses better than V. He's so different. One night he got me drunk, and..." She winced at the memory of her indiscretion.

Charlotte giggled. "My word you're a prude, Noli Braddock. By the way you're blushing, one would think he got you undressed and under the covers."

Noli's mouth dropped open at her friend's blunt words. "I..."

"You wished he did, didn't you? I can't believe it." She clapped her hands to her chest.

"He's nothing but a lying rake and rogue—no good will ever come from falling for such a man," Noli replied, saying the words she needed to believe.

"What of V? How do you feel about him?" Charlotte studied her.

"I..." Noli's heart raced. "I've felt something for him for a long time. I enjoy being with him. We're best friends. We have a lot in common. I don't know why he's acting so odd."

"It sounds as if he's under a lot of stress. Men under stress sometimes behave strangely."

"They do?" Noli blinked. She'd never heard that before.

Charlotte nodded. "When my father was alive some-times he'd be in terribly foul moods when things were difficult at work."

"Oh." Her father hadn't been like that. Could her mother be on edge all the time because she felt stress? It *was* difficult for her mother to run the shop, pay the bills, and raise Noli.

"How *do* you feel about V?" Charlotte put a hand to her mouth and laughed.

"I like to kiss him. In real life as well as in dreams." Noli's cheeks burned at her admission. "How can I be attracted to two so very different men at the same time?"

"It's normal. Girls speak of being attracted to multiple men all the time, of their affections being torn." Charlotte grinned. "Especially between who's proper for them to marry, and who made their heart race and insides tingle."

"Really?" Noli laughed. It felt scandalous to speak so freely. Charlotte seemed to know so much for someone so young. Then again, Noli never could be bothered with such things previously.

"Really," Charlotte replied.

"When V kissed me earlier... " Noli closed her eyes to shut out the painful images and her voice cracked. "He pushed me away—physically. He yelled at me and told me to leave."

"He did?" Charlotte frowned and stroked her hair. "Then what?"

"I left. Then Kevighn found me and told me I should be with him."

"And?"

"V came, apologized, and you came." So many emotions welled inside her, overwhelming her to the point where she didn't know what to think.

"Ruffians are often attractive only because we know they're bad for us," Charlotte replied. "Like stuffing yourself with sweets because they're tasty even though you know you'll have a bellyache in the morning. Also, he's a liar who tried to seduce you on orders and wishes to kill you. Remember?"

It sounded so clear-cut when Charlotte said it. "You're right."

In all honestly, Kevighn never had a real chance. V had always been the one she wanted.

A sigh escaped Noli's lips and she wished all those emotions could escape with it. "I still feel so selfish. I don't want to give up my life—even for a people, even to live in comfort with nearly every wish fulfilled."

"You're not selfish. But this is quite a predicament." Charlotte tapped a finger to her lips.

"How can you be so cheerful and positive when—" Noli's mouth clamped shut. How could she say such a thing?

"Life is what you make of it. I know my days are numbered. I choose to live those days as happily as I can—and thanks to James ... " A silly grin spread across Charlotte's pale face. "Thanks to him, I'm in no pain, and I've found someone who loves me. And I love him. We might not have much time together, but it's worth it."

"What if he can fix you? What if you could have more time?" They'd just been reunited.

"If I can, I will, but I'm not going to fret over it." Charlotte smiled. "And neither should you. We should spend our time together happily."

Noli's face contorted. "Does it hurt you that I want to go home?"

"You have a place to go." She shook her head, red hair flying. "If anything, I'm jealous—but only a little. I'll miss you when you do. I think I'll like it here with James."

The idea of staying with Charlotte was certainly tempting.

"I need to make up with my mother. I need to ask her forgiveness. I…I want to try to be a better daughter—perhaps not a perfect one, but a better one," Noli finally replied.

Charlotte patted her knee. "That sounds like a good plan to me."

Noli had trouble understanding Charlotte's attitude. She had just found someone she loved. How could a brief time together be as good as a lifetime?

She sighed again. "This is all so hard."

"No, it's not," Charlotte retorted. "Be happy. I choose to be happy."

"What can make me happy?" The obvious would be going home.

"Only you can decide that." Charlotte snuggled closer, eyes drooping. "I'm sleepy."

"Take a nap." Noli tucked her friend in.

Be happy. Could it be that easy? Did V make her happy? As her best friend, he did. Could he make her happy as more than her best friend, present behavior aside?

As Charlotte fell asleep, Noli thought about it, hard. Drifting to sleep herself, she realized the answer was yes.

THIR+Y

It's Just Not Fair

Noli awoke; Charlotte was snuggled against her, using her as a pillow. Darkness cloaked the room and her stomach rumbled. Carefully edging Charlotte's head onto a proper pillow, Noli climbed out of the bed and padded off to find something to eat—or V. Butterflies fluttered in her belly when she thought of him.

Yes, Kevighn might awaken feelings deep within her, but she wanted V. Was he even still awake?

She checked the library first. Soft, concerned voices came from within.

"It's imminent?" James' voice dripped with uncharacteristic defeat and worry.

"I believe so. According to the books I've found, that's just not something we can cure." V sighed. "I'm not even sure if we could make it so she could walk again. I don't know about you, but my magic's behaving oddly. Also, it might take awhile, and from the look of it, I'm not sure how much time she has. We could try to seek outside help, but..."

"I know; who would help us? Especially to save a mortal." James' voice turned bitter.

Standing outside the door of the library, angling her body so they couldn't see her, Noli's knees buckled as the realization hit. Charlotte was going to die, and they couldn't save her.

She sank to her knees on the hallway rug. What was the point of having magic if they couldn't save anyone?

Wait. That wasn't fair. There was a difference between talking to trees and healing tumors. Noli wasn't even sure what a tumor was other than a death sentence. Certainly it escaped mortal doctors. Still...

"Don't cry, Noli." V crouched down in front of her. "I guess you heard."

"Why does everything here have to end with people dying? It's not fair," she sobbed.

"It's *not* fair. Life isn't fair—and that's not fair, either." He shot her a lopsided grin that reminded her of better times.

"Why *is* that?" Noli felt like the turtle who carried the world on her back.

"I don't know." V held out his hand. "Charlotte's asleep?"

She allowed him to help her up. "Yes. I'm hungry."

"Come sit with us." Putting an arm around her waist, he ushered her into the library. "We're going to do all we can. I'm not sure how much of a help we can be other than keeping her free of pain."

"For her that's important."

"I know." James looked up from his perch in one of the big, comfortable library chairs. "When I found her, she was in so much pain she could barely talk. She was dirty and starved, and more people had hurt her."

Noli could only imagine what life on the street held for a defenseless young woman. Her hands fisted in anger. "How could her uncle do such things?"

James shook his head. "There are terrible people in all worlds, Noli."

"Charlotte's a good person." Her face contorted as she took a place on the settee. "Why do such bad things happen to her?"

"And that is a question the great thinkers have pondered for eons." V sat down next to her on the settee. "Here." He handed her a piece of fruit from a bowl on the table.

"I wish we could do something." James put his head in his hands. "How will I tell her?"

"You *are* doing something." Noli remembered what Charlotte said about happiness. "I don't think she'll take it nearly as hard as you think. She has a different outlook."

"She's very upbeat, all things considered," James admitted.

"This is someone who chose to not play the game at Findlay House because she didn't want them to win, because she didn't want to be the soulless drone they wanted us to be," Noli said. "Look where it got her."

"She told me stories." James shuddered. "Sounds dreadful."

Just the thought of that place made Noli shiver. "It was terrible."

"What of you?" V's look turned pensive. "Did you play their games?"

"I wanted to go home, but I didn't want to be like those girls, those vapid, pretty dolls. That's why we were going to run away. If only we'd worked faster, run away *before* her uncle came. This all would have been avoided." Guilt churned inside her. If she could do it over…

"It's not your fault." V put a hand on hers. "The two of you on your own would have been a target for all sorts of scoundrels."

She made a face. "Because of how Sparky we both are?"

"Who told you that?" V's forehead wrinkled in concern.

"Kevighn." She shrugged. "He spoke to both of us once, back at the school, through the fence. Did you know there's a joy house on the other side?"

V's look shifted from concern to horror. "Kevighn knows about Charlotte?"

James' expression turned solemn. "No one can know she's here, then."

"Exactly," Noli agreed. Unlike her, Charlotte couldn't fight back. "How much trouble are you two going to be in for all of this?" she asked. "I know how strict your father is, and this is much worse than hoverboarding in the hills without a license."

V made a face at the thought. "I don't relish facing him,

but we will eventually, and we'll take whatever punishment he doles out as befitting our station."

James rolled his eyes. "I'm so glad I'm the younger son."

"You're not going to escape it—especially since you plan on staying here with Charlotte," V warned kindly.

"You won't see me being all stiff-backed, taking it like a man without a word of dispute." James leaned back in the chair and crossed his arms.

"Oh, I think you will." V's voice lowered.

Eventually, James left, leaving her and V alone in the library.

"I'm sorry for causing you stress." She leaned her head on V's shoulder, wishing they were sitting in her tree house at home, looking at the stars.

"What?" V yawned as he paged through another big, old book.

"You've been in an odd mood. Charlotte says you're stressed. I'm sorry I caused this."

His lips brushed the top of her head. "It's not your fault, Noli."

Sleep pressed down on her. "I don't want Kevighn."

"What?"

"I don't want Kevighn—even if he weren't a roguish liar who wants to kill me." It felt so good to say that aloud.

Chuckles brushed her ears. "I'm so glad to hear that."

"Do you know who I want, V?" Against her will, her eyes closed, weighed down by fatigue, as she leaned against him.

"Who?" His voice took on a breathy quality.

"I want you." Again, saying it felt *right*, like uttering the words out loud made it so.

"You don't mean that, do you?" Fright colored his voice.

"Of course I—" Before she could finish, his hand pressed over her mouth. Her eyes flew open as memories of suffocation back at the school crashed down on her.

"You don't know what you're speaking of. You're tired," V snapped.

"What?" Noli sat up, ramrod-straight, shocked, hurt, ripping his hand away from her. "Why don't you tell me what's going on?

He didn't look angry. No. V looked utterly terrified.

"Please, Noli, just go to bed," he whispered desperately.

What was going on? Oh. What if…

"Fine," she huffed. "I thought you felt something for me as well." Without looking at him, she stomped out of the library.

What a stupid girl she was. She was mortal; he was a prince of the Otherworld. She'd read enough stories to know how *that* usually turned out.

• • • • • • • •

Shoving his hands into his pockets, Kevighn Silver once again skulked down the dark, foggy streets of San Francisco, his soul heavy with defeat.

This time there was no way around it. Despite what he'd told the queen about knowing where to find girls with the Spark, it wasn't as if he could just burst into Findlay house and take someone. They were all going to die, and if he was going to die, he wanted to die happy—oblivious and in the arms of a willing, beautiful woman.

If only that woman were Magnolia…

Despite princes being bad for girls such as her, for girls such as Creideamh, the princes always won. It just wasn't fair.

As he strolled past Findlay House, he gazed into the soulless eyes that passed for windows—barred, lifeless, nary a light on. Taking a deep breath, he cleared his mind and tried to sense how much Spark lurked within.

The result made him stagger backwards as if drunk. A lot of Spark dwelled inside that place. Whether it was from one girl, or the collective Spark that he felt, he didn't know. It wasn't as if he could simply burst in and look. *Excuse me, ma'am. Might I please see how many of your students have the Spark? They're actually not willful, rebellious hoydens; rather, they're special. By the way, I'd like to take a few back to the Otherworld with me.*

Yes, that would go over about as well as a lead zeppelin. Perhaps tomorrow he could spy a few hanging wash, gardening, or playing a game. Tonight…

He walked through the gates of the Red Pearl and knocked on the door. Who knew, maybe one of the girls here had the Spark. This took talent, right?

"Ah, Mr. Silver, welcome." Mr. Chun opened the door, welcoming him in. "What do you wish for this evening? Priscilla is free."

Kevighn gave him his coat. Which one was Priscilla? It didn't actually matter. Taking a wad of money from his billfold, Kevighn handed the money to him. "I'd like the works."

THIR+Y-⊕NE

Charlotte's Solution

"Here you go." Steven poured Noli a cup of tea and handed it to her. Silently, she took it. She hadn't spoken much all morning—especially to him. Charlotte hadn't said much to him either, and he had a feeling he'd become the victim of female solidarity.

He deserved it. Once again, he'd been tender with Noli only to push her away. Why didn't he just tell her that every time he touched her, kissed her, he felt the magic swirling around her, trying to use their feelings for each other to seal her fate as the sacrifice? That he wasn't pushing her away because he hated her, but because his love for her ran so deep that if the magic bound her, he'd never forgive himself? He'd always been able to tell her everything before.

His efforts to protect her were hurting her. And, well, Noli never had liked being protected.

Yes, he should tell her as soon as they had a moment alone.

He poured a cup of tea for Charlotte, who sat wrapped in a blanket on the settee, a deck of cards abandoned on the table from the game she and Noli had been playing.

James intercepted the cup, then handed it to Charlotte. "Here you go, Lottie love."

Steven shook his head. His brother possessed all sorts of obnoxious nicknames for Charlotte. He had none for Noli. The only one he could think of was *little blossom*, since a magnolia was a flowering tree. But that was quite stupid.

Girls did often like stupid things.

He took a piece of fruit out of the bowl. Simple fare got old, but there was no kitchen staff to make and serve meals and it wasn't as if he could go and get things for them to eat.

The queen might tolerate him being here for now. If his uncle found out…

Steven wasn't ready to face his uncle yet. For the time being, they'd have to make due with the garden's bounty. James had offered to cook—a frightening prospect.

"What happens when a sacrifice is found?" Charlotte's earnest question startled him from his thoughts.

"The magic of the Otherworld will stabilize," he replied. "Which means no more creatures die, and the sick should get better." Looking at Noli, he recalled her tears for the little wood faery. "Those who've already been lost won't come back to life, but our magic will cease being erratic, and those who've lost it completely should get it back. The areas of our world that have faded should return." But he wasn't certain. "Things won't completely return to normal until the sacrifice is complete."

"Oh." Charlotte put a hand to her chin, her expression pensive.

That morning, James had told Charlotte that they didn't think they could fix her, but that he'd take care of her, keep her free of pain, and extend her life as long as he could. She took it well, stating she'd rather have a few months free of pain with someone who cared for her as much as James than a lifetime alone and hurting. Sage words for someone so young.

"Noli's not the sacrifice yet, right?" Charlotte's eyes widened a little as she spoke.

"Not yet." But not for the want of the magic. Steven kept feeling it poking and prodding around her, trying to find some way in.

"All the magic needs is someone with the Spark, right? Not Noli in particular?"

Where was she going with this? He searched his mind for everything he knew about the matter at hand. "Due to circumstances I won't go into, the sacrifice needs to be strong in the Spark. But that's all—just a Sparky girl whom the magic accepts."

He *had* found it poking around Charlotte when she and James played what Noli termed "kissy-face."

"I see." Charlotte nodded. "In return, the girl gets whatever she wants, right?"

Steven tried to recall exactly what happened. "Usually she lives in the high palace with the queen. They throw her parties. She wears pretty dresses and eats fine food. Everyone lavishes attention on her. She's pampered and revered."

"Then no one will die—not you, not James, not Noli?" Charlotte asked.

A sinking sensation consumed him. "No. None of us will die. Where are you—"

"I'll do it." She took a sip of tea, as if she'd just said nothing of consequence.

"What?" three voices said simultaneously.

"You have no idea what you're saying, Lottie." James stood up, his eyes flashing with terror. "Steven, you promised not to say anything to her. I know you don't want Noli to die, but—"

"Stop." Charlotte raised a tiny hand. "I made this decision by myself. I don't want an entire people to die—nor do I want Noli to. She has her whole life ahead of her, and people who love her. My life is at its end. I wouldn't mind spending my final days being the center of attention, living without pain, living with James." She made doe eyes at him.

Steven could feel the magic whirl like a dervish around Charlotte, seeking her, testing her, building quicker than he ever thought possible as she made her decision.

"Lottie, stop, please." James' face contorted in pain, his voice a near wail.

She squeezed his hand. "I know I'm crippled, I know

I'm dying. But I want my life to mean something. If the magic wants me, I'll take the job."

The magic exploded like a million fireworks going off at once—both deafening and staggering. If Steven hadn't been sitting, he would have stumbled.

"Charlotte, no." Noli shot up off the settee, as if her actions, her protests, could do something to stop it.

Too late.

"Flying figs." James' eyes widened.

Steven felt the magic continue to shift and swirl in a kaleidoscope of power and upheaval, expanding, contracting, and finally, relaxing into a pleased state. An odd feeling settled down on him like a wet wool blanket.

"It's done." Steven's voice hushed. Charlotte was the sacrifice.

Noli's steel eyes flashed with fear, anger, and sadness. "Lottie, what have you done?"

Tugging on her hand, Charlotte pulled Noli back down onto the settee with her. "I'm choosing to be happy. James, you'll stay with me, right? Could we stay here instead of the palace? Please?"

James stood behind the settee, putting his arms around her protectively. "If you want me to be your consort, I'll gladly accept the honor. We'll stay wherever you want. Personally, I like it here better than at the high palace."

"I don't want you to die." Spinning on her heels, Noli ran out of the room.

Steven followed. Now that Charlotte was the chosen girl, he no longer had anything to fear from comforting Noli.

• • • • • • • •

It seemed to Noli that all she did of late was run away with tears streaming down her face like a weepy heroine in a penny dreadful. She ran outside and scaled the oak tree in the corner of the little garden outside the library.

Pulling her knees to her chest, she wrapped her arms around her legs and put her head on her knees as she sobbed. Many emotions bombarded her, the two main ones being anger and despair. Despair because Charlotte had condemned herself to death. What had possessed her to do that? There was still a chance James and V could do *something* to help, or that another healer might have a solution.

Her anger was directed at herself. She hadn't been willing to offer herself as a sacrifice to save a people, even though she loved V. Charlotte, who'd only just met James, voluntarily offered herself up, not only to save his people, but to save Noli. Such a beautiful, selfless act. One that made Noli feel like a fiend.

Someone entered the garden. V, mostly likely. Still hurt from the previous night, she ignored him. She'd tried to profess her love and he'd shushed her, telling her she didn't know what she said. Wouldn't she know her own mind?

V scaled the tree. When he hauled her into his lap, she didn't fight, but she didn't help, either. She laid her head in the space between his neck and shoulder as sobs wracked her body.

"Go ahead and cry." One of his hands rested in her loose hair as the other stroked her back.

"Why did she do that? I can't believe it." The words came out as little gasps between her sobs. "I don't want her to die."

"I know, I know." His soft, sweet whispers brushed her ear. "But I already feel the magic stabilizing. That act of giving herself over proved enough for the magic to bind her quickly and forcefully. Nothing will get worse, and soon all will be well again."

"At what cost?"

"The same cost we pay every seven years, and will continue to pay for all eternity, or until we finally fade away." The motion of his hands was soothing.

"I don't understand. Why does someone have to die anyway?" Noli cried.

"That's the way things have been here for a very long time. Father tells the story best, better even than Quinn; we should get him to tell it to us." Doubt rang in his voice.

"Your father tells good stories?" Her eyebrows rose. She hadn't known that.

His eyes swam with memories. "Amazing ones."

"I don't want Charlotte to die." She peered at him through tear-laden eyes.

"It's her choice. No one suggested it—not me, not James. And we can't cure her, Noli. She *is* dying." He rubbed his face. "It's a beautiful act, actually. One that proves a point. I've always thought we didn't need to trick the girls; that even in this day and age, there still are mortals willing to give their lives to save others."

"So you're going to be the queen's huntsman now, looking for girls who are in pain and misery, offering them a few parties in exchange for their lives." Oh, how bitter she sounded.

"I'd never hunt for her. Even if she ordered me to." V straightened with resolve. For a moment he studied Noli with his unspectacled green eyes. "That's part of this, right? You didn't want to die, and Charlotte offering herself unsettled you."

Noli exhaled, her chest shaking. "I'm a selfish, selfish girl."

Taking her face in his hand, V forced her to look at him, albeit gently. "No you're not. No one thinks less of you because you didn't willingly—or unwillingly—become the sacrifice. Charlotte isn't doing this for nothing, either."

They were quiet, and he ran his fingers lightly through her hair. It felt so nice when he did that.

"I really like how you've been wearing it down lately," he murmured.

"You don't think it's dreadfully improper, me running about with bare arms and unbound hair?" Her eyes narrowed, daring.

He planted a little kiss on her nose, sending shock waves through her body. "No, I don't."

Noli laughed. "I actually don't mind the sleeveless dresses. I think I want to take this one home with me." Today's gown was dark green, loose, and flowing—another gown ideal for fixing autos. "It's perfect for doing all the things I do—proper enough, but not constricting."

"Well, you really are a vision in green." V leaned closer.

"Things are different here than in the mortal realm, especially our attitudes about propriety and social conventions." His lips caught hers.

Her hand darted out, pushing him away, preventing him from kissing her. "Oh no you don't, Steven Darrow. I'm done with having my emotions toyed with." Jutting out her jaw, she scooted off his lap onto the branch next to him.

"I'm sorry." He snaked an arm around her waist.

She crossed her arms over her chest. "Explain. Now."

"Gladly." V sighed, as if exhaling the weight of the world. "I was going to tell you as soon as we had a moment alone—only Lottie had to go and bind herself to the magic before I got that chance. You see, I was afraid that if we went far enough the magic would bind you, because you would accept me as your lover and that you belonged here with me. Even last night, when you tried to profess your love for me, I sensed the magic wanting you, waiting for you." His lips brushed across her forehead, making other parts of her tremble.

She eyed him. "Why didn't you tell me sooner? We had time alone before now."

He blushed to the roots of his hair, eyes on his lap. "I didn't tell you because I wanted to protect you, like I always have, and will continue to do. Then I realized that bringing you heartache wasn't protecting you. I should have told you sooner." His fingers brushed her face, trailing down her cheekbone. "I never wanted to hurt you. I'm sorry I made you cry. I'll never do it again. We don't have to deny our feelings anymore."

Their faces hovered dangerously close. Yes, they definitely weren't children anymore. But this...this was nice.

Maybe even more.

"If you ever do that again, so help me." Noli poked him in the chest. V had always sheltered her, protected her, taken the blame, so this didn't come as any real surprise. But that didn't mean she had to like it. "You said you'd always be honest with me—even if it hurt."

"I did. I...I'm sorry." He buried his face in her shoulder. "I won't do it again."

She didn't doubt his sincerity, but she wasn't done with the subject. "You would have saved the both of us a lot of heartache. Do you know what it did to me, you kissing me one moment, shouting at me the next?" The memories made her wince. "Do you know how long I grappled with my feelings?"

It seemed almost improper to speak of these things. But she wanted him to know. "I felt like such a dollymop. Then, when I sorted everything out, my mind finally decided what my heart had understood all along." Reaching out tentatively, she cupped his face with her hand. "It's what I've always wanted, but never wanted to admit to myself."

V lifted his head from her shoulder and once again his face got very close to hers. His breath came out ragged. "What is that, exactly, Noli?"

"I want you." She met his gaze. Her heart skipped a beat. Would he reject her again?

A surprised look swam through his eyes. "Why didn't you want to admit it?"

"I'm a hoyden, my mother *works*, and I enjoy fixing things and playing in the dirt." Her words got faster, as if they might fade away into nothing if she didn't get them out quickly enough. "You're from a respectable family, and now I find out you're a prince, and you know how that always ends in the stories—"

His warm lips covered hers, silencing her before she could finish. She found herself pulled back into his lap as he kissed her, reigniting the inferno in her belly. One of his arms tightened around her; the other tangled in her hair as he pressed his body into hers. She wrapped her own arms around his neck, trying to anchor herself; otherwise she'd float away on clouds of pleasure.

He broke it off, both of them gasping for breath. V's fingertips brushed the length of her face as he gazed into her eyes with an intensity that made her soul burn.

"Those are just stories, Noli. This is real." Then he kissed her again.

THIRTY-TWO ⊕

As the Dust Settles

"Shall we?" Priscilla giggled, hooking her arm through his. Or was it Pamela? Perhaps her name was Persephone. It didn't matter; she was just another mortal joy-girl.

"Of course." Kevighn led her off for a walk in the gardens. This morning he possessed an alternate agenda. Otherwise, he'd be lying in the dark with more of Mr. Chun's rather fabulous—and potent—opium.

Steering her close to the fence of the school, he kept watch for any of the girls. He needed to figure out some way to obtain entrance, perhaps by touring the school as a potential place to send a fictional sister.

As they strolled past the fence, he spied two girls in gray dresses, hanging laundry under the watchful eye of a dour-faced matron. For a moment he paused, recalling when he'd seen Noli and her friend doing the same task. These girls didn't laugh or smile.

One possessed the Spark, but not enough; not like Noli or her red-haired friend.

As they continued to stroll, the joy-girl nattered away about womanly nonsense. Noli wasn't a chatterbox. By the Bright Lady, he missed her.

There were no other girls outside at the school today. The little faery garden lay empty; he didn't even see any wood faeries. Perhaps they'd all died. He could feel the weak state of the magic, and last night he'd had difficulty lighting a single candle.

Fictional sister it was. Though it seemed a betrayal of Creideamh's memory.

He still didn't have a clear idea as to why girls ended up here, other then they didn't behave the way society thought they should. Stupid mortals. They hadn't learned much in the time he'd been interacting with them, and they were easy to influence.

"I think it's time we return," he told the harlot. She made eyes at him, but he steered her toward the opium den. He'd need to wear a better suit, one that said "respectable gentleman" rather than "high roller." What should his sister's ailment be? Perhaps he'd use what Noli told him, that she was a willful hoyden prone to youthful disobedience. What poppycock.

What else did he need?

Before he could make a mental list, the magic went haywire, searing right through him like one of the queen's energy bolts. A maelstrom of magic built rapidly, binding a girl with a ferocity he'd never felt before. The sheer force of the magic made him stumble backwards.

"Are you feeling poorly?" The trollop steadied him.

"Yes. It is quite warm today, don't you think?" He struggled to catch his breath. Someone had been chosen.

Anger coursed through him. He'd never regain favor with the queen if someone else had found a girl. Or bound Noli; his gut twisted at the thought. Either way, his failure meant that he probably shouldn't bother returning to the Otherworld.

No, he needed to return. Surely, if Noli was the sacrifice, she'd understand—forgive him—give him a chance.

Also, Queen Tiana would send someone to look for him if he took the coward's way.

The joy-girl smiled, revealing dimples, unaware of his thoughts or what had happened. "Let's go inside. I'll make you feel better."

Oh, she was a winsome one. One sultry look weakened his resolve. It wouldn't delay his return by much.

He smiled at her. "I think you're just what the doctor ordered."

• • • • • • • •

Steven awoke to sunlight streaming through his window. As with the other bedrooms in the nursery, it still contained all the relics of his childhood. His box of playthings had amused Noli, but hearing her laugh at his tales had made it all worthwhile.

A bigger bed wouldn't be unwelcome. A beam of light shone on the sleeping beauty lying on his chest, giving her the appearance of an angel in her white nightdress. Tangling her braid around his hand, he planted a kiss on her forehead.

All had been forgiven last night. They'd made their peace, as had Noli with Charlotte. He and Noli had stayed up late, lying on his bed, talking. She'd spent the night in his arms; however, both of them had remained fully clothed.

Parts of him felt frustrated, especially considering where one of her soft hands currently rested as she slumbered peacefully, using him as a full-body pillow.

Their evening hadn't been fully chaste. No, he'd gotten plenty of her sweet kisses and had been rewarded with her cute little noises of satisfaction as he'd kissed, stroked, and touched her. For the moment he was happy to hold her, to love her without fear, the way he'd wanted to for years.

Well, his father still wouldn't approve. Charlotte and James were different, since Charlotte was the chosen girl. That was temporary.

Noli, being mortal, was temporary in her own way. But one thing at a time. The magic possessed her sacrifice—now, he needed to help Noli return home. He'd yet to find any way to make it happen. Pity that Quinn wasn't here. Maybe James had an idea.

He eased Noli off him and onto the bed, then padded

down the hall to James' room. Rapping softly on the partially open door, he walked in.

James lay asleep in his own little bed. The weapons on the wall made Steven smile.

A dainty pair of milky shoulders peeked out of the blanket. Red hair contrasted with James muscular chest. Someone else hadn't gone to bed alone, and judging from the bare skin, their night probably hadn't been as chaste as his.

"James?"

His brother cracked open a single eye. "I'm sleeping, Stio."

The childish nickname made Steven grin. "I see that, and not alone, either."

"Oh, don't give me any mortal nonsense." Sleepily, James stroked Charlotte's bare shoulders. "She was completely willing, I promise. *You* didn't go to sleep alone."

"Our clothes stayed *on*." He eyed the heap of discarded clothes on the floor.

James' eyes popped open. "Why?"

"Noli's a lady." And unused to their ways.

"So is Charlotte."

"They're two different girls in two different situations," Steven retorted.

"I'm sure you'll convince her eventually." James flashed him a rakish grin.

"In time." At least she'd forgiven him for pushing her away. And as much as he looked forward to eventually being with her in that way, she was so much more to him than that.

"Why are you here?" James closed his eyes again.

"I need your help. Noli wants to go home."

"What do you want me to do, wave my wand?" James turned over, his back to Steven. "Let me go back to sleep."

"I can't find anything in Father's books. Should I venture home and ask Quinn?"

James snorted. "As soon as father sees us, we'll be on restriction until manhood. Besides, you know what your other option is."

Steven raked his hair with his hand. "Yes, I'd wished to avoid that option."

"Well, I suppose she knows a girl's been bound." James curled his body around Charlotte protectively.

"The acceptance by the magic was so forceful I'm sure *everyone* felt it. It's only a matter of time before her majesty visits." Steven wasn't looking forward to that, either.

"I'm not allowing her to take Charlotte to the palace. She wants to stay here." James' voice held quiet ferocity as he continued to cradle the sleeping mortal in his arms.

"I'm sure the queen will try to tempt her, but she'd never force her, not now. Charlotte has the right to live where she pleases in the Otherworld, with whomever she pleases. The queen could probably even get you out of trouble with Father, *if she wished*."

James made a face. "The key phrase is, 'if she wished.'"

"Yet you think I should ask her to release Noli?" Steven shook his head.

"She *is* our mother, as I've said. Now, I'm going back to sleep." James faked a snore.

With a shake of his head, Steven left.

....

"Will you hand me the wrench, V?" Noli held out a tanned and calloused hand.

Steven handed her a wrench and couldn't help but grin. Outside in the library garden, Noli was attempting to construct a wheeled chair for Charlotte from pictures she'd once seen of something called a "bath chair." James had found her a tool box and some goggles.

She was wearing the brown dress he'd given to her, and he could see how it made a good work-dress. He'd also found her a leather waist-cincher, which Charlotte had adorned with loops and pockets for tools and such. Charlotte had made her a matching leather bracelet as well, though Steven wasn't exactly sure of the point of it.

"I'd really like to design something with a reclining seatback, a foot rest, and suspension so James can take her for walks. It should also be stylish." Noli tightened the wheel onto the axles she'd made from random things James had procured.

"Stylish?" The contraption seemed to consist of a wicker chair and the wheels from Elise's old tricycle. It didn't look practical *or* comfortable.

"Yes, stylish. So Charlotte can be the belle of the ball."

Noli picked up the handle from a wagon. "This will do for the moment. If only I knew how the queen's chariot works."

The queen herself probably had no idea how her chariot worked, not in a way that would satisfy Noli. Oh, how he loved seeing her happy. She practically glowed with joy.

A shadow fell over them. Frowning, he looked up from his place on the grass next to Noli and her invention.

"Whatever are you doing?" Queen Tiana looked down at them, her face scrunched in puzzlement. She wore a diaphanous gold gown with trailing sleeves. The front of the dress cut up in an asymmetrical arc, revealing a myriad of pale gold ruffles beneath. On her shoulder perched a gold mechanical bird.

Well, he had expected her to come eventually.

The wrench nearly dropped from Noli's hand as she eyed the queen dubiously. "I'm building a chair for Charlotte, Your Majesty."

The queen's cold blue eyes narrowed. "You are not the chosen girl."

Noli cocked her head, still sitting on the grass, not standing. "No, Charlotte is."

"Good morning, Your Majesty." Steven stood and bowed. "You remember Noli."

"I do." She eyed Noli, who still hadn't stood.

Noticing, Noli sighed heavily and got up. She pushed the goggles on top her head and curtseyed.

"James and Charlotte are inside." Steven jerked his head toward the house.

The queen looked around. "Séamus is here? Ailís as well?"

"James is here. Elise isn't."

"Oh." For a moment the queen's face filled with disappointment—or it could have been the light.

She cast her eyes around the garden. "But who is this Charlotte?"

A few guards and courtiers joined her. A brunette wearing what looked like a gold and leather fishnet waved at Noli. Noli waved back, and Steven stifled a laugh—Noli was still holding the wrench. Only Noli.

"Why don't you let me introduce you, Your Majesty?" He gestured toward the house.

Queen Tiana's eyes went alight with curiosity. "That would be splendid, Stiofán."

He looked to Noli. "Would you like to come with us?"

"I'll stay here." She held up the wrench. "Tell Lottie I'm nearly done."

"Of course." He wished he could stay. Ignoring his mother, he leaned over and gave Noli a kiss on the cheek. "I'll return soon." He turned to the queen. "Shall we?"

They walked toward the house, the queen's entourage trailing behind. Noli pulled down her goggles and returned to her project.

Queen Tiana looked down her nose at him. "So you found another mortal. I'm disappointed in you. You could have had everything you wished."

"Still, I found you one." Well, not truly. Charlotte had bound herself.

"Indeed. You may keep your mortal." The queen's lips pursed into a self-satisfied smirk. "I hope she's worth it."

"She is. Wait—Noli is mine? You swear it?" By giving Noli his sigil, with his particular intentions, he'd made her his, but the queen allowing him to "keep" her was another matter entirely. Of course, Noli would be relieved to know that neither term implied that she was property, and it really didn't translate into mortal terms. It had more to do with alliance and protection than possession.

Tiana's expression contorted. But only for a moment. "You are your father's son." She held up a dainty, pale hand. "I swear that Noli is yours until you decide otherwise, entitled to all rights and privileges therein." Her eyebrow rose. "Satisfied?"

"Yes." He gave a satisfied nod. Now Noli could safely visit the Otherworld. Well, once he figured out how to take her back to Los Angeles.

He led the queen into the library, where Charlotte and James sat in the window seat playing a game of cards. She was leaning heavily on him, so Steven wasn't precisely sure how their game worked. Not that James was any good at cards.

The queen stopped in her tracks. "My, Séamus, you've grown."

"Good morning, Your Majesty, I wondered when you'd arrive." James sounded resigned, not pleased, at their mother's appearance. He set down his cards, stood, and bowed. "Your Majesty, may I present Charlotte Wilson. Charlotte, this is Queen Tiana, our high queen."

Charlotte inclined her head. "Pleased to meet you. Please pardon me if I do not stand."

The queen looked her up and down, confusion dancing in her eyes. The mechanical bird on her shoulder let out a little squawk. "Why?"

"I can't stand or walk, Your Majesty." Charlotte reached out and squeezed James' hand.

"Charlotte knows—about everything. She's chosen me as her consort." James stood stiff-backed and proud, for once acting like the man he looked like. "She also wishes to stay here, at the House of Oak, not at the high palace."

"The palace is much more comfortable. You must at least come and see for yourself." She smiled one of her phony smiles. "Certainly, it would be more convenient."

"Of course, Your Majesty," James replied as Charlotte simply nodded, a bit more pale than usual, her freckles standing out.

"It's nice to see you, Séamus," the queen said. "I look forward to getting a chance to catch up. Perhaps you could send for Ailís? I'll arrange for a small staff, if you insist on staying. If Ailís comes, I'll make sure she has what she needs—a governess, lady maids, playmates."

Could their mother *miss* Elise?

"I'm not sure Father will allow her to come, Your Majesty," Steven interjected. "She's still quite young." And she thought their mother was dead.

Her eyebrows arched as her attention turned to him. "Will you be gracing us with your presence as well, Stiofán?"

"I hope to return Noli to her mother as soon as possible, but yes, I'll visit."

"I give you the mortal and you wish to take her back to her own realm?" The queen laughed heartily, as did her courtiers. "How exactly do you plan on accomplishing that?"

Steven tried to remain calm and ignore her amusement at their plight. "I haven't precisely figured that out, Your Majesty. Perhaps you have a suggestion?"

Her lips pursed as if holding her real reaction inside her mouth. "For the right price, I might consider helping you."

There was always a price—a high one.

"You would grant me the knowledge?" That would be preferable.

She laughed again, tossing her golden hair over her shoulder. "You are so funny, Stiofán. Certainly, you didn't get that from your father." She turned to James and Charlotte. "I'll see you both tomorrow for tea."

Without waiting for a reply, she flounced out, her entourage trotting after her. Steven wished he had a brick wall to smack his head against.

"That went well." Rolling his eyes, James plopped back down on the window seat and picked up his cards.

"If you say so." Steven shoved his hands into his pockets. "I'm going back outside. Oh, Charlotte, Noli wanted me to tell you the chair is nearly finished."

But they'd already resumed their game.

Decisions

Kevighn returned to the House of Oak. His sources told him Noli still dwelled there. A girl like her *would* prefer it.

Laughter greeted him as he approached one of the bigger gardens on the property. An abundance of Spark resided there, and not all of it felt like Magnolia's. Making his way into the garden, he saw her speeding across the grass, pushing a redheaded girl in a chair with wheels on it. He recognized the girl as her friend from the school, the one who'd been dragged away, who possessed quite a bit of Spark in her own right.

That earth court prince watched the girls from the sidelines. Another young man stood with him, one with darker blond hair and a more manly appearance, but he, too, was naught but a child by their standards. He wore the same sigil around his neck. Ah, the other exiled prince.

Had Quinn the Fair and the exiled king come as well? Kevighn had a score to settle with the both of them.

"Go faster," the redhead squealed as they ran.

"If you say so, Lottie." Grinning recklessly, Magnolia ran faster, steering the chair over the uneven grass.

"Careful, Noli," Stiofán called. As he spoke those words of caution, the girls hit a bump. Lottie, Magnolia, and the chair all went flying.

"Lottie!" The other prince ran toward the girls.

"Noli!" Stiofán took off after him.

For a moment Kevighn's insides twisted. Was she all right?

The girls erupted in fits of laughter.

"We're fine, V." Magnolia stood up, brushing the grass off her green and brown gown.

"Truly, we are." Lottie grinned as the other prince fussed over her. She, too, wore green. So, both young princes had found themselves mortal girls with the Spark.

Which one was the sacrifice?

"Be careful, Noli," the younger prince chided. He scooped the redhead up in his arms as if she were a small child.

Lottie rolled her eyes. "Noli, I thought V was the fussy old bodger, not James."

"Me too," she laughed.

No. Now that he saw her, he could tell Magnolia wasn't the chosen girl. Relief cascaded over him. How *had* they managed that?

It didn't matter. A sacrifice had been found and it wasn't her. Excitement coursed through him.

He continued to watch as James fussed over the red-head, putting her back in the chair, which Stiofán righted.

"Please be careful, Noli," James added, tucking a blanket around Lottie.

"I'm crippled, not made of spun sugar. Besides, I like the chair Noli made me." Lottie grinned, tipping her face up for a kiss, which the young prince gave her.

Crippled? Kevighn could never remember a crippled chosen girl before … extremely ugly, dumb as a post, not right in the head, but never crippled. Still, the magic only needed the Spark, not a sound mind or body.

"I'll make you a better one, I promise. I really, really want to find out how the floating chariot works. A bath chair like that would be glorious." Magnolia put her arm around Stiofán.

Watching them cut Kevighn to his very soul. Stiofán would break her heart.

The prince stiffened, then focused on Kevighn and his place on the sidelines of the large garden. "What are you doing here, huntsman?"

Magnolia froze when the prince spoke, and Kevighn suppressed a smile at her reaction.

"Why do you think I'm here, prince?" Kevighn said "prince" as if it were a dirty word, his lips curving into a dangerous grin.

The prince wrapped his arms around Magnolia. "She's *mine*. The queen gave her to me."

He saw her bristle. "Did she now? What am I, a marble to be lost or won in silly boy games?"

Stiofán ran his fingers through her unbound hair. "No, that's not what it means here. It's protection. It keeps people like *him* away from you. It also enables you come and go, so when we return you to your mother, you can still come visit Lottie."

"Oh." Magnolia nestled back into the prince's arms.

Anger and jealousy raged within Kevighn. His hands fisted. Usually he didn't hurt children, but Stiofán was near enough to a man that he didn't care. Except for the brat being the high queen's son. The thought made his fists unclench. He was in enough trouble as it was.

"Wait—you told her she could *return*?" Kevighn smirked. "What other lies are you feeding her?" Privately he hoped Magnolia would smack the prince. Hard.

Stiofán shook his head. "I didn't lie. She knows it's something we have to work on."

"How *are* you going to do that?" Kevighn scoffed. The prince could simply ask his mother, of course, but he'd turned down the earth court throne for a mere mortal— even if the mortal *was* Magnolia.

The prince shot him a privileged look as he ran a possessive hand through her hair. "We'll figure it out together."

Sure they would. If the whelp believed that, Kevighn had waterfront property in the middle of fire court territory to show him...

"Go away, Kevighn. I have no use for men like you." She didn't meet his eyes, but he could tell from her body language that she was teeming with inner conflict. His heart leapt.

"He's bad for you." Kevighn took a step closer, speaking as if they were alone in the cabin's kitchen, not in the middle of a garden with an audience.

"No. V is a good, kind, smart, respectable man. You're nothing but a lying rogue. All the good looks and sweet words in the world won't make up for your errant ways," she scolded.

So she thought he was good-looking. His belly jumped.

"Leave, Kevighn." Stiofán shot him a hard look.

His attention returned to the prince. "Give her to me. You might be earth court, but you princes don't grow and nurture love—especially with girls like Magnolia—no, you destroy it." Memories of his sister grew and built, like a powder keg ready to explode. "Don't you know how bad you are for her? You're going to hurt her. Please, Magnolia." Turning to her, he itched to take her hand. He should have brought her the firestone necklace—or some flowers. "Come with me. I'm done being huntsman. We'll live in the cabin, you can work in the garden and do all the lovely things you did to make it a home again."

He reached out to her, praying to the Bright Lady that she would step away from the prince and take his hand, but knowing deep down that she wouldn't. "You don't understand," he repeated. "He's going to hurt you. I don't want you to suffer at the hands of an earth court brat like Creideamh did..."

"And suffer with a rake and liar instead? A cheating fiend

353

who frequents opium dens and consorts with fancy women? One whose job is to trick innocent girls into dying?" Her cheeks flushed with anger.

He wasn't a cheat—well, except at cards. Everything else she said held true.

Kevighn took another calculated step forward, ignoring the venomous looks from both princes. "I know how to care for someone like you. We'll do whatever we want, whenever we want. There's so much I could show you."

She stepped out of the prince's arms. Kevighn's heart skipped a beat. Would she actually choose him over the prince?

"I'm sorry, but as fun and interesting as you might be, you're not what I need." Yet her eyes told him that he was what she wanted.

"I can be." Even though she possessed an earth spirit, like Creideamh, he could feel the fire, the passion, within her. That he could nurture.

"No!" She held out her hand, as if trying to physically sever the connection between them. Magnolia turned away, her arms wrapping around her chest as if trying to hug herself. "No." Her yelp sounded like the mew of a helpless kitten. "I made my choice, Kevighn. I didn't choose you. I chose V."

Prince Stiofán held her to him, a smug look on his face.

Unfair. Why couldn't she run into his arms like every other girl? Not only did his heart ache because this would end badly for her, but the rejection itself stung. He never got rejected by women—especially mortal ones.

The prince's eyes met Kevighn's. "Leave. Now."

Kevighn gave Stiofán a mock bow, his voice snide. "Yes, Your Highness." His expression and tone softened as he focused on Noli. "Magnolia, my little blossom, when he breaks your soul, you can still come to me. I'll still love you. I promise."

"My brother asked you to leave." The other prince was holding a sword, eyeing him menacingly.

What was it with princes and their swords? It was as if they were compensating for something.

Oh wait, they were.

"Of course." Kevighn's voice dripped with disdain. "Your Highnesses, ladies."

Spinning on the heels of his boots, he left the House of Oak. Maybe the queen would put him out of his misery quickly.

No. That wasn't her way. Besides, if she killed him, he wouldn't be around to help Magnolia when the brat hurt her. No matter what that puppy of a prince might intend, he would hurt her eventually. Kevighn could tell from her words, her look, that she wanted him, desired him.

He was a huntsman. Eventually, she would be his.

• • • • • • • •

Noli buried her face in V's shoulder. She hadn't counted on Kevighn returning and asking for her to come with him. She hadn't expected that facing him, and stating her choice, would be so difficult.

"Kevighn can't hurt you; he can't take you from me. You're safe." V whispered sweet words over and over as he caressed her hair, her shoulders.

Kevighn hadn't even apologized for deceiving her. The fiend.

Noli's mind wandered back to last night with V, which had been quite ... satisfying. Even though he'd never touched her bare skin, she still felt a little naughty.

"I made the right choice," she whispered.

"You did." His lips trailed little kisses down her neck. "I'm not sure what his problem is with earth court princes, but I'll take care of you. I'll never hurt you."

She groaned softly at his caresses. James cleared his throat. Charlotte giggled.

His lips pressed her forehead. "I love you, Noli."

He took her hand and led her to his room, shutting the door. "I need a new nickname for you. I'm not about to call you *my little blossom* now."

They sat down on his bed. "I don't need little syrupy nicknames like James and Lottie use."

"Good." He attacked her throat, sucking and teasing with his lips and tongue. His other hand roamed. Her body went aflame at his touch and she kissed him back, trying to pour all her feelings into that kiss.

They fell back onto the bed, lips still entangled. When he tugged at her dress, her eyes flew open and she broke off the kiss, her heart thumping.

"Please?" His eyes were half-closed, his voice rough and low.

It took a moment for her to process what he'd asked. "Give myself to you? As if we were man and wife?" The idea made her feel a bit dizzy and, well, not dirty, but definitely wicked. "I … I … "

His lips met hers, silencing her, but her mind sped. He wasn't tugging at her dress now, but his kisses were no less passionate. She loved V, but if she lay with him, she would be unmarriageable, and what if his father didn't permit them to marry? How much more could she possibly shame her family? Her absence alone could prove suspect. The double standard just wasn't fair.

"Don't tremble." His hands glided over her body, lingering on her uncorseted breasts, making them yearn for his touch. What would it feel like for him to kiss them?

"I'm … " Oh, how she wanted him. He could quench that ache inside her. "I'm not ready, V. Not to do *that*." Parts of her protested, but common sense won out.

"We could do other things." His lips brushed her breasts, the heat of his breath making its way through the brown fabric.

"Things that wouldn't ruin my reputation?" She laughed as he attacked her with kisses, which tickled.

"I don't understand why you're worried. Things are different here." His hand trailed down her stomach, which also tickled, as they lay on their sides, face-to-face.

She eyed him, but didn't bat his hand away. "I'm pretty sure things work the same way here. Right?"

V smiled. "What I mean is that while back in Los Angeles it's considered a duty, a way to ensure more sons to carry on the family name, here…" He gave her a little kiss on the lips, his hand tangling in her hair, his face hovering inches from hers. "Here, it's love. Here, it's a way for two people who love each other to express their feelings."

The urge to kiss him, to let him show her everything, threatened to overpower her; she remembered her conversation with Charlotte about the possibility of it being pleasant. But they weren't going to remain in the Otherworld forever.

Her eyes met his as fear struck through her like an arrow. "What about when I return? I will return, right?"

"Oh, Noli." He bundled her into his arms and curled his body around hers. "Would you consent to stay here with me?"

Invisible hands choked her. "I want—no, I need—to go home." She struggled to sit up. "If you really love me, you won't keep me here."

"I do really love you." His lips brushed the back of her neck. "But knowing the queen, I still think I'll have trouble finding a way to send you back without making a bargain with her."

Noli leaned into him. "She can do that?"

"She could release you, and send you home, but," V warned, "it has a price. Everything has a price. With her, it's always a high one."

"Like what? What could she want from you?" The idea of bargaining with Queen Tiana made her shiver, but if it was her only hope…

He stroked her hair as they lay on the bed. "Remember

when I told you she cast my father out because he made a choice she didn't like?"

She nodded, remembering.

"The choice was that he wouldn't give up his kingship of the earth court for her. There's no such thing as a high king in the Otherworld, but the high queen's consort can't have his own elemental court, either—it would upset the careful balance of power. Every court has an opposite."

Dour Mr. Darrow, consort to Queen Tiana? The thought seemed as ludicrous as her mother and Officer Davies. Noli recalled the five-circle symbol in the high palace. "What would the converse of the high queen be?"

"The dark king—he leads the dark court," V explained. "The high court unites the four elemental courts. The dark court isn't actually part of the unification, yet is just as necessary."

Noli pondered that. "For every action there's an equal and opposite reaction?"

V laughed. "Something like that."

"The high queen wished to court your father?" She still couldn't imagine the two of them together. They were so, well, different.

"She wasn't high queen when they met; just the high queen's younger sister. Father was king of the earth court. She broke a promise to him, then cast him out." V's face contorted in pain.

Noli kissed his forehead, trying to sooth his worries away with her touch. "Wait, that means..."

He nodded slowly. "Once we called her Mum, before she chose her position over us."

Noli blinked, mind swimming. "I thought your mother was dead."

"She is. To us." He closed his eyes, as if shutting out the pain. "It was easier to tell Elise that our mother was dead than tell her she'd abandoned us. Father plans to tell Elise the truth when she's older."

That didn't seem to be the smartest idea. Personally, Noli would feel betrayed and hurt.

"James and I support our father's decision," V added.

"That's why you never call her Mother?" Noli asked. V's mother was high queen. Queen Tiana had cast away her own husband and children. Certainly, that didn't make her seem very likeable.

"Exactly." He stroked Noli's arms lightly.

They were silent. Then Noli said, "So, as far as me going home, what would the price be?"

V thought for a moment. "I don't know. I'd have to word it very carefully, to be a single task with a time limit, so that I'm not bound to her for eternity."

"Be careful when making deals with the fae?" Her fingers brushed the length of his face.

Grabbing her hand, V kissed her fingertips. "Precisely. The last thing I wish to do is to become her new huntsman. She'd delight in the irony of the situation."

Noli scrunched her nose. "Isn't Kevighn the huntsman?"

"He failed. At the very least, she'll banish him, but if

she's in the right mood, she'll kill him." V looked happy. The thought made Noli shiver.

Misunderstanding, V pulled the butter-soft green blanket over them. "I don't want to go to her unless we have to. But I'm willing to, if you wish. We'll simply have to bargain carefully."

"You'd do that for me?" Noli gazed into his eyes. Entering into a bargain with the queen was much different than simply convincing her.

"I'd do anything for you." He kissed her on the nose. "You are my love. Regardless of how much trouble we get in, I'll love you forever and stay with you always."

His sweet promise made her insides quiver. She brushed his lips with hers. "I love you, too. I really would like to see what she could do to help—after all, if we don't like the bargain we don't have to accept, right? We could keep looking."

"If we don't accept her first offer, the price will go up a hundredfold should we ever have to go back to her," he warned.

"I can only imagine." She enjoyed snuggling in V's arms. So safe, so comfortable.

"We could go tomorrow. James and Lottie have a royal invitation, and we should be good friends and accompany them." His smile grew pained. "We'll speak with Queen Tiana afterwards."

"Thank you." She touched a finger to his nose. "I mean it."

"Be careful, or I might take advantage of you." His warning came between delectable kisses that started at her temple and worked down her jaw, her neck, her collarbone, making every inch of her body become alive with anticipation.

"You may do anything to me you wish, as long as my dress and your trousers remain firmly *on*, and it's nothing that would sully my reputation." Wrapping her fingers in his golden hair, she steered him to the spot where her neck met her shoulders, which especially liked to be kissed.

"Really?" His eyes danced with mischief.

"Really. I rather liked last night." She caught his lips with hers.

"Me too." His hands, his mouth, increased their intensity, stoking her internal inferno, making her gasp, pant, and moan with pleasure and expectation.

He took off her boots. His hands worked their way up her dress.

She swatted at him. "Our clothes stay *on*, remember?"

V's grin became devilish as he reached under her skirt and undid the ties to her bloomers."

"I remember. But you said nothing about your drawers." He slid them off and dangled them in front of her, chuckling in delight.

"V!" Fear and anticipation swirled in her deepest places. "That's not what I meant."

His face drew close to hers. "Always word your bargains with the fae very carefully. We'll take advantage of you to the full extent."

A sharp gasp escaped her lips as his fingers caressed her bare skin in a place she'd never even touched herself.

He smiled. "Oh, you like that."

She did—too much.

"I won't do anything they can check for, promise. Not that the mortal idea that it can be checked for is accurate." His gentle touches firmed and she moaned. "The things I can show you…"

"Like what?" Her words became gasps as his mouth fastened onto her covered breast.

"Patience, Noli." His mouth worked down her body as his hands continued to tease her.

She writhed in pleasure meeting his touches, running her hands over his firm body as the heat within her continued to build. What would happen when it came to a head? Would it tear her apart? As anxious as she was, she didn't fight it.

When his breath brushed her bare thighs, the inferno within exploded. Every fiber of her being became alight with fire for the man who kissed her where no one had ever touched her before.

THIRTY-FOUR

The High Queen is Law

The few things Kevighn cared about in his palace chambers fit in a leather rucksack. Regardless of what the queen said, he was finished being huntsman.

She'd probably already found his replacement anyway. As he walked through the marbled halls bustling with servants and courtiers, he realized that while he'd grown accustomed to this life, he wouldn't miss it much.

It didn't take long before he found the queen, bustling through the halls in a flurry of pink silk, followed by a trail of flustered servants, guards, and courtiers.

Stopping short, she looked down her nose at him as if he were something distasteful. "What are *you* doing here?"

He bowed deeply. "I've come to give you my resignation, Your Majesty."

"Pity. I had hoped to send the wild hunt after you and watch them rip you to shreds." She said this as easily as she might inquire what fabric someone used for their new ball gown, or demand a new mechanical toy or game.

"And resignation?" she scoffed. "You failed, Kevighn Silver. Failed." Anger raged in her voice. "You could have killed us all, yet you don't seem to care. Do you care about anything, anymore?" She tossed her golden hair, which someone had woven into hundreds of tiny beribboned plaits, over her shoulder. The pink ribbons matched her diaphanous pink gown, which seemed to be made of many layers of sheer fabric. She looked like a rose in bloom.

What a curious question. He didn't have anything to care about, not anymore.

"You are relieved of duty for substandard performance." Her eyes narrowed at him.

His belly clenched. Would she order his death? Or perhaps have her guard haul him off to be publicly flogged as entertainment for her tea?

"Killing you is too lenient a punishment. Kevighn Silver, also known as Kevighn Silver-Tongue, I hereby banish you from the high court and the four elemental courts. We owe you nothing, and you are nothing to us. All that should be yours is hereby taken from you." She waved her hand in the air.

Kevighn sensed the magic tighten around him and prayed to the Bright Lady it disagreed. He felt no such rebellion. His stomach sank. Banishment meant he wasn't welcome in this court or any of the elemental courts. It also meant that his parents' lands were lost to him; they held no enchantment like the House of Oak did.

His cabin and Creideamh's grove would also disappear. That cut deeply—as it was meant to.

"We no longer recognize you as one of our own. Guards, take this exile away. Do as you will, then cast him out," she ordered, a little too happy for his comfort.

The guards descended upon him gleefully, dragging him down the hall as the queen looked on, cackling in delight.

· · · · · · · ·

Noli sat on an uncomfortable purple chair next to V's in the queen's opulent library, holding his hand in a death grip. This place didn't feel comfortable like V's library at the House of Oak. It didn't even seem often used; no, with its cold marble floors and unwelcoming walls of books, it seemed like a place designed for one thing. Intimidation.

The high queen across from them looked prim, a smug expression on her pretty face. "What do you wish to talk about, son?"

The queen laid the last word on thickly, ignoring Noli and stroking LuLu, who lay on her lap. Actually, the queen had ignored Noli all through their tea, which Noli didn't mind. Poor Charlotte had gotten a lot of tough questions. Right now James was taking her for a walk, to soothe her.

"I'd like to speak with you about helping Noli return to the mortal realm. Though she's still mine. I'm not giving her up." V spoke slowly, carefully, and Noli flashed him a reassuring smile. He'd been practicing, trying to make their bargain so airtight that even the queen couldn't manipulate it.

She waved her hand in a dismissive gesture. "What do you see in this mortal, anyway?"

"I love Noli's spirit, her independent nature, her individuality." V looked at her and smiled in a way that made her feel warm inside. "I love her curiosity and inquisitiveness. I love how she's so different from all the girls they call *ladies* in the mortal realm."

"Why do you wish to go back to the mortal realm in the first place, Magnolia?" The queen's face scrunched in puzzlement. "It's much nicer here. We have fine gowns and parties and feasts, you don't have to go to school if you don't wish to, and no one will yell at you or punish you. Also, Charlotte is here. Don't you wish to stay with your friend until it's time?"

Her tone and expression made Noli feel like a heel for even thinking otherwise. "I'm not averse to returning to your realm, Your Majesty. In fact, I plan on it." She looked at V, who nodded. "But I miss my mother, and I don't want her to worry. After all, she's my mother and I love her. Even though I love V, all I want is to go home."

Queen Tiana didn't look moved. "But you ate faery food, which means you are ours."

"Kevighn tricked me, Your Majesty." She smoothed the green skirt of her dress, trying not to fidget.

The queen smirked. "We invented trickery, my dear Magnolia. If you're not clever enough to figure it out, perhaps I'm doing the mortal world a favor by keeping you."

V's hand tugged on hers and she realized she'd stood up.

"This is why we wish—I wish—to strike a bargain, Your Majesty," V interjected.

"Do you now?" A predatory smile spread across the queen's lips like an ink stain. "What do you wish to bargain, Stiofán?" She was practically rubbing her hands together in glee.

V took a moment to compose himself. Noli knew he needed to offer her something she'd take, yet worded to prevent being trapped in her service for eternity—or doing something distasteful.

"I wish to offer myself for a future favor—" V started.

"A quest, a task?" The queen perked up, her lips curved into something resembling a smile but lacking the warmth.

A quest? V had a definitive set of rules for his favor; how was a quest any different?

Rubbing his chin, V nodded. "If it follows normal questing rules and traditions, yes," he replied. "I need advance notice, and the single quest or task cannot be designed to take more than two mortal months. It can't be impossible or involve harming my family—and it needs to follow all traditional rules." His eyes met the queen's.

Noli wondered exactly what those rules were. V hadn't wanted a task involving anything that could render him incapable of eventually reclaiming his family's throne.

V looked to Noli, as if asking her wordlessly if he'd remembered everything. In her head, she went over her list, then nodded slowly.

The queen stroked LuLu, who wagged her metal tail. "That is it?"

They exchanged glances. V replied, "Yes, that is it."

"My, what a bargain. You are my son after all, aren't you?" The queen looked the tiniest bit smug.

V looked away as if insulted.

"I still don't understand why this mortal is so important to you. Especially with your aspirations." Queen Tiana shrugged. "Children."

"Oh," V added. "The task can't be anything that requires harming any of my family or friends, nor can it be something my father would disprove of."

Noli squeezed his hand. Good save. But would she accept so many stipulations?

"You are no fun, Stiofán." Queen Tiana tossed her golden braids over her shoulder in annoyance.

"I stand by my conditions. In return, you release Noli and immediately return her to Los Angeles. And she'll still belong to me. She'll be returned as time is now, not to find that many years have passed, and she has safe passage while in the Otherworld, and the ability to travel back and forth as we do. Time will pass as it does for us, but it won't cause her to age unduly, she won't be bound to stay a certain amount of time, and her trips will not be limited." He exhaled sharply.

So far, it was going as planned. Noli couldn't help but feel the tiniest bit of excitement in the deepest pit of her belly. She couldn't wait to see her mother.

The queen considered the proposal for a few moments, each second feeling like an hour. "Anything else?"

Furrowing his brow, V thought. She could almost hear him going over his mental list.

He finally shook his head. "Noli?"

Closing her eyes, she went over her own list one last time. *Check. Check. Check.* No, they seemed to have gotten everything. She nodded, biting her lip in apprehension.

He squeezed her hand; she could practically feel his nervousness. "That's all, Your Majesty."

"I accept your bargain." The queen's expression became carefully neutral. She sat primly in her chair, her hands folded in her lap, LuLu climbing down and curling at her feet.

"You do?" Noli wanted to jump up and down. V shot her a warning look.

"I do." Her lips curved into a fearsome smile. Noli's stomach sank. "I have the perfect task for you, Stiofán—when you're ready, of course."

V went as pale as a sheet.

"Come here, Magnolia."

Suddenly, this didn't seem like such a good idea. Noli's stomach knotted. She prayed this would work out for the better—and in their favor. V squeezed her hand.

"Yes, Your Majesty." Noli curtseyed, trying not to squirm.

The queen noticed her nervousness and flashed a predatory smile. "You look dreadful in that color. I detest green. I shall release you, returning you as time is now, granting you both safe passage and the ability to come and go as set forth in the agreement. Come closer."

Taking a deep breath, Noli approached the queen. She had a sinking feeling that she and V had walked into a trap, and no matter how carefully they'd worded their bargain, the queen would get them coming and going.

"Don't worry. This won't hurt ... much." Her face curved into a ferocious grin as she cupped Noli's face with her hand.

Everything went black, as if she were back in Dr. Martin's isolation box. Only this time an invisible weight pressed on her chest, pain pricking her like a million pins. A high-pitched scream ripped from her throat as the pain consumed her.

A Bad Bargain

As soon as the soul-scraping scream slipped from Noli's lips, Steven jumped to his feet. Queen Tiana's face radiated pure joy as she reveled in Noli's pain.

"What are you doing, Your Majesty?" he yelped. All she needed to do was grant their wish; there was no need to hurt Noli.

But he hadn't stated that in the agreement.

His stomach sank all the way to the smooth marble floor. What else had he left out?

Alight with glee and malice, the queen's eyes were riveted on his. "I'm doing you a favor. This way, you won't come to me in a decade when she starts to grow old." Her hand still clutched Noli's arm. "You're my son. It's the least I can do."

"Stop. Please." His voice choked.

"What, you mean you didn't want me to change her?"

She placed a hand over her mouth in mock horror. "Oops. You didn't state that in your bargain."

His knees threatened to give out. She was right. He hadn't told her not to alter Noli. Stupid. Stupid. Stupid.

"What ... what are you doing to her?" How he wanted to cover his ears so he didn't have to hear Noli's pitiful screams, close his eyes so he didn't have to see her writhe in pain. Instead, he took her hand. If he tried using magic to fight the queen, or even physically broke the connection, it might kill Noli.

"I'm making it so she may leave us, of course, and may come and go freely, like we do, oh, and so she may stay with you always—since I know that's what you want." Her lips curved into a cross between a sneer and a smirk.

"Stop, please. I beg of you, Mother." Knees giving out, Steven sank down next to her stupid dog, Noli's hand still in his. He realized what was happening—the queen was turning Noli into one of the fae. And since they hadn't specified it in the bargain, she'd get to choose what sort.

Her laugh came out cool and maniacal, her eyes flashing with her own kind of insanity. "It's better this way for both of you. Don't worry; she'll be earth court—and a pretty one, too. You rattled off all sorts of nonsense, but I know what men really want."

Steven's mind raced as he went through the list of earth court fae. "Flying figs."

The prettiest court folk also tended to be the stupidest. He remembered when she'd asked what he loved best about Noli. It felt as if he'd been run through with a sword.

The queen was not only taking away Noli's humanity, but also everything that he loved about her, everything that made her different, special—and he'd caused it by simply not stating that Noli needed to be returned as she was.

Truly, he was an idiot.

"I take it back," he cried with such ferocity LuLu looked at him. "I take it back."

"Too late." Triumph etched on her regal face, Queen Tiana released Noli from her clutches. She slumped to the ground. Evil laughter tickled his ears as he gathered his love's crumpled body into his arms.

The queen loomed over him, glowing with satisfaction. "Didn't anyone ever teach you to be exceedingly careful when bargaining with the fae? Also, never, ever bargain with a high queen. You'll pay far more than your wish was ever worth."

That was for certain.

Tears of betrayal—and for his love—welled up inside him, but Steven held firm. No weakness could be shown in front of her. He'd shown far too much already.

"I'll be in touch ... son." Chuckling insanely, she left, her dog trotting at her heels.

Already, he could see the transformation taking place in Noli. He'd have a little time, but only a little. They needed to return to the House of Oak quickly. Noli's lifeless body in his arms, he ran out of the room, hoping James and Charlotte hadn't wandered too far.

They were exactly where Steven expected, a night-blooming garden with a gazebo that had always been

James' favorite as a child. They'd come here often with their mother to visit her older sister, back before Tiana had decided that she wanted to be the high queen.

Actually, his mother wasn't a very good high queen, but he'd never say that out loud. Not even to Noli, James, or Quinn. He valued his life far too much, and the queen possessed ears everywhere. Even in the mortal realm.

James looked up with a start when Steven tore into the garden. His eyes fell on Noli. "By the Bright Lady, what happened?"

"I made a bad bargain." Stupid. Stupid. Stupid.

James' mouth formed an "o" of horror. "You did it? Flying figs, I didn't think you would."

"I wish I hadn't." Steven pressed his lips against Noli's pale forehead. "She wanted to go home; I didn't know what other choice I had."

James put a hand on his arm. "Only three people can help you in this situation."

"I know." But that didn't make him feel better.

"Approaching the Bright Lady or the magic itself would be even more fearsome." James' eyes flashed with fear. The queen, the magic, and the Bright Lady were a triumvirate of power, keeping the balance, keeping each other in check, each one representing a different aspect of the Otherworld. Every one of them was beautifully terrible.

"I don't understand." Charlotte's voice lowered as she looked at Noli's still form.

"Steven and Noli asked the queen to free Noli so she

could go home," James explained. "You must word things carefully when dealing with the fae."

"I *know*." Steven wanted to bang his head against a tree. "I made a list; I thought I'd covered everything." His expression contorted as pain and regret exploded through him, threatening to tear him into a million pieces. "But I hadn't … and stupidly I thought that perhaps, deep down, she was still our mum."

James' eyes glistened as he shook his head slowly. "Me too. But she isn't, is she?"

"No." He shifted Noli in his arms. "We have to get her home. Will you help me?"

"What do you think we can do? We can't reverse anything the high queen does."

"We have to do something. Noli wouldn't want to be this way." It was everything she fought against at that dreadful school, everything she fought against in society.

"What did she do?" Charlotte's eyes filled with tears as she clutched James' arm.

"James, what are the prettiest of the earth court fae?" Right now Steven couldn't think straight. His finger traced Noli's ear, which held the slightest of points—not a good thing.

"Flying figs. Is she turning green?" James examined Noli's hand. "If she turns green, she'll be some sort of wood nymph."

Wood nymphs were tied to a piece of land such as a hill or a grove. If that was destroyed, they would be, too, and they couldn't be gone from it long without getting ill.

"No. No green that I can see. She's probably some sort of sprite." James sighed in dismay. "Cruel, cruel woman."

"I should have known better," Steven muttered. His mother liked to keep sprites in her entourage as courtiers, despite their beauty, because they made her feel clever. Given that sprites were the exact opposite of Noli, that was probably what she was becoming.

"I was the one who told you to go to her; I never thought she'd do this..." James shook his head. "Come on. Let's get Noli home."

"Yes, let's." He planted a kiss on Noli's cool forehead. "I'm so sorry, darling. I'll fix this. I promise." He wasn't sure how much he could do, but he had to do something. Now.

....

Steven held Noli in his arms, the green blanket pulled over them, as he dozed in his bed, waiting for her to wake. Over the past few days he and James had worked so hard to fight the transformation and try keep Noli's mind and spirit intact as she became fae. He could deal with her having the body of a sprite. Her having the mind of one would be hard on them all. She'd need him to take care of her, to protect her. Sprites weren't one of their kind who went into the mortal realm much.

He'd made this mess, and he wouldn't abandon her. Eventually, they'd find a way to fix his mistake and make her his Noli again.

Clearly, they'd never be able to reverse her transformation

from mortal to fae. Noli's humanity was gone. As for the rest of her...

He and James tried; they'd tried so hard to keep Noli's personality and all that made her special, to keep her from becoming a silly, flighty, nitwit of a sprite. But he feared they'd only made it worse. In his attempt to amend the queen's spell, he'd managed to preserve Noli's memories, but he wasn't sure what else. She hadn't been awake long enough for him to truly tell. They were still trying, and he refused to stop.

If her memories alone were intact, it would be beyond cruel—to remember how she'd been, but be forced to act in ways, as her sprite instincts took over, that would be appalling by her own standards. Hopefully they'd kept enough of her spirit that she'd be able to counteract the sprite.

Even then, it would be difficult for her, and she'd need him.

Sprites cared little about the past or future, living only in the moment. Though not clever or intellectual, they certainly were fun and upbeat. They could also be vapid and frivolous, easily strayed by parties, dresses, and shiny things—much like the society girl Noli never wanted to be.

Her eyes fluttered open. "Hi, V."

"I love you." He gave her a kiss on her perfect nose.

The first time she'd woken up, she'd been appalled by her appearance—by her womanly curves and how her wild curls had straightened to more manageable waves. The biggest physical difference was the slight point on her ears, but it wasn't very noticeable, especially if she continued to wear her hair unbound.

The other differences, however ...

She giggled at his kiss. Hearing herself, her eyes widened.

He pressed a finger to her lips. "I told you, we'll figure this out. I'm going back with you; I'll stay by your side. None of this changes how I feel about you." He held up his hand. "By the Bright Lady, I promise."

The war going on inside her played across her eyes like a moving picture. Hopefully they'd managed to keep enough of her, otherwise there would be a constant battle in her mind, her longing to be who she was while helpless to change herself. A horrible, terrible fate.

"I trust you." She kissed him back.

He hoped he'd prove himself worthy of her trust—and that he could keep his promise.

THIR+Y-SIX

Homecomings

Now that he was banished, Kevighn didn't know where to go. Well, there was a place, but he wasn't certain if they'd take him back after all this time.

First he needed to do something. This was a fool's errand if there ever was one. His cabin, and everything in and around it, including the grove and his parent's house, was gone, his right to them taken away when the queen had banished him.

Still...

When he walked up the familiar path to the cabin, limping from his injuries the guards inflicted when they'd cast him out, he'd expected to be greeted with the pure chaos of wild magic instead of his home.

A sharp gasp escaped his lips. The cabin stood there, awaiting his return as always.

Kevighn scrubbed his eyes. A trick?

He put his hand to the door of his cabin and it opened as usual. A quick tour showed everything in its proper place. Bursting into the back garden, he saw that it—and Creideamh's grove as well—still remained.

His parents' land was gone. But that wasn't important to him.

Still... how? Why?

As he went inside to add a few things to his rucksack, he thought long and hard about this unexpected turn of events. There was only one person who could keep his lands intact. Really, he should go to him. If anyone would take him in, exile and all, it would be him.

But not yet.

He strode back out the front door, his favorite bow slung over his shoulder, and gave his cabin a long look, his heart wrenching. If only things had been different. Eventually he'd return.

No longer did he have a job. Noli was in the arms of that whelp of a prince. He wasn't welcome amongst most of his kind. For the time being, he might as well go back to the mortal realm and drown his sorrows in women and opium.

He knew just the place.

•••••••

"Ready, Noli?" V came up behind her and gave her a kiss on the cheek.

"I think so." Noli fidgeted in front of the mirror as she

fixed her hair. Her new waves were much easier to braid, but part of her missed her wayward curls. She still couldn't get over her appearance. Or what was happening to her. "What will Mama say … about me?" She wasn't totally unrecognizable, but the points on the tops of her ears bothered her.

"It will be fine. You still look like you—everyone's just going to think you finished maturing at school and that growing was, um, kind to you. It does happen, you know."

He ran his fingers down her covered arm. Today she was wearing a many-hued green dress with long, narrow sleeves and a full skirt.

She grimaced as she worked to cover the tops of her ears with her hair. "I liked my old self better."

"I liked your old self better, too. We're going to find a way to fix this." V kept saying this, over and over, probably as much to reassure himself as to reassure her.

Taking his offered hand, she stood up. Excitement at returning home and seeing Mama coursed through her. Everything would be fine, just like V said.

"I'm going home." A vapid giggle escaped her lips and her cheeks burned. How she hated when that happened. She felt like a puppet.

V handed her a cloak, giving her a peck on the cheek. "Yes, you're going home."

She adjusted the dark green cape in the mirror and turned a little, studying her reflection. "Do you think green is my color? Blue might bring out my eyes more."

Her mouth clamped shut. She kept saying and doing

stupid things. It was as if someone else had taken control of her body, and all she could do was watch in horror, powerless to stop it.

V wrapped his arms around her. "I love the way you look in green."

Noli shouldn't care what *anyone* thought about her appearance, but her heart fluttered. She turned away. She didn't want V to know how hard this was on her; how it took every ounce of willpower she possessed to fight from succumbing to that other girl—the one who just wanted to drown herself in frivolity, completely unaware of the bigger picture.

Even then, it didn't always work.

It physically hurt, both to resist and to see what she'd become. But she'd continue to fight against becoming the girl who giggled and cared only about her appearance and having fun.

If she didn't fight, the high queen would win.

"I'm going home." Noli focused on the moment. Finally, she could return to her mother like she'd wanted to all along, from the moment she'd been left at Findlay.

Yet, as with her wish in the tree, she regretted how it had all unfolded. They never should have made the bargain with the queen.

"Please don't." Taking her face in his hand, he covered it in kisses. "We could still stay here if you'd like, but I know you won't."

For the briefest moment, that other girl wanted to. It would be much more fun here, with balls and parties... Noli gave that girl a mental shove, wishing she could lock her in the attic.

"You'll stay there with me?" Noli wanted to smack herself. She sounded so clingy, so stupid.

V gave her another kiss. "Of course." He rummaged in his pocket and pulled out an old brass key hung on a new bit of green ribbon.

She stared at the object in his palm. "Is that..."

Pink tinged his cheeks. "I found it, in the garden, when we went to Findlay to look for you. I'm not sure why I took it. Would...would you like it?"

"It is a pretty key." Noli took the key and turned it over. "I was going to lock the garden and keep this, but the tree had other ideas." It seemed so long ago.

"I locked the garden. It's unsafe to have a tree with a mind of its own at a school like that," V told her. "One day we should figure out why it's there."

"Yes, we should." She put the key in her cloak pocket.

He took her hand. "Let's go say goodbye to Lottie and James. We'll be back soon."

"How exactly will we do that? We'll have to follow societal conventions again. We can't sneak away together without causing a scandal. Besides, we'll be punished for ages." Although it would be worth it to see her mother again. She'd try to be a better daughter, to take care of her mother, just like she'd promised Jeff.

"I'll figure it out. I'll be on restriction for life, but you won't." He led her toward the library. "It will look like you're being sent home from school because you've been cured."

Noli winced. In a way she had. If she wasn't vigilant, she'd become the insipid society ninny they wanted her to be.

"I'm sorry," he soothed her. "I should have used another word."

They walked into the library. Noli ran to Charlotte and hugged her. "I will miss you."

"I'll miss you, too." Charlotte smiled. "You're coming back soon?"

"Of course. And I'm going to build you a better chair. Someone has to know how the queen's floating chariot works … if not, perhaps I can base it on the workings of a hoverboard." She'd tried to see what she could design, but thinking often made her head hurt. Hopefully it would be easier to think back home.

"I can't wait." Charlotte gave her one final embrace.

Noli gave James a hug. "Bye, James."

"Hurry back." James grinned.

James clapped his brother on the shoulder. "I don't envy you, but I appreciate you working things out with father for the both if us."

"I am the eldest." V smiled. "Besides, you're the one who has to deal with Her Majesty regularly. I don't envy you there."

The queen kept dropping by, either to try to lure Charlotte back to the palace or to gloat over Noli and their bad bargain. Noli had learned her lesson; she'd never bargain with the fae again.

Taking her hand, V looked at her. "Ready?"

"Could we go check on the wood faeries first? Please?"

Noli still possessed that connection with them, and with the flowers and trees. If anything, it seemed stronger.

"Of course." He smiled.

They made their way to the faery tree in the middle of the hedge maze. They'd buried all the little wood faeries who'd died, and been checking on the ones who survived as they grew stronger. The wood faeries weren't strong enough to fly around, but they did come out from their knothole, probably hoping she had treats for them in her dress pockets.

"I'm sorry, but I don't have anything for you today," she told them.

"I do." V took a handkerchief out of his coat pocket, a little pink cake inside. "But you have to share." He broke it up and doled out pieces to all the wood faeries, who bickered and fought over crumbs of varying sizes.

She smiled at their antics. "Will you let wood faeries move into my tree?"

"If it'll make you happy." He took her hand. "Everything's going to work out."

"If you can't fix it, no one can."

He smiled wryly. "That's not precisely true, but I appreciate the vote of confidence."

"How could I not trust you?" She fingered her medallion. "You're my best friend ... and so much more. You defied your father to rescue me—and I know your father." Noli grinned. "You even faced the high queen."

His face crumpled. "I'm sorry. I'll fix it. We'll fix it."

She ran her fingers through his wayward hair. "It's not your fault. I don't blame you."

Even if she wanted to. She found it difficult to feel negative—or complex—emotions for long, which was another thing she hadn't told him. He had enough to worry about.

Capturing her fingers, he kissed the tips, sending sparks of pleasure shooting through her. All those sensations had become more intense—and harder to fight.

"I don't deserve you." He intertwined his fingers with hers.

"Funny, I feel the same," she replied.

His eyes gazed deeply into hers. "This does nothing to affect my feelings for you. It's merely a setback. All relationships have setbacks."

She thought of her parents, how her mother still pined for her father. "That's true."

Fingers still intertwined, he pulled her closer. "Magnolia Montgomery Braddock, I love you, and I promise to love, cherish, and protect you always."

He kissed her, slowly, madly, deeply, as if trying to connect their souls. She kissed him back, trying to take everything he offered—love, comfort, stability—and drink it in.

She broke it off before it became more, despite that other part of her thinking it crazy to break off a kiss with such a handsome man, and a prince to boot.

"I love you." She gazed into his eyes, enjoying this last moment. As hard as it would be, they'd have to be more cautious at home where, once again, propriety ruled. Taking her hand, he smiled. She squeezed it. Home. In a few moments she'd be able to hug her mother again.

"Can I tell you how excited I am?" Allowing the anticipation to take over, she grinned again.

He kissed her. "You just did."

Noli linked her arm through his. "Come on, V. Let's go home."

Home Again

Noli's heart sputtered like the Pixy's engine as she walked up the steps of her house. A flying auto passed overhead, and the thought of her broken Pixy in the shed made her sigh.

V's brow furrowed. "Are you all right? Look, you're *home*."

Suddenly, she felt lighter. "That I am." She gestured to the house. "I like the paint."

V grinned. "I'm glad. We tried to keep the place up for you."

"It looks so pretty." She winced at how she sounded. The front of the house looked dark, but this time of night her mother would be in the kitchen, sewing. Really, she should make her mother a proper sewing room.

Putting her hand on the doorknob, Noli hesitated. "Are you sure they're going to believe this?"

"Yes, they will. Now, go on." His hand found the small of her back, pushing her forward.

Stealing herself, she turned the knob. She'd wanted to come home more than anything, and here she was.

He put his hand on top of hers, smiling. "*We* can do this."

"Yes, we can." She smiled back. Hiding everything from Mama would be difficult, even with V's help.

They walked through the foyer and the dark front room. Flickering light came from the kitchen. Her mother sat at the table, slumped over a half-made dress, asleep, the room lit only by candles.

How many times had Noli found her like this? That was it—no matter how difficult it now was to focus, she would build a steam-powered sewing machine for mother. Oh yes. She could put it in her new sewing room.

"Mama?" Her voice choked with so many emotions.

Edwina Braddock's eyes flickered open. They blinked, several times. "Noli?" Her voice sounded sleepy. "Noli, is that you?"

Heart in her throat, Noli nodded, not bothering to hide her tears of joy. Letting go of V's hand, she ran to her.

"Noli." Standing, her mother embraced her, pressing her face into Noli's hair. "Oh, Noli, you've grown so much. I'm glad they didn't keep you for year like they said they would."

"I'm sorry, Mama," she sniffed. "I'm so sorry. I'll be a better daughter, I promise. I love you. Please don't send me away again. I missed you so much."

Her mother cupped her face with a pale, delicate hand,

tears streaming down her pretty face. "I know. I'm sorry, too. I love you so much. I missed you. I won't send you away again, I promise." Her lovely face had aged a little, creased with worry and fatigue, but it radiated pure joy. "Oh, just look at you. You've grown up so much I barely recognize you. What a lady you've become. But you're home." She wrapped her arms around Noli. "That's the most important thing of all."

Suddenly, all the difficulties, all the sacrifices, seemed worth it. Mama was happy—and she was *home*. At last.

THE END

Author's Note

The Victorians loved faeries and fairy tales, as do I, and I drew on both that love and the classic tales to create what you read here. I also love steampunk, and *Innocent Darkness* takes place in an alternate version of 1901, a peek into what might have been. I've taken significant liberties with history, both in changing things completely, like adding flying cars and hovercops, and in moving things forward or backward in time.

For example, there was no "pleasure pier" in Los Angeles until 1916, and the carousel didn't appear there until 1922. The San Francisco Earthquake was real; however, it happened in 1906 and was caused by a rupture on the San Andreas fault, not magical backlash from the Otherworld. A good deal of the city had to be rebuilt from the earthquake and subsequent fires. Over 3,000 people died. Many things in this story are based on actual history: the sensory deprivation box was used to treat different sorts of "imbalances," and women and girls really were institutionalized for things like willfulness, hysteria, and nymphomania. The ancient Greeks considered aether the fifth element, and aether appears in a variety of alchemical theories and in early physics.

As for faeries … they could very well walk among us. *Be careful what you wish for* is always sage advice, no matter when and where you live.

—Suzanne Lazear

Acknowledgments

Books aren't written in a vacuum, and so many people helped, supported, and inspired me along the way—more than I can name here. I thank you.

Thanks to Rachel for making this "her" story, to Reina for giving the series its name, and to my dance gurlz who made me write YA in the first place. This novel never would have gotten written without Candace Havens and her fast draft class, where it all started, or NaNoWri-Mo, where it finished.

Thanks to those who helped me become the best writer I could be, especially the regulars at SFFHOWW, the ladies of LARA, the night owls at the FF&P water cooler, and my critique group. Thank-you hugs to Sandy, who told me to query both my editor and agent. Thanks to my ever-vigilant critique partners, Cecilia and Jenn, who reassured me it didn't suck; Kris and Cassie, who suggested the quotes used in the story; and Kathy Bennett, who helped with the flying car infractions and hovercops. Thanks to the ladies of Steamed and the Twitter Steampunk Community, for inspiration and information on all things steampunk.

The journey didn't stop after I sold the manuscript. Thanks to the Apocolypsies, the Class of 2k12, and my amazing mentor Kiki Hamilton for holding my hand and sending me virtual cupcakes, and to Julie and Harmony—who give the world's greatest Twitter pep-talks.

There really is a YA sisterhood. Thanks to all the amazing YA authors who allowed me to learn from their experience, especially Shelley, Simone, Leanna, Kady, and Inara. Also, thank you so much to Kim Harrison and Jeanne Stein, who taught me more about writing than they'll ever know.

Music is a huge source of inspiration for me. I need to do a special shout-out to Emilie Autumn: I listened to "Across the Sky," "Shallot," and "Opheliac" on continuous repeat for a bulk of my drafting process. Plague rats forever.

A lot of work goes into a book behind the scenes. This book wouldn't be possible without my editor, Brian, and the whole amazing Flux team, as well as my fabulous agent Laura Bradford. Thank you so much for having faith in me, taking a risk on my story, and helping me shape this into what you see here.

Last but not least, huge hugs to Missy and the hubby, for believing in me, going to the movies when I was on deadline, and most importantly, never letting me give up. I love you and never could have done this without you.

Photo by John Lazear

About the Author

Suzanne Lazear (Los Angeles, CA) loves both faeries and steampunk and has been known to build faerie houses in the backyard and make rayguns to match her ball gown. She's a regular blogger at *Steamed*, a group steampunk blog. *Innocent Darkness* is her debut novel.

To learn more about the world of the Aether Chronicles, please visit www.aetherchronicles.com.